Allon

Book 7

Dangerous Deception

Shawn Lamb

Allon Books

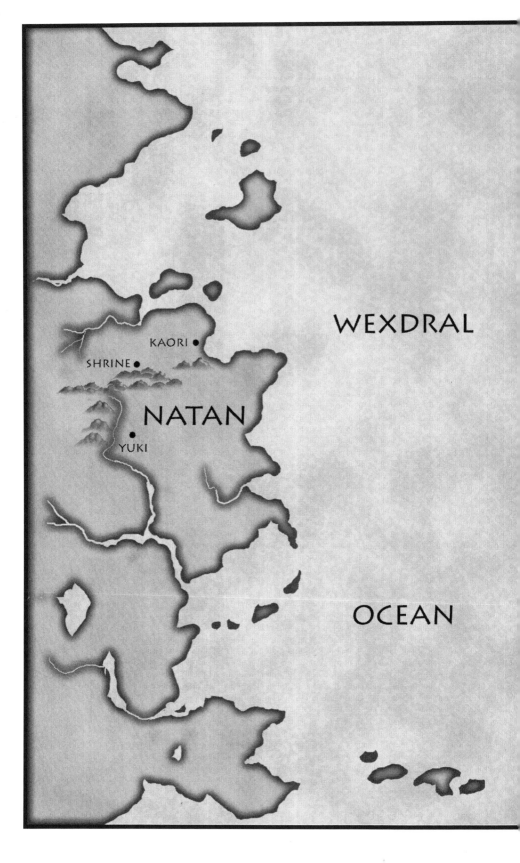

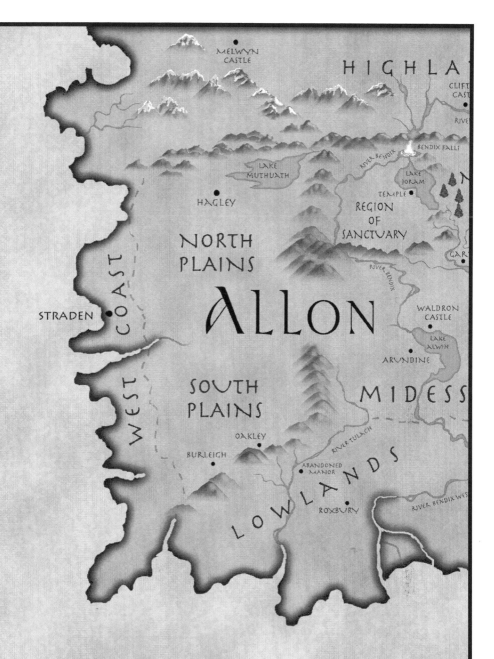

ALLON ~ BOOK 7 ~ DANGEROUS DECEPTION by Shawn Lamb
Published by Allon Books
209 Hickory Way Court
Antioch, Tennessee 37013
www.allonbooks.com

Cover design by Robert Lamb

International Standard Book Number: 978-0-9891029-1-9

Other Books by Shawn Lamb

Young Adult Fantasy Fiction
ALLON ~ BOOK 1
Published by Creation House, a division of Charisma Media

Published by Allon Books

ALLON ~ BOOK 2 ~ INSURRECTION
ALLON ~ BOOK 3 ~ HEIR APPARENT
ALLON ~ BOOK 4 ~ A QUESTION OF SOVEREIGNTY
ALLON ~ BOOK 5 ~ GAUNTLET
ALLON ~ BOOK 6 ~ DILEMMA
PARENT STUDY GUIDE FOR ALLON ~ BOOKS 1-4
THE ACTIVITY BOOK OF ALLON

For Young Readers – ages 8-10
Allon ~ The King's Children series
NECIE AND THE APPLES
TRISTINE'S DORGIRITH ADVENTURE

Historical Fiction
GLENCOE
THE HUGUENOT SWORD

Coming from Allon Books

ALLON ~ BOOK 8 ~ DIVIDED
ALLON ~ BOOK 9 ~ IN PLAIN SIGHT

ALLONIANS

King Tyrone – age 37
Queen Tristine – age 30
Prince Nigel, Tristine's brother, the King's Champion – age 33
Princess Mirit, wife of Prince Nigel, the Queen's Champion – age 30
Prince Titus – son of King Tyrone and Queen Tristine – age 12
Chad, squire to Prince Nigel – age 21
Barrett, companion to Prince Titus – age 14
Baron Mathias, Lord of the West Coast, father of Mirit – age 72
Lord Allard of the Meadowlands – age late 60s
Kasey, first mate of the Protectorate

NATANESE

Admiral Kentashi Yoshiru, under-sheriff of Lord Norkiru Akari
Lady Hoshi, number one wife of Kentashi
Captain Hodi, over Admiral Kentashi's soldiers
Jiru and Makito, soldiers
Lord Norkiru Akari, one of Natan's ruling warlords
General Ryo, Lord Norkiru's commander

GUARDIANS OF JOR'EL

Captain Kell – Commander of the Guardians of Jor'el
1st Lieutenant Armus – Guardian Advisor to the King and Queen
2nd Lieutenant Avatar
Virgil, a warrior
Egan, Overseer of Prince Titus
Ridge, a ranger
Gulliver, a Sea Guardian
Chase, a Sea Guardian, Trio Leader of the West Coast

NATAN'S SUPERNATURAL BEINGS

Raiden, ancestral protector of Kentashi's family
Akido, dragon, friend of Raiden
Onedo, king of the underworld
Hoshiki, goddess of the night

Chapter 1

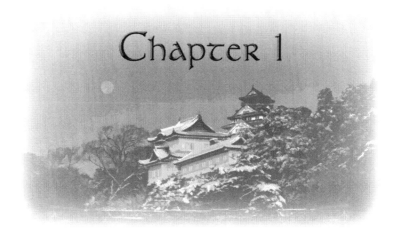

ON A CRISP CLEAR SPRING DAY, KING TYRONE, PRINCE NIGEL and Princess Mirit rode ahead of an entourage en route to Straden, the main port of the West Coast province of Allon. At age thirty-seven, Tyrone towered above most mortals, standing six feet, eight inches tall, lean and strong and every inch pure muscle. Being half-mortal, half-Guardian showed in his appearance with black hair in striking contrast to cool light gray eyes, bold evidence of his heavenly half. An intense look from him made one aware he possessed a perception beyond mortal comprehension. He wore a mauve color traveling suit with black accents, matching short cloak and feathered cap.

At thirty-three, Nigel was three years older than his wife Mirit. They dressed similarly in the uniform of their stations of the King and Queen's Champions; rich azure blue, close-fitting knee length jackets with side slits trimmed in silver and gold braid. Each wore a royal medallion to signify their station. Instead of helmets, they wore small brimmed feathered caps. Her auburn hair was wound in a coiled braid on her head in a way to accommodate the hat. The only difference between their uniforms was the crest on the left breast of Nigel's jacket symbolizing his status of Jor'ellian Knight of the Temple. The tri-part crest contained the ancient symbol of Allon, an eagle, a wolf and a crown surrounding a sword.

Guardian warriors Avatar and Virgil walked behind Nigel and Mirit. They stood seven and half feet tall and didn't need a mount to keep pace with the mortals on horseback. They did not wear the royal blue and silver uniforms rather the Guardian uniform of an embossed tan close fitting knee-length jacket trimmed in gold with slits in the side from the hem to the hip. The tan breeches were tucked into leather boots. A large leather and gold belt held a sword and dagger. Guardians also had different and brilliant colored eyes compared to mortals. Virgil's eyes shone a crystal blue, almost translucent and similar in lightness to his blond hair. Avatar's bright silver eyes proved a marked opposite to his bronze hair and goatee.

Behind the Guardians rode Nigel's twenty-one-year-old squire, Chad. A short distance behind Chad came Tyrone's twelve–year-old son, Titus, along with his companion Barrett, a lad two years older than the prince. Titus stood taller than most boys his age with very dark brown hair and mortal-colored blue eyes. Following a discreet distance behind Titus's horse came Egan, another Guardian warrior. Black hair stood in stark contrast to his vividly bright blue eyes. Twenty yards behind Egan came a royal carriage, two loaded wagons, and a mounted troop of royal soldiers.

Tyrone turned in the saddle to look past Avatar and Virgil to Titus. The boy remained downcast and did not respond to Barrett.

Nigel followed Tyrone's considering glance. "You can't blame him for being disappointed."

Tyrone faced forward to reply. "He has to learn to mask his feelings, for with his station comes responsibilities not always to one's the liking."

"Such as you not being able to go to Natan and having to send Mirit and me instead?"

Tyrone tried to contain his annoyance, but it crept into his voice. "Being king does have some limitations. But you need to stop making excuses for him."

"I'm not making excuses. I'm saying I understand his disappointment. Same as I understand you not being able to travel freely. Remember, I was once the royal heir."

Tyrone did not respond, rather regarded Nigel, long and hard, the grey eyes betraying irritation.

At the rising tension, Mirit said, "We'll bring you back a gift." She flashed an uncertain yet lighthearted smile when Tyrone turned his attention to her. His expression softened, but not quite into a smile as he made a retort.

"Only be discreet. The last time someone gave me gift, Tristine flew into a fit."

Her smile grew at his acceptance of her intervention, but short-lived when he looked again to Titus. This time Titus spoke to Barrett, the latter deeply frowning. "Poor Barrett. Titus can be a handful," she again tried speaking with levity.

"Barrett holds his own," said Nigel.

"Like Chad does with you?"

Nigel chuckled. "No, not as well as Chad."

Tyrone audibly sighed in frustration. "I hoped Barrett's influence would soothe Titus, but instead, his behavior of late is growing intolerable."

"All boys go through a rough time or two before they fully mature and come to their senses."

"Excuses again?"

"No, personal experience. It took my crippling to teach me some harsh lessons."

Mirit laid hold of Nigel's hand. "You've come a long way since then."

He smiled. "I'm not feeling sorry for myself. Merely expressing my hope that his maturing years are less painful."

Tyrone huffed to the contrary. "He's been kidnapped and seen death and war. I don't know if that's less painful."

Nigel confronted Tyrone. "Why are you so easily offended? I'm trying to be encouraging, not anger you or make us all depressed."

Abruptly, Tyrone faced forward and a deep silence fell between them.

"You can't be serious, Highness," said Barrett in low protest.

"Hold your tongue," scolded Titus. He made a nodding motion of caution toward his father.

"I would be remiss in my duty if I didn't speak."

"You are remiss in your duty by not keeping my confidence!"

Barrett stiffened in offended remorse. "I would not betray you, Highness. But I—"

"But nothing! Not a word, Barrett."

The determination and inflexibility was clearly evident on the prince's face, so he yielded. "Ay, Highness."

"Is there a problem?" asked Egan.

Titus' expression changed to a placid smile when turning to his Guardian Overseer. "Merely a debate to pass the time. It's a long ride."

Egan stared at Titus. Along with unusually bright colored eyes, Guardians had the ability to search a mortal's intentions with a mere glance, if they chose. More often the look was a warning before employing their heavenly senses.

Titus scowled. "Nothing! Why must you always be suspicious?"

"I'll stop when you start giving me reasons not to be."

With a huff, Titus turned forward.

By nightfall they reached Dunemore Castle, the home of Baron Mathias, Lord of the West Coast, a member of the Council of Twelve, and Mirit's father. The enormous two-hundred-year-old castle overlooked the bustling port city of Straden. Storms from the sea weathered the stone to a dark foreboding gray. Despite the age and weather, the wood and iron portions of the castle were well maintained and in good working order.

After passing through the massive gate, the caravan entered a huge courtyard capable of mustering several hundred troops with wagons and horses. Mathias stood in the threshold of the main house. Even at seventy two years old, he cut a dashing figure with a full head of gray hair, neatly trimmed beard, and deep green eyes. His smile grew at seeing Mirit dismounted to greet him.

"You look well," he said after they hugged.

"I am. But I've missed you." She hugged him again.

Mathias flashed a wry grin at Tyrone and Nigel. "Forgive me, Sire. I realize this isn't protocol and I should have greeted you and the prince first, even if he is my son-in-law."

Tyrone laughed and Nigel quipped in response, "Since when do you stand on protocol, father-in-law?" They exchanged hearty handshakes and large smiles.

"Where do I stand on a greeting, Mathias?" asked a merry female voice from behind Tyrone and Nigel.

Tristine, Queen of Allon, moved from the carriage to stand beside her brother Nigel. She came just two inches shy of his height of six-foot two. She was an attractive woman of thirty with long golden hair and crisp hazel eyes. Her charming smile held an impish edge. Accompanying her was a burly Guardian warrior named Armus, whose bright chestnut eyes sparkled with lively joviality. An older nobleman in his late-sixties and a ruddy complexion also escorted Tristine.

"Majesty!" began Mathias in surprise. "This is a most unexpected pleasure." He took her hand and kissed her knuckles.

"I could never resist visiting one of my favorite places."

"I thought Mylton was your favorite," bantered Allard, Lord of the Meadowlands and fellow Member of the Council of Twelve. Keen shrewdness reflected in his mortal green gaze and with vitality to his character obvious upon first meeting him.

Mathias smirked at his peer. "You, I expected."

Allard heartily laughed.

11

"I came also, my lord," chided Titus. He stood with his chin raised in a display of childish pride.

"Indeed, Highness. It is always an honor to see you." Mathias bowed to Titus.

Tyrone gave his son a disapproving frown and the boy changed his tone to pleasant.

"I am glad to see you, Mathias. Sometimes Aunt Mirit can't speak of anything else than coming home for a visit."

"If only to get away from your badgering for a while." She chuckled and ruffled his hair, which nearly dislodged his hat. He scowled in annoyance. He removed his hat to brush his hair back into place and replaced the hat.

The adults chuckled, smiled or laughed.

"Shall we go inside? The night still grows chilly and a warm fire and dinner awaits," said Mathias.

After dinner, everyone retired to the drawing room. The clock on the mantle showed the time of eight in the evening.

"A few hours remain until the tide is right for departure, Sire. Any or all may rest. I have rooms prepared," said Mathias.

Surprised by the statement, Titus asked Nigel, "When are you leaving, Uncle?"

"Midnight."

"Why? You said you weren't leaving until tomorrow night."

Nigel noticed Tyrone's steady regard of him during Titus' questioning. Rather than reply, Nigel shrugged and took a drink.

Tyrone answered. "Gulliver sensed an incoming storm that could delay departure and advised leaving before it arrives. I approved of the change in schedule." He spoke concerning the most formidable sea Guardian.

Titus huffed and plopped into a nearby chair. Egan placed a hand on Titus' shoulder only to be brushed off. Again he gripped the boy's shoulder and spoke.

"Rest is a good idea if you want to attend the departure fully awake."

"Excellent suggestion, Egan," said Tyrone, but his eyes never left Titus.

"I'd rather spend time with Uncle before he leaves. I may not see him for several months!"

At Tyrone's annoyance, Nigel said, "Do as the king, your *father*, says."

"Ay, sir." Titus stood, gave Tyrone a stiff bow and left, passing his mother without an acknowledgement. Egan and Barrett followed Titus.

"The young prince seems rather put-out," said Mathias.

"That's a polite understatement," began Allard. "He didn't like it when the king told him he could not accompany us. He thinks his experiences in Tunlund uniquely qualifies him to meet the new young emperor."

"He was only seven."

"Now he acts like twelve going on thirty."

"With such an attitude he could do more harm than good to any future relationship with Natan."

Tyrone swallowed his drink before speaking. "Which is why I refused his offer. He's too young, brash and inexperienced, despite what he thinks."

Mathias looked confused. "Then why not leave him at Waldron?"

"Because he has perfected Tristine's knack for escape." Tyrone cast an irate side-glance to Armus.

For all his burliness, Armus possessed an easy-going nature, but to the accusation he grew stiff with insult. Tristine laid hold of his arm to delay his reply.

"It's not Armus' fault Titus has a rebellious streak. If anyone, I bear blame. Many times I gave my father reason to be angry and concerned as you are now," she said.

"Not so," insisted Allard. "Ellis loved you and naturally expressed concern."

A tolerant smile crossed her lips. "You're being kind. I know I vexed him, and some times on purpose. Such as Titus did now." She sighed with regret. "I see my youthful tendencies in him."

"Ellis was just as pigheaded and stubborn in his youth," said Armus.

"Along with another member of the family," said Avatar with a nod to Nigel.

He took the cue. "Admit it, sister, stubbornness is a family trait."

Tyrone's scowl deepened. "Family trait aside, it is better to confront his attitude than let it fester or wonder if he'll be at Waldron upon our return."

Tristine sent Mirit a prompting glance. Mirit responded with a slight nod to Tristine then slipped her arm around Nigel's arm.

"I think rest is a good idea. I don't sleep well on ships," said Mirit.

"Since when?" said Mathias in amused dispute. "You were practically raised on a ship."

She flashed a frustrated toothy grin and steered her husband out of the room.

Once in the hall, Nigel spoke. "Mathias is right. I don't recall you having trouble sleeping on any of our other voyages."

"I need to speak to you in private."

Conversation ceased until they were in their quarters. Mirit closed the door and pursed her lips, guarded in her demeanor, which made Nigel suspicious.

"What is it?" he asked.

"Tyrone is right, you need to stop making excuses for Titus."

"I didn't think I was. Nor did I answer him when he asked about the change in schedule. I deferred to Tyrone."

"True, but he disputed Tyrone in public and didn't leave until *you* said something."

He scowled and nodded. "I noticed that."

"There is more. Why do think Tyrone has been short with you of late?"

He heaved an uncertain shrug. "Because of Titus?"

"Ay. Titus idolizes you and turns to you for answers rather than his father."

He began to pace, his habit when agitated. "I never meant to inspire such admiration! Nor take Tyrone's place."

"I'm not saying your have, but frequently you say things in defense of Titus which should not be said."

He sat on the edge of the bed, a frown of vexation on his face. "I was often accused of making excuses for Tristine when we were younger. I thought I was helping not enabling her behavior. In time, I accepted some truth to the accusation. Now I'm doing the same with Titus."

She sat beside him. "We know your actions are driven by love."

His earlier suspicion returned. "We?"

"Tristine and I discussed the subject at length. She told me of Tyrone's struggle with the issue. He loves you dearly, but Titus is his son. Neither she nor Tyrone want to wound you or destroy the bond you share with Titus, but—"

"I know!" he snapped and stood. "Perhaps it is best to be gone for a while." He paced again.

"Tyrone plans to use the time to confront Titus. However," she said, rising to stop his pacing, "when we return, it cannot be the same. For all concerned, you must restrain yourself and allow Tyrone to deal with Titus as he feels necessary."

"I'll try. I just don't like being stern or unfeeling toward children."

"Because you are tenderhearted toward your family. Other people's children are a different matter. Still, he's not only your nephew; he will be king some day and *you* are the King's Champion. To help him respect his father *you* must demand the same respect from him you do of others."

Nigel's brows knitted in consideration. "I suppose I have let that aspect of our relationship falter. After Tunlund ..." His voice trailed off into a soft sigh.

She continued her gentle yet probing argument. "How do you think Tyrone feels? Surely he told you about his horrible vision of Titus' sacrifice at the ruins."

Her statement surprised him. "He told you?"

She shook her head. "Tristine did."

He tenderly stroked her cheek, his gaze distressed. "Did she tell you about him seeing you in his vision?"

"That I was present. Only Hueil wanted to kill Titus, not me. He didn't foresee my intervention so he didn't convey it to Tyrone when projecting the vision. However, I'm not the issue."

He went to reply when there came a knock at the door followed by, "Uncle." He gave Mirit a hapless look.

"Be strong, for his sake, and Tyrone," she said and nudged him to answer the second call.

Upon opening the door, Nigel discovered Titus fully dressed. Despite the boy's smile, he spoke to his nephew's attire. "Your father told you to go rest. Why are you still dressed?"

"He didn't say I had to change to do so. And I wanted to see you before you leave."

Nigel's ire flared. He never tolerated an insolent, disrespectful attitude. "I will not help you further disobey him by speaking to you. Now go to bed."

"But, Uncle—"

"No!" To Titus' pout of stubborn resistance, he added, "Must I take you to bed and undress you like a child?"

"No, sir," the boy grumbled.

Rather than waiting for Titus to leave, Nigel closed the door. He listened to Titus' grumbling departure before speaking to Mirit. "You're right, things can't continue this way. He's taking to open defiance and using me as excuse. I cannot accept such behavior or unwittingly encourage it any longer."

She smiled. "Perhaps by recognizing it and taking action, Tyrone will feel less threatened and not act as combative towards you."

"I can only hope. I hate this tension between us, not to mention learning I'm the cause of it."

"Not the cause, rather the object of Titus' actions and behavior. That is what Tyrone plans to confront during our absence. You must support him when we return."

"Perhaps I should speak to Tyrone before departure."

"No, let him deal with Titus. Until he sees a genuine change in Titus' behavior, I don't think he'll listen, rather consider it another excuse." Seeing the answer not to his liking, she made him look at her. "Let Tyrone come to you. This way, he can feel he succeeded without help or even good intentions."

He simply nodded.

Chapter 2

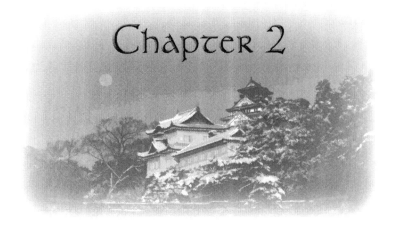

B Y ELEVEN O'CLOCK, THE CARAVAN ARRIVED AT THE DOCKS where Mathias' flagship the *Protectorate* was loading and preparing for the midnight departure. Lit by lamps and lanterns for work, the impressive warship loomed with four masts, three main deck levels, two quarterdeck levels, eight guns on the main deck, four aft and four astern and thirty cannons below, fifteen on each side.

At the bottom of the gangplank stood a silver-haired Sea Guardian with brilliant green eyes coordinating the loading. "Don't let that line go slack, lads!" He turned from the loading to greet the arriving group. "Evening, Sire."

"Gulliver. How goes it?"

"We'll be ready to leave on time."

"Even loading what we brought?"

Gulliver noticed the wagons. "More trinkets?"

Tyrone grinned. "I consider them good-will gifts."

"Mister Kasey!" Gulliver called to an officer on board. "See to loading the *gifts* from the wagons."

"Ay-ay, Captain."

Nigel, Mirit, Tristine, Chad, Titus, Barrett, Mathias, Allard, Armus, Avatar, Virgil and Egan joined Gulliver and Tyrone.

"Are the cabins ready?" asked Nigel.

In his dry witted manner, Gulliver surveyed the group. "I thought only you, Princess Mirit, Chad and Lord Allard were going."

"Don't forget Avatar and Virgil," added Nigel with a prompting smile.

Gulliver heaved an indifferent shrugged. "Warriors can sleep on deck."

Tyrone chuckled. "Let's go onbroad. I want to have some final words of instruction and prayer before departure."

As the others moved to follow Tyrone up the gangplank, Titus held Barrett back and whispered, "Remember what I told you."

"I remember. I just don't agree."

"You agreement isn't important, obedience is."

"Ay, Highness," he droned. He followed Titus onboard and into the wardroom.

Tyrone was speaking when they arrived. "Remember you are guests of Admiral Kentashi Yoshiru, who is under-sheriff of Lord Norkiru Akari, one of Natan's ruling warlords. If you manage to find favor with Norkiru, he will introduce you to the young emperor Tirigato."

"That's why you insisted upon so many gifts, as bribes," quipped Nigel.

"Not bribes," began Armus, seriously. "The Natans are an ancient people and strict on formal conduct and manners. You will be given some leniency since you are foreigners, but it is a great insult to arrive empty-handed and not offer something to each host."

"With this storm coming, can we still meet Kentashi in four days?" Nigel asked Gulliver.

"Naturally."

"Don't you mean *un*-naturally? The trip to those coordinates is reported to take ten days," said Avatar, trying to hide a smirk.

"What is *unnatural* for mortal sailors is *natural* for me."

Titus groaned and grabbed his abdomen. "My stomach! It's been hurting since dinner. *Ohhh!*" He doubled over. Barrett grabbed him in support.

"I can call for the surgeon," said Gulliver.

"No! I just want to go back to bed. I felt better when lying down."

Tristine brushed the hair from Titus' face to feel his forehead. "No fever."

"I think it was something I ate." With a pitiful expression, he spoke to Tyrone. "Please, sir, can I go back to lie down?"

"What did you have to eat?"

"One too many deserts," he moaned.

"The tart or pudding?"

"Tart."

"That could cause a belly-ache—" Nigel stopped when Mirit poked him.

Tyrone tossed a scowling side-glance at Nigel before speaking again to Titus. "We won't be much longer. Wait in the carriage and we'll return together."

Barrett helped Titus leave the wardroom. Egan followed.

On the walk down the gangplank, Titus noticed crates from the wagons being loading into the cargo hold. One trunk in particular had not yet been loaded.

"Did you follow my complete instructions?" he whispered to Barrett.

"Ay, but Egan's behind us."

"Get in the carriage."

Once inside, Titus made a loud moan and began to heave. Barrett spoke to Egan, before the Guardian reached the carriage door. "He's getting worse."

"I'll fetch the surgeon." Egan left.

Seeing Egan board the ship, Titus said, "Now!" He shoved Barrett toward the window nearest the ship then carefully slipped out the other side door.

"Drive on quickly!" shouted Barrett to the driver then to Egan, "He's vomiting, I'm taking him back to the house! Tell the king!"

From behind another wagon, Titus watched Egan rush into the wardroom. He had to act fast. He ran to the trunk, unlatched it and got inside. A special lever was fixed to latch and unlatch the trunk from inside. There were also several holes of various sizes in the trunk, a blanket, flask and pouch of food. After re-latching the trunk, he used the blanket to cover himself to keep from being seen through the largest hole beside the lock. He barely got situated when the trunk was prepared for loading. Soon he felt himself lifted into the air.

In the wardroom, Tyrone and Tristine received the news of Titus' condition with mixed reactions, she showed concern and he annoyance.

"Fetch the surgeon and take him to Dunemore," he told Egan, who promptly left.

"I hope it's nothing serious," said Tristine but added at Tyrone's skepticism, "He wouldn't go that far."

"How far did you go?"

"I was never so dramatic in feigning illness."

An impulsive breath caught in Nigel's throat, forcing him to cough.

"Your brother seems to differ."

"My brother shouldn't talk unless he wants to trade stories about running away since the Natans are similar to the Morvenians!" said an irate Tristine.

That stung! Nigel stood to his full height, jowls tightened and glared at her.

His reaction concerned Mirit. "Is that significant?"

Armus placed a restraining hand on Tristine's shoulder while he replied. "The Morvenians once tried to form an alliance by way of a marriage proposal, but," he added when Nigel's harsh gaze turned to him, "the negotiations became interrupted and never resumed."

Avatar moved alongside Nigel to mediate. "Which was good since their beliefs run counter to ours."

"Ellis managed to avoid war with Morven," said Allard. He then spoke to Tyrone. "However, Natan is more powerful and we can't afford to make them an enemy, Sire."

Tyrone kept careful watch of Tristine and Nigel during the heated exchange. "Then let us pray and we'll leave so preparations for departure can be complete."

Arriving at Dunemore, Barrett pulled a long, thin stuffed bundle out from under his seat, dressed in some of Titus' clothes. He hurried out of the carriage before it completely stopped. He shielded the bundle from the driver's complete view, but enough to see he held something.

Once inside, Barrett raced upstairs, carrying the stuffed bundle to the chamber where Titus was supposed to sleep. He tossed back the covers and tucked the bundle underneath to make it appear as if Titus slept. When he made a passable lump, he observed his handiwork with a fretful expression, gnawing on his lower lip. Voices and footsteps in the hall startled him. He rushed to the door and peeked out. Egan and the surgeon arrived! Frantic, he stepped into the hall, waved them silent and spoke in an urgent whisper.

"He's asleep now."

"Asleep?" asked Egan.

"Aye. He was so exhausted from being sick he barely made it into bed."

"I should examine him," said the surgeon.

"No!" Barrett intercepted him. "I mean to do that, you'll have to wake him. Isn't it good for someone who is sick to sleep?"

The Guardian went to the door, Barrett at his heels.

"Gently," said the lad in warning.

Egan opened the door enough to see a form lying down and facing the far wall. Barrett seized Egan to stop him from entering.

"If you wake him I'll get blamed. You know his stomach has troubled him in the past. And after a good night's sleep he's fine."

Egan eased the door closed and spoke to the surgeon. "He's had this complaint before and recovered."

"What about the vomiting?"

Barrett shifted his feet in an awkward manner when Egan looked to him for an answer. "Dry heaves."

The surgeon reached into his satchel, pulled out a small packet and handed it to Barrett. "If he has need, mix this in some warm milk."

"I will."

"Fetch me if the situation changes." The surgeon left.

Egan appeared thoughtful. "Stay with him. I'll be back in a few minutes."

Barrett sagged in relief and returned to the room.

In the courtyard, the surgeon mounted his horse and rode out the gate while Egan went to the carriage house and stables. He found the driver taking care of the horses.

"I heard the prince became sick in the carriage."

"I heard him, but there isn't a mess to clean up."

"No?" Egan inspected the inside of the carriage. He plucked a couple of pieces of straw off the floor near the seat.

"I was surprised at finding nothing. By the sound and look of it, he was pretty sick."

"You saw him?"

"He was all bent over when Barrett help him out of the carriage and into the house. I would've helped, but they got out before I could stop and get down."

"And this straw? I found it inside." He held it up for inspection.

The driver shrugged. "Could have come in on anyone's shoe."

Egan's considering glance shifted from the carriage to the straw. In light of Titus' recent brash and suspicious behavior, the situation warranted investigation. However, the driver witnessed the incident and he sensed no deception in the man's answers or demeanor. He dropped the straw.

"Thank you," he said and returned to the house.

In the room, Barrett sat beside the bed staring at the packet of medicine. He didn't like deceiving people, especially the king and Egan, but what could he do? To tell what he knew would betray the prince. He bolted to his feet when the door opened and quickly moved to prevent Egan from coming fully into the room.

"You told me to stay with him. But if I'm to keep him from being disturbed you need to stay outside and keep people from coming in."

Egan drew Barrett into the hall. "There was no mess in the carriage."

"I told you, dry heaves."

Skeptical, he eyed the lad. "You could have waited at the dock for me to fetch the surgeon."

"He managed say *go* before another heave. I just did what I was told."

"Did you eat the same food he did?"

Barrett shrugged, a bit taken back by the question. "Ay. Except dessert. I can't eat sweets. Have you ever experienced an upset stomach?"

"No. Food isn't necessary to Guardians like it is to mortals. The only time I ever experienced sickness was from exposure to stygian metal."

"What's that?"

"One of the two elements that can render a Guardian helpless."

"Egan."

Tyrone, Tristine, Mathias and Armus approached. Barrett swallowed back his sudden fear. Fortunately, the king spoke to Egan.

"How is Titus?"

"Sleeping, Sire."

"Did the surgeon examine him?"

"No, when we arrived, Barrett said he was asleep and we didn't want to disturb him. The surgeon left a packet of medicine should there be need."

"I have it." Barrett held up the packet.

"Then it truly is an upset stomach," said Tristine.

"So it appears, Majesty," said Egan. "Barrett will remain with him while I stay in the hall to prevent any servant from inadvertently disturbing him until he is recovered."

Tyrone's expression relaxed. "Very well. Inform us if his condition changes. Good night." He and the others left.

Gulliver manned the helm when Nigel, Mirit, Avatar and Virgil joined him. "Mister Kasey, all hands to their stations. Cast off the lines."

"Ay-ay." Kasey repeated the orders to the crew.

Nigel glanced up. Numerous clouds moved across the moon. "Will we leave before the storm hits port?"

"Ay, we'll make it," said Gulliver with certainty.

"But will we meet the storm at sea?" teased Avatar and poked Virgil. The other warrior snickered under his breath.

"If we do, you better hope I can get us through or I'll feed a certain lieutenant warrior to the sharks to quiet the waters."

Virgil laughed out loud at the retort, but bit his lip at Avatar's scowl.

In triumph, Gulliver smiled. "You can sleep peaceful, Highness. Even if we encounter the storm, it won't be for at least a day."

Nigel's smiling glance passed from Gulliver to the warriors. "Hope you two find a comfortable spot on deck." He and Mirit left the helm.

Once in their cabin, Mirit asked the obvious question since the heated exchange between Nigel and Tristine. "What did Tristine say to make you so upset?"

"She made reference to a painful time," came his evasive answer.

"The Morvenian marriage proposal. It was you?"

In reluctance, Nigel nodded. "Although not at first. Emperor Kamu offered one of his daughters to my father to seal an alliance, but he refused. That is when the ambassador asked about me. Shortly thereafter, things went from bad to worse."

"How so?"

He shook his head, his expression showing his reluctance to speak on the subject. "It happened years ago, when I was sixteen."

"But not long enough for the wound to heal."

Avatar entered without knocking.

Nigel became relieved at the Guardian's arrival, and a natural diversion. "Is there a problem?"

"No. I just though you might want help in explaining what happened earlier," he replied and glanced toward Mirit.

"That would nice since he is again reluctant to talk about his past to his wife," she groused.

"Because of the accident."

With sudden understanding, she asked Nigel, "You were crippled because of the Morvenians' visit?"

At Nigel's persistent reluctance, Avatar continued, "You've avoided the topic for too long. It is time to speak."

Nigel stared at Avatar, the prompting and encouragement clearly seen in the Guardian's silver eyes. Nigel took Mirit's hand, and together sat at the table.

"After the Morvenians left to convey our counter proposal, Father and I went on a hunting trip to discuss the circumstances. I had not been comfortable the entire time of their visit, only I didn't know how to tell him the reasons why."

"The problem goes deeper than feeling uncomfortable," said Avatar.

Again, Nigel met Avatar's probing eyes. "Ay," he admitted. "For several weeks, I experienced horrible nightmares and a deep sense I was not meant to be king. Yet, as his heir, everything aspect of life was to groom me for some day becoming king. How could I explain this strong, but vague sense without wounding him? I proposed the hunting trip so we could talk. Unfortunately, it didn't go as I planned," he lamented. "When I spoke, my words were clumsy and ill-conceived. He felt I rejected him and the throne. Trying to explain only made him angrier. No use pursuing the conversation until we cooled our heads, so we went in search of prey." He paled and his brow leveled. "We found a stag and several does in a meadow near the river and split up. I rode along the cliffside to come at them from upwind. My horse grew skittish, not like him at all. When I saw why, I tried to calm him, but he moved too close to the edge."

She gasped in fearful horror. "You fell over the cliff?"

"Pushed, actually. An assassination attempt by forces using the Morvenian visit to cover their intent."

Avatar spoke. "A Guardian named Morrell became swayed by the Dark Way to enact revenge for Ellis killing Latham and destroying Dagar. The whole scheme culminated in an attempted coup five years later by Latham's mistress and their son. Ellan, Nigel's sister, betrayed her family in favor of the Dark Way and participated in the coup. Fortunately, they were defeated, and Tyrone identified as the Great King of Prophecy."

In stunned sympathy she turned back to Nigel. "Your sister. Now I understand why this is so painful."

From under the collar of his tunic, Nigel pulled out the chain of stones he wore around his neck. It contained two purple stones, one blue stone, one amber stone, one ruby and one black. "Her stone is black."

Tentatively, Mirit touched the necklace. "I always wondered about that stone. You said it was for one no longer with us. Is she dead?"

He shook his head and replaced the necklace under his tunic. "Exiled. We don't speak about her much."

"So because the coup failed you were healed?"

"Not exactly." A teasing smile of gratitude appeared and he jerked his thumb at Avatar. "It was all his doing. Little did he realize the trouble he would have since."

The Guardian widely smiled. "Oh, I knew, but did it anyway."

His answer confused her. "How? I know Eldric has healing power, but you too?"

"No. Kell and I accompanied Ellis and Nigel, but Morrell used the Dark Way to incapacitate me and carry out his plan. When I learned Nigel survived, only crippled, I took it upon myself to set right my failure and the treachery by one of my kind." He held up a hand to stop Nigel's expected protest. None came, but he continued. "I broke all protocol in approaching Jor'el directly. He granted my petition after determining Nigel bore no ill will or bitterness for what happened."

Nigel said, "Over time, I realized neither my father nor Avatar were to blame. Also, I met Tyrone during my first year of wandering and we became friends. In fact, I discovered his identity before he did, and pointed Tristine to his smithy when her horse threw a shoe. In my spirit, I sensed they were meant to be together." He smiled in remembrance.

"Tristine knew about you?" she asked.

"No. Our meeting happened by chance, or rather providential. She didn't recognize me." He motioned to the left side of his face and body. "My entire left side from head to toe was crushed and disfigured."

"That is how we met, a cripple and an orphan," said Chad.

"We didn't hear you come in," said Nigel.

Chad grinned. "I've learned how to move without disturbing you. We're leaving." As he spoke, they felt the ship's movement.

"Tell me, do you feel better having discussed it?" asked Avatar.

Nigel cocked a grin. "Ay. Yet I wouldn't mind some sleep."

"Sounds good." Mirit yawned. "Must be past midnight."

In the cargo hold, Titus squirmed to get comfortable. He removed the blanket from the hole to allow air to pass. He felt cramped, but had to stay hidden until the ship put out to sea. If caught before departing the harbor, he would be taken back and that wouldn't do. He knew he faced punishment for his actions, but he had to prove his father wrong and this was the only way he could think to do so. Of course, convincing his uncle would be easy once he revealed his presence. Nigel always acted reasonable; so with him, he doubted encountering much trouble.

He did slam the door in my face earlier. He shook the thought from his head, as it must have been fatigue. *Ay, wanting to rest before the journey.* He yawned. Rest would be nice considering the late hour, but he didn't want to close his eyes until the ship put safely at sea.

His heart raced at shouting coming from above, only the words muffled and not distinct. Had his escape been discovered? It would so be like Egan to spoil his plans. He seethed against the Guardian. Although dedicated to duty, Egan wasn't Jedrek, thus not understanding his desire to be taken seriously. It still troubled him how Jedrek died, but he couldn't dwell on that when hearing more voices. He placed the blanket back over the hole and waited.

A few anxious moments passed, but no one entered the hold. He heard a few more unclear loud voices; then he felt it, the swaying of a moving ship. He smiled. A half-hour at most, and the ship would be out of the harbor and in open water.

Chapter 3

THE FOLLOWING MORNING EGAN FOUND THE KING, QUEEN AND Mathias gathered in the dining room for breakfast with Armus in attendance.

"How is Titus?" asked Tyrone.

"Barrett said he had a fitful night."

"Did he need the surgeon?"

"Not that I was told."

"You weren't in the room at the time?" asked Tristine.

"I remained on watch outside the door and heard nothing to indicate a problem. Otherwise I would have summoned the surgeon, Majesty. This morning, Barrett came out and asked me to fetch Titus breakfast."

"He wants food. That's good," she said to Tyrone.

Tyrone motioned Egan toward the side-table. "Not too much. Eggs, toast and cider will do for now."

"Ay, Sire."

Egan fixed the prescribed plate for Titus, filled another for Barrett and returned upstairs. He knocked on the door, but received no reply.

He knocked again. Still nothing. "Barrett? Highness?" He tried the door and found it unlocked, so he entered.

The figure still lied on the bed facing the far wall only Barrett was not there. Egan put the plates on a small table near the door and approached the bed. "Highness? Titus." He reached to shake the lump.

Feeling something unusual beneath the covers, he ripped off the blanket and discovered a thin stuffed bundle dressed in Titus' clothes. His jowls tightened and a low throaty growl of anger escaped. In two strides, he crossed to the window overlooking the courtyard. He caught sight of Barrett running into the stables. Egan vanished in dimension travel and reappeared inside the stables. He snatched Barrett, nearly taking the lad off his feet and into the air.

"Where is Titus?" he demanded.

Barrett stood mute with fear at the Guardian's imposing wrath.

"What have you done to him? Answer me!"

"Nothing! He's not harmed!"

"Then where is he?"

Barrett's lips quivered. "I think he's on the ship, but I'm not sure."

"How?"

"A special trunk he ordered me to fix for him."

Egan jerked Barrett out of the stables and headed for the main house. The lad stumbled in his effort to keep up, so Egan practically carried him inside.

The blustery entrance placed Armus on alert, clasping the hilt of his sword ready to face whatever entered. He only slightly relaxed at seeing Egan, as their visual exchange told of trouble.

"Is something wrong with Titus?" he asked.

"Indeed." Egan turned to Tyrone. "No stomach ache. In fact, Titus isn't here and this boy will explain!" He shoved Barrett toward the table.

"What do you mean not here? Where is he?" demanded Tyrone.

Barrett trembled. "I believe he's on the ship, Sire."

Tyrone flushed red with anger. "How?"

Barrett swallowed back his fear to reply. "A special trunk among the luggage from Waldron the prince ordered me to fix for him—"

Enraged, Tyrone stood. His action knocked a full tray of plates from a male servant, who scurried back, startled. He ignored the servant, hot to confront Barrett. "He's been planning this since then?"

Overcome with terror, Barrett dropped to his knees. His voice shaky yet urgent in pleading, "Sire, I'm sorry! I wanted to tell you, but every time I objected, the prince scolded me about obedience and how telling you would be betraying him."

"Tyrone, please." Tristine seized his arm and motioned to the wary servant gathering the split food and broken dishes.

The scene only mildly helped Tyrone to contain his temper, as told by the strained voice asking Mathias, "Where can we talk in private?"

"My study."

By the time everyone reached the study, Tyrone regained his temper. Still firm in features and voice, he addressed Barrett. "Start from the beginning and leave nothing out."

The lad took a deep calming breath before proceeding. "The prince was angry about your refusal to let him go. He felt you were wrong and he had to prove it. That is when he began formulating a plan to stowaway."

"Did anyone else know of the plan or help in this?"

"No, Sire. The prince said he trusted only me, and anything other than my full silence and cooperation he would consider betrayal. I knew it was wrong, but didn't want to betray him." His voice cracked with emotion and fear.

"You told me you weren't sure if he made it onto the ship, how is that?" asked Egan.

"Once we were in the carriage we had to think of a way to get you to leave so he could exit the other side and slip into the trunk. He got out, but I never saw if he reached the trunk before being loaded."

"So he could still be at the dock."

"Why? If his goal is to sneak onboard, he could have found another way," said Mathias.

"Ay, but if he failed, returning here would be risky. Barrett was heading for the stable when I discovered the stuffed bundle of clothes to give the appearance of Titus in bed asleep."

"It was all his idea!" insisted Barrett in desperation. "We hid the bundle under the carriage seat."

"Which is what the driver saw and mistook it for the prince," said Egan.

"Ay."

Tyrone turned the lad to face him, but Barrett balked, shameful and glanced to the floor. "Barrett, look at me." The light grey eyes of his Guardian heritage were intimidating and commanding and Barrett flinched. Tyrone kept a firm hold to prevent retreat or avoidance. "Why did you keep up the lie when at anytime you could have told Egan? Titus wasn't around to stop you with threats."

"I love him like a brother and I didn't want to betray him. That maybe wrong for a servant to say of a prince. I'm sorry!" He wept.

"Mathias, have Barrett taken to a room and kept under guard until the king decides what is to done," said Tristine.

"Truly, I'm sorry, Sire!" Barrett wept louder when Mathias laid firm hold of him and they left.

"Blind loyalty," groused Tyrone.

"The same could be said of Chad where Nigel is concerned. Or Avatar, even Armus," she said.

"Titus took advantage, the others have not."

She went to dispute but Armus intervened. "Sire, I suggest an immediate search of the dock to make certain he made it onboard ship and nothing worse has happened."

"Ay. Go."

Armus and Egan saluted and left, but not without Armus whispering a word of warning to Tristine. She nodded and spoke in a more controlled tone after the door shut.

"What are you going to do about Barrett?"

Tyrone shrugged and poured himself a drink from a decanter on a small side table. "I don't know. There must be some punishment. Helping Titus under duress in his presence I can accept, but not continuing the ruse on his own."

Mathias returned. "Barrett is secure, Sire. And I ordered my men to aid Armus and Egan in their search of the dock. Sire, about Barrett," he began with deliberation. "I had a similar case brought to me a few years ago concerning a servant who helped the daughter of a local noble family run away with a man she wanted to marry against their wishes. He was a slow-witted, good meaning fellow, who also claimed his action was for love and loyal of the daughter. He wanted to see her happy. Fortunately, we found her and prevented what we learned would have been a disastrous marriage."

"Barrett isn't slow-witted."

"No, but I believed him, as I think you did."

Tyrone nodded since he drank, then asked, "What did you do to the fellow?"

"I gave him fifteen lashes and thirty days in prison. He didn't return to work for family. In fact, he came to work for me and served as your carriage driver last night."

Tyrone glared in admonishment at Mathias. "You baited me."

The baron flashed a grin. "Only a little, but the story is true."

"Very well. Order your sergeant-at-arms to administer fifteen lashes and keep him locked up until we learn what's become of Titus. After that, he will be discharged. And don't take him in or help him find employment."

"No, Sire."

***

Armus, Egan and fifty men split up to scour the docks, houses, streets and alleyways of Straden. The search took all day and at sundown they met where the *Protectorate* originally docked. Being unsuccessful in finding Titus, they headed back to Dunemore.

"We can tell the king he made it onto the ship," said Armus.

Egan growled with great irritation. "I feel like a complete idiot! Fooled by two mortal boys and a sack of cloth."

Armus wryly grinned. "Welcome to world of Guardian and mortal relationships."

Egan shook his head. "I thought we moved past his objection of me taking Jedrek's place as his Overseer."

"This has nothing to do with you—"

"He still resents me! And you know it."

"*This* action was in direct defiance of Tyrone."

"Maybe, but I was still duped. What do we do now? He's spent a whole day at sea."

"Continue to Dunemore, I'll be along shortly."

Egan grabbed Armus to stop him leaving. "What are you going to do?"

Armus calmly removed Egan's hand, yet looked directly at him. "Trust me and go." He gave Egan a gentle nudge to encourage his continuance before he turned and ran down one of the alleys.

Egan complied. Despite what Armus said, he believed some residual bad feelings lay behind Titus' actions. After all, the plan included deceiving him in a most elaborate manner.

And he asked why I'm suspicious of him? As if that isn't obvious. He glanced skyward and complained. "Why, Jor'el, did you assign me such a difficult and ungrateful mortal?"

Suddenly everything stopped: time, the soldiers and surroundings. Everything came to a standstill. A hazy cloud appeared in front of Egan, making him wary of what was happening. Eyes of bright opulence emanated from the cloud and the voice, kind yet firm, spoke.

"That is not a question you should be asking me, Egan."

Realizing who spoke, Egan fell to one knee, head lowered in a submissive bow. "Jor'el! I lashed out in frustration. I didn't mean to question your wisdom."

"Egan," said Jor'el with parental indulgence. "I know your stouthearted nature, but you have allowed frustration to rule in your dealings with Titus. You could have discovered his intention if you had been more persistent and not abandoned him to his own devices. Get his own *comeuppance* as the mortals say."

"Ay, I hoped he would be caught by someone else."

"Why do you think I placed you as his Overseer?"

Egan dared an uncertain glance at Jor'el. "In all honesty, I'm not sure."

"You are a brave and strong warrior in battle, but timid and uncertain where mortals are concerned. Perhaps that is because you fear another failure in protecting your charge?"

Pricked, Egan's mouth opened to speak in defense. Meeting Jor'el's eyes, he couldn't object, and lowered his head in shame. "Ay," he whispered in distress.

"Egan," began Jor'el in tender compassion. A trail of mist from the cloud turned into a hand and lifted the warrior's chin to look at him. "Do you trust me?"

"Of course, Mighty One."

"Then be as fearless in dealing with Titus as you are in battle and the outcome will benefit you both."

"As you command it shall be done." Egan bowed his head, making the Guardian salute of his right fist to his left breast.

The hazy cloud vanished.

"Egan? Are you all right?" asked a soldier.

The question made Egan realize everything returned to normal, only he remained on one knee with soldiers looking curiously at him. He stood. "Ay. Why do you ask?"

The soldier shrugged. "Do Guardians always get on their knee when one is leaving? I mean, I know Armus is imposing but—"

"No," said Egan with an embarrassed chuckle. "I must have tripped."
He pretended to rub his left knee before continuing on their way back to
Dunemore.

Tyrone and Tristine remained in the study waiting for results of the
search. He stood beside the desk shuffling through maps of the city. She
gazed out the widow to the courtyard for any signs of returning.

"He must be on the ship or Armus would have found him by now.
He always tracked me down when I slipped away."

"Did you ever board a ship ready to set sail?"

"No," she began with a growing smile. "But I did meet a cocky,
sarcastic blacksmith."

Tyrone chuckled. "Whatever became of him, I wonder?"

She moved from the window and hugged him. "I married him."

He tightened his embrace. "Where did I do wrong with Titus?"

"You didn't. Titus acted on his own."

"Perhaps, but his presence could prove a difficulty on this mission."

"Nigel will make sure he behaves—"

"No! Titus is *my* son." He abruptly moved from her.

"Tyrone—"

Egan's return interrupted her. Mathias accompanied the Guardian.
"Sire. Majesty. I'm afraid, the prince is not in Straden."

"Then he succeeded," chided Tyrone.

Egan bowed, his face and voice contrite. "For that I apologize, Sire. I
let myself be fooled by boys."

Tyrone waved it aside. "They fooled us all."

"What now? Can you dimension travel and fetch him off the ship?"
she asked.

The Guardian shook his head. "I'm afraid not. I don't know where
the ship is. We can dimension travel from place to place on land because
they are fixed points, but a ship at sea can be anywhere. I'm sorry,
Majesty."

"Can Avatar bring him back from ship to land?"

"No, and for the same reason. Although the land is fixed, he wouldn't know in what direction to go. Sea Guardians like Gulliver and Chase are skilled in finding land when at sea by constantly sensing the water."

"But Elgin did so when the Sorens invaded," she continued her argument.

"That was a singular event permitted by Jor'el and for the expressed purpose of aiding you and Princess Mirit. It is not a normal ability for Guardians to dimension travel between land and sea. The best Gulliver can do is turn the ship around and head home."

"A doubtful choice, Sire, since it would delay them in meeting Kentashi and cause great insult," said Mathias.

"Then I go to fetch him back."

"I can have a ship ready within an hour."

"I'll go with you, Sire," said Egan.

"Tyrone, you can't go to Natan," she said in strenuous objection.

"I have no choice."

"You do. Send for Kell and have him dispatch Chase."

"No!"

"Tyrone, be reasonable. You are the king. You can't just leave Allon. At least speak to Kell and see what he advises."

"Hang what Kell thinks!"

"I'm sorry you feel that way, Sire."

All were caught off guard by a new voice and turned to see the captain, along with Armus and another unfamiliar Guardian. Kell wore the formal Guardian white and gold uniform. Instead of a belt, a purple sash held his impressive sword and dagger. His midnight black hair contrasted his bright golden eyes.

"Kell. I'm glad to see you," said Tristine in relief.

He grinned. "Thank you."

Already angry, Tyrone confronted Armus. "I should have known you'd send for him. I can handle this!"

"Sire, I bring help for you to find Titus, not advice," said Kell.

"What?" asked Tristine with surprise.

Kell ignored her and kept speaking. "Chase is readying the *Sentinel* to set sail. This is Ridge," he indicated the new Guardian. "He is a ranger, a master woodsman, trapper and tracker. If for some reason Chase can't catch Gulliver at sea, Ridge can find anyone on land."

"Sire." Ridge saluted. He stood the same height as Kell only slender, with red hair, thin beard and light golden eyes, a shade less striking than Kell. He wore the clothes of a forester, black and brown and was armed with a large dagger at his hip and quarterstaff slung across his back.

"You're tall for not being a warrior," said Tyrone.

Ridge cocked a grin. "Thank you, Sire. I've defeated many warriors in hand-to-hand combat training."

Armus objected with a cough to one-side.

The reaction made Tyrone curious. "Have you defeated Armus?"

"We called it a draw after six bouts."

Egan's angry narrow blue eyes stared at Ridge from the moment he entered. His jowls tightened and voice strained. "We don't need his help, Sire. I can find the prince well enough alone."

Kell stepped into Egan's line of sight to draw the warrior's marked attention from Ridge. He spoke with firm authority. "He is going with the king."

"No!" Tristine continued her objection, only louder since ignored earlier. "Kell, Tyrone can't go. How would it appear if the King of Allon arrived in Natan unannounced? It could cause war."

"Who said I am going as king?"

"Then as whom?"

He grinned. "A cocky, sarcastic blacksmith."

"You're not talking sense, Tyrone," she shot back, not accepting his humor.

"He's talking perfect sense," said Kell. "Only I suggest being disguised as a royal officer sent with a message for Prince Nigel from *the* king."

Seeing her frustration, Tyrone took her by the shoulders so she faced him. "There isn't any serious risk. You know the invitation was for dignitaries to come and greet the new emperor in hopes of opening Natan to new allies and trade. Nor have they ever seen me."

"You're using this as an excuse because you wanted to go in the first place!"

"It's not an excuse."

"No? You accuse Nigel of making excuses when he is trying to explain something. He'll see Titus is safe."

Tyrone grew hot. "I am the one dishonored and disobeyed, not Nigel, and I will deal with Titus!" He waved for Kell, Egan, Mathias and Ridge to follow him out.

In angry concern, she turned to Armus. "Well?"

"In this case, I agree. Tyrone must curb Titus' reckless impulsiveness and teach him to respect his duty and his father. You had to learn the same lessons before becoming queen, and Titus will someday be king."

Not liking the answer, she glared at him, but the Guardian of her youth didn't flinch and returned her stare. She lashed out, "I hope they all get some sense knocked into them!" She stormed from the room.

Egan began to follow Tyrone into the chamber intent on helping the king prepare for the venture when Kell prevented him. Ridge stood opposite Egan. The captain's fixed features and golden eyes shifted between them, but he didn't speak until the door closed behind Tyrone.

"The animosity between you two must stop!"

Egan couldn't fully look at Kell, his grip tightening on the hilt of his sword in an attempt to curb his vehement disagreement. He caught a glimpse of Ridge. Even though the ranger stood stiff shouldered and straight backed, he could meet Kell's firm gaze.

"That maybe easier said than done, Captain," said the ranger when catching Egan's glare, which immediately placed the warrior on guard.

Kell seized Egan's arm, jerking it to get his full attention. "It is by Jor'el's command Ridge accompany the king."

Egan's brows drew level in surprise. "Jor'el?"

"Ay. Do you question the Almighty again like you did earlier?"

Egan balked at Kell's knowledge and the challenge. It was bad enough being confronted by Jor'el personally, now others knew. He shouldn't be surprised by Kell knowledge, but Ridge was different. Kell's grip tightened on his arm, prompting an answer. "No, Captain."

"Then somehow, someway, there must be an end. Do you understand?"

Everything within him didn't agree, but to dispute the captain could bring unthinkable consequences. Thus in reluctant agreement, Egan nodded. "As Jor'el commands, it shall be done, Captain."

Kell's fixed gaze turned to Ridge.

The forest ranger offered the Guardian salute. "As Jor'el commands, Captain."

Kell released Egan. "Both of you go to the ship. Armus and I will accompany the king for departure." He didn't wait for an answer and entered the chamber.

Fighting anger and shame, Egan pushed passed Ridge to depart. He did, however, hear footsteps from behind. Kell was right. Something had to be done: find Titus before the ranger.

"We could dimension travel to the ship and not let the mortals see our discord," said Ridge.

Egan halted at the top of the stairs and seized Ridge by the collar. "Know this, ranger. Any hint of danger from you toward my charge, and I will act."

"Against Kell's orders and Jor'el's command?" asked Ridge in brazen rebuke.

Egan released Ridge so hard the ranger took a step back to catch his balance. Egan vanished in dimension travel. He reappeared on the dock next to the *Sentinel,* the ship Chase commanded, and hurried on board.

"Egan, lad, where's the king?" asked Chase, only to be ignored. But the Sea Guardian wouldn't be put off and followed the warrior to the bow. "Egan."

"Oh, sorry, Chase, did you say something?"

"Where's the king?"

"Kell and Armus will escort him when he's ready." Egan stiffened upon sight of Ridge making his way onboard.

"How many others are coming?" asked Chase.

"One too many!" Egan moved to the furthest extent of the bow. He heard someone approach. He grabbed the rigging to contain his anger at hearing Ridge's voice.

"We can't avoid each other, so know this. Despite our differences, I will do my duty to the mortals and Jor'el. And I hope, for their sakes, everything turns out well."

"Better hope for your sake also," chided Egan, glaring sideways at the ranger.

"I'm not the one harboring centuries of anger. Look to yourself, warrior. You know where unbridled passion can lead." Ridge turned on his heels and left the bow.

Indeed, Egan knew. He curbed his anger in Jor'el's presence and even managed to contain his temper when dealing with Kell, but Ridge—that was difficult. Jor'el's question echoed in his mind, *Perhaps that is because you fear another failure in protecting your charge?*

"I won't fail Titus!"

"Who said you would?"

Stunned at hearing Tyrone, Egan whirled about. "Sire!"

Tyrone wore the blue and silver uniform of a high-ranking royal officer. "Egan. What makes you think you have or will fail Titus? He deceived all of us."

"If I had been more persistent he wouldn't have succeeded."

Tyrone shook his head in disagreement, a small wry smile appearing. "Only if you were better corralling Titus than Armus was with Tristine." He clapped Egan's arm. "Take no blame. Titus bears sole responsibility."

"I'll try, Sire."

"Now, come. Chase wants to cast off immediately."

Ridge acknowledged Tyrone with a bow when he and Egan passed on their way to the helm. He remained at the rail rather than join them.

Chase issued orders to cast off when Tyrone and Egan arrived.

"How long will it take to intercept Gulliver?" asked Tyrone.

Chase glanced up at the wind guidon then briefly closed his eyes for a moment of meditation. He frowned and opened his eyes. "Two or three days since the storm is strengthening."

"Couldn't the storm slow him down also?"

Chase flashed a mischievous grin. "If you want to have Priscilla join us and add her special touch to stall Gulliver, it can be arranged."

Tyrone chuckled despite initially frowning at the suggestion. "No. We have time before they are scheduled to meet Kentashi."

"Ay, Sire. Only I would enjoy seeing Gulliver's face learning she thwarted him." He then shouted to his crew, "Prepare the sails for full once we're out of the harbor! Let's take advantage of the wind."

"With or without Priscilla's help, I wonder," said Egan to Tyrone.

Tyrone grinned, but the humor didn't reach his eyes. In fact, he looked to Ridge sitting deck, the ranger's back to the helm. "So, Egan, what can you tell me about Ridge."

"Kell told you, he's a ranger," came the flat reply.

"That's not an answer. Nor does it explain why you are so vehement against him accompanying us." Tyrone kept focused on Ridge.

"As the prince's Overseer, I can find him."

"It is obvious there is history that has caused strong feelings between you two."

"Centuries ago and not relevant."

"No?" Tyrone turned to face Egan. "Look at me and say it won't interfere if we must search for Titus on land."

Egan met Tyrone's stare. His blue eyes equaled the intensity to Tyrone's grey. "Will your feelings interfere with how you confront Nigel in respect to Titus?"

Tyrone stiffened at the counter-challenge. Whereas his gaze intimidated most men, in this exchange, Egan held the advantage of being full Guardian. Tyrone averted his eyes, and his jowls flexed at the thwarting. "I'll be in the captain's cabin." He left the helm.

Chase confronted Egan. "What are you avoiding, lad?"

"Just keep your mind on your task and catch Gulliver." Egan made his way to the stern. From there he watched the vanishing coastline.

Two situations he thought dealt with came crashing back in one day. He hoped the day at the Temple when Titus ran from Virgil and to him for help, was the beginning of a change in their relationship. Titus loved Jedrek, who had been his Overseer from birth. Being felled in the line of duty is one hazard of a Guardian's physical existence and something a warrior didn't fear.

Egan understood Titus' attachment along with some hesitation to accept another. In fact, Titus prayed for Jedrek's return. That day at the Temple, the boy mistook Virgil for Jedrek. Although twins, there were differences in their eyes and personalities. Jedrek had fiery amber eyes compared to Virgil's light, icy blue. Jedrek had a more soft-spoken personality compared to his witty brother, but both compassionate. Only Virgil's character became impacted by his four hundred year imprisonment in Soren. It reflected in his eyes and mannerisms. Perceiving the change is what frightened Titus and sent him fleeing to Egan for comfort and protection. The realization that Virgil wasn't Jedrek returned proved the final blow to the boy's hope of seeing his beloved Guardian again.

For a couple of months, Titus became friendlier toward Egan, especially those times he encountered Virgil at Waldron. This reinforced his hope of an improvement in their relationship. Then, as Titus grew more comfortable with Virgil, his old craftiness returned. The constant scheming and making him look like a fool grew tiresome.

Egan knew Tyrone brought Barrett to Waldron in an attempt to give Titus an older companion and avert his attention from scheming. Egan would have preferred Ellis, Baron Fagan's son, named in honor of the late king. A year older than Titus, Ellis had a more stalwart character equipped to counter Titus compared to Barrett's easy-going manner.

Now he was on a ship in a race to catch Titus after pulling off his most brazen escape to date.

"You have allowed frustration to rule in your dealings with Titus. You could have discovered his intention if you had been more persistent and not abandoned him to his own devices," Jor'el's words echoed in his ears.

"Maybe, but Ridge? Why?" he asked, glancing skyward. "I do not ask in rebuke or rebellion, rather wondering what good it can do at this time? I don't want to lose another—" He couldn't finish for painful vexation. He glanced over his shoulder to the main deck. He didn't see Ridge. He moved to the helm rail for a better view of the whole deck. Chase manned the wheel, but Ridge was nowhere. The last time he lost sight of the ranger proved disastrous.

"He went to the captain's cabin," said Chase.

Egan hastened to the cabin. He didn't fear Ridge harming the king, but he wouldn't lose track of the ranger until he secured Titus and this incident ended. His blustery entrance startled both Tyrone and Ridge. Tyrone sat at a table with Ridge carrying a plate of food he was about to set in front of the king.

"Is there a problem?" asked Tyrone.

"No, Sire. I thought I heard you call me."

Ridge didn't speak or react to the obvious deflection, rather set the plate before Tyrone.

"Ridge convinced me I should eat. I think breakfast was the last time I ate."

"You should keep up your strength, Sire."

"Anything else, Sire?" asked Ridge.

"No, this is fine. Thank you."

Ridge nodded. "I'll see if Chase is able to keep the wind in the sails, preferable without Priscilla's help." The ranger flashed a half-hearted smile and left.

"Join me, Egan." Tyrone used his knife in motioning to the food on the sideboard.

The warrior did as bade and crossed to the sideboard specially made to keep food from sliding onboard ship. He put the barest amount of food on his plate. Tyrone pause in eating when Egan joined him at the table.

"At least Kell and Armus know how to take advantage of an invitation."

Egan grinned, genuine in his attempt to add levity. "Armus is spoiled by mortal food and always teases me about being a picky eater."

Tyrone smiled, also wanting to change the mood. "Would it help to know Armus prepared the meal special for this trip?"

"It might at that." Egan rose and piled more food on his plate.

Chapter 4

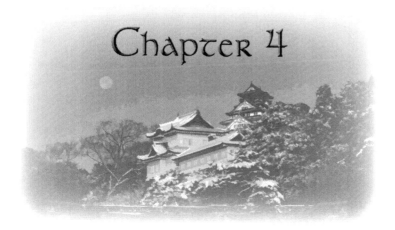

I N THE CARGO HOLD OF THE *PROTECTORATE*, TITUS DIDN'T KNOW
how long he remained inside the trunk or how far the ship sailed.
He slept for quiet a while and grew hungry for something other than
the biscuits, cheese and sausage Barrett packed. He drank enough of the
cider that he needed to find a privy.

He carefully opened the trunk and got out to search the hold for a
place to relieve himself. He found an old pot, not a privy but would
serve. When finished, he covered the pot using an old canvas. He noticed
the ladder leading up to a large deck hatch. Leaving by way of the hatch
would make too much noise and draw attention. He found a regular door
to the hold but he didn't know where it led. Still a door was better than
the hatch. He became annoyed to find it locked, meaning he had to use
the hatch.

He climbed the ladder and tried to move the hatch with his hands but
it wouldn't budge. Being large and strong for his age, he placed the back
of his shoulders against the hatch and tried to use his legs as leverage to
lift the hatch. It moved slightly, but came down on his shoulders. He
slipped down several rungs yet managed to keep from falling completely
down the ladder. He held his breath, listening and waiting to determine if

anyone heard. Nothing. He climbed down the rest of the rungs and sat on a nearby crate to consider his situation.

With both the hatch and door locked he either had to call for help or wait until someone came to fetch something from the hold and sneak out. True, he couldn't stay hidden the entire voyage, but the longer he did, the less chance of being sent back. Calling for help wasn't what he wanted to do, but who knew how long until someone came to the hold? He might starve if the food ran out before then. No, there were numerous crates and sacks. Perhaps some contained food.

He investigated the marked cargo. Most bore labels of pottery, cloth, silverware or other such commodity. There were sacks of grain and seed but nothing immediately edible. In fact, everything was sealed and he couldn't access a crate or sack without prying or ripping it open thus giving away his presence.

This brought him back to his original problem, locked in a hold with little food and drink. He would have to make do with what remained in the sack and flask. He glanced to the corner. At least he had the pot. But how would he dispose of the waste? This wasn't going according to plan.

At the stern rail, Nigel stared out to sea in the direction of Allon, watching the third sunrise of the journey. Since leaving, he wrestled day and night over the situation concerning Titus. Although he hoped and prayed the boy felt better, it disturbed him to again be accused of favoritism. He believed he loved all his sisters equally just like he believed he loved all his nephews and nieces equally. His youthful illusion became shattered when at age sixteen, Ellan accused him of favoring Tristine. When she pressed him, he had to admit his partiality and tried to correct his behavior. Now he was accused of the same favoritism toward Titus.

The more he thought, the more he understood how, when and where he gave that impression. Yet during his introspection he realized it wasn't the fact of Titus being Tristine's son, for she had four children. It was Titus' kidnapping to draw Allon into war that infuriated him! How dare anyone use a seven-year old boy in such a manner? He didn't hesitate going to Tunlund to rescue Titus, for nothing short of finding him alive and whole would satisfy. Mirit told him how during their captivity by Hueil, Titus remained strong in his faith in Jor'el and his unwavering belief Nigel would find them and Tyrone defeat the enemy.

In Tunlund, Nigel met Mirit. Thought of her made him smile in recalling how contentious their relationship began. She proved her bravery when unselfishly trying to save Titus from being sacrificed at the cost of her own life. The memory made him wince. Seeing her struck down was one of the worse moments of his life while her miraculous restoration by Jor'el proved one of the happiest.

Still, in reflection, he recognized where his relationship to Titus had taken a turn. The boy's steadfast confidence in him bolstered his ego. Since Tunlund, Titus mimicked his training and every move just like Tristine did in their youth. She followed him everywhere, trying to do everything he did from riding, to swordplay, to archery, anything. He never intended to capture Titus' admiration or intense interest, it simply happened.

Rather than discourage, or at least corral him, I allowed it to flourish, which is why there is such tension between Tyrone and me. The admission pricked him. Besides his father and Darius, he loved no man better than Tyrone. Their friendship formed during his days as a wandering cripple and Tyrone a simple country blacksmith. He couldn't allow such a bond to deteriorate any further. Upon return, he would rectify his behavior toward Titus and hopefully allay Tyrone's defensiveness. For now, he yawned and stretched, as the lack of sleep caught up to him.

Mirit appeared next to him. "Who doesn't sleep well on ships?"

He frowned at her humor.

"What is troubling you? Meeting the Kentashi?"

He shook his head. "Thinking about Titus and what you said. At the first opportunity to show I understand I made an excuse for his bellyache."

"I'm sure he's feeling better."

"I hope so. Still, it will be difficult when we return."

She chuckled and tried to wipe the amusement from her face at his irritation. "Some habits are harder to break then others."

"You mean keeping my tongue?" he chided.

"No, habits of the heart. Your deep concern for those you love guides your actions. So consider this, during our absence things may be mended between Tyrone and Titus, which might make it easier for you."

Avatar and Virgil approached. "Gulliver says we're making good time and by tomorrow morning we should reach the coordinates Kentashi sent," said Avatar.

"Ahead of schedule may be good," said Nigel.

"Chad has breakfast ready," said Virgil.

Avatar flashed a wry glance toward Nigel while speaking to Virgil. "Unless his appetite is like his sleep and mind, absent and disturbed."

Nigel smirked to Mirit. "Remind me to have Avatar help Gulliver with the bait next time there are sharks present."

Virgil laughed and Avatar grinned; both watched Mirit and Nigel return to the cabin.

"They are a handsome mortal couple. Shame they can't have children," said Virgil.

"Eldric says it is a side-effect of her restoration."

"Could that be why he so favors his nephew?"

Avatar shook his head. "No. Titus reminds him of Tristine in their youth. They have always been close and he made excuses for her while she mimicked him in everything."

"The same as Titus does now."

"Ay." Avatar grew thoughtful. "Only there is an uneasiness with Tyrone. Titus' behavior in Straden was unacceptable and I'm surprised Nigel didn't react more forcefully when the boy rebuffed Tyrone."

"Actually, I thought him wise to remain silent. After all, if his excuses are causing the tension, silence may be the best course."

"Perhaps."

"Captain! Dolphins off the port bow," called the watch to Gulliver.

Avatar and Virgil moved to where several deckhands peered over the side to watch the playful dolphins swimming parallel to the ship.

"A good sign we're getting closer, lads," said Gulliver.

"It also means we've left the sharks behind," said one deckhand to another.

"How so?" asked Virgil.

"Sharks steer clear of dolphins."

"I didn't think sharks feared anything."

"Most sharks are loners while dolphins travel in numbers. They kill sharks by ramming them in a group."

"And saved a number of sailors by doing so," said the other.

Avatar smiled and looked to the helm. Gulliver focused on the wind guidon. Virgil pulled on Avatar's sleeve to divert his merry attention from the Sea Guardian.

"Let's help Chad with breakfast."

In the captain's cabin, Chad served Allard, Mirit and Nigel a breakfast of hard-boiled eggs, cold roast beef, cheese, bread, and apple cider.

Avatar was still grinning when he and Virgil arrived. "Doesn't look like Gulliver will need any bait. Dolphins have chased the sharks away."

Nigel laughed into his cup and took a drink.

Chad turned from the sideboard carrying a silver tray with a fancy pitcher full of cider and two cups when Allard stood up, knocking the tray from Chad's hand. The pitcher and cups broke, spilling the cider.

"I'm sorry," said Allard.

"No, my lord, it's my fault. I know better than to use such finery on a ship, but I thought for appearances it would be better than pewter." He carefully picked up the broken pieces.

"You mean for the Natanese?"

"Ay. I wanted to set a nice table tomorrow night when we entertain the admiral."

"Do we have more?" asked Nigel.

"In the cargo hold. I had a second set packed just in case."

"I'm truly sorry," said Allard.

Chad's reply became interrupted when he cut his left hand on a piece of broken porcelain.

"How bad?" Allard reached to examine Chad's cut.

"Not too serious."

"All the same, it should be bandaged."

"Avatar." Nigel indicated Chad. "Virgil, fetch the second set from the hold."

"You'll need to get the key from Gulliver. That section of the hold is secured for the journey," said Chad.

Titus nestled in the corner nearest the trunk to take a nap. There wasn't much else to do but sleep. He reckoned several days had passed. However, with no portholes he estimated time by the shafts of light through the hatch. The food and cider were long gone and he grew very hungry, yet uncertain if alerting someone to his presence was a good idea. His stomach growled and he squirmed to get into a position to quiet it. He had to make a decision soon or else starve! He stirred at hearing something and took a moment to recognize voices. He scrambled to hide behind the trunk yet tried to see the speaker.

"Whew! What stinks in here? I thought it was only cargo?" said Virgil.

"Ay, it is only cargo," groused Gulliver. He took a whiff. "Mortal not animal. Stowaway, I'll wager."

Titus tried to get into the trunk, only his movement made noise. Before he realized it, someone jerked him to his feet and spun him around. He came face-to-face with Virgil.

"Titus?" said the astonished Guardian.

"Let go." Titus tried to break loose, but Virgil held fast.

"What are you doing here? You became sick and left the wardroom with Egan."

"Ay. Barrett called to say he was taking you back to the castle," said Gulliver.

Titus again tried to be free of Virgil. "I said let go!"

"Not until we get some answers. How did you get in here?"

Titus clamped his mouth shut in defiance.

"Very well. You don't have answer us, but your uncle is a different matter." Virgil started to move, but Titus resisted. He forced the boy from the hold.

Avatar finished tending Chad's hand when the door opened. Gulliver entered first.

"I'm afraid, we found more than dishes," he said.

Nigel began to ask for clarification when Virgil arrived, and with a struggling boy in tow. "Titus?"

"By the heavenlies," murmured Mirit. "How did you get here?"

"We found him hiding in the cargo hold," said Virgil.

"The cargo hold?" Nigel's brief surprise turned into anger when Titus folded his arms in resistance. "You faked illness and snuck onboard. How?"

"With Barrett's help, no doubt," chided Allard.

Titus looked away in a refusal to answer.

Nigel seized him. "Answer me! How did you get onboard?"

Visibly startled by the forcefulness, Titus blurted out, "I climbed out the other side of the carriage when Egan went to fetch the surgeon and hid inside a trunk being loaded."

"You've been in the hold for three days?" asked Mirit with disbelief.

"I had Barrett place provisions in the trunk."

Nigel's grip on Titus tightened. "This was planned and not impulse?"

"I wanted to come with you, Uncle. I know I can help."

"Help?" Nigel's rough release made the boy stumble. Mirit caught Titus to keep him from falling, though her expression far from supportive.

"No!" began Allard in angry rebuff, "Your presence will be a complication not easily explained. Although women aren't scorned like in Morven, it took delicate negotiating to allow Princess Mirit to participate in what they view as a man's business. For a boy to suddenly be involved in matters of state is something I don't believe the Natanese will agree with."

"I'm the royal prince of Allon. The new emperor isn't much older than I."

"You went against your father, the king! And by doing so, placed us in a very awkward position of which you cannot comprehend!" In frustrated anger, Allard turned to Nigel yet gestured at Titus. "This defiance can't be allowed."

He didn't reply to Allard. The weight of the Titus' scheme and the consequences showed in Nigel's intense silent regard of his nephew.

"Can we take him back before we reach Natan?" asked Mirit.

"To turn back means we'll miss the rendezvous," said Gulliver.

"Out of the question," refuted Allard.

"May I make a suggestion, Highness?" asked Virgil.

Nigel waved with impatience for the Guardian to proceed, though his gaze never left Titus.

"Fortunately, he didn't wear his best suit and after three days in a smelling cargo hold, his appearance could pass for a servant and not a royal prince."

"Ay, he could be Chad's apprentice," added Avatar. "Which would require not calling him *highness* or any reference to his station. And for him to act accordingly," he stressed to the boy.

Titus scowled in offense. "You want me to act like a servant?"

"If you don't, it may prove dangerous to all of us."

Titus recoiled at the formidable Guardian's glare. Next to Kell and Armus, Avatar ranked among the elite leadership and there was more to his silver eyes than just the normal heavenly prodding common to other Guardians.

"What about having Gulliver take him back after the rendezvous?" asked Mirit.

"That would be my choice," said Nigel.

"I don't want to go back."

"You will do as you are told!"

"He didn't listen to his father, the king, what makes you think he'll listen to you?" asked Allard.

"You are too bold, my lord," Titus scolded Allard.

The tightening of his jowls and features signaled the end of Nigel's temper. "Gulliver! Place him in the brig until I decide what to do."

"Uncle?" he gasped in astonishment. He resisted when Gulliver took hold of him.

"Virgil." Nigel waved at Titus. The Guardian promptly helped Gulliver take the boy from the cabin.

Avatar closed the door upon Titus' loud protests. Nigel sat at the table, lips pressed and eyes narrow in fuming anger. Mirit moved beside him to offer support.

"Don't take the blame. He did this himself," she said.

"To be with me!" he argued then took a breath to curb his temper. "I see my excuses have led him to believe he can act his will even with the king."

"No, *he* is taking advantage of *you* to excuse his wrongful behavior. You can't allow that," said Avatar.

"Ay. Tyrone must be furious and Tristine beside herself with worry."

"Worry isn't the word I would use to describe Tristine's feelings about this," said Mirit with certainty.

"You must speak to him," said Avatar.

Nigel nodded, his look determined. "Only let him cool his heels in the brig for awhile. It may cause him to think about what he's done."

Titus tried to prevent the cell door from closing, but not possible with both Gulliver and Virgil present. With an angry huff, he turned from them.

"I would not want to be you when the king learns of this," said Gulliver.

"What could he do but take me back?"

"With that attitude he could do more."

Titus stuck out his chest, his chin tilted in pride. "I'm his son and heir."

"Then start acting like it!" Gulliver turned on his heels to leave.

"What's that supposed to mean?" he shouted, but received no reply save Gulliver slamming the brig door. Virgil moved to sit at a nearby table. "What did he mean?"

"You're acting more like a spoiled child than a prince who understands his responsibility."

"You're nothing like Jedrek. He wouldn't have spoken to me like that."

"Are you're saying my twin wouldn't have told you the truth?"

Titus clamped his lips together in an angry sneer.

"Then you didn't know him as well as you claim."

Titus jerked on the bars to test them.

"Even if you got out, you wouldn't get past me. I suggest you make yourself comfortable. There is more room in that cell than a trunk."

Titus' stomach growled with hunger. "Can I at least have something to eat?"

Virgil heaved an indifferent shrug. "Certainly, but you'll have to wait till someone comes down here. I'm not leaving."

Titus plopped down to sit into the far corner. He groaned and drew his knees up to his chest to rest his forehead. This did not turn out like he hoped. He carefully peeked up to watch Virgil. The Guardian sat at the table appearing disinterested. Virgil and Jedrek might have been twins with blond hair and same facial features, but different color eyes and personalities. He knew Virgil spent centuries imprisoned by Shadow Warriors. Still, every time he saw Virgil he remembered Jedrek. Although five years passed since Jedrek died trying to protect him from the Tunlundian kidnappers, Titus missed him.

Egan becoming his Overseer was not easy to accept. Eventually he came to tolerate Egan. The most difficult part of his plan was figuring how to deal with the Guardian's constant presence and suspicion. If Egan got wind of his plan, he would not have made it onto the ship.

All the same, he succeeded in stowing away, only to end up in the brig, which brought him back to his original depressing thought of failure. He knew Nigel would be put out, but to lock him up? What kind of treatment was that? *Nigel is usually reasonable. How could he be so mean?* He expected harsh treatment from his father, but not Nigel. He thought about ways to convince his uncle of how his actions were for the best. Of course, providing he gets a chance to speak to Nigel before they reach Natan. *But why wouldn't they talk? Nigel has always been willing to talk or listen to him in the past.*

He locked me in the brig! It will be temporary. Aunt Mirit will help him see reason. He sighed and lowered his head.

Chapter 5

NIGEL ENTERED THE BRIG. FOR A BRIEF MOMENT, HE AND TITUS regarded each other. He noticed a look of defiance in his nephew similar to Tristine in her youth, but a glint of meanness different than his mother. Tristine pushed and prodded, yet understood when she went too far and her responsibilities. These were concepts Titus had yet to grasp and by the look of him, it would take some doing. Thus, he asked, "Have you given thought to what you've done?"

"I did it to be with you, so we can show Father I'm capable—"

"Oh, no! Do not include me in your rebellious act of defying the king."

"I didn't mean it as rebellion."

"It cannot be taken any other way. You planned this!" Nigel took a deep breath to regain his temper before continuing. "I know I made excuses for your misbehavior in the past and I was wrong to do so. By this action, you have abused and misused my intentions of aiding you by turning it into defiance and rebellion against your father. That I cannot and will not tolerate!"

"Uncle, I didn't mean any of that."

Nigel said nothing in response, which made Titus scowl.

"I didn't think you would act like Father and dismiss me like a child."

"You are a child! You won't reach the age of manhood until next year."

Titus turned away. His selfish action manifested in his posture and expression.

Through the bars, Nigel seized Titus by the collar. "Look at me!" It was a sideway glance, and done in reluctance, but he had Titus' attention. "*I* was heir to the throne, only willingly yielded when another born to be king was discovered."

"Father."

"Ay. Although I stepped aside, I have not shunned my duty nor scorned the station to which I was born—like you." He roughly released Titus, but he could see some of the boy's stubbornness begin to weaken.

"I've not abandoned anything."

"No? I wear the uniform of the First Jor'ellian Knight and King's Champion. I have sworn oaths to give my life to protect the king, Jor'el and Allon. What have you done but dispute him in public and disgraced him by carrying out this escapade to suit your own pride? I won't be there to defend you when we send you back." He turned to leave.

Stunned, Titus seized the bars. "No! Uncle, please! You can't send me back."

Nigel stopped at the door when Virgil caught his arm and whispered something in his ear. He tossed a casual glance over his shoulder at Titus.

"Uncle?" asked the boy, hopeful.

Nigel left. Ten minutes later, a sailor brought food for Titus.

Nigel paced the cabin. At various times Mirit, Chad, and Avatar sought to counsel him. However, to be told how personal behavior affected someone is different than witnessing the behavior manifested.

"You can't take this upon yourself," said Mirit.

He shook his head. "I'm not, though I feel some responsibility. Mostly, I'm trying to think of how to explain this to Tyrone without sounding like I'm making excuses."

"You locked him in brig, which shocked him."

"Not enough of a shock to curb his brashness."

"Maybe you should throw him overboard. Egan would," said Avatar in deadpan seriousness. "Until he called for help, that is," he added at Nigel's chagrin.

"If I can add my voice, do not make the same mistake with your nephew you did with me," said Chad.

In confused curiosity, Nigel regarded his squire. "I didn't think I made a mistake in befriending you."

Chad kindly smiled. "Not in friendship, in your tolerance of my unruly behavior in Soren."

"I don't see how I could have stopped you."

Chad took a step toward Nigel to press his point. "You are the prince, my lord and master. You didn't press the issue for fear of my reaction and *I* took advantage. Much like Titus is doing to *you* now. Locking him in the brig must be only the beginning."

Nigel nodded. "I reminded him if I had not stepped aside for Tyrone, I would be king."

His sober tone made Mirit ask, "Do you regret it?"

He waved aside the question. "No. I'm troubled by his attitude. Not the brashness, rather a defiance beyond anything I encountered from Tristine."

"Ellan," said Avatar.

Nigel flinched as if waking from a bad dream. His voice barely rose above a disturbed whisper. "You think Titus exhibits similar tendencies?"

"When confronted about his actions, he displayed the same obstinacy Ellan manifested after she became heir. She wielded her will and even tried to pull rank on me. She never understood the relationship between Guardians and mortals, but used her advantage to sway Ellis. I think if those around Titus don't corral and tame his strong will then there is a possibility it could grow more intolerable."

Nigel shivered in disturbance. "I pray to heaven you're wrong. That he doesn't follow Ellan ..."

Mirit seized Nigel's hand. "Avatar isn't saying Titus will, only he *could*. We all could if not for harsh lessons."

"Which is what I meant earlier," began Chad. "I'm just a squire of little significance but Titus is the royal heir. There is much more at stake with him."

The door burst open and Allard rushed in. He beckoned to Nigel. "You'll want to come see this."

They all hastened out of the cabin and to the quarterdeck.

Gulliver stood at the helm. Kasey stood beside him looking through a spyglass to a ship on the horizon silhouetted by the late afternoon sun.

"The *Sentinel.* Seems Chase caught up to us," said Gulliver to their arrival. "They must have discovered the prince's disappearance and came to fetch him."

"Thank Jor'el," said Mirit in relief.

"By the heavenlies!" exclaimed Kasey. He looked from the spyglass to the others. "It's the king!"

Nigel snatched the glass from Kasey and focused the glass on the large rowboat heading for their ship. "Tyrone. Along with Egan and another Guardian I don't recognize." He handed the glass back to Kasey.

"The king! Prepare for boarding," shouted Gulliver to the deck hands.

Nigel and the others made their way to the port side where the crew prepared for boarding. Below, the rowboat pulled alongside. Tyrone waved to Nigel, who signaled in response. When Tyrone came aboard, he said, "No need to ask why you're here."

"Where is he?"

"In the brig."

For a long stern moment, Tyrone stared at Nigel. "Avatar, bring my son to the wardroom, only don't tell him I'm here." He made his way across the deck with the others following.

Nigel spoke once they inside the wardroom. "Why did you come? I planned to send him back with Gulliver."

"He's my son. Nor are you the one he disgraced. Only the object of his action."

"Don't you think I know that? That's why I put him in the brig."

"I'm surprised you took such action. Usually you make excuses."

Nigel stood to his full height, shoulders squared at the rebuff. Further words were prevented when Avatar arrived with Titus.

Titus gasped and his eyes went wide in fearful surprise. "Father!"

"How long did you think it would be before you were discovered?"

Titus' initial surprised turned to belligerent defense. "They didn't find me until this morning."

"Maybe they weren't looking hard enough."

"How should we know? Last we saw he was sick and being taken back to Straden," argued Nigel.

"As if you hadn't fallen for feigned illness before."

Before a piqued Nigel could reply, Egan spoke. "Sire, he fooled all of us and I was with him; Prince Nigel was not."

Tyrone took a deep, steadying breath before confronting Titus. "What do you have to say for yourself?"

"I'm sorry," he grumbled, but sounded far from sincere.

"Sorry you disgraced the king or were caught?" asked Egan.

Titus turned from the Guardian without replying.

Tyrone made Titus face him. "You have much to learn, beginning with humility. I'm not only your father, but also the king."

"I know! *Uncle* reminded me how *he* would be king if he hadn't stepped aside," chided Titus.

"Not in so off-handed a manner," said Nigel.

Tyrone flashed an irate glance at Nigel, but continued with Titus. "So you think if he were king he would be more lenient than I?"

Nigel lost his temper. "I don't condone what he did and blast you for implying I do!" He stormed out of the wardroom.

"Highness!" Gulliver called to Nigel. "The Natanese have arrived and a longboat is heading this way."

Nigel rushed to the helm where Kasey gave him the spyglass. "Six ships to our two. Let's hope we can get Tyrone and Titus away before continuing to Natan." He focused on the boat. "Must be the admiral." He gave the glass back to Kasey. "Stall them!" He scrambled down the steps from the helm and returned to the wardroom. "We have a problem! Kentashi is here."

Stunned, Allard grew pale. "What? He isn't due until morning."

"He's early, and with *six* large ships," he emphasized the number to Tyrone. "He's in a long boat about to pull alongside."

Allard gaped at Tyrone. "You're not supposed to be here, Sire."

Tyrone waved. "Calm down. Notice I am dressed as a royal officer not as king. Nor did we fly the royal standard. We anticipated a possibility of having to catch you on land and not at sea. I didn't want to offend or cause alarm."

"They told me to be a servant," Titus complained of Virgil and Avatar.

"A suggestion of what to do with him upon discovery," said Avatar.

"My option was to send him back, but that may not be so easy now, considering the numbers," groused Nigel.

"Perhaps we can still return without incident if you explain the *Sentinel* is an escort vessel," said Egan.

"Let's hope so. "

They heard the whistling on board of a visiting dignitary.

"Try not to look so fearful," said Tyrone to Allard.

"I'm sorry, Sire."

"Captain Fraser—at least for now. I don't think my grandfather would mind temporary use of his name. After all, he has a namesake in a great-grandson."

"Then I'm to be a servant?" asked Titus in disdain.

Tyrone laid a heavy hand on his son's shoulder and leaned down to speak low and harsh. "We must do some play acting for the moment to avoid unwanted trouble."

The door opened. Gulliver escorted an imposing looking man of forty years of age and five Natanese warriors. Admiral Kentashi Yoshiru appeared every inch a capable and seasoned soldier in his exotic plate armor, two swords and elaborate helmet. He was taller than his companions by about four to five inches. They too were dressed similar to Kentashi.

"Admiral, this is a surprise. We weren't expecting you until morning," said Nigel.

"Winds favorable. We make good time. You Prince Nigel?"

"I am. This is Lord Allard and my wife, Princess Mirit, the Queen's Champion."

"My lord admiral," said Mirit with a regal nod.

Kentashi stiffly bowed while the others slightly sneered in surveying Mirit's manly appearance. "We not expect wife to be dressed like warrior."

"If you recall, Admiral, I wrote to inform you of the princess' station as the Queen's Champion and her prowess in combat," said Allard.

Kentashi grunted. His gaze passed to the others, but more intense scrutiny on the towering Guardians. "Who?"

"They are Guardians of Jor'el. Avatar, Virgil, Egan and ..." Nigel stopped, realizing he didn't know the forest Guardian.

"Ridge," said Tyrone. "He is with my command."

Kentashi regarded Tyrone with the same intensity as the Guardians. Then again, Tyrone's height of six feet eight inches, black hair and light grey eyes always drew attention. Also, like the Guardians, he stood much taller than the Natanese. "You?"

"Captain Fraser of His Majesty's army and this is my son, who is being considered as a apprentice to Prince Nigel's squire, Chad." He indicated Titus and Chad respectively.

Titus began to react, but held his peace when Tyrone squeezed his shoulder. The boy made a partial bow to Kentashi.

"When you have finished we sail for Natan," said Kentashi to Nigel.

"Of course." Nigel turned to Tyrone. "That will be all, Captain. Tell His Majesty we appreciate him sending you as escort. As for your son, we'll discuss his future another time."

Tyrone made the Allonian salute then with Titus in hand, he, Egan and Ridge headed for the door.

"You not leave. All go to Natan," said Kentashi.

Nigel moved to stand beside Tyrone. "The captain is just escorting us to the rendezvous, he has no part in this."

"Emperor order all ships of visitors to port for time of stay. You comply."

Tyrone and Nigel exchanged brief conferring glance and Tyrone shrugged. "Who am I to dispute the emperor?"

"Father—?" began Titus, but stopped at a firm, swift jerk of his shoulder by Tyrone.

Nigel spoke in a bit louder voice to cover Titus' outburst and draw Kentashi's attention from the boy. "Of course, Admiral. We wouldn't want to disobey the emperor."

Kentashi stoutly nodded. "Have ships follow my ships." He spoke a few guttural words in Natanese to his companions. Two took up position by the door. "They help find way." He bowed to Nigel and left with the rest.

"We don't have to go with them do we, Father?"

Tyrone drew Titus away from the Natanese at the door. "We don't have a choice."

"But you're the k—"

"Captain," he forcefully corrected and snatched a glance at the soldiers. They didn't appear to understand. He made a slight motion of his head to Virgil, indicating the soldiers.

Virgil approached and began speaking in Natanese, surprising them. After a brief conversation, he led them from the room.

"He's taking them to Gulliver to help with navigation," said Avatar.

"Why do we have to go with them? As king you could have refused," insisted Titus.

"Not going would be a great insult and create unnecessary danger."

Titus shook his head. "It doesn't make sense. Why should they be insulted because a king didn't want to go? He's just an admiral."

"You don't understand the area of diplomacy!" declared Allard. "The king replied to the invitation with the names of those he was sending as an envoy, myself, the prince and princess with an small entourage. Your name was not on that list," he stressed. "Any last minute change of plan is not diplomatic protocol. And certainly *not* the sudden appearance of a king or meddlesome young prince!"

"But why?"

"The arrival of kings are stately affairs arranged well in advance and *only* with permission from the host country. I told you, your presence could be troublesome. Now we'll have to keep up the charade and hope they don't learn your true identities before we can find a way for you both to leave."

Titus shook his head, frowning in confusion. "I still don't understand why they would object to a visit from another king."

At Allard's unbridled frustration at dealing with the young prince, Avatar took over the explanation. "Natan is a closed country and only recently opened their ports in hopes of trade. Negotiations are a delicate matter, and normally done between representatives of the king. The unknown, or unwanted presence, of a foreign king on their soil could provoke them."

"That's why I put on the uniform, to avoid trouble," said Tyrone. Seeing Titus not convinced, he made the boy sit on a window seat with him and asked, "Do you remember why the Tunlundians kidnapped you?"

"To force you into war."

"To draw me onto their soil so they could claim I invaded and kill me in self-defense, and by doing so, defeat Jor'el and proclaim Helmer god."

Titus' brow grew level in remembrance. "That's why I was to be sacrificed, only Aunt Mirit saved me."

"I would do so again," she said.

Tyrone made Titus turn back to him. "In Tunlund, a trap was laid by others for evil purposes and had to be sprung. This is different." His voice grew stern. "You forced me into this position by your selfish action. Now we must play our parts or risk the lives of others if we are discovered. And this time, if something goes wrong, Jor'el may not allow Mirit, Nigel, or any of us to survive. Do you understand?"

Titus shrunk back, the impact evident on his face. "Ay, sir."

"Chad. Take him and find more suitable clothes, and teach him what you can before we reach Natan."

"Ay, Captain."

Tyrone motioned for Egan to go with Chad and Titus.

When the door shut, Allard voiced further objection. "This arrangement is going to be problematic. He is too young, too inexperienced and too arrogant to keep his tongue."

"I am well aware of the situation," said Tyrone, in waning patience.

"Really? Then why are you here? Why not let me handle it?" asked Nigel.

"He is my son!"

"This is not the time for arguing!" scolded Mirit.

"He accuses me of leniency when I was caught completely unaware of knowledge he claims," refuted Nigel.

"You were ignorant of his plan?" asked Tyrone.

"Ay! And never would I agree to or sanction any action against you! I'm sworn to protect you. Although how I'll do so on this trip, I don't know, *Captain Fraser.*"

Allard intervened by asking Tyrone, "How did he get past Egan and sneak on board?"

"By a very elaborate scheme he started planning and preparing for at Waldron."

Nigel's sarcasm came spilling forth. "Well, that alone should vindicate me, since Mirit and I met you in Burleigh and haven't been to Waldron in a month!"

"Can we save this argument until we get home?" she lashed out. "We have a serious situation and must face it united or risk lives."

"The princess is right," said Avatar.

"Although blame should be placed where it belongs—on Titus," said Allard.

"Blame matters little under such circumstances."

"But necessary in planning our response to protect all concerned."

To Allard's logic, Avatar nodded in agreement.

Tyrone took a deep, calming breath before addressing Nigel. "You tell me how he was discovered and I'll tell you what happened in Straden."

Chapter 6

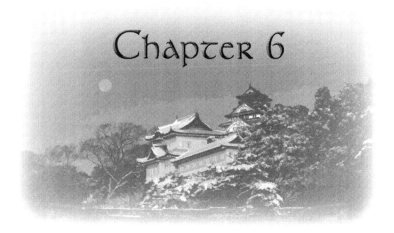

L ATE IN AFTERNOON OF THE SEVENTH DAY SINCE LEAVING ALLON, they entered the harbor of Kaori, Natan's main port city. Tyrone, Nigel, Mirit, Avatar, Virgil and Allard stood on the quarterdeck with Gulliver. Titus waited on the main deck alongside Chad, Ridge and Egan. Titus wore a uniform of a cabin boy in the king's marines, similar in style to Tyrone's royal blue and silver uniform.

The sprawl of Kaori stretched across the horizon, as far as the eye could see. The city rose sharply in elevation from the harbor to a plateau. The architecture ranged from squalor to a massive majestic fortress perched on the plateau overlooking the city. The multi-layer roofs of the fortress were of tile cut at sharp angles and upturned corners with some kind of statues indistinguishable at that distance, but large enough to be seen from the water. Beyond the fortress rose impressive mountains, taller and more rugged than any in the Highlands of Allon. Although spring at the lower elevations, snow covered most of the mountain peaks.

"Incredible," began Chad. "There must be tens of thousands of people living here. I can't recall seeing so many, even in Panos Point."

Titus wrinkled his nose. "What is that smell?"

"Low tide, rotting fish, sewage. Who knows with this many people?"

As the ships drew closer to the dock, faces and the state of the people proved fascinating. Their simple manner of dress was quite different from Allon. Both men and women wore a form of pants with long straight shirts closed to one side or a padded coat. The hats were made of tightly woven straw with broad brims. Even when shouting, the dockworkers spoke fast and unintelligible.

"Egan. Can you understand what they're saying?" asked Titus.

"Ay, but I wouldn't translate such base language. In over two thousand years, I've not heard the servants and peasants of Allon speak so vulgar."

"So you're among the Originals," said Chad.

"Ay."

"What is an Original?" asked Titus.

"Those among the first group of Guardians created, with Kell the premier. Other Guardians were created in two hundred year intervals ending after eight hundred years. *He* being in the next to last group and six hundred years younger than me." Egan jerked his thumb at Ridge.

"Despite being among the Originals, you haven't been abroad much," said Ridge in sarcastic rebuff.

"Mind yourself, ranger."

"Or what, warrior?"

At the terse exchange, Chad asked, "Is there a problem?"

"Not with me," said Ridge and assumed a nonchalant expression.

"Nothing for you to be concerned about. Just concentrate on your role playing," said Egan.

"That may be harder for some than others," chided Chad.

"I'm doing my best, but I wasn't born a servant," complained Titus.

Egan's hand gripped Titus' shoulder in warning. "Don't speak so loud and open about yourself."

"If I can't understand them I doubt they can understand me."

Egan leaned down and spoke in a low voice of warning. "You want to bet your life and the lives of everyone else on that assumption? Remember, Kentashi speaks Allonian."

"Speaking of, the admiral and others are heading this way." Ridge pointed down the dock.

The crowd scurried out of the way when barked at, pushed or struck aside by the lead soldiers. A pair of two wheeled carts, each drawn by a single man, followed Kentashi and his men mounted on horses. The carts appeared in function to be for transporting people and not cargo.

Nigel, Tyrone, Mirit and Allard joined them on the main deck. Avatar and Virgil moved to secure the gangplank. By the time the Guardians finished, Kentashi and his men reached the ship. After a guarded glance to Tyrone, Nigel led the group down the gangplank.

Kentashi dismounted, clasped the hilt of his sword and bowed to Nigel. "I officially welcome you to Natan, honored guests." His men followed his lead to bowing.

"Thank you, Admiral. On behalf of His Majesty King Tyrone, I offer greetings from Allon and wishes for a successful first exchange."

"On behalf of Emperor Tirigato, I accept king's greeting and make same wish for Natan. I mean Allon."

Nigel grinned. "I understand. You speak Allonian well. Where did you learn our language?"

"From Raiden. He teach many things to me and ancestors before me."

"Raiden?"

Kentashi motioned toward the mountains. "Raiden live in mountain and is ancestral protector of my family."

"He sounds very old," said Mirit.

"Raiden eternal, mighty spirit. Mountain rumble when he is angry but mostly Raiden kind. Now, please, come. It will be dark soon." Kentashi turned to his men and spoke a few curt words. In turn, one man shouted and waved. Immediately three of the two-wheel carts arrived. "Please, prince and wife. Way to Kaori."

"I thought this was Kaori?" asked Mirit.

"Town named after fortress." He motioned to the impressive structure that dominated the pinnacle.

71

Nigel and Mirit got into the cart Kentashi again indicated. Tyrone and Allard sat in the cart behind them.

"You, you and you follow first cart," said Kentashi to Avatar, Virgil and Ridge. "You, you and you follow second cart," he said to Titus, Chad and Egan.

As they took up position, Titus noticed the curious and askew looks being given them by the Natanese. "Why are they staring at us?"

"Aside from being oddly dressed, wouldn't you stare at a being twice your size carrying a lethal sword?" Chad grinned and indicated Egan.

"Or red hair." Egan flicked some strains of Chad's hair.

"As if I hadn't heard that before."

Kentashi shouted in Natanese to the soldiers before mounting his horse.

From the dock, the narrow streets wound through the city up the plateau to the fortress. Those in the path of the soldiers and carts quickly made way, bowing when the carts passed. Not once did the soldiers' pace slow or the men pulling the carts falter.

The fortress walls rose to impressive heights, thirty feet with ornate battlements and lookout towers. The statues on the corners of the numerous roofs were unusual creatures; some resembled a reptile with scales and wings, others with the face of a dog, body and arms of a man with the hindquarters and tail of a lion.

The massive main gate was constructed of lumber five feet thick and held together with forged iron of intricate workmanship. Through the large gate they entered a courtyard alive with a stunning array of blooming trees and flowers of pink, white, red and green. The courtyard gravel was carefully raked. Twenty servants, male and female, stood behind a beautifully dressed lady, all waiting in front of the main structure.

Her garments were colorful and flowing, her black hair meticulously arranged in an elaborate style. She wore make-up of white powder on her face, bright red lips and exquisitely painted eyes. She made a most elegant acknowledgement of Kentashi's arrival. He gave her a nod and began barking commands to his soldiers.

Although short of breath from running to keep up with the carts, Titus gazed in wonder at the fortress. Columns of ornate design rose, topped by elaborately carved wood beams, lentils and frames, but he couldn't see any windows.

"Where are the windows?" he asked Chad between breaths.

"Look." Chad pointed to a male servant opening what appeared to be panels from floor to ceiling that slid sideways. "I guess they don't have windows, rather open those opaque doors for light and air."

Kentashi spoke. "Welcome to Kaori, my ancestral home."

"Impressive, Admiral," said Tyrone.

"Thank you, Captain." He continued up the steps then paused. "This is Lady Hoshi, number one wife."

"An honor, my lady," said Tyrone.

She smiled, bowing at the waist and speaking Natanese.

"She does not speak Allonian, but bids you welcome," said Kentashi.

He made the introductions to Hoshi in Natanese, to which she offered greetings to each. However, she stopped at seeing Mirit, obviously disturbed by the uniform. She spoke a few words to Kentashi, who made a curt reply. Hoshi curbed her initial reaction to greet Mirit.

"She too surprised by princess man clothes."

"Well, I must say, I'm impressed by her most splendid dress," said Mirit, smiling and motioning to Hoshi.

Kentashi made a brief explanation, to which Hoshi smiled and this time her response to Mirit was genuine. She made a gesture indicating the house, which they took to mean a bid to enter. Kentashi confirmed the action by moving toward the house only he paused at the entrance to allow a servant to remove his boots.

Servants went to remove their boots, but the Allonians and Guardians appeared confused and resistant.

"Custom not to wear outside shoe in house," said Kentashi. He placed his foot into a wooden sandal-like slipper the servant held. "They place shoes near door for later."

The Allonians and Guardians removed their boots and accepted the sandals. Of course, this added several inches in height to the Guardians, who already towered two feet above the Natanese.

"It's like walking on a wooden plank," said Chad.

Kentashi chuckled and led them inside to what appeared to be a foyer. Although the furnishings were sparse the house was immaculately clean and organized with superior craftsmanship of painting, wood engraving and construction. Again Kentashi spoke fully throated and servants scurried to fulfill his command. He placed his arms up and two male servants began to remove his armor plating from shoulder to legs, his helmet and sword. A female servant put a wonderful shimmering robe of black and red design on him and tied it closed. The servants offered to take the cloaks and weapons of the Allonian, but again they hesitated about yielding their weapons.

"Please. Also custom not wear weapon in home. No harm. My warriors protect."

"So will ours," said Nigel concerning the Guardians.

"They impressive, but that one not wear sword and have strange color hair like squire," said Kentashi of Ridge.

"I'm a ranger. I don't need a sword. Just this." He whipped out his quarterstaff and twirled it.

"What ranger?"

"One who knows and protects the wilderness."

"Ah, a Sen," said Kentashi with understanding. "Please, also give staff."

Ridge complied and handed it to a small old man, who rocked under the weight of the staff before shuffling off.

Kentashi led them through the foyer to a room set up for a meal. A long low table sat about two feet off the floor with many embroidered cushions and pillows where chairs would normally be placed. "Sit."

Chad held Titus back when the boy moved toward the table with the others.

"You two also. Today. Tomorrow begin serve."

In a formal acknowledgement, Chad nodded to Kentashi and steered Titus to the far end of the table. "Remember your place," he whispered.

Titus frowned but said nothing as he sat beside Egan. Mirit sat beside Nigel with Avatar and Virgil flanking them. Tyrone and Allard sat on the opposite side with Ridge.

Once seated at the head of the table, Kentashi nodded to Hoshi. She clapped her hands and many servants began bringing the meal. She spoke to the Allonians, which Kentashi translated.

"Eat. Enjoy," he said.

"Will Lady Hoshi join us?" asked Mirit. Hoshi stood to one side and busy with issuing short instructions or hand gestures to servants.

Kentashi laughed. "She see to your needs as good host. Now eat."

"First we shall bless our food," said Nigel.

"Bless?"

"A prayer of thanking Jor'el for provision and a safe journey."

"Ah," said Kentashi with understanding. He watched them bow their heads and Nigel speak a quick prayer.

The Allonians looked at their plates and bowls trying to find utensils.

Mirit leaned toward Nigel and discreetly ask, "What do we with eat with?"

Kentashi heard her and laughed. "Knife to cut. These to eat." He picked up two slender pieces of wood. "Hold this way and bring food to mouth." He demonstrated then laughed when his guests tried to mimic his demonstration with varying degrees of success. The only one who didn't have any problem in mastering the wooden sticks was Ridge. Yet despite their obvious frustration, they too grew amused.

"You must always be hungry if the food keeps falling before you get it in your mouth," said Tyrone.

Nigel reached for the table knife. "I think this would be easier."

Kentashi smiled and nodded. "For now, perhaps. But if invited to eat with Lord Norkiru or the emperor would be insult."

"Then I better practice."

"Or go hungry," said Tyrone. Once gain, a piece of meat fell off the stick.

"What's this?" Nigel held up his table knife.

Tyrone picked up the piece of meat using the sticks and succeeded to eat. He flashed a smile of satisfaction.

"What is this drink, Admiral? It's warm but colorless," said Allard referring to the small porcelain cup from which he drank.

"*Sakiri*. Rice wine. Warm for soothing and enliven spirit."

Titus smiled at hearing the word *wine* and downed the contents of his cup. He refilled his cup from a ceramic bottle.

"That's enough for you, young man," said Tyrone.

Egan removed the bottle from Titus' reach.

Kentashi grinned and spoke to a servant. "I order tea for son."

"Thank you, Admiral."

"Can I finish this?" asked Titus, holding up the cup for Tyrone's approval. By his father's steady look, he knew the answer and handed the cup to Egan without taking a sip. Instead of pouring the wine back into the bottle as expected, the Guardian drank it.

Hoshi made certain the food was plentiful and the guests entertained with unique music on string instruments and interesting percussion. An hour later the meal concluded and servants began lighting lanterns for the night.

"If you like to retire, rooms are prepared," said Kentashi.

"That would be nice. The voyage was long and tiring," said Nigel.

Kentashi spoke to Hoshi, who bowed and went to dismiss the servants. Kentashi led the Allonians from the room and upstairs. He paused in the hall between two rooms of sliding doors.

"This for prince and wife. This for Lord Allard but made room for Captain Fraser." He motioned to each as he spoke.

"What about us?" asked Titus.

At Kentashi's disapproving sneer, Chad intervened. "Forgive him, Admiral. I'm still training him. It is our custom to sleep near our masters."

"Sleep at end of hall. I have blankets brought. Guardians sleep with soldiers, unless there is an objection?" He again glared at Titus. This time the boy didn't speak.

"There are no objections, Admiral," said Tyrone. "Please forgive my son. He often speaks out of turn. It is a habit I'm trying to get him to break."

"My son had same habit. Sent off to war and he learn to hold tongue."

"I hope to meet him while we're here. Maybe he can give my son some advice."

"He is dead. That is how tongue became silent."

Tyrone offered a respectful bow. "My condolences, Admiral."

Kentashi gave his expected curt nod and short bow. "Good-night."

Titus moved beside Tyrone to watch Kentashi leave. "He frightens me."

"Good. You need a little fear at present."

"Do I have to sleep out here?"

"What do you think?" came the terse reply.

Titus said nothing, rather tugged on Chad's sleeve and moved to the end of the hall.

"Egan, stay with him. The rest of you go to the barracks."

"We won't leave any of you, Captain," said Avatar.

"We don't want to offend them."

"We can make it appear as if we're not here."

Tyrone wryly smiled. "Your concern is always appreciated so I suggest a compromise. You and Egan remain while Virgil and Ridge circulate among the soldiers. See what the Natanese are like."

"Fair enough."

Mirit yawned. "It'll be good to sleep on something that doesn't move."

Nigel chuckled and slid open the opaque panel to their room. Mirit followed him inside. The room appeared empty except for two small tables each with lit lanterns, a paneled screen, a two-inch high mat with a folded blanket at one end and two scooped out wooden pieces placed side-by-side at the other end. Two of the shimmering fabric robes were laid on the mat.

"Where is the bed?" she asked.

"I guess it's the mat," he said.

"You must be joking? Where are the pillows, the mattress?"

Tyrone and Allard appeared behind them. "Their room looks the same," said Allard.

"Only I think that is a single bed where we have separate mats."

"Do you believe this?" she began. "First sitting on the floor to eat with sticks and now I'm to place my head on a wooden block to sleep."

"I suppose we're to wear these." Nigel picked up one of the robes and held it in front of him. It barely covered his torso.

"Too short for you. I think it's for Mirit," teased Tyrone.

She blushed and snatched the robe from Nigel. Muffled laughter came from behind where Chad and Titus stood in the threshold. "Out! All of you."

Virgil and Ridge made their way to the barracks. Despite being a ranger, Ridge equaled Virgil in height at seven and a half feet tall. Other castes of Guardians were shorter than warriors, but not under seven feet. Even vassals were taller than most Allonians by at least a foot. Compared to the Natanese, the height nearly doubled. Servants wearily regarded them and some backed away bowing, muttering in what sounded like anxiety.

They found the barracks located across the large compound from the main house. Upon approach, three of Kentashi's soldiers moved to accost them. They were the same three who accompanied Kentashi. One pointed at Ridge and spoke sarcastically to his companions.

"Your red hair is the object of a joke," said Virgil.

"Did he just call me a sunburned tomato?"

"No, he made reference to a woman's face paint."

The soldiers laughed.

Ridge flashed a sarcastic smile at the soldier making the joke and spoke in Natanese. "You must be very familiar with women's ways to know how to use face paint."

At first he was startled by Ridge's command of the language then said, "Your hair is not a man's color."

"Oh, and what is a man's color?"

"Black or brown are colors of strength. Red is the color of celebration. Or a concubine's robe." He laughed to his snickering companions.

Virgil seized Ridge's arm to stop any physical retaliation to the insult. Instead, Ridge made a verbal reply.

"Where we come from red is the color of fire and power."

The soldier smiled and nodded in approval. "You give as well as you take. We haven't seen your people before."

"Wait. This was a test?" asked Virgil.

"Yes. A test of words since hospitality forbids challenging guests to a test of battle strength." He flexed his arm.

"Somehow I think we have the advantage."

The soldier confidently smiled. "Height isn't everything. Often smaller opponents can react quicker."

"True."

"I am Hodi, captain of Admiral Kentashi's soldiers. This is Jiru and Makito."

"I am Virgil and he is Ridge. We are Guardians of Jor'el."

"Who is Jor'el and what are his Guardians?"

"Jor'el is the Almighty Heavenly ruler of Allon. He created us to serve him and his mortals."

"You are spirits?" asked Makito, his voice tentative and eyes shifting between Virgil and Ridge.

"In a manner of speaking," began Ridge. "We are physical manifestations of the spirit from which we were created. Virgil is a warrior and I'm a ranger, one who knows and protects the creatures of the wilderness and those who travel it."

Makito's apprehension increased. "You were not born! You are immortal."

"Ay."

Frightened, Makito ran from the group.

"Wait!" called Virgil. "Where is he going?"

Jiru also appeared uncertain of the Guardians. "To the shrine to pray to Raiden and the ancestors to protect him."

"We're not here to harm anyone."

"Only Raiden and the ancestors will know if you are good or evil spirits."

"Where is this shrine?" asked Ridge.

Hodi lead the Guardians to a small building between the barracks and the main house. One side remained open for easy access. Inside, under an altar stood smaller carved versions of the winged reptile found on the corners and apex of the fortress. Colored lanterns lit the shrine and many sticks burned but didn't give off light, rather strong, pungent scents. Makito knelt with his head to the ground before a carved wooden altar of a man standing beside a winged reptile twice his size.

"Makito," said Hodi.

He scrambled to his feet and pointed at the Guardians. "They should not be here!"

"We mean no harm," said Virgil.

"Tell that to Raiden." Makito motioned to the statue.

"I don't think he can hear us, it's a statue."

"He will know. Speak!"

Virgil studied the statue, icy blue eyes narrow in concentration then asked, "Which is Raiden, the man or creature?"

"Both. Raiden can be man or dragon," said Makito.

"Dragon? Is that what it's called?" Virgil spoke lowly in the Ancient. "Creatures are more your domain, though I don't sense evil."

Ridge stared at the stature, his golden eyes momentarily flaring in brightness of concentration. "Seems harmless."

"What do you say?" demanded Makito. "Speak in Natanese."

Virgil addressed the statue in Natanese. "Raiden, we are travelers from a distant land and mean no harm to you and your people. Accept our visit in friendship."

A thunderclap startled the mortals. Heavy rain fell on the shingled roof and the lanterns extinguished by a sudden gust of wind.

"I thought you said it was harmless," Virgil chided Ridge in Allonian.

"Raiden does not believe you!" said Makito.

"Wait!" Ridge seized Makito to stop him from leaving. "Raiden means god of thunder. So thunder is a sign of his presence, which mean he accepts us."

Makito turned to his companions for their opinion.

"He could be right," said Hodi. "Thunder and rain have showed Raiden's favor."

A bell began to toll.

"An alarm?" asked Virgil.

"No, the signal to change the watch," said Hodi. He, Jiru and Makito left the shrine with Virgil and Ridge following a few paces behind.

"That was quick thinking," said Virgil in the Ancient.

"I'm just glad it worked. We can't have them believing we're here to do harm and possibly jeopardize our first visit." Ridge saw Hodi waiting for them. "For now, let's just be pleasant guests."

Chapter 7

LYING IN A COOL HALLWAY WITH A BARELY PASSABLE blanket didn't seem to bother Chad, who fell asleep easily. Egan assumed the Guardian meditative position for the night so nothing troubled him. Titus couldn't get comfortable on the hard, cold floor. He didn't know when he finally fell asleep, but it didn't feel like long before someone tried to wake him. He batted the hand away. The next grip on his shoulder tightened and a firm voice told him to wake up. He opened one eye to see Chad.

Behind Chad, came other voices. Egan towered over the Natanese manservant, who held a lantern because the hallway was still dark. The man did not appear intimidated by Egan and spoke in quick, agitated phrases, gesturing toward Chad and Titus. Egan tried to turn him away but he wouldn't budge, standing his ground even against the Guardian.

"Is he awake yet?" asked Egan with impatience.

Chad yanked the blanket off Titus. "He is now."

"Hey!" The boy tried to grab the blanket back, but Chad moved away. "It's cold."

"There is work to do. We're to help with breakfast."

Titus stretched and yawned. "What time is it?"

"About an hour before dawn," said Egan.

"What? I only get up this early to go hunting."

"*Shhh!* You'll wake the others," said Chad. He pulled Titus to his feet. "Come. This is our duty."

The man gestured for haste. Titus delayed in moving, groggy and uncooperative, so Chad practically dragged him down the hall. Avatar stood outside the door to his father's chamber. Titus heard Egan say something under his breath to Avatar in passing and Avatar chuckled.

"What did you say?"

"Private joke between Guardians."

"About me, I bet."

"Not everything is about you."

The Natanese man stood at the top of the stairs making an impatient waving motion.

"About him?"

Egan just shrugged and fought a wry smile. Titus huffed in annoyance and began to follow Chad downstairs. He slipped slightly and caught the rail to keep from falling.

"Watch your step in the dim light," said Chad.

When they reached the first floor, other servants rushed about yet silent in their duty. Titus yawned, large and loud, which angered the man holding the lantern.

Egan translated. "He says you must learn to keep your fatigue to yourself."

Titus rolled his eyes. "I don't know why anyone gets up this early."

"To tend to the needs of their masters. The servants at Waldron do the same," said Chad.

"They do?" asked Titus. He tried to stifle another yawn.

Chad slowed the pace to speak privately to Titus. "Haven't you noticed what goes on around you? When do you think they gather the fresh eggs for breakfast, or get the milk and cream? Many tasks are done before you rise and still others are done after you go to bed."

"I guess I never paid much attention."

"Sadly most nobility don't and take for granted what their servants do. Fortunately, your uncle and father aren't like that. What about you?"

Titus made a considering frown. "I don't know. I'm still not awake yet."

"Awake or asleep, you have an important role to play and you better do it well."

They reached the kitchen. In contrast to the quiet servants in the main house, this place was a noisy hive of activity and brightly lit by lanterns and cooking fires. Shouting of unintelligible orders came from every direction.

The man set the lantern on a table and began speaking to Chad and Titus. He pointed at what to do and which direction to go. He picked up a rod with a bucket attached to each end and shoved it into Titus' hands.

"You're to fetch water from the well for cleaning dishes," said Egan.

"I don't know where the well is."

The man gave the lantern to Egan and shoved Titus toward the back door. The boy stumbled. Egan caught Titus and said a few curt words to the man. The servant shrugged with indifference to what Egan said and took Chad across the room. Egan and Titus left the kitchen by a rear door.

They found the well fifty feet from the kitchen. Titus set the rod and buckets down to survey the well. "How am I supposed to get the water?"

Egan smirked in disbelief. "Are you telling me you can't figure out how to draw water from a well?"

Titus scowled. "At least place the lantern so I can see."

Once Egan put the lantern in its place, he took a seat on a nearby bench.

"You could help, you know?"

"Why? You're perfectly capable."

With a bucket already lowered into the well, Titus located the crank. He began turning the crank and felt the weight of a loaded bucket. He tried not to show the strain, or rather his annoyance at the labor. When the bucket came within reach, he grabbed it. He pulled too fast and it hit the side of the well, spilling the contents and dousing the front of his pants.

Egan laughed. "You could have used the privy earlier."

Titus snarled at the humor. He lowered the bucket for more water. This time when he raised the well bucket, he carefully brought it to the side and filled one of the fetching buckets.

From the back door the man called, waving at Titus. The boy started to leave but Egan stopped him.

"No, he wants to know what's taken you so long."

"What do you mean, so long? I just got here."

"According to him, you're taking too long."

"Well, if you'd help me it wouldn't take so long."

The man arrived, seized Titus and scolded him.

Egan translated. "He calls you lazy and selfish because you won't do your task properly and wonders if all Allonians are like you." Egan spoke to the man. The servant sneered at Titus and left, muttering under his breath. The Guardian moved close to speak to Titus. "You've brought disgrace to Allon, your father and Jor'el by your behavior."

"I wasn't meaning to disgrace anybody. I just wanted to prove myself."

He leaned down to look directly at Titus and spoke in a low, firm voice. "I would die to protect you just like Jedrek did, but you have placed more lives at risk than mine. Tell me, is proving yourself worth their possible deaths for failure?"

Titus paled and muttered, "No." He shied from Egan's steady and penetrating bright blue eyes. "Please, help me with the first load. I'll do the rest myself."

Egan filled the second bucket and place the rod over Titus' shoulders for him to take back to the kitchen.

Inside, Chad washed dishes in a cauldron over a low fire. A woman working with Chad spoke to Titus. She pointed to the cauldron next to where Chad worked.

"The water needs to heat for the next load of dishes," said Chad.

"Isn't the water hot?" asked Titus. He poured the first bucket into the cauldron.

"No. I pushed open this lever to add cold water to get the right temperature."

Titus observed the wooden lever from a trough hanging over the cauldron. "If there is way to bring water in then why am I fetching it from the well?"

Chad smiled. "Probably to get you to do some work."

"Ha, ha."

"This pump draws hot water from the heating cauldron. Once the cleaning water is too dirty, they tip it over with this lever and the water runs down that grate." He pointed to the floor on the other side of the cauldron.

"How do you know all that? I didn't think you spoke Natanese."

"I don't. The woman showed me. Very similar to the devices used in the privies at Waldron."

"We don't tip over the tubs to drain."

"I said similar, but the construction is a bit cruder."

After Titus emptied the second bucket, she shooed him away with a few words and indication to fetch more water.

Dawn broke and several roosters crowed. Titus made a dozen trips between the kitchen and the well. He grew tired and his shoulders ached. All the while, Egan sat on the bench next to the well in silent observance. In some ways Titus was glad for the silence, as Egan made his point clear. Still, it was hard to think past the task at hand to what the Guardian said.

Titus went to grab the rope of the filled well bucket when his hands cramped and he lost his grip. The rope slipped. He loudly hissed in painful surprise and released the rope. The bucket would have fallen back down the well, except Egan caught it.

"What's wrong?" asked the Guardian.

"My hands cramped and the rope slipped."

Egan set the bucket on the side of the well to inspect Titus' hands. He discovered several red marks. "Rope burn. It'll smart for while, but no serious damage."

Titus rubbed his hand. "Could you please finish?"

Egan filled the buckets. "You must bring it in."

Titus sighed and positioned himself so Egan could lift the rod and buckets onto his shoulders.

Inside the kitchen, the light of dawn filtered through the windows. The noise level and activity increased with the sunlight, even drowning out the roosters from outside. His fatigue manifested in the difficulty of lifting the first bucket to refill the empty cauldron.

Chad helped to pour the last bucket into the cauldron. "You've done well."

"My hands hurt." He rubbed his palms on his pant legs.

Chad examined Titus' hands. "Take my place with the dishes. I'll fetch water."

Titus flashed a grateful smile. He placed his hands in the water, only to hiss and withdraw them.

"Too hot?" asked Chad.

"No, they sting."

"Because of the burn. The water will soothe them and the soap help to prevent infection."

Apprehensive, Titus lowered his hands into the water then relaxed once they were submerged.

Chad chuckled and picked up the rod and buckets. "Do a good job. The cook is very particular."

Withdrawing his hands from the water, the palms changed from red to looking like very wrinkled prunes. Well, at least he didn't have to lift anything heavy. Surprised, he backed away when several pots were dropped into the cauldron and splashing dishwater doused the front of his pants.

A man laughed and pointed at Titus' pants. He obviously made a joke of the wetness before walking away.

Mirit stirred in her sleep at hearing voices then felt a tug on the blanket. She tugged back, though her eyes remained closed. At another, harder tug she opened her eyes. Two women knelt at the end of the bed;

each held a part of the blanket. Startled, she yanked it from them, which made her fall back into Nigel.

He woke with a start. He didn't wear the provided robe and slept bare-chested, the blanket covering him from his waist down. "What's wrong?"

"They were trying to take the blanket off."

The women giggled. One spoke, motioning to Nigel and waving toward the door.

"I think they want me to go with them."

"Not undressed," protested Mirit.

They heard chuckling and Avatar appeared in the threshold. He translated. "They were trying to wake you. Admiral Kentashi ordered a morning bath for Nigel. He is to accompany them wearing only his robe."

"With them to a bath? I don't think so," she chided.

The women again spoke and waved for Nigel.

"They are only to escort him to the admiral," said Avatar.

Nigel wore a mischievous grin as he said to Mirit, "A bath sounds good," then to Avatar, "Tell them to wait in the hall."

Avatar relayed the statement. The women bowed to Nigel and Mirit before departing. The Guardian slid the paneled door closed.

"That was a rude awakening," she groused.

"Why? You should be used to servants milling about." Nigel rose. He wore his personal undergarments to bed.

"Not trying to take the blanket off while I'm sleeping. And what's with you willing to go with these women to a bath?"

He chuckled and put on the robe and slippers. "They're just the escort." He knelt beside her, his smile taking on a roguish edge. "Care to join me in the bath?"

"Not here! It's too strange. I feel we're being watched."

He laughed. "Someone didn't sleep well."

"Did you?"

"Actually I did. My back ached from the ship's bed but not now. I'll see you at breakfast." He kissed her forehead and left.

In the hall, Tyrone emerged from his room. He also wore a robe and sandals.

"They woke you too?" asked Nigel.

"Ay, only Allard isn't feeling well so he went back to sleep."

"What's wrong with him?"

"Tired from the voyage and not accustomed to the food."

Nigel didn't see Chad, Egan or Titus. "Where are the others?"

"They were sent to help with breakfast," said Avatar.

The women spoke and motioned for them to follow.

"Stay with Mirit and Allard," said Nigel to Avatar.

The women led them downstairs and through a plain back hallway to a room off the main house that appeared dedicated to bathing. A huge wooden tub four feet deep by six feet in diameter stood in the middle of the room. Steam rose from the milky and pleasant scented water. Several steps led to the tub. There were wooden benches and hooks along the wall for sitting and hanging clothes. Kentashi was in the water.

"Ah, prince and captain. Good morning. Where is Lord Allard?"

"He begs to be excused as he is not feeling well," said Tyrone.

"Should I send him physician?"

"I don't think it's serious. At his age, the voyage was long and difficult."

Kentashi nodded. "Please, join me."

Nigel hesitated and glanced at the women. They giggled under their breath.

Kentashi said something to the women. They bowed and left, sliding the door closed. "Please."

Nigel and Tyrone stripped and joined Kentashi in the tub.

"Is this the common form of bathing?" asked Tyrone.

"Ay. Is bathing not common in Allon?"

"No, it is common. Only usually alone."

"Oh!" said Nigel in surprise when he slipped and landed on something that prevented him from submerging. "There are benches underwater."

"To sit and be bathed," said Kentashi smiling. He clapped his hands and the door slid open. This time three different women entered and dressed in what appeared to be undergarments only. They placed themselves at the rim of the tub behind each man.

Taken back at the sight of the women, Nigel sunk further under water. One began to massage his shoulders. Another tried to do the same to Tyrone, who also grew wary of the attempt.

"You not like bath?" asked Kentashi at their reactions.

"A bath, ay, but not this." Nigel tried to stop the woman from bathing him further.

"Not understand. Captain say bath common in Allon."

Tyrone avoided a woman's attempt to bathe him. "Ay, but not a woman bathing a man."

"Wife not enjoy bath?"

Nigel caught her hand on his chest. "That's different."

"Have wife join us. I call for Hoshi, she like bath too."

"No!" Nigel moved to one side to get away from her.

Kentashi spoke to the women and they left. "If not with woman how you enjoy bath?"

"Bathing is to get clean," said Tyrone.

Kentashi shook his head in mild confusion. "In Natan bath is more than cleansing of body. It is," he brought his hands to bring together, "how you say tie hands?"

"Bind?"

"Ay, bind family, friends." He clasped his hands together.

Tyrone and Nigel exchanged brief puzzled glances before Tyrone said, "You mean your entire family bathes together?"

"Ay, wife, son, daughter. We," said Kentashi, pointing to each of them, "here binding." Again he used his hands to demonstrate.

Tyrone chuckled. "So the point of this is to establish a relationship."

Kentashi laughed, jovial and loud. He clapped Tyrone on the shoulder. "You understand. Good. I call them back …"

"No," said Tyrone and amended his speech at Kentashi's curiosity. "Let us enjoy this time of binding among men." He used his hands like Kentashi to interlace the fingers. "Women tend to be a distraction when important matters are to be discussed."

Kentashi smiled in approval and turned to Nigel. "Your king sent captain as escort, but he is wise and well with words."

"Indeed," said Nigel with a forced smile. He sent a skewed glance at Tyrone.

"After breakfast, I have arranged trip to dock for unloading. Captain Hodi will be escort."

"Thank you. We hope the gifts and trade samples will show the fine quality of Allonian goods."

"Our wool is highly regarded in other countries," said Tyrone.

Kentashi grunted and made curt nod. "We hear of such wool. What type sheep?"

For about ten minutes or so they spoke concerning Allonian goods and trade when the door opened and Avatar appeared.

"Pardon me, Highness, but Lord Allard inquires if you and the captain will be joining him and Princess Mirit for breakfast?"

"He feels better?"

"Ay. Chad brought him some herbal tea and it seems to have cured his headache and fatigue."

"We have many goodly teas for—how you say—help be unsick?" said Kentashi.

"Remedy," said Tyrone.

"Tell Lord Allard and my wife, we'll be along shortly." Nigel got out of the tub.

Tyrone also exited the tub and toweled off. "This was a fascinating experience, Admiral."

"Please to bathe anytime, Captain. Prince."

"Thank you."

Making their way back upstairs, Nigel chided Tyrone. "I'm surprised you agreed with him about *binding*."

"No, I was avoiding him recalling the women. Still, you must admit it is a rather unique way to make a first impression by having everyone strip down and get in a bathtub together." He laughed. "Oh, the hapless look on your face trying to get away from her."

"You weren't much better. Now, you can use your *wise* and *well words* to explain this to my wife."

Captain Hodi led a troop of escort for the two carts and six empty wagons from Kaori. Not until the trip did Tyrone see Titus, and by the boy's deep frown he wasn't happy in his role-playing. Tyrone privately smiled and faced forward in the cart he shared with Allard.

"Something amusing, Captain?" asked Allard, overly exaggerating the title.

"Titus doesn't look very happy this morning."

"And you find pleasure in his unhappiness?" Allard wore a wry grin.

"Same as you do."

Allard chuckled. "He is young, with much to learn. And I admit I see familiar traits in him."

"Tristine."

"Ellis," countered Allard. "He was brash and outspoken as a child, more so than Tristine. Angus held a firm hand while Darius countered him. But," he said with a reflective sigh, "when his true destiny was revealed, those rough edges smoothed out." He glanced back to Titus, Chad and Egan following the carts on foot. "In feature he resembles you, but there is much of his grandsire in him."

"I thought I was holding a firm hand."

Allard turned back at hearing Tyrone's stern tone. "I didn't mean to imply you weren't. But with children, discipline sometimes falls short and experience is the better teacher."

"So I am hoping."

"And why you were smiling," said Allard, which made Tyrone chuckle.

The carts pulled alongside the *Protectorate*. Mirit got out of the cart in front of them and marched up the gangplank. Tyrone reached the cart when Nigel dismounted.

"Is she still not speaking to you?"

"Your diplomacy about the women didn't help."

Tyrone shrugged and flashed a rueful smile. "I tried."

"Tell that to Tristine after Mirit speaks to her about our *binding*." Nigel, Tyrone and Allard made their way up the gangplank.

Titus pulled to a weary stop beside Chad. Short of breath, he gestured at the men pulling the carts. "They must be more than mortal."

Chad chuckled. "For their small size, they are surprisingly fit and strong."

"Someone needs to pay more attention to his fitness exercises," said Egan.

Titus rolled his eyes and took a seat on a dock pillar. A Natanese man pulled him to his feet, chattering in a cross voice. He shoved Titus toward the ropes.

"You're to help unload," said Egan.

"My hands are still raw from drawing water."

The man spoke more and made angry gestures at Titus. Chad nodded to the man and took hold of Titus' elbow.

"Remember your place," he whispered. He drew them to join the group of Natanese men readying the nets and ropes for unloading.

"I know, but can't we rest?"

"That doesn't happen until bedtime. Now take this." Chad gave Titus the end of a rope used for guiding a load in the air. "Watch me and do what I do, when I do it."

Allonian sailors prepared the cargo for unloading. The Natanese scrambled to receive the first load. For two hours, Titus helped with the cargo, pulling and steadying the rope until his hands cramped.

At a break in the work for those onboard to prepare the final load, Titus slipped away. Finding a spot across the street, he sat to rest and inspected his hands. There were several small cuts and rough spots while the skin red and his fingers and palms ached. Gingerly, he tried to rub the aching away. He glanced to the ship. Nigel and Tyrone spoke to Gulliver. Had they even noticed him doing hard manual labor? He was supposed to be assisting Chad as a squire not a hired hand.

Titus smelled food, which made his stomach growl. He didn't eat much at breakfast, too busy drawing water and washing dishes. He followed the scent, his steps taking him away from the ship. He stopped at what appeared to be either a bakery or inn but unsure which. Before he could enter the shop, one of Kentashi's soldiers seized him. Titus may not understand what the soldier said, but he understood the angry tone and rough hands dragging him back to the dock. He struggled to get free, but the soldier proved strong and unyielding, even making a threatening gesture with the whip he carried. Finally, Titus kicked the soldier in the groin and broke free. The soldier blindly struck back with the whip handle. Instead of striking Titus, he hit Chad in the back of the head and sent him sprawling to the ground.

Titus gasped when the soldier coiled the whip to strike Chad. "No!"

Egan seized the soldier's arm to prevent the attack. The soldier tried to break free, but the Guardian held fast. At the second attempt to break loose, Egan shoved the soldier aside and rebuked him in Natanese. The soldier sneered at Egan, yet wary of the Guardian's size and wrath. The soldier's hostile look passed to Titus. He spat on the ground. Hodi arrived in a rush and spoke to the soldier.

"What are they saying?" Titus asked Egan.

Hodi answered instead. "Keno say you were someplace not permitted and was bringing you back when you struck him."

Chad touched the back of his head and flinched in pain. "You struck him first?"

"He grabbed me, hard, and began dragging me back!"

Both Chad and Egan showed great displeasure at the response. Chad spoke to Hodi. "We were coming to retrieve him when I got struck from behind."

Keno spoke, motioning between Titus and Chad.

"He say, you got in the way of punishment for being attacked," said Hodi. He spoke again to Keno, who bowed and left. "Return to ship and stay there," he ordered the Allonians.

Titus helped Chad to his feet. "Are you badly hurt?"

"Since when is being hurt good?" Chad managed to make it back to the ship, but had to sit and hold his head for pain.

Mirit rushed over. "What happened?"

"I stepped in where I shouldn't have and got struck by a whip handle," he chided.

She noticed blood and called up to the ship. "Avatar! The medical bag."

Nigel, Tyrone and Avatar quickly joined the others. Nigel did his own inspection of his squire's injury. "What happened?" He moved aside to let Avatar cleanse the wound.

Hodi motioned to Titus. "Boy leave work and my soldier find him in forbidden place, start to bring him back when boy strike him. This one," he pointed at Chad, "received punishment meant for boy as mistake."

Tyrone's anger was immediate. "You struck a soldier for doing his duty?"

"He was dragging me back," came the boy's feeble excuse.

"You leave work. Others must take your place, make task harder, and he is hurt for you," said Hodi in rebuke.

Titus bit his lip, lowered his head and shoulders hunched in regret.

"I assure you, Captain, my son will be properly chastened. My thanks to your soldier for finding him."

Hodi made a curt nod and moved off.

"Thanks?" began Titus in surprised dispute. "The soldier raised his whip to strike Chad only Egan stopped him—"

Tyrone yanked Titus onboard ship and into one of the private cabins. "What were you doing away from the ship that put Chad's life in jeopardy?"

"I didn't mean for anyone to get hurt. Egan stopped the soldier—"

"You left the dock! Now, why?"

Titus grew sheepish and looked at his hands. "I wanted to rest and stop my hands from cramping." He showed the injured palms to his father, who only gave them a passing glance before continuing his reprimand.

"Captain Hodi said you were found somewhere you shouldn't have been. How far did you go to *rest* your hands?"

Titus shrugged and rubbed his hands. It was more a fretful action than for pain. "I don't know. I smelled food. I didn't eat much at breakfast because of hauling water and washing dishes."

Tyrone grew incredulous. "So you selfishly followed your stomach and as a result Chad got hurt."

Titus frowned in hurt and distress. "I didn't mean it! And I never got anything to eat. The soldier caught me before I went inside."

"Is that when you hit him?

"No. He grew rough and mean in bringing me back. I kicked him and broke free. That's when Chad went down."

"Now I understand what Hodi meant about Chad being punished by mistake. The soldier went after you for hitting him, but Chad intervened."

"I guess," murmured Titus. "It happened so fast."

Tyrone took Titus by the shoulder to make the boy look at him. "You must be more careful. Next time it could be worse."

Titus' face screwed up in regret. "I'm truly sorry about Chad." He took a sober, thoughtful breath. "Everything is so strange. I'm not used to such work or treatment. You've never raised a hand to me in anger like that soldier did."

"No, but you haven't been without strong discipline when needed, which makes your behavior puzzling."

"I just want to prove to you I can help and do as well as Uncle in such matters."

"You don't understand what you're saying! Nigel is a grown man, you are a child." He put up a stern hand to stop any dispute. "You vaguely remember what happened in Tunlund yet claim because of your experience you can deal with the young emperor. Now, you abandon duty when hungry and placed another in danger of being killed! Nigel never would have done that."

Titus plopped into a chair as Tyrone continued his rebuke.

"I know you idolize Nigel and there is much to admire, but if you wish to imitate him, do so with full understanding of his character, both good and bad. He is not the infallible person you make him out to be."

"I know! He put in the brig."

A knock at the door was followed by Nigel's voice. "Captain."

Tyrone answered the knock. For a moment he and Nigel regarded each other before Nigel's gaze shifted to Titus, anger visible.

"How is Chad?" asked Titus, sheepish.

"Fortunately it appears to be glancing blow resulting in a shallow cut. But any injury to the head tends to bleed."

"I'm glad it wasn't worse."

"Only thanks to Egan." Nigel turned back to Tyrone, his tone and expression changing to more agreeable. "The unloading is finished and Kentashi is expecting us for supper." He cast another severe glance to Titus before turning on his heels and leaving.

Tyrone beckoned Titus to join him in leaving, but first said, "From now on, stay near Chad and Egan. And do what you're told."

"Ay, sir."

On the dock, Tyrone nudged Titus to join Chad and Egan. The boy complied. Nigel and Mirit were already with Kentashi. Nigel and the admiral conversed about departure. Tyrone joined them. At a break in the conversation he spoke.

"Highness. May I have the honor of escorting the princess back to the compound?"

"I'm sure Allard and I can find something to discuss," said Nigel. He grinned at her and proceeded to enter the second cart with Allard.

Mirit flashed a wry, knowing smile when Tyrone escorted her to the cart and they climbed in. "Further explanation isn't necessary, Captain," she said once underway.

"Oh, but it is. Knowing your husband as you do, there should be no doubt to his honor after what I told you happened at the bathhouse. Which was nothing."

"The same as there should be no doubt to his honor in respect to you and your son."

Tyrone frowned at the retort, but she continued.

"Search your heart. You know Nigel would do nothing to harm you or Titus."

"Our situation is more complex than a single incident of misunderstanding."

"Only if you make it so," she insisted. His frown deepened and she laid hold of his arm to get his attention. "Why are you acting as if there is something to be jealous of?"

"Aren't you acting jealous of other women without cause?"

"Oh! You can be as infuriating as Nigel with your circular reasoning. You want me to trust your word that nothing happened between Nigel and those women. Why won't you give me the same trust with what I say about Nigel in respect to you and Titus?"

"If I do, will you stop being angry at Nigel?"

"I will stop when you stop."

Tyrone scowled, frustrated by her counter-argument. "You call my reasoning circular. You don't play fair."

"There is nothing fair about unjust anger. Of all people, you should know Nigel's heart towards you, towards his entire family." She put up a hand to stop any argument and quickly continued. "So I propose a truce for the remainder of this trip. A truce between all parties involved. Agreed?"

For a moment Tyrone pressed his lips together, studying Mirit. He couldn't find fault with her acting in defense of her husband. That thought struck him and he said, "For acting the part of a jealous wife, you defend your husband most vigorously."

"Same as you defending a man you claim injured you."

He snorted an irked chuckle. What he hoped to do in curbing her annoyance toward Nigel didn't go the way he intended.

She leaned closer and spoke low in the Ancient. "A truce, brother? To help our family." A small hopeful smile appearing.

Another unfair entreaty, but one he couldn't ignore. "Ay, a truce."

⁕

At Kaori, Kentashi and Hoshi waited on the porch. He wore a satisfied expression at seeing all the wagons. Hoshi was not as elaborately dressed as when they arrived, but still elegant and refined in her day gown.

"You bring many gifts. Lord Norkiru will be pleased," he said.

"Thank you. Our desire is to make a good impression," said Allard.

Kentashi nodded in approval. "Refresh and rest before eating. Maybe bath?" He tossed a teasing smile to Tyrone, who grinned. "With wife alone?" he continued his good humor to Nigel. He laughed when Nigel received a withering glare from Mirit. "Come."

After the customary yielding of weapons and receiving of house sandals, they retired to their chambers. In Nigel and Mirit's room stood a portable wooden tub filled with hot, sweetly scented water. He laughed at her flush of embarrassment.

"Don't worry, no one will get past Avatar."

"Or overhear us," she spoke the Ancient in a private tone.

"Ah, so it worked and you convinced him."

"I convinced him to call a truce, since he became defensive and I didn't want to press him further. Like you, he will talk when ready. I hope my prodding makes that time sooner than later. I'm uncomfortable about this visit."

"The Natanese are different, but that shouldn't make you uncomfortable. Especially not after our other trips were more combative. This is simple diplomacy."

"Complicated by two unexpected participants."

He grinned and nodded. "Ay, a unique wrinkle. You know Tyrone is clever and can handle himself."

"Well, for a moment I thought you agreed too quickly and made him suspicious."

"Better than the original idea of feigning an excuse I needed to speak to Allard so he'd have to ride with you. I'm already accused of making excuses for Titus."

"Now, don't go taking blame."

He kissed her cheek and wrinkled his nose.

"What? Is there a problem?"

"You smell like fish."

She playfully struck him. "I do not. That's just an excuse to get me to take a bath."

He widely smiled.

Chapter 8

VERY EARLY THE FOLLOWING MORNING TITUS WAS WOKEN BY the same Natanese servant, only this time from a sound sleep. Being exhausted, sleeping on the hall floor didn't trouble him. The man held the lantern in such manner that blinded Titus. He heard the low guttural sounds of Natanese.

"Ay, ay," he grumbled, waving the man away so he could sit up. He noticed Chad standing and folding his blanket. "Are we to help with breakfast again?"

"No. This morning the caravan is leaving for Yuki and we're to help with the horses and harnesses." Chad reached for Titus' blanket, but the boy jerked away.

"I can take care of it." He yawned and stood, not paying attention to how he folded the blanket.

The man snorted a few annoyed words and snatched the blanket from Titus.

"Hey!"

"He says you're still lazy," said Egan.

"I just woke up. Give me a minute."

The man motioned for Chad and Titus to leave.

"Do you think we'll get something to eat and drink before we start work?" asked Titus.

"Doubtful. Although food will be brought to us before we leave," said Chad.

Titus lumbered down the stairs, yawning and stretching. They followed the man to the stables where Natanese soldiers and grooms already worked. The man called to another then spoke to Chad and Titus.

Egan translated. "He says this is Dai, the head groom, he'll tell you what to do."

The man nodded at Egan and left.

"Do you speak Allonian?" asked Chad.

"A little," said Dai. He led them to where four handsome bay horses stood tethered in a line. "For masters. Saddles on wall," he pointed behind them. "Go." He made a shooing motion using both hands to Chad and Titus.

"Well, this I can do." Titus moved to fetch a saddle.

"Aren't you forgetting something?" asked Chad.

"What?"

He held a grooming brush out to Titus. "You brush and prepare the horse first, then the bridle, and finally the saddle."

Titus grabbed the brush. "I know. I was testing you." He began brushing a mare.

Chad chuckled and picked up another brush. "These are fine looking horses. As well-cared for as those in the royal stables." He glanced over to the saddles and bridles. "Not to mention splendid harnesses."

Titus paused in brushing to view the saddles, only he noticed Virgil observing them from across the compound. "As if I'm not watched enough by Egan."

"You mean Virgil?" asked Chad a bit perplexed.

"I can't look at him without thinking of Jedrek."

"Virgil isn't the only one who makes you think of Jedrek," chided Egan.

Titus went back to grooming the horse. "I'm not angry at you anymore."

"No? Then face me and say so."

Titus managed a sideways glance.

"Fully, and in the eye," the Guardian challenged.

Titus stopped grooming and faced Egan, but hesitated, appearing at a loss for words.

"I didn't think so," said Egan in annoyance.

"I'm not angry," insisted Titus, but balked at Egan's skepticism. "You and he are so different. It's hard." He motioned toward Virgil.

"This is difficult for us as well. You only knew Jedrek for seven years. He was Virgil's twin and my friend for over a thousand years."

Titus heaved an awkward shrug and went back to grooming. "I guess I never thought of it that way."

"Virgil is just as brave and skilled a warrior as Jedrek."

"Ay," began Chad in agreement. "He saved me from Jor'el's wrath when the Almighty rained his judgment upon the Sorens. He was seriously wounded and dying when he did so."

"Really?" asked Titus. His glanced across the compound to Virgil, only his attention brought back when Chad spoke again.

"I know your father and Nigel told you what happened."

"Ay. Again, I haven't given it much thought," he said in sheepish admittance.

"You haven't given many things the consideration they deserve. It's time you start," said Egan.

"Maybe," he muttered. Silence fell as he and Chad continued to groom the horses.

Egan slipped away and spoke a few words to Virgil, who left the area. By the time Chad and Titus finished saddling the four horses, Virgil returned carrying a tray of food and drink.

"They seem more interested in packing food for the journey than eating, but I managed to scrounge up some breakfast." He placed the tray on a tack box and handed a bowl to Chad and Titus then gave them eating sticks.

"Rice," grumbled Titus.

"This time with some vegetables and sauce," said Chad. He picked at the small, diced pieces of vegetables.

"Scraps left over from last night. I thought you would prefer them to raw squid," said Virgil. He grinned when Titus rolled his eyes yet spoke with his mouth full.

"Thanks."

"Nearly dawn, so I better get back. The others are probably awake." Virgil left.

"He's not all bad. I would have hidden some squid in the rice," said Egan, a cunning smile appearing.

"He did," said Chad in strained voice. He swallowed hard.

Titus' face screwed up at Chad's distress. With a suspicious frown, he poked the sticks into his rice, but stopped at hearing laughter. "He didn't hide squid in your rice."

"No, but worth it to see your expression." Chad took a drink. Suddenly, he spit out the liquid, gagging and grimacing.

"Oh, please! I'm not going to fall for that again."

"No, really, this is awful. Taste for yourself."

"No."

Chad held the cup out to Egan. "It is horrid."

Egan took the cup and sniffed it. "It does have a peculiar smell compared to the tea we drink. Maybe that is where Virgil put the squid."

Chad screwed lips in a queasy expression. "I've lost my appetite." He set the bowl on the tray.

Dai appeared and frowned in disapproval. "Eat when finished."

"We are finished." Chad used the sticks to point to the horses. "The horses are saddled and ready."

Dai inspected the horses and harnesses. He made a stout nod of approval. "Good. Finish eat and do more horses."

"I'm afraid not," said Ridge, who appeared behind Dai and startled him.

"Why?" asked Dai, annoyed and tried to recover from the fright.

"Because their master needs them to prepare for departure. You wouldn't want to interfere in their duty, now would you?"

"No." Dai bowed and departed.

"That was timely. Thanks," said Chad.

Ridge wryly grinned. "Not at all, but you are needed." He led them back to Nigel and Mirit's room. Both were up and wore their formal uniforms.

"Ah, good. We'll need help when Avatar returns with our armor," said Nigel.

"Armor? But we're only traveling, aren't we?" asked Chad.

"Apparently, full formal armor is normal for a *shiagoto's* procession." Nigel's glance passed to Titus. "You and your father both need to be cleaned and pressed before leaving since you don't have any dress uniforms. Egan, see what you can do with him."

"Ay, Highness." Egan ushered Titus across the hall.

Allard and Tyrone were in the midst of dressing. In fact, Tyrone only wore his undergarments.

"Where have you been?" he asked.

"Grooming and saddling your horses," replied Titus.

"Well, smelling of horse won't do. The water's not too dirty." He indicated the portable tub. "Egan, take his uniform and see what can be done to make it more presentable. Virgil already took mine. Don't tarry. We need to be ready in less than two hours."

"Ay, Captain." Egan waited for Titus to strip and get into the water. He gathered his uniform, leaving the undergarments, and departed.

"The water's cool," said Titus.

"No time to soak, just wash off the smell and grime." Tyrone tossed Titus a small bar of soap.

He sniffed the soap. "At least it doesn't smell like fish or rice."

"Actually, the aroma is pleasant. They call it sandalwood," said Allard.

"Cleans well too," said Tyrone. "Do your hair, and don't cheat."

Titus frowned and took a deep breath before dunking himself underwater to wet his hair. He lathered up the soap in his hands and washed his hair. His eyes were closed due to the suds on his head and face. "Is this good enough, sir?"

"Ay." Tyrone pushed Titus' head underwater for a rinse. Titus gagged when Tyrone let him up.

"I wasn't ready!"

Tyrone laughed and dried off his hands and arms with a towel. "Finish washing, dry off and put on your undergarments."

"I hope Egan comes back soon, it's too cool to be naked."

Two hours later the large caravan prepared to depart Kaori. Banners of various colors and symbols would be in front and at various intervals of the caravan. The soldiers were fully armed and an impressive sight in their plate armor with intricate metalwork and embroidered undergarments. Kentashi wore more elaborate armor than when he met them on the ship.

The Allonians sat upon the horses, waiting. Nigel wore his complete King's Champion and Jor'ellian battle armor; only used on special state occasions. Mirit wore more ornamentation on her uniform and the Guardian warriors dressed in their formal white and gold uniforms with some battle armor. Avatar appeared the most decorated with purple accents surrounding the golden embroidered border, the crest of Jor'el at the apex on his chest and matching gauntlets, all signaling his high rank among the Guardians. Even Chad wore his military squire's uniform and Allard formally arrayed in his Council robes. Ridge's forester uniform was embellished with formal trappings and appeared richer in color. Even in clean and pressed royal uniforms, Tyrone and Titus were less splendid than what the occasion called for. Titus even wore a sword.

"I feel underdressed," said Tyrone to Nigel.

"This isn't the time or place for *your* armor," quipped Nigel.

Kentashi arrived and reined a feisty white stallion. "All is ready."

"Then let us proceed," said Nigel.

Kentashi shouted and servants opened the main gate. Trumpets sounded. Standard bearers on horseback led the way with Kentashi, Nigel and Tyrone followed by Allard and Mirit. Behind them came the Guardians, who chose to walk since there weren't any horses big enough to carry them. Chad and Titus rode behind the Guardians followed by Captain Hodi, a company of soldiers, two wagons, more soldiers, two wagons, more soldiers, the final two wagons and ending with a company of soldiers.

Where the road forked down to the city or further inland, Kentashi turned the caravan to head inland toward the mountains.

After the caravan made the turn, Chad looked at Titus. He smiled and winked before speaking. "Virgil. What was that drink you gave us for breakfast?"

"Fermented rice and bamboo tea. They say it helps invigorate you for the day."

"No squid?" said Titus with a sarcastic smirk.

"Squid?" Virgil looked over his shoulder. "What would make you think that?" Egan laughed and immediately Virgil grew suspicious. "Never mind, I know." He scolded Egan, "He already doesn't like me; you don't need to make it worse."

"I never said I didn't like you. You're just different," said Titus.

"Is that supposed to make me feel better?" Again, Virgil glanced over his shoulder. "You realize when Jor'el created Guardians he didn't just give us strength and power but feelings and emotions also?"

"I haven't thought about it that way," Egan mimicked Titus' voice before the boy could answer.

"Well, I haven't! And I know, you're going to tell me again how I should."

"Well, you should," said Egan and Virgil in unison.

Titus sat up in the saddle. "You're both forgetting who I really—"

Egan immediately drew back to Titus' horse. A firm grip on the boy's arm stopped Titus' speech. At seven-and-a-half feet tall, he looked directly at Titus even when the boy sat on horseback. His was voice stern yet low. "You are constantly forgetting we are Guardians of Jor'el and not lackeys to a spoiled mortal boy. We are not obliged to obey you. Beware of trying our patience and that of Jor'el with your continual prideful and obstinate behavior. If you doubt what I say, remember your Aunt Ellan." He released Titus and rejoined Virgil.

"Ellan?" muttered Titus with disturbance.

"I'm certain you've been told about her," began Chad. "How she betrayed your grandfather, abused your mother, and nearly turned Allon over to the Dark Way."

Titus stared at Chad.

"You don't know?"

"I know," replied Titus in a harsh whisper. "I just never—" He clamped his mouth to stop his typical response.

"Thought about it?" Chad finished the sentence.

Titus slumped in the saddle, shading his eyes from looking at anyone.

Up ahead, Nigel and Tyrone rode alongside Kentashi unaware of the verbal exchange happening behind them.

"How long will it take to reach Lord Norkiru's castle?" asked Nigel.

"We must pass through the mountains, and if Raiden blesses our journey, we should reach Yuki in four days."

"You said Raiden taught you our language, so I assume you've seen him. What does he look like?" said Tyrone.

"Sometimes Raiden is a man, sometimes a dragon."

"Have you witnessed him change shape?"

Kentashi shook his head. "I have seen Raiden and I have seen dragon, but they are one spirit."

"How can you tell?" asked Nigel.

"I heard dragon speak."

"It spoke to you?"

"Ay. Often dragon fly over Kaori to protect my people in time of danger. After, I go to mountain and speak to Raiden."

"Does Raiden speak to anyone else?"

"No. I am *shiagoto* of this region like my ancestors before me. To my family Raiden speaks." Kentashi grew somber. "Kiyoshi would have taken my place when I join the ancestors, but now no one will take my place."

"I thought you said you have a daughter?" asked Tyrone.

Kentashi sneered in displeasure. "Akira is married to Rukan Shokita, Lord Norkiru's nephew."

"You don't like him."

Kentashi waved aside the statement yet shook his head. "Like not matter when obliged to lord. Akira cannot become *shiagoto* so Raiden not speak to her." He glanced back to Mirit. "Now wife is—how you say—strange woman?"

Tyrone laughed but stopped at Nigel's piqued reaction. "I don't think he meant it in a bad way."

"No, no. I mean different, not like other woman."

"Unique?" asked Nigel.

"Ay, unique," repeated Kentashi with some difficulty.

Nigel grinned. "Oh, she is unique."

"Can she become *shiagoto* in Allon, like you?"

"She became a princess when we married, though she is of nobility. Her father sits on the Council of Twelve."

"Can she take father's place when he join ancestors?"

"We go to the heavenlies to be with Jor'el or someplace else if we reject the Almighty." Nigel shrugged and looked briefly to Tyrone as he continued. "I don't think there has been a female on the Council."

"Allard might know, or better yet, Avatar. He was alive before the Council was formed," said Tyrone.

"Avatar? Which spirit is he?" asked Kentashi.

"Goatee and silver eyes."

"His eyes like yours. Not normal color." Kentashi studied Tyrone, which made Tyrone fidget in his saddle.

To avert Kentashi's marked attention, Nigel called to Avatar and waved the Guardian forward.

"Ay, Highness?"

"Admiral Kentashi asked a question about the Council of Twelve we couldn't answer, but at your age, you should know," he said with a wry smile. "Has a female ever sat on the Council?"

"Actually, there was one. Lady Jocelyn, the wife of Baron Winslow of Midessex. She assumed his seat shortly after his death and for two years acted on her son's behalf until he became of age."

"When did this happen?"

"Shortly after King Tristan formed the Council. There hasn't been a female since."

"Why?" asked Kentashi.

"No need."

"So there is no law forbidding woman from man's world?"

Avatar shook his head. "Only from being a Jor'ellian Knight."

Kentashi turned back to view the group following them. There was enough distance between the groups that they couldn't hear the conversation, but he caught Mirit's eye before turning back to Avatar. "Princess dress like knight."

"Princess Mirit is the honorary Queen's Champion. Although a skilled fighter, she has not been formally trained and cannot hold the title of knight."

Kentashi became angry. "Then Lord Allard deceived me!"

"How so?" asked Tyrone.

"He say princess knight, but spirit say otherwise."

"I'm a Guardian," said Avatar.

"*Spirit* say princess not knight," insisted Kentashi, ignoring Avatar.

"There is a way to clear up any misunderstanding," said Nigel. "Lord Allard, come here!"

Allard kicked his horse and moved forward. Mirit started to move, but Nigel put up a hand and shook his head. She reined her horse and held back.

"How can I be of service, Highness?"

"There appears to be a misunderstanding regarding the princess."

"You say she knight, so I allow her to come, but spirit say she cannot be knight," said Kentashi.

"I'm a Guardian."

"You spirit! Immortal and not born," snapped Kentashi.

Tyrone signaled Avatar to hold his peace.

"If I may, Admiral," began Allard calmly. "I wrote that Princess Mirit is the Queen's Champion. In trying to explain her function and duties, I may have compared her to her husband, who is a knight, but I do not recall saying she is an actual knight."

"No difference," said Kentashi with impatience.

"There is a difference, Admiral," said Avatar. "Just like there is a difference between you and Captain Hodi. Both are trained and skilled, but you are *shiagoto* and he is not. Does that make Hodi any less a good soldier?" He looked directly at Kentashi.

The admiral stared into the Guardian's silver eyes. "No," he said, a bit begrudging.

"Neither is Princess Mirit less of the Queen's Champion than Prince Nigel is the King's Champion, though he is a Jor'ellian Knight and she is not."

Kentashi made his usual snort of agreement. "You make argument good. Almost as well with words as Captain Fraser."

"Thank you, Admiral," said Avatar, and sent a private smile to Tyrone.

Nigel patted Avatar's shoulder and instructed him to fall back.

Avatar returned to his fellow Guardians and Virgil asked, "What was that about?"

"The admiral had some questions about women serving on the Council of Twelve and accused Lord Allard of deceiving him concerning the princess and her status."

"Why?"

"I don't know what prompted it, but I made certain he understood her position and respects her accordingly."

"Was Raiden mentioned?" asked Ridge.

Avatar glanced at the ranger with curiosity. "No, but he kept referring to me as a spirit. Why do you ask?"

Ridge motioned to the soldiers following them. Makito and Jiru were in the front ranks. "The other night when Virgil and I mingled among the soldiers there was an incident regarding Raiden."

"Virgil told me. What does it have to do with the admiral's questions?"

"Ever since, the one called Makito avoids us, yet speaks in hushed tones to his companions concerning us and Raiden."

"He still believes it was a judgment against us?" asked Virgil.

"Ay, but I didn't want to cause trouble by appearing to eavesdrop or contradict him. Do you know anything about Raiden?" he asked Avatar.

"Never heard of him."

"Really? I thought at your age you would know of beliefs and customs outside of Allon."

Avatar scowled. "You are the second one to mention my age."

Virgil flashed a mischievous grin and nudged Ridge. "I guess we were mistaken to think wisdom comes with age."

"Senility more like it."

Avatar rolled his eyes and grumbled, "Children. Kell burdened me with children."

"*Doragon!*" a Natanese driver shouted.

From the highest peak of the mountain range an enormous winged reptile began a descent toward them.

"Looks like an overgrown kelpie," said Ridge.

"Stay here with the others," Avatar told Egan and Ridge. He and Virgil raced forward to be near Nigel, Tyrone and Allard.

Egan glared sideways when Ridge whipped out his staff to place at the ready.

Ridge noticed the guarded expression. "We're here at Jor'el's command. You think I'll defy him and let you defend them by yourself, warrior?"

Egan faced forward, jowls flexed in anger. "It maybe best for them if you did."

Ridge moved his staff to a defensive position, only stopped just shy of touching the underside of Egan's chin. "Any more comments?"

Egan's lips snarled, but said, "No."

Ridge lowered the end of the staff from Egan's chin.

Wide-eyed in fear on the creature, Allard muttered, "What is it?"

"*Doragon*. Dragon, in your language," said Kentashi.

Avatar and Virgil arrived, ready to draw their swords when Kentashi hurried to speak.

"No! Dragon will not harm us."

"Are you sure?" asked Nigel.

"Ay. Remember I tell you Raiden and dragon are one." Kentashi called for the caravan to halt.

The dragon landed on the road in front of the procession. It's wings folded against its side. In height it stood ten feet at the shoulders, perhaps fifteen feet to the top of its head and nearly twice as long from nose to tail.

Kentashi bowed at the waist and continued to speak in Allonian. "Greetings, Akido, friend of Raiden."

"Greetings, Kentashi," said Akido.

"It speaks in our language!" marveled Allard.

The unnatural action made Nigel's cautious focus change from the dragon to the Guardians. Virgil and Avatar stared at the creature, hands on the hilts of their swords. Further back, Ridge and Egan took up position in front of Mirit, Titus and Chad. Egan stood ready to draw his sword and Ridge held his quarterstaff. Mirit appeared tense, Titus anxious and Chad watchful. Nigel's attention returned to the dragon when it spoke again.

"You bring strangers to the mountain, Kentashi."

"They are from Allon and come to pay respect to Emperor Tirigato."

Akido's head rose at hearing *Allon*. "Worshippers of Jor'el." He moved his head to survey Nigel. "Who are you?"

"I am Prince Nigel, the King's Champion."

"Your father?"

"Ellis, the Son of Tristan."

"How long has he reigned?"

"He died five years ago. Tyrone, the Great King reigns."

To this, Akido spread his wings, lifted his head skyward and roared, a loud and piercing roar, making everyone cover their ears. He then stretched his head toward Nigel.

"Nigel!" Mirit kicked her horse to move forward.

Akido looked past Nigel at her outcry. Virgil intercepted her horse to stop her advance. Akido stared at Mirit, which made her tremble but she couldn't look away. Nigel moved his horse to block Akido from Mirit. Tyrone and Avatar joined him to form a defensive line between the dragon and Mirit.

Akido's gaze passed to Tyrone where it lingered. "Who are you?"

"I'm Captain Fraser of his majesty's army."

"He is wise and well with words," said Kentashi.

Akido titled his head to survey Tyrone. "Just a captain?"

"Ay." Tyrone returned Akido's stare.

Akido laughed and drew back to a less threatening posture. "You may pass." That said, Akido took off, the wind from his wings scattering debris and dust from the road.

Kentashi smiled. "This good sign. Come." He shouted a command in Natanese and the caravan proceeded.

Nigel, Tyrone, Allard and Avatar waited for Mirit to catch up before following Kentashi. Virgil walked beside her horse. She appeared pale and nervous.

"Are you all right?" asked Nigel.

"Me? I thought it was going to bite your head off!" Her voice slightly quivered with fear.

"I wondered the same," he said, flashing a wry smile.

"It's not funny."

He held her hand in a reassuring gesture. "Avatar and Virgil were ready to strike. You should have stayed back."

"It's a huge flying reptile that talks!" she insisted, disconcerted. "I've never seen anything like it before." Akido circled high above. "It's still here."

"Kentashi said it is a good sign," said Allard.

"As long as it stays visible, we should be fine," said Tyrone.

Virgil detained Avatar enough for the mortals to move ahead. He spoke in the Ancient. "When it stared at her, she grew horribly pale and trembled. I thought she would faint, only she stared back, unable to move. I sensed some kind of connection from her, but sensed nothing from the beast. Did you?"

"No," said Avatar, a cautious glance at the dragon. "Yet beasts do not naturally speak. Not to mention the strange reaction when hearing about Tyrone then questioning him." Again he turned his attention to Akido, this time a more concerted effort on his face, silver eyes growing narrow. "If there is a connection, we should sense something from the beast. The fact we don't concerns me. We must be on guard. I want you to stay close to Mirit. I'll stay near the captain. Have Ridge act as scout, only quietly."

"No need to tell me how to be quiet."

Avatar flinched at hearing a voice in his right ear then scowled at Ridge. "How much did you hear?"

"Everything. And I agree," he turned to Virgil, "old age is showing. First his mind and now his hearing."

Virgil laughed.

Chapter 9

THE REST OF THE DAY THEY TRAVELED FURTHER INTO THE mountains, the temperature grew cooler at higher elevations. By dusk, they reached a mountain meadow to make camp for the night. Akido landed on a rocky outcropping overlooking the meadow.

Titus dismounted beside his father and the others. "Do you think it means to harm us?"

Tyrone stared at Akido. "I'm not sure if it is waiting to attack or standing guard."

"Have no fear. We'll be on watch all night," said Avatar.

Somewhat uncertain, Titus looked to Egan and Virgil. Egan nodded and Virgil tapped his sword in salute. The boy shied away.

Unaware of the exchange, Tyrone's focus changed from Akido to Avatar. "What did you sense from the creature?"

"Nothing."

Tyrone found the answer surprising. "No evil or sense of danger?"

"No. It is strangely void of any sensation."

"How is that possible?" asked Nigel.

Avatar shrugged and shook of his head. "I'm not sure. Usually, there is some sense about a creature." He studied the dragon, his voice growing cautious and concerned. "Even before it appeared I sensed nothing about to happen."

"Neither did I," said Virgil.

Egan and Ridge also agreed.

"Between four Guardians we should have sensed something," said Avatar.

"Could it have a shielding medal?" asked Tyrone.

Avatar pursed his lips in brief consideration. "Possible, but that would indicate the Dark Way, and again, we should sense something."

"And why use a shielding medal? That is a formidable creature," said Virgil, motioning toward Akido.

Mirit rubbed her arms as if warding off a chill. "An unnerving one."

Nigel placed a comforting arm about her shoulders.

Avatar regarded her; studious yet intrigued. "Mirit is experiencing the most sensation."

"And I don't like it."

Kentashi approached. "After tents raised we eat." Mirit's disconcerted expression remained fixed on Akido and the admiral smiled. "Akido keep watch for evil spirits and creatures that roam the mountain."

"I'm sorry, but I hardly find that comforting."

"No dragons in Allon?"

"No."

"In Natan, dragons are goodly and help us."

"Good? I thought it was going to bite my husband's head off!"

"Dragons not attack unless provoked. He test to see if intention honorable." Kentashi took her hand and spoke in a reassuring tone. "You see come morning. We pass night safely."

"I hope so."

Kentashi offered a bow and departed.

"We should help put up the tents." Chad tugged on Titus' sleeve.

The boy nodded. Out of the corner of his eye, he noticed Egan followed. When they reached the wagon where the tents were being unloaded, he confronted Egan.

"Why, after what you said, are you still willing to protect me?"

"Because Jor'el gave me charge of you. And despite our differences, I will not shirk my duty." He placed a hand on Titus' shoulder and drew him a short distance away from the wagon. "Being around Guardians all your life, I understand you've grown accustomed to us. Familiarity can sometimes bring contempt and being taken for granted. The challenge is preventing that from happening, or correcting it when it does."

"How?"

Egan's expression grew kind yet compelling. "By taking a deep look inside your heart to learn why. Then armed with knowledge and understanding, alter your attitude and behavior."

"Sounds hard."

"Ay. It takes personal courage and faith in Jor'el to take the first step on the journey to maturity. The question is, are you willing to start?"

Titus' became vexed by uncertainty. "I'm not sure."

"Well, at least that's an honest answer. Perhaps the first one you've given me in a while."

They heard shouting. A Natanese soldier scolded Chad.

"Enough talk. Think while we work." Egan steered Titus back to the wagon. He spoke in Natanese to the soldier. The soldier chuckled and patted Egan's arm before going back to work.

"What did you say?" asked Chad.

"I told him the three of us will erect a tent by ourselves." Egan tossed the bundled canvas of tent, rope and spikes over one shoulder.

In an hour, all the tents were completed, with the Allonians' tents erected side-by-side. They took dinner in Kentashi's tent, the largest of camp yet divided into three parts. The two smaller sections were for sleeping while the biggest section easily accommodated everyone for dining and relaxing. Hodi joined Kentashi, the Allonians and Guardians.

118

Titus again helped Chad and the Natanese servants in attending those at dinner. When he bent down to pour his father some more to drink, Tyrone whispered in his ear, "You're doing well. I'm pleased." The truth of the statement reflected in his father's eyes. Titus smiled and continued his task.

Hodi motioned to Chad and Ridge. "Like hair. They kin?"

"No," said Nigel, chuckling. "Ridge is a Guardian and Chad my mortal squire."

"And mine," said Mirit. She tossed a smiling wink at Chad, who grinned and bowed.

"Squire serve you?" asked Hodi.

"Ay."

Skeptical, Hodi surveyed her with a harsh, impertinent glance not to Nigel's liking. "Mind your manners toward the princess, *my wife*, Captain Hodi."

Hodi immediately corrected his expression to apologetic and made a submissive head bow to Nigel.

Kentashi spoke. "Forgive Captain. In Natan, woman never do such thing as to wear sword. Stay at home. Make children, keep house. Princess unique."

Nigel fought a smile. "Ay, she is not conventional."

"Would prince permit wife to demonstration?" asked Hodi in a polite manner.

"You mean fight? No, she is not an exhibition." His earlier sternness returned.

"Woman rarely brought before emperor," began Kentashi. "If we are to convince Lord Norkiru she is worthy, we must be convinced."

"Put that way, I don't know if we have a choice, Highness," said Allard.

Nigel frowned in consideration, making Mirit touch his arm to get his attention.

"I've done it before, so it is not unusual. And fitting to my unconventional status."

He wasn't too pleased by her reasoning and using his words. He sent a considering glance to Tyrone, who shrugged and said, "She's your wife, but we came to see the emperor."

At the reply, Nigel relented. She, in turn, addressed Kentashi. "What kind of demonstration, Admiral?"

Kentashi and Hodi both grinned with satisfaction before Kentashi answered. "In morning before we depart, you face Captain Hodi in mock combat for all to see."

"And the terms of the bout?"

Titus lingered in refilling her cup to hear the exchange.

"Only to disarm. I do not wish to harm or dishonor," said Hodi.

"Neither do I." Mirit raised her cup in a salute.

Hodi smiled and returned the salute.

Titus tried to hide his grin. When she finished drinking the salute, he bent down to catch her eye. She smiled. He withdrew from the table to join Chad near the tent opening to wait for their next assignment in serving.

"Won't Hodi be surprised," he whispered to Chad.

"Ay, but remember he is a soldier and will be a strong opponent."

Twenty minutes later, Mirit made excuse to retire earlier so she could prepare. The others joined her for departure.

Crossing the camp back to their tents, Titus, Chad and Egan trailed the others. Titus caught several suspicious sneers and glares from Kentashi's soldiers, especially Keno, Makito and Jiru.

"I don't think they like us," he said.

"You haven't exactly made a good impression," said Chad.

"I said I'm sorry. How many times must I apologize?"

Chad took Titus' arm to slow the pace and widen the gap between the others to speak privately. "It's not just about being sorry but also learning from your mistakes and correcting them so nothing like it happens again."

Titus appeared downcast. "I really didn't mean for you to get hurt."

He stopped Titus and looked directly at the boy, his voice low. "I would not have been hurt if you weren't here. How many more things will happen or be prevented from happening because of you? How many more of us will get hurt? Or worse?"

Titus shook his head in confusion and fear, unable to answer.

"My speech may be inappropriate, even harsh, but I've been charged with your care and feel it's important to speak my mind for all concerned."

"I suppose," murmured Titus.

Egan cleared his throat to get their attention. "We need to keep moving."

The others were out of sight and several soldiers eyed them. Chad nudged Titus to keep moving. They went inside the tent they shared with Tyrone and Allard.

"Is there a problem?" asked Tyrone at Titus' downcast expression.

Titus didn't answer and went to his mat to lie down.

Chad spoke a low reply. "I gave him food for thought and not just his stomach."

Tyrone fought the impulse to smile and gave Chad a discrete pat on the arm before moving to his mat.

<hr />

Well after midnight, Mirit emerged from the tent, a cloak wrapped about her nightclothes. From the tent, the outcropping and silhouette of Akido could be seen, illuminated by the campfires. She stopped a few feet from the tent, staring at Akido.

Virgil sat on a crate at the tent entrance. "Is something wrong, Princess?"

She didn't answer, just kept staring at the dragon. When she shivered and drew the cloak closer around her, he hopped off the crate to join her.

"What about the creature disturbs you?"

She spoke, her voice barely above a whisper. "There's something frightening, yet tragic about it that touches me."

Suddenly, she cried out in fear, seized Virgil and buried her head against him. Holding her, he turned his back to the creature to shield her from danger. Avatar and Ridge responded, taking up position in front of Virgil and Mirit with sword drawn and staff ready.

Nigel emerged from the tent. "Mirit?"

She went to Nigel and Virgil explained, "Something about the dragon frightened her."

Tyrone, Titus, Egan, Chad and Allard appeared, also armed.

"Mirit?" asked Tyrone.

Nigel comforted his wife. "Unharmed, but frightened by the dragon."

"I don't understand? It hasn't moved." Titus pointed to Akido; the dragon remained perched in its watchful position.

"It looked at me and—" she whimpered, clinging to Nigel.

"Hush." Nigel took Mirit back inside. He tried to coax her back to the mat, but she resisted. "You must get some rest. You have a bout in the morning, concentrate on that."

Mirit sat but would not lie down.

Virgil entered and knelt beside her. He gently placed both hands on the sides of her face for her to look at him. He spoke in the Ancient. *"Cluinn mi, Mirit, nighean de Mathias as leth Jor'el. Cluinn agus bi aig fois."* She still appeared fretful so he repeated. "Hear me, Mirit, daughter of Mathias on behalf of Jor'el. Hear and be at peace." She began to relax so he helped her to lie down. "Sleep and rest with ease." She closed her eyes, and shortly fell asleep.

Nigel quietly thanked Virgil. Avatar entered yet remained near the flap. Nigel drew Virgil from Mirit to confer with Avatar.

"You said the dragon frightened her, how?" he asked Virgil.

"I don't know. She came outside and stared at it saying there was something tragic about it that touched her. Again I tried, but sensed nothing from the beast then she cried out and grabbed me. I didn't hear it speak or see it move."

"Strange," mused Avatar.

"Indeed. I'll remain inside to make certain she doesn't leave again, either on her own again or drawn away."

"If you can't sense anything how will you know the difference?" asked Nigel.

"I may not be able to sense the beast, but I sensed a great conflict immediately rise up in her when we first encountered it. She has been unsettled ever since."

"I told Virgil to remain close to Mirit since he's developed a perception for her. I will stay close to the captain because of the beast's interest in him. Egan remains with Titus, leaving Ridge to mingle and scout out anything unusual," said Avatar.

"Let's pray nothing else happens," said Nigel.

"We shall while keeping watch," said Avatar.

Titus wasn't ready to go back to sleep, though he lay down when his father told him to. Tyrone spoke a few words to Egan before going to his mat, taking off his sword to place beside the mat and lied down.

Chad lay on the mat next to Titus. He turned on his left side to face the boy. "Are you troubled by what happened?" he asked in a quiet voice so as not to disturb the others.

"More confused. Why would the dragon protect Aunt Mirit and why would someone want to harm her? We've never been to Natan so how could anyone know her?"

"I don't know, nothing is clear right now."

"The answers will come in time," said Tyrone.

They were surprised to find Tyrone still on his mat, but looking at them.

"We didn't mean to disturb you, Captain," said Chad.

He grinned. "It is difficult to return to sleep after an unsettling experience. Trust Jor'el and have patience."

"Lord Allard doesn't have trouble sleeping," said Titus.

"That's because I'm old," said Allard. His eyes remained closed as he continued speaking. "The old can fall asleep quickly at anytime, but," he turned to them with opened eyes, "wake up just as quickly to chattering children. Listen to your father and get some rest. We are being watched over and protected."

The others did so, but Titus still couldn't go to sleep. Egan sat in the Guardian meditative position: his legs crossed, sword on his lap, hands folded and eyes closed. Quiet, so as not to disturb the others, Titus crawled over to Egan. At his light touch on the Guardian's arm, Egan's eyes snapped open.

"Something troubling you?" he asked in whisper.

"What do you do when you keep watch over me at night?"

"I sit in a state of prayer yet sensitive to any approaching danger and ready to respond." He tapped his sword. "Why do you ask?" he spoke in a tone suggesting he knew the answer.

Titus shrugged. "I thought I should know."

Egan grinned. "Return to your mat and be at peace."

"Thank you." Titus flashed a shy smile and crawled back to his mat to lie down.

Chapter 10

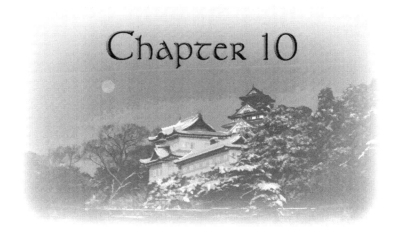

MIRIT PASSED THE REST OF THE NIGHT PEACEFULLY AND WAS surprised at how refreshed she felt upon waking. Virgil sat in the Guardian meditative position near the entrance, which meant he spent the night in watchful prayer over her and Nigel.

"Morning, sleepyhead," teased Nigel. He was up and getting dressed.

Virgil's eyes opened. He smiled at Mirit. "Sleep well, princess?"

"Ay. Thank you."

From outside, they heard the noise of camp breaking down.

"They'll be here for this tent soon, you better get ready. You don't want to keep Hodi waiting," said Nigel.

"At least he's mortal," she dryly quipped and rose to get dressed.

Virgil left.

Fifteen minutes later, Natan soldiers arrived requesting permission to dismantle the tent. With Mirit dressed, they vacated the tent for disassembly and joined the others around a small fire for a light breakfast Chad and Titus fixed.

Titus handed Mirit a small bowl of rice with some kind of gravy. "How are you feeling this morning, Aunt?"

"Better," she said with a soft smile and whispered, "But you can't call me *aunt* too loudly."

"Oh! I'm sorry, I forgot."

She ruffled his hair.

He frowned and pushed his hair back into place. "I wish you wouldn't do that in public," he grumbled and went back to serving breakfast.

Tyrone grinned and spoke sideway to Mirit. "I thought his attitude was improving."

"It is. I just do that to annoy him."

By the time they finished eating and cleaning up from breakfast, Kentashi, Hodi and two other Natanese officers approached.

"Camp is nearly down, time for bout," said Kentashi.

"If the captain is ready," said Mirit with a gracious smile.

"I always ready for combat," said Hodi, returning her smile.

Kentashi spoke to the other officers, who saluted and departed. "They prepare area for bout. Come."

The Allonians followed Kentashi and Hodi to a pre-selected area where the officers barked orders for specific arrangements.

Tyrone took her arm and leaned down to ask, "Are you ready for this?"

"I used to do this for living, remember?"

He partial grinned. "Actually, I never saw any of your performances."

She laughed and motioned to Nigel. "Just ask *Niki*, he was my combat partner for several weeks."

Tyrone's amused look found Nigel. "Is that what they called you in Tunlund?"

"Among other things."

A large circle formed. Kentashi stepped forward and began speaking in Natanese. Hodi entered the circle, and by the admiral's gesture toward the captain, the Allonians knew he spoke of the bout. When the admiral waved to Mirit, she stepped into the circle to join Hodi. After a few more words, Kentashi stepped back.

Hodi drew his sword and saluted Mirit. She returned the warrior's gesture. When he assumed his beginning stance, she took the Jor'ellian first position, right sword arm raised above her head, left arm straight out before her for balance.

Hodi moved to attack, and Mirit brought her sword down in an arc. The blades clanged in several exchanges during which they switched places. Hodi grinned with satisfaction before launching another attack. Mirit parried but misjudged his riposte and skidded, falling to one knee with her back partially turned to him. She quickly moved her sword over her right shoulder to deflect his expected attack then rolled to one side and came up facing him.

"She is very good," said Tyrone.

"Ay, and she anticipates well. You should bout with her sometime," said Nigel.

"You know my strength is overpowering," he replied in a discreet voice.

Mirit's move sent Hodi stumbling sideways and drew comments and chuckles from the Natanese soldiers and servants. Hodi scowled in great displeasure at the reactions and launched a fierce attack. He drove Mirit back to the edge of the circle. He feinted a thrust she was forced to parry and used his arm to strike her. She fell hard to the ground and didn't have time to recover to her feet when he hacked at her. She gripped her sword in both hands to use like a staff to stay his attack then kicked him hard in the knee. When he bent over in pain, she rolled on the ground, using her legs to trip him. She scrambled to her feet and swung down at him, knocking his sword away.

Reaction from the Natanese at Hodi's disarming by a woman was measurable. Hodi rolled to retrieve his weapon, but Mirit stepped on the blade and leveled her sword at his face. Anger, frustration and disgust showed in his narrow regard of her.

Kentashi stepped into the circle and began to speak when Akido roared, loud and long. The dragon took off from his perch.

At the same time of Akido's move, Avatar drew his sword and shouted, "Evil!"

From out of the surrounding trees came one hundred grotesque creatures half-dog, half-man standing eight feet tall on two legs. Their faces were mostly human with facial hair and a wild, deadly look in yellow eyes, drooling growls and three-inch fangs. Fur covered most of their bodies and their arms were shaped like a man only with large paw-hands of five fingers and razor-sharp claws. Their legs bent in the shape of a canine with feet-paws capable of speed and powerful leaps.

Wagon drivers and servants dove for cover as the soldiers, Guardians, and Allonians battled the creatures.

Titus raced to aid Chad. The loyal squire was making a stand against a dogman, taking several swiping claw blows that tore both sleeves and his collar but fortunately, no deep cuts or serious wounds.

Titus wasn't certain what to do only that he had to help. He swung his sword at the beast. The blade nicked the beast in the left arm. It growled in anger and turned on him, swinging massive claws and snapping at him.

Chad took advantage of the distraction and sent a savage slash to back of the beast. It staggered and made a defensive move at Chad. Titus thrust his sword into the beast from behind. The weight as it fell, forced Titus to release his sword. He stared at the dead beast.

"I think it's the first time I killed anything in anger."

Chad stepped on the carcass and yanked the sword out. "You don't have time to think about it. There are more to deal with." He handed the sword back to Titus and moved to engage more dogmen.

Titus followed, but soon they became separated and he faced a beast alone. Everything happened so fast, he only had time to react; thus surprised when landing a gash to its abdomen and it retreated. This proved a temporary reprieve. The beast charged again, forcing him back. He fell to one knee and barely managed to block the attack using the same method as Mirit, holding the sword like a staff. When it reared back for another swipe at him, he rolled away, coming quickly to his feet. He turned in anticipation of a charge; only Egan killed the beast.

"Are you all right?" asked the Guardian.

He swallowed back the momentary ill of seeing more death to reply. "Ay. Have you seen Chad? We got separated."

"Over there."

Titus began running in the direction Egan pointed. The Guardian followed.

Together, Tyrone and Nigel faced half-a-dozen beasts. Tyrone's half-Guardian strength proved helpful in handling four. Nigel's Jor'ellian training and experience in mock combat with Avatar aided in his battle against two creatures.

Nigel moved to avoid one creature's swing. The blade missed Nigel, and instead, sliced the hide of the second beast. In retaliation of being wounded, it lunged at the other's throat, massive jaws clamping down and killing it. Enraged by the wounding and wild in triumph of defeating the offending attacker, it launched at Nigel. He tripped in ducking the head high attack and fell onto his buttocks.

Tyrone used his sword to block one beast then sent a vicious kick in the midsection of another, causing it to fall backwards and into the one attacking Nigel. The beast turned on the one that interfered and knocked it aside with its paw.

Nigel scrambled to his feet, speaking, "Seach Jor'el's an luiths!" and thrust at the wounded one. His sword passed completely through the body. Without pause, he jerked the blade out and slashed the one Tyrone kicked, nearly cleaving it in half. Now the odds were three to two.

Avatar arrived, and the remaining beasts fell beneath the Guardian's added attack.

"Either of you seen Titus?" asked Tyrone. He barely broke a sweat in battle.

"No," said Avatar.

Nigel shook his head, trying to recover his breath. Even using his position as First Jor'ellian to call upon the Almighty's strength, fighting unnatural creatures took a lot of mortal energy.

"Let's find him."

Allard did his best against a beast, but most of the time he dodged massive claws. He landed a few minor blows, but nothing stopped it. When he fell to the ground for the fourth time, his left hand hit something hard, a large rock. He seized the rock and threw it at the beast, striking its face and making it stagger. Allard stood and thrust his sword into the beast's midsection. It collapsed to the ground.

He took a deep breath of recovery before turning to leaving. Something caught his left leg with sharp and intense pain. He cried out and fell to his knees. Three-inch fangs buried deep into his calf, and powerful jaws crushing against his bone. He tried to hit the beast with the pommel of his sword to make it let go, but the angle was wrong.

A blow between the beast's shoulder blades with a staff made the bite worse at first. The creature released Allard to deal with Ridge. In a blur of speed, the ranger twirled his staff, came up under the chin and sent it flying some fifteen feet into a tree. He finished the beast by throwing his dagger, the hilt buried deep into its throat. He made certain it was dead then withdrew his dagger and wiped the blade clean.

He returned to Allard, who groaned in pain and reached for his leg. Ridge knelt to examine the wound. "A nasty bite." He glanced around the battlefield in search of the nearest shelter. Wagons stood nearby. "Let me get you to safety and treat the bite."

Above the noise of battle came an ear-piercing cry of a bird. Over the treetops, flew an enormous black creature with a fifteen-foot wingspan and body bathed in flames.

"Firebird!" shouted Kentashi in both Allonian and Natanese.

Mirit heard the warning but only caught a glimpse of the firebird since she was engaged with a dogman. The beast knocked her off her feet, her sword falling away upon impact with the ground. The beast jerked her up and turned her around. The firebird dove at her with talons out stretched. Before it reached her, Akido's hind legs sent it tumbling through the air.

A blast hit the dogman in the head. Dazed, it released Mirit but came face-to-face with Virgil. She stumbled to avoid the beast when the flat of the Guardian's blade sent the dogman flying through the air and into a tree. Despite being further stunned, it tried to rise and attack, but Virgil beheaded the beast.

He hurried back to help Mirit stand. "Are you all right, princess? I didn't hit you, did I? I tried not to."

She brushed off the dirt and debris while taking stock herself. "No, I'm unscathed. Although I think the dragon saved me."

Akido fought the firebird, both throwing flames from their mouths at each other and dodging attacks.

"At least it distracted the beast until I could get to you."

She glanced around to see Natanese, Guardians and Allonians send the dozen remaining dogmen retreating to the trees. The battle proved costly, with dead and wounded soldiers scattered across the meadow.

"Any one of us hurt?" she asked.

"I don't know. But we wandered too far from the caravan." He took her by the arm and they ran back to the wagons.

Nigel sat on a tailgate examining his wound. Tyrone and Avatar were with him.

The sight startled her. "Nigel?"

He flashed a gallant smile. "Just a cut from one of the beast's claws. What about you?"

"I'm fine." She inspected his wound for herself.

Chad arrived with Titus and Egan. Titus held a bloody sword. His face was sweaty and dirty while his doublet torn at the shoulder.

"Master?" Chad took a quick look at Nigel's arm.

"A minor wound."

Tyrone observed Titus. "Are you hurt?"

Too winded to answer, the boy shook his head.

"He fought well. I arrived before the beast did any harm," said Egan.

With a relieved smile, Tyrone clapped the back of Titus' neck.

Ridge came running and calling, "Avatar! Bring the medical pouch. One of those creatures gave Allard a nasty bite."

Avatar and the others followed Ridge to where Allard sat against a wagon wheel, pale and grimacing in great pain. The serious bite on his left leg starkly visible. Tyrone knelt on one side while Avatar the other. The Guardian took the medicine out of the pouch.

"How did this happen?" asked Tyrone.

"I thought I killed it, but I was wrong. It bit me when I turned to leave. I thought its jaw would crush my leg. Thankfully, Ridge arrived."

Kentashi appeared. "Is he bad hurt?"

"One of those things bit him. What were they?" replied Tyrone.

"*Sheshian*. Evil spirits commanded by Onedo, king of the underworld. A bite is poison. You have strong medicine?"

"What kind of poison?" asked Avatar.

"Infection bad enough to cause loss of limb or life. You have something? If not, we seek Tani. He knows magic medicine."

"We have medicine capable of countering evil, along with our prayers to Jor'el."

Allard squirmed in discomfort. Despite the pain, he spoke with determination to Kentashi. "I think we'll try our remedy first. I have confidence in Jor'el. Beside, I'm too ornery to let a wound incapacitate me."

Avatar proceeded to treat the wound with salve and bandage.

"What about a cut from its claws? Is that poisonous also?" asked Mirit. Her worried eyes shifted from Kentashi to Nigel and indicated his cut arm.

"No, poison comes from mouth. That why wet." Kentashi made a motion with his hand of drooling. "Akido try to warn us of sheshian and firebird."

"He saved me from the firebird."

"How?" asked Nigel.

"One of the beasts held me and the firebird came to grab me," she said, making gestures with her hands, "but Akido knocked it away. Virgil arrived and killed the beast."

Kentashi stoutly nodded. "I tell you Akido good. Firebird would take you to Onedo for sacrifice."

Her eyes grew wide in terror and she gasped.

Titus seized her arm. "We won't let that happen, Aunt."

Kentashi's interest became piqued at the miscue.

Tyrone stood and spoke to divert Kentashi's marked attention. "How many casualties, Admiral?"

"That is still being determined. But Onedo knows we are here, so we must leave."

"We'll be ready when you are, Admiral."

Kentashi nodded, yet tossed another thoughtful glance at Mirit and Titus before leaving.

"I told you to be careful. Now he may suspect you are not who you claim," scolded Tyrone.

Titus frowned in shameful regret.

Mirit placed a comforting arm about his shoulders. "I know you spoke out of concern."

"I'll try to be more careful, sir." He shied from his father's gaze.

Tyrone lifted Titus' chin and spoke with assurance. "We will all make sure nothing further happens to her."

"Let me treat your wound, to be certain," said Avatar to Nigel. He finished with Allard and turned his attention to Nigel's arm.

"Can you ride, my lord, or I should we find you a spot on a wagon?" asked Ridge.

"I don't know. Help me to my feet and we'll find out." Ridge aided Allard to stand. He gingerly placed weight on his leg but flinched and held onto Ridge to keep from falling.

Ridge lowered him back to sit on the ground. "I'll find you a seat on a wagon."

"We'll fetch the horses," said Chad concerning him and Titus.

"Egan and I will come with you," said Tyrone.

Mirit stepped away from Avatar and Nigel to watch Akido. The dragon lowered its head when a cloaked man appeared beside it. The man spoke to the dragon and Akido nodded. The man looked down at her before disappearing behind Akido. Virgil came alongside her and she seized his arm.

"Did you see that? A man appeared and spoke to the dragon then looked at me and left."

Virgil shook his head, watching the dragon. "No."

She scowled in frustration. "Don't tell me I'm seeing things along with experiencing unusual feelings?"

"Is there a problem?" asked Nigel. Avatar finished the bandage and he rolled down his sleeve.

"I guess not," she groused. Chad approached, leading her horse. She moved to take the reins and mount.

Before Nigel could question Virgil, Kentashi called for the caravan to move. Tyrone arrived leading two horses and handed one set of reins to Nigel.

Leaving the meadow, they traveled deep into the dense forest. Everyone kept a wary eye out for danger. The mountain pass was well traveled and wide enough to ride three abreast and for large wagons. Mirit rode between Nigel and Tyrone. Several times she glanced up, but it proved difficult to see through the trees.

"Looking for the dragon?" asked Tyrone.

She heaved an awkward shrug, her eyes turning forward.

"You told Virgil there is something tragic about Akido, yet claimed it saved you," said Nigel.

She shook her head in confusion. "I don't know how to explain my feelings. I've never felt anything like this before. It's as if I know the dragon and it knows me, only I don't know how or why. After the battle, a man appeared beside Akido and spoke to it then looked at me before leaving. Something about him also felt familiar."

"Kentashi said Raiden and Akido are one. Perhaps you saw him," said Tyrone.

The answer didn't satisfy her and she groused, "I suppose, or else my mind is playing tricks. Virgil said he didn't see anyone."

"Unfortunately the Guardians haven't sensed anything where the dragon is concerned," said Nigel.

"Avatar sensed evil before the attack, as did I," said Tyrone. "Which makes me wonder if two different forces are at work. One that can be sensed and one that cannot."

"Except by me," she complained. She uneasily shifted in the saddle to glance around before speaking to Tyrone. "To answer your earlier question, we're being watched, which is why I keep looking for Akido, but I can't see anything through these trees."

Tyrone leaned closer to reply. "The Guardians may not be able to sense what you do, but they will protect us with their lives."

"I know. My hope is it doesn't come to that," she said with sobriety.

Titus rode beside Chad about fifty yards behind the wagon carrying Allard and Ridge. His eyes focused on the group ahead of the wagon, his father, Nigel and Mirit. Allard's wound was troublesome, but to hear Kentashi speak of Mirit's possible sacrifice unnerved him since that is what happened in Tunlund. The only difference is he was the intended sacrifice until she saved him, now she could be the intended.

"You did well, if that is what troubles you," began Chad. "I know killing for the first time is hard to deal with."

Titus shrugged and smirked. "At first, but after a short time it seemed the right thing to do to something so dark and evil." He waved toward the wagon. "I hope Lord Allard's wound heals and the poison doesn't affect him."

"Avatar used Guardian medicine that has cured evil illness before."

"What if it doesn't?"

"We still have our prayers."

"So you agree with Unc—I mean the prince, that Jor'el can hear us anywhere outside of Allon?"

The question surprised Chad. "I thought you did too? You were so confident in Tunlund, why question now?"

"I guess I'm questioning a lot things now," he droned.

Chad firmly took hold of the boy's arm. "Your faith is something you should cling to, not question or become discouraged. Use your faith and belief in Jor'el to draw strength."

"I'll try." Titus faced forward and watched Allard move in the wagon in an attempt to get comfortable. "I'll help Lord Allard when we stop for the night."

Chapter 11

B Y DUSK, THE CARAVAN HALTED AT AN ALCOVE IN THE SIDE OF the mountain. Moss and vines covered stone architecture built into the mountain. Virgil took hold of the horse's bridle when Mirit dismounted, concerned by her curiosity directed at the edifice. Tyrone and Nigel joined her in observation.

Kentashi drew his horse alongside them. "This shrine to Raiden and half-way point to Yuki. We stay here tonight. No evil spirits dare come near shrine. We will be safe but can only put up a few smaller tents between the trees. Can you share?"

"Ay. That won't be a problem," said Nigel.

Mirit regarded the shrine while Kentashi and Nigel spoke.

When the admiral left, Tyrone questioned her. "Do you sense something?"

Her eyes never left the shrine. "Something stirs under the mountain."

Nigel moved closer to his wife, intrigued yet concerned. "Can you tell what?"

She shook her head. "No, and I really don't like this." Her voice quivered slightly.

He held about her shoulders. "There has to be a reason."

With a weary sigh, she glanced down to the ground.

"You need to rest." He kissed her bent head.

She snorted a short hollow chuckle, raised her head to scowl at the shrine. "Somehow I don't think that will happen until we get home."

"Try. Virgil, stay with her while we see about the tents." Again he kissed her on the forehead then left with Tyrone.

She spoke when Virgil touched her shoulder. Perhaps he wanted to divert her attention, but she kept gazing at the shrine. "How do you cope with such uneasy feelings?"

"For a Guardian it is natural."

"Have you ever asked why?"

"On numerous occasions, especially during the early centuries of my captivity. In time Jor'el provided the answer with my restoration. He'll do the same for you."

"I hope it's soon, otherwise I might wonder if I'm going crazy." A tremor of doubt shook her words.

Virgil made her look up at him, his crystal blue eyes unwavering in certainty. "Your mind, heart, and spirit are sound. Nigel is right, there is a reason. Trust and believe and all will become clear."

"Thank you."

He smiled warm and generous. "Come sit and take your focus off this place while the tents are erected." He guided her to a fallen stone positioned so that her back was to the shrine. He stood in such a way that if she turned, his frame blocked her view of the shrine.

A few moments later, Nigel and Tyrone returned. Nigel carried a knapsack and softly smiled at her. "I have something to help you— help all of us."

"What?"

The smile turned cocky and he indicated the knapsack. "I'm a Jor'ellian. I never travel unprepared. I had Kentashi's baker make bread before we left Kaori to go with our wine. After the attack, we could all use refreshing in prayer."

She visibly relaxed.

Ridge climbed out of the wagon. Titus joined him to help Allard get down. Allard winced in pain, his grip on Titus' arm tightening in an attempt to stay on his feet. Titus caught him about the waist for extra support.

"You should have waited in the wagon until the tents are finished," said Titus.

"Tried of playing a squire that you're a doctor now?" said Allard with biting sarcasm.

"No, sir. I'm concerned for you."

Allard took notice of the boy's sincerity. "What brought this about?"

Titus didn't answer rather looked away, and in doing so, spotted a fallen log. "You should sit while Egan finishes arranging your mat."

Allard didn't argue and let Titus help him to the log and then to sit. He grunted in discomfort. "It does feel better to be off my feet."

Ridge knelt to examine Allard's wound by rolling up the pant leg. "Starting to swell. The boy is right, you should have stayed in the wagon."

"Well, I'm out now so I'll make the best of it."

Ridge patted Titus' shoulder. "Stay with him. I'll help Egan so he can lie down again."

Titus sat beside Allard. A brief awkward moment of silence passed before he said, "I'm sorry about your leg, my lord."

"This isn't your fault."

"I'm still sorry. And I intend to help you until your leg is healed."

"Really? What about your squire duties?"

"I don't think Unc—the prince will mind. Besides, Chad is a better squire than I."

Tyrone approached. "How is your leg?"

"A bit troublesome, but such is the nature of wounds, Captain."

Tyrone's attention shifted to Titus. "Aren't you supposed to be helping with the tents?"

"He graciously offered to help me while the Guardians erect the tents so I can rest again. As if I haven't been doing enough of that," he groused.

"You have to rest for your leg to heal," insisted Titus. "And I will help him get that rest, sir." For a moment he and his father regarded each other before adding, "With permission from you and the prince, of course."

Tyrone's smile was small but noticeable. "I grant permission and I will speak to the prince, but I don't think he'll object."

"Thank you, sir."

"Once all is ready and we occupy a tent, the prince will conduct the Jor'ellian refreshing ceremony."

Allard sighed in relief and rubbed his leg. "Splendid idea, Captain."

After a brief nod, Tyrone withdrew.

Allard looked along his shoulder at Titus. "You may resemble your father, but in character and action you are like your grandfather when he was a boy."

Titus sat up straight, a proud smile on his lips. "I take that as a compliment."

Allard shook his head, adamant and firm in feature and voice. "I knew him from a baby, same as I have known you. Despite his reckless impulsiveness, those of us who knew him gave him some leeway because he was likeable and intelligent. Since we believed him to be Angus' second son, we didn't expect much of him. Then again, we didn't know his true destiny at the time." He leaned closer to Titus, eyes direct on the boy. "You and I know what destiny awaits you. How do you think your grandfather would feel about your behavior?"

Titus shrunk back from Allard. This was not a question he wanted to answer since it was obvious. His grandfather would wholeheartedly disapprove. Images of the last year of his grandfather's life flashed through his mind. As a gift to his eldest grandson before passing onto the heavenlies, Ellis took Titus on a five-month tour of Allon to visit each member of the Council of Twelve.

Having just turned seven years old, Titus was very excited for only Armus and Jedrek would accompany them on the journey. His parents and younger brothers remained at Waldron. What a special time with his grandfather, and something he would never forget. Despite all the youthful faults Allard alluded to, he remembered his grandfather as a king much admired at home and abroad for his wisdom, courage and dedication to Jor'el. Surely he inherited some of those good qualities or was he just fooling himself into believing he had? Others told him differently, and not just any others, but his father, his uncle, Egan, Chad, and now Allard. This trip was definitely not turning out like he hoped.

After the tents were erected and furnished, Titus helped Allard inside one. They entered first so Allard could be made comfortable. Normally those who partook of the refreshing ceremony sat in a circle. With Allard's wound, Ridge and Egan prepared a special place for him to sit on the floor with his back against a solid object and legs extended. The others sat around his position. The tent became a bit cramped, but no one complained.

On the white cloth in front of Nigel, sat a cup, the bottle of wine, large loaf of bread, a candle and matches. Although not a priest, his position as First Jor'ellian Knight qualified him to conduct the refreshing ceremony.

He spoke in the Ancient. "Great Jor'el, creator of the universe we come before you with bread and wine to pay homage, beseeching you for strength and wisdom." He stuck a match. "May this, your light, give us insight into this enemy who threatens us." He lit the candle.

"*Tangiel*," said the others.

He poured wine into the cup. "May this wine give strength to our hearts and spirits to complete our task." He drank then handed the cup to Mirit, who sat on his left. She repeated what Nigel said before drinking from the cup and passed it to Chad, who did the same, as did, Egan, Titus, Allard, Virgil, Avatar, and Tyrone, who sat to the right of Nigel. When Tyrone finished drinking, he placed the cup back on the cloth.

Nigel took the bread. "May this bread give strength to our frail bodies joined with the wine to strengthen our hearts." He broke off a piece and ate. The rest did the same in turn. When Tyrone placed the bread next to the candle, Nigel spoke, "To your will we commend our prayers, our lives, and our mission. *Tangiel*."

"*Tangiel*," the others repeated.

Uncomfortable, Allard squirmed. "It will be cramped in here tonight with so many."

"We'll be outside," said Avatar of him and his fellow Guardians. "How is your leg?"

"Sore. Kentashi called those creatures *sheshian*. Have you encountered anything like them before?"

"There are similar to a creature that appeared prior to the Great Battle called *madah-dune*."

"I don't recall their bite being poisonous," said Egan.

"No. Yet I felt a same sense of evil just before the attack," said Avatar with emphasis not easily ignored or missed.

"You think that's significant?" asked Chad.

"Perhaps. I want to be certain before saying directly. Natan is so different and our inability to sense anything until now is puzzling."

"You will tell us when you know?" asked Titus.

Avatar flashed a smile at the boy. "Of course."

"We should fetch supper. Lord Allard needs to eat to keep up his strength," said Chad to Titus.

"More rice?" groused Allard.

"I don't think they eat much else."

"Except the large horrid slimy thing with round sticky holes," said Titus with a disgusting smirk.

"Octopus. Similar to squid." Chad chuckled at the boy's disgusted reaction and steered him from the tent. Egan followed.

Tyrone rose to leave but Mirit intercepted him. For a moment they stared at each other, silent and conferring before she released him and he left. Avatar accompanied Tyrone.

"Is something wrong?" Nigel asked Mirit.

She bit her lip, the debate of whether to answer evident on her face. She shook her head and left. Virgil signaled Nigel to remain and left after Mirit.

Mirit joined Tyrone, who stood in front of the shrine. His narrow grey eyes focused with intensity on the edifice. Since they stood in the open, she spoke in the Ancient for privacy and less risk of being overheard and understood. "You also sensed something during the ceremony. Something we need to discover."

He didn't immediately answer. Only when she touched his arm did he react. His voice was low and hesitant as he replied in the Ancient. "Ay, but unclear and unsettling. And I don't know if I want to risk finding out what."

Avatar and Virgil stood behind them. "The sense is growing," said Avatar.

"You too?" asked Mirit, her gaze hopeful of the Guardians.

Avatar made a partial inclination of his head in acknowledgement.

"Perhaps you will tell us what you wouldn't tell Titus," said Tyrone, and in tone unreceptive of denial.

"Once I am certain. There is too much uneasiness and vagueness to speak and cause undue alarm."

"Another one with an annoying answer," she chided and nudged Tyrone's arm.

"My reasons are more personal—your welfare," he said.

"And mine is for everyone's welfare," insisted Avatar.

"Then we're back where we started from with vague senses, and I don't like it!" she groused, though more uneasy than angry.

Tyrone held her shoulder to get her attention. "Despite the circumstances, I glad I'm here—*sister*." He added the kinship term with an affectionate smile.

She gripped his hand and grinned. "So am I. Titus aside, there is something here far beyond what we expected of a simple diplomatic journey."

"Avatar!" Nigel rushed over, but spoke in normal Allonian. "Allard's wound is badly infected, the likes of which neither I nor Ridge have seen before."

All headed back to the tent to find Allard in extreme pain, pale and sweaty. The visible wound was horribly swollen with a greenish crust and ooze.

"Infected, only I've never seen such discoloration," said Ridge to Avatar when the lieutenant knelt across from him. "He suddenly developed a fever."

Avatar felt Allard's forehead then examined the infected wound.

"Doesn't look normal. What did you use?" Tyrone asked Avatar.

"The same suave used for kelpie and *madah-dune* bites. The dog-like creature I described earlier."

Tyrone gently inspected the wound. "You said their bites weren't poisonous."

"The creature is similar, so I hoped the remedy would be also."

"Maybe a local remedy will work better. Try to make him comfortable. Ridge." Tyrone waved the ranger to follow him and they left to find Kentashi. "Admiral!"

"Captain Fraser. Is there problem?"

"Lord Allard's wound is badly infected and he has developed a sudden fever. Our medicine doesn't appear to be working. Is there a local remedy for such a bite?"

Kentashi shouted and a moment later, a smaller, older man appeared. Kentashi briefly spoke to him and the older man nodded while replying.

Ridge translated for Tyrone. "Tani says we could try a paste made from two local plants, the sukiruish and amayna."

"Are there some close by?"

Ridge spoke to Tani, who by his gestures appeared to be describing the plants. Ridge sent a confident grin to Tyrone. "I'll be back shortly."

"Tani go with you to help make paste when spirit returns," said Kentashi.

Tani scurried to follow Tyrone, his short legs moving rapidly to keep pace with Tyrone's long, hurried strides.

"This is Tani, Kentashi's physician, I guess. At least he knows local remedies. Ridge is looking for the plants now," said Tyrone upon arrival.

Tani knelt to examine the wound, a constant stream of Natanese emanating. Avatar conversed with Tani, but the old mortal sounded adamant in his speech, which appeared to frustrate the Guardian lieutenant.

Virgil translated for the others. "He's scolding Avatar for not seeking him out sooner and using *foreign* medicine."

Avatar's sharp glance conveyed his displeasure at the translation. "You two see what's keeping Ridge," he said to Virgil and Egan, despite Tani still speaking to him.

Ridge tried to be quick about his business. He first found the *sukiruish*, a mushroom type fungus, and dug up several whole plants just to be sure to have enough. The *amayna* proved more elusive. He finally located some a mile from the campsite. He knelt to inspect the low growing weed when something jumped onto the back of his neck. He heard clicking and snapping and felt a nip at his collar but grabbed it before being bit on the neck. He tossed it on the ground and pinned it with his dagger. The slimy insect was the size of a rat with huge mandibles and gave off a noxious odor when killed. He backed away to clear his nostrils. Hearing more clicking, he ripped up three plants and left before more creatures appeared.

Returning to camp, he found the creatures everywhere and soldiers doing their best to deal with the stench of the insects they killed. Virgil and Egan didn't fair much better than the mortals in handling the creatures.

Virgil swatted the insects with his sword. "What are these things?"

"They remind me of *drusi*," said Egan.

"One almost bit me as I gathered the plants." Ridge grabbed a log from out of the side of a nearby fire. "Fire kept drusi at bay. I need to get these plants to Avatar." He handed the safe end of the burning log to Egan and left.

Virgil gabbed another log and joined Egan by waving fire at the insects. The insects angrily hissed, but backed away from the flames.

"What's going on?" asked Mirit when Ridge arrived. Two insects followed him into the tent and one leapt at her face.

In swift motion, Avatar bolted to his feet and snatched it in midair. The force of his grip snapped the creature's neck and it stunk. Mirit turned away, covering her face at the awful smell. He dropped the creature, uncertain of what to do with the smelly residue on his hand. He reached between the floor mats for a handful of dirt to *wash* his hands.

Nigel avoided a second insect leaping at him. Ridge batted it out of the air with his hand then crushed it beneath his foot. More stench.

"What is it?" asked Mirit with a crinkled face at the smell.

"Egan thinks they're like a drusi. He and Virgil are chasing them away with fire," said Ridge. He handed the plants to Tani, who again chattered in Natanese of what to do with the plants for the wound.

"Help with the medicine while I deal with the insects," Avatar instructed Ridge before leaving.

Outside, he summoned his fellow warriors. He led them to the center of camp, drew his sword and placed the pommel in front of his face. They mimicked his action only held the tips of their swords pointing down.

Avatar raised his sword above his head and said, *"Jor'el's a'lasadh dion an aghaidh olc!"* then made a quick downward turn of the blade and thrust the point into the ground. Virgil and Egan did the same.

The entire camp became illuminated with light radiating from the struck swords, up and through the trees. They heard some startled outcries from the Natanese, but soon a chorus of eerie insect screeching drowned them. After several moments the forest grew silent.

When the light faded, all the creatures and their stench were gone. The Natanese nearest the Guardians stared at them in awe. Others gaped, looking around and not seeing the creatures.

Avatar pulled his sword from the ground and sheathed the blade. He sent displeased glances to his comrades before they all headed back to the tent.

Kentashi and Hodi intercepted the Guardians, both in a state of amazement.

"You are most powerful, spirit!" said Kentashi.

"For the last time, I'm a Guardian! Servant of Jor'el and not one of your spirits," said Avatar, not hiding his impatience or annoyance.

Kentashi balked and fell silent. However, when Avatar, Virgil and Egan continued to the tent, he and Hodi followed.

Chad and Titus were now present, having returned from their attempt to fetch food. Tyrone, Tani and Ridge tended to Allard's leg.

"Admiral," said Nigel.

"Creatures gone thanks to spir—them," he said of Avatar, Virgil and Egan. "I come see if all is well."

"We gave him something for the fever. I'm about to apply the suave," said Tyrone.

Tani spoke instructions that Ridge translated. Tyrone followed the instructions, speaking a prayer in the Ancient as he did.

"You speak to your god?" asked Hodi.

"I was asking for his mercy to heal Lord Allard."

"Maybe he protect us more like tonight."

Mirit's accosted Kentashi. "You said no evil spirits would dare to attack near Raiden's shrine but they did. Why?"

Kentashi appeared perplexed. "It never happened before."

"Unlike the earlier attack."

"That unusual too. Sheshian not attack in such numbers or in daylight."

"I wonder what stirred them." Her harsh stare went to Hodi at hearing the captain snarl under his breath.

Kentashi scolded Hodi in a terse exchange of Natanese.

"Apparently he thinks we're the cause," said Avatar, not pleased.

Hodi momentarily glared at Avatar before turning away from the Guardian lieutenant's intense silver glare.

Tyrone rose to stand beside Mirit. "Is that true, Admiral? Does Captain Hodi believe our presence is responsible?"

Hodi's unfriendly focus shifted to Tyrone and he said something in Natanese to Kentashi.

"He doesn't like your insubordinate look, Captain," said Avatar.

"Whether he likes it or not, is of little concern. Is it true, Admiral?" Tyrone face's and voice showed he was in no mood to be tolerant.

For a brief moment, Kentashi stared up into the fierce grey glare. Tyrone's size was enough to intimidate, but joined with the severity of his scrutiny, few could withstand him. The Natanese admiral proved no exception. He gave a short assenting nod to Hodi, who spoke to Tyrone in Allonian.

"I not mean you specific, but foreign presence bring opportunity to enemy of Lord Norkiru."

"How so?"

To this question, Kentashi replied. "Death of old emperor bring divide to shiragoto. Some choose Norkiru when he side with Tirigato others with Lord Rukan Shokita and his claim to power."

Tyrone's initial probing turned to guarded curiosity. "Your son-in-law?"

The admiral made a reluctant nod. "Rukan, how you say, want of power."

"Ambitious."

"Ay, ambitious. Jealous of uncle, Norkiru, and not like Natan become open. Keep closed and worship Zekar."

"Zekar?"

"Gods of the spirits."

"There is more than one?" asked Mirit.

"Ay. Raiden and Onedo among the Zekar. Yoshia is goddess of water, Sukiui is goddess of sun and wind, Kinkini is god of forest, Nobuku is god of justice—"

Nigel put his hand up for Kentashi to stop. "We get the idea you have many gods among the Zekar."

"Most powerful and most evil is Onedo and Hoshiki. She is goddess of the night and controls sheshian and firebird," said Kentashi with gravity.

"Lord Rukan is devout worshipper of Onedo and Hoshiki," said Hodi.

"So you believe he is using us as an excuse to go against Norkiru and employing these gods to do so?" asked Tyrone.

"Ay. He make you fall like goat."

Nigel tried not to grin at the miscue. "You mean use us as *scapegoats*. Blaming us for the evil that is happening."

"Ay," said Hodi with an embarrassed shrug. "My Allon not so good."

"I thought stopping here would shield us. I was wrong," said Kentashi. "My apologies." He made a short bow to Nigel.

"It's not your fault. Only I wish you told us after the earlier attack."

Kentashi's own studious gaze found Tyrone. "Not know you, make me cautious. Again, my apology, prince." He spoke the last sentence to Nigel.

Allard stirred and groaned in his sleep.

Nigel steered Kentashi and Hodi toward to tent flap. "We appreciate you and Captain Hodi informing us. We'll help in anyway we can to make this a more trouble free journey."

"That explains some of the problems," said Tyrone after Kentashi and Hodi left.

"And how the Dark Way is involved," said Avatar with gravity.

"The Dark Way?" said Titus, disturbed but ignored when his father and Avatar continued speaking.

"That might be what we sensed."

Avatar nodded. "Dealing with the creatures confirmed it."

"How?" asked Titus more forceful, and tugged on Avatar's sleeve.

"Because my power completely destroyed them." At the boy's confusion, Avatar continued. "I went out to use my power of light to drive them off. I did not expect to destroy them. For a Guardian's power to be that effective, the evil has to be of Dark Way origin, otherwise the results vary."

"I think I understand."

In his unconscious state, Allard moved, muttering something under his breath.

Ridge felt Allard's forehead. "His fever is down. The restlessness maybe a side-effect of the medicine."

"We'll take turns watching him while the rest get some sleep and prepare for what may face us tomorrow," said Avatar.

Chapter 12

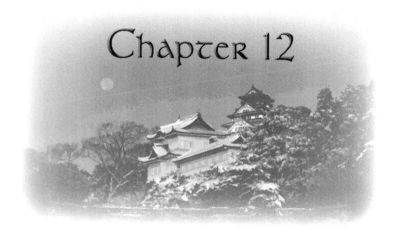

Titus didn't sleep well. Every time he tried to sleep, disturbing dreams began. Dreams of events in Tunlund he hadn't thought about in years, or even consciously remembered. The most disturbing was reliving Mirit's death when she saved him from being sacrificed to Hueil. Thankfully, Jor'el restored her life as a sign of his power in contrast to Hueil's false claims of godhood. To hear Kentashi speak of her possible sacrifice to Onedo and Avatar's belief of the Dark Way being involved and responsible for Allard's wound, deeply troubled him and prevented sleep.

Around midnight he decided to sit up with Egan and Avatar to keep watch of Allard. Tani left but Tyrone and Chad remained, both sleeping. Nigel and Mirit retired to the second tent along with Virgil. Ridge stood watch between the tents.

"Why aren't you sleeping?" whispered Egan.

Titus knew Egan asked the question to probe him; something Guardians did. What Egan said earlier was true about his familiarity with Guardians, only he never thought about taking them for granted. Still, he didn't want to discuss the subject so he shrugged in avoidance of speaking.

"Allard's wound or Mirit's sacrifice?"

Titus' head snapped up at Egan mentioning what he thought about.

"Both," said Avatar. His also kept his voice low in an effort to not disturb the others.

Titus' stupefied gazed passed to Avatar. One Guardian's comprehension was hard enough to deal with, two proved difficult. He nodded. Egan placed a comforting hand about his shoulder. Titus didn't rebuff him or retreat. In fact, he leaned against Egan without saying a word.

Titus didn't realize he fell asleep until voices woke him. Chad and his father spoke to Avatar about Allard. The tent seemed lighter, perhaps dawn, which meant he slept where he was, against Egan's side.

"How long did I sleep?"

"A couple of hours," said Egan.

He sat up. "Does your side hurt?"

Egan chuckled. "No. Any more nightmares?"

"No, actually, I feel rested," replied Titus in mild surprise. "How is Lord Allard?"

Tyrone answered, "His fever is down, but no improvement in the infection."

Titus moved beside his father. "Is that good or bad?"

"Hard to tell just yet. How long were you awake?"

"I don't know. I couldn't sleep. Well, not at first. Egan helped me."

Ridge arrived bringing breakfast. "How is he?"

"No fever, but the wound is not much better," replied Avatar.

Titus stared at the bowl of rice Ridge gave him. He didn't have much of an appetite, not because eating rice at every meal grew tiresome, rather being troubled and concerned.

"Eat some. We have a long journey ahead," said Tyrone.

Titus only took a few mouthfuls but stopped when Allard stirred, uneasy and in pain. He placed the bowl down, anxious to watch Avatar and his father tend Allard.

"I don't like moving him like this," said Avatar.

"We have no choice," said Tyrone.

"He'll have to stay still and quiet in the wagon to prevent the infection from spreading."

"I'll make sure he doesn't move. I told him I'd stay with him until he is recovered," said Titus.

Nigel and Mirit arrived. "They're breaking camp and Virgil is making the wagon ready for him," said Nigel.

A few moments later, Virgil arrived. Together, he and Avatar carried Allard from the tent to the wagon. One Guardian could easily carry a mortal, but they were careful to keep his wounded leg immobile. The arranged cushions for Allard, made a tight fit for the injured lord. Allard woke during the transfer and bit back the great pain of moving.

"There doesn't appear to be room for me," said Titus, disappointed.

"No. I had to place the cushions to ensure he wasn't jolted and injured further," said Virgil.

"We'll ride behind the wagon," said Chad.

"Do not hesitate to call if you have need, my lord," said Titus.

Due to pain and fatigue, Allard only nodded.

Avatar and Virgil accompanied the others ahead of the wagon. Ridge walked beside the wagon. Egan remained with Titus and Chad.

Titus watched Allard try to get comfortable during the ride. The tongue-lashing he received onboard ship echoed in his mind, followed by the question about his grandfather. Soon, he began to regret coming. However, regret didn't change reality.

He looked past the wagon to his father. Although a king with strength and power, he willingly took on the role of an army captain, subjecting himself to others for everyone's safety and welfare. That would not have happened if he had not deceived him. At first he didn't like the idea of acting as a servant, but watching his father, experiencing danger and witnessing injury, he understood the necessity.

Feeling a tap on the arm, Titus realized someone spoke to him. "What?"

"I asked, what are you thinking about so hard?" said Chad.

"Everything," he said with a deep, dejected frown.

"I thought so. I gave my situation in Soren much consideration after far worse happened."

Titus' brows knitted in recollection. "I remember a time you and Uncle had a falling out, but I don't know why."

"Beware of speaking so freely."

Titus flushed with embarrassment at not realizing he called Nigel *Uncle* instead of highness. "Sorry," he murmured. He looked around, but none of the Natanese seemed interested in them.

Chad discreetly spoke. "*He* and I did have a falling out. You were eight at the time. Sadly, it happened because of a girl," he said with a deep sigh. "Or rather what I thought were my feelings for her, when in actuality it was my own selfish discontentment."

"Discontent with what?"

"Being his squire."

"Really?" said Titus in surprise. "I didn't think he treated you bad."

"He doesn't. I couldn't ask for a better lord and master. As I said, my own selfishness made me discontented. During the mission, I lashed out at him for petty reasons, all of which he took and never once said a cross word to me. In fact, he, Avatar, and *she* tried to counsel me, but I stubbornly wanted my way and wouldn't listen. Finally, when the girl became involved, I did the unthinkable and broke my pledge and left him to marry her, which is why he returned without me."

Titus grew thoughtful while listening. "I wondered why I didn't see you. Although he said I might see you again. Which I did at the wedding."

Pricked, Chad winced. "After all I did, he never gave up on me and I was so ready to give up myself. Truth be told, I wanted to die the day the Sorens invaded and faced the queen in battle. I didn't want to live the rest of my life knowing what I done, not only to him, but also to Bergeta. If not for me, she would have remained in Soren and be alive today."

Titus gaped, wide-eye and barely able to speak. "She died?"

Chad nodded, his voice thick. "Long ago Jor'el pronounced a curse upon the Sorens and fulfilled his judgment on the battlefield. Virgil protected me and I survived the Almighty's wrath."

A long moment of silence followed the somber explanation before Titus asked, "How did you and he reconcile?"

"Undeserved grace, mercy and forgiveness." Chad motioned Titus' attention toward Nigel and the group ahead. "He found me grieving and guilt ridden with shame. I couldn't even look at him, but he embraced me and forgave me. To this day I don't understand why, yet have come to accept it, and with Jor'el's help have not acted so foolishly since."

Titus' gaze passed to his father when he asked, "You said I was eight, how old were you then?"

"Seventeen. I met him when I was eight."

Thoughtful, Titus turned to Chad, who kept speaking.

"I also met your father, mother and grandfather the same day. In fact, as a reward for helping *him* during a certain coup attempt," he pointed to Nigel, "I received instruction from the master-at-arms alongside him and your father." At Titus' consideration, he added, "When I told you it isn't only about being sorry, but also learning from your mistakes and correcting them, I spoke from personal experience. My selfishness ended in tragedy. My hope and prayer for you is you don't suffer the same guilt and shame I did from not learning soon enough to appreciate blessings and guard them with all your might."

Titus slumped in the saddle. A heavy silence fell, as he struggled to absorb all Chad told him.

By mid-day the caravan left the forest behind and climbed to the summit of the mountain, a plateau bare of trees. The temperature was much colder with patches of snow on the ground. They paused to rest and refresh before the descent. The summit offered a commanding view of the valley and beyond. Tyrone, Nigel and Mirit stood at the edge of

155

the plateau gazing down at the vista. An impressive fortress stood miles away, surrounded by a village.

Kentashi joined them. "That is Yuki."

"Appears larger than Kaori," said Tyrone.

"Ay. Lord Norkiru is very wealthy and powerful."

Titus came running. "Father! Lord Allard's infection is worse."

They followed Titus back to the wagon. Ridge and Virgil gathered around Avatar, who tended the exposed wound, the green crust larger and signs of bulging under the crust. Allard remained unconscious.

"Avatar?" asked Nigel.

"We're going have to drain the infection or it will spread further."

"How?" asked Titus with fear.

"By cutting it open." Avatar nodded at Ridge.

Ridge withdrew his hunting knife and took a small torch from Virgil. He heated the blade. Avatar took firm hold of Allard's leg to hold it still. Ridge made two long cuts on the greenish crust over the wound and immediately green foul smelling pus oozed. Allard barely moved and only made a slight groan.

They heard a familiar yet muffled call. Overhead, Akido appeared and held something in his mouth. He descended and landed beside the wagon.

Mirit stopped Virgil and Egan from drawing their swords. "He means no harm."

Akido held a leather strap in his mouth, which appeared to be carrying something. He lowered his head and gave it to Mirit. She removed the strap to reveal a covered jar.

"Let the wound finish oozing, then use the paste and bind it well," said Akido.

She handed the jar to Avatar. He removed the lid to discover a pleasant smelling paste.

"What's in it?" he asked.

"Herbs and plants you are not familiar with but will cure a sheshian bite."

For several moments they waited for the wound to finish oozing then Avatar applied the paste directly to the wound and tightly wrapped it with fresh bandages.

"He should recover in a few days," said Akido.

"Thank you," said Avatar.

Mirit regarded Akido. "Where were you last night?"

Akido spoke to Kentashi rather than answer her. "Have you told them?"

"Of Onedo and Hoshiki."

Akido replied to Mirit. "Recovering from my encounter with the firebird. Since joining Hoshiki, Onedo has grown more powerful, even to the point of infiltrating Raiden's mountain. Once you enter the valley, you will be completely in his territory. You must be whole to face what is to come. That is why Raiden provided your friend's cure."

Tyrone took several steps toward Akido, grey eyes direct on the dragon. "We didn't come to confront Onedo and Hoshiki."

Akido returned Tyrone's stare. "No. Their fight is with Raiden, and you are caught in the middle. If you want to survive, you should turn back now and leave Natan. But I do not believe you will, *Captain*." He deliberately spoke the title.

"Since being here, backing down and leaving also has great risk."

"You must count the cost of both options, Captain. For the good of those in your charge."

Nigel grabbed Tyrone's arm to stop another reply. "The captain appreciates your counsel. We've never encountered a dragon before, but you speak wisdom."

"May wisdom guide you as it did your father, Son of Ellis." Akido spread his wings in preparation to take off.

"Wait!" said Mirit. "Will we see you after we leave the mountain?"

"For me to venture into Onedo's territory is very dangerous. Still, I will be Raiden's eyes, watching." Akido stepped away from the wagon and took off.

"Well, *Captain*, do you chose to turn back or continue?" asked Kentashi in a probing voice and eyes fixed on Tyrone.

Tyrone shrugged, his glance shifting to Nigel. "You should ask the prince, Admiral. I'm just the escort."

Kentashi was slow to turn from Tyrone to Nigel.

"Lord Allard needs time and attention to recover. Being we are closer to Yuki then Kaori, we continue."

"Ay." Kentashi bowed to Nigel, yet tossed another studious glance at Tyrone before leaving.

Nigel drew close to Tyrone and scolded him. "You tell Titus to be more careful, you should heed your own counsel!" He stormed off.

Titus came alongside his father. "Why is he angry? You did nothing wrong."

Tyrone watched Mirit catch up to Nigel and answered Titus. "No, nothing wrong, but I interfered where it wasn't necessary."

"Like he has done with you and Titus, so why be jealous?" Avatar spoke in Tyrone's ear while passing in pursuit of Nigel and Mirit.

Tyrone winced at hearing the word *jealous* again, first from Mirit and now Avatar. He curbed his pricked reaction for Titus' sake. Only Titus didn't appear to hear what Avatar said, rather kept focused on Nigel and Mirit. They mounted when Kentashi shouted orders for departure.

"Come. Time to leave." Tyrone steered Titus to the horses.

Once on horseback, they separated. Titus took up position behind the wagon, and Tyrone moved his horse beside Nigel for the ride down the mountain. The trail leading down didn't appear wide enough to allow the three to ride abreast as in the forest so Mirit rode ahead of them with Virgil accompanying her.

Nigel barely glanced at Tyrone, but what he saw appeared more hurt than anger. Although he and Nigel spoke onboard the ship about Titus and came to an agreement on how to handle the current situation, he wondered about the basis for that agreement. Nigel tended to withdraw or make concessions to soothe personal situations. He always acted strong and confident in matters relating to his position as First Jor'ellian

Knight and the King's Champion, but possessed a tender heart towards family. He would rather yield than inflict hurt or disappointment. Marriage to Mirit helped him curb the habit and deal more straightforward with family issues. Only this turned into a full-blown argument, and Tyrone heard the voices replaying certain exchanges.

"How long did you think it would be before you were discovered?"

"They didn't find me until this morning." Titus rebuffed him.

"Maybe they weren't looking hard enough."

"How should we know? Last we saw he was sick and being taken back to Straden," argued Nigel.

Later in the argument:

"Uncle reminded me how he would be king if he hadn't stepped aside."

"Not in so off-handed a manner," said Nigel.

"So you think if he were king he would be more lenient than I?"

Tyrone cringed at his callous words, but more so at Nigel's heated response.

"I don't condone what he did and blast you for implying I do!" He stormed out of the wardroom.

Tyrone sighed at the obvious truth: he started the argument and one that remained unresolved. Why? *Because I came to confront Nigel about Titus' disgraceful and wrongful behavior,* he admitted to himself. Despite Barrett's confession of being Titus' sole aid in the escapade, he faulted Nigel for being the object of Titus' plan. Nigel's denouncement of Titus' behavior, his action of locking him in the brig and even Egan's speech on behalf of Nigel, did little to dissuade his course.

Kentashi unexpected arrival changed everything. In the midst of their role-playing, resolving the matter took second place to making the mission a success. Or had it? Avatar and Mirit accused him of jealousy toward Nigel. How?

The thought made him reflect on their relationship. A time not long ago, he and Nigel's attitude and actions complemented each other with no offense. They first met when he lived the isolated, lonely life of a blacksmith, ridiculed and scorned for his size and heritage. That changed when a wandering cripple stumbled upon his cottage during a fierce storm. Since then a deep friendship developed, and became a brotherhood upon marriage to Tristine. True Titus was his son, but no other man loved the boy more than Nigel. He was an attentive and good uncle to all their children.

Again the word *jealousy* sprang to mind. He couldn't recall being jealous of anyone. Oh, there were times in his youth when his forced isolation weighed on him. Tristine became jealous when a woman from Soren tried to drive a wedge between her and him. Her jealous anger came about by emotion, nothing he did.

Of all people, she should know me better—the thought stopped when he recalled Mirit's statements, *Of all people, you should know Nigel's heart towards you, towards his entire family. Search your heart. You know Nigel would do nothing to harm you or Titus.*

Indeed, he knew. In fact, Nigel risked his life to save the boy—*Tunlund.* Without hesitation, Nigel went to Tunlund to rescue Titus, and Mirit died to protect him. They did what he failed to do: save his son. But he confronted Hueil and refused to yield to the dark Guardian's terror, setting the stage for the battle to come. After the rescue, Titus began to idolize Nigel, and fondness for an uncle turned to admiration and imitation. So why minimize him to Titus?

"Jealousy," he spoke under his breath. He winced at finally acknowledging the truth of what others said. *I'm the one who allowed jealousy to affect us all. That's why he backed down and agreed: to keep peace between us.*

Gripped by sudden remorse, he noticed that in his preoccupation, Nigel pulled ahead. He kicked his horse into a trot to catch up. Fortunately, Kentashi and Hodi rode a safe distance in the lead, and in front of Mirit. Still, he spoke discreetly in the Ancient. "Nigel. I'm sorry."

Nigel only gave him a sidelong glance and half nod.

He took hold of Nigel's arm to get his full attention. "I mean, I'm sorry for being jealous of you with Titus."

The statement took Nigel by surprise. "I never meant to make you jealous."

"I know. It's my fault for allowing it to fester and come between us. It's what brought me here rather than allowing you to deal with him. It's what made me confront Akido."

"Confronting Akido wasn't due to jealousy, rather your nature, who you are. Unfortunately, Kentashi is more suspicious, which could jeopardize us and," he leaned toward Tyrone and tapped his Champion's amulet, "I'm supposed to be the protector. I can't do that if you keep asserting yourself, *Captain*."

Tyrone laughed and said, "I should know better than to doubt your motive." By Nigel's careful glance ahead, he realized he grew a little too loud. Not that Mirit's attention caused concern, but Kentashi.

Nigel made a friendly wave and spoke in Allonian. "A private joke, Admiral." He added a chuckle for effect and Kentashi faced forward. Nigel quipped out of the corner of his mouth in the Ancient. "At present, you can do good for my motive by shutting up."

Tyrone straightened in the saddle and clamped his lips closed. The difficultly of keeping a smile from his face was quite evident. Not for amusement, but grateful relief that Nigel would not hold anything against him.

At one point, the descent became steep and winding between trees and sheer cliff, forcing them to ride single file. The drivers frequently used the brakes to keep the loaded wagons from going out of control. Skillfully they navigated the dangerous slope and arrived at a small mountain glen with the load intact. Thankfully, Allard slept all the way.

Kentashi ordered the caravan to stop for the night. Although two hours remained until dusk, he explained to the Allonians the need to rest the horses and inspect the brakes. The glen was large enough to accommodate all the tents being erected.

Once finished making camp, Ridge and Chad carried a sleeping Allard inside. Titus held several extra pillows, ready for when needed. Allard woke when Ridge laid him on the prepared mat.

"How are you feeling, my lord?" asked the ranger.

"Weak and tired."

"What about your leg?" asked Titus.

Allard thought for a moment before answering. "It doesn't hurt as much."

Ridge unwrapped the bandage. Avatar and Tyrone arrived. Avatar carried some cloth. They waited to see how the wound appeared. The greenish hue of the crust appeared half gone, replaced by the normal dark red scab.

"Looks better. How does this feel?" Ridge gently prodded around the wound.

"Tender, but not painful."

"Fresh bandages." Avatar handed them to Ridge.

Allard glanced around at the tent. "Where are we?"

"Half-way down the mountain. Kentashi said we should reach Yuki tomorrow," replied Tyrone.

"Really? The last I remember we arrived at Raiden's shrine."

"You've been asleep since, and it's been rather quiet."

Allard grinned. "Well, now that I'm awake I can make up for lost time. First tell me what has happened."

Tyrone chuckled. "After you have something to eat."

"I'll get it," said Titus.

"More rice?"

Titus paused at the entrance and smiled at Allard. "I don't think they eat anything else. But I'll see what I can get."

Allard flashed a wry smile. "Oh, how I see Ellis in him."

"He has given you trouble?" asked Tyrone.

"No. He's been quite diligent. Like Ellis in his youth, words seem slow to penetrate."

"The Son of Tristan was more a man of action than words," said Avatar.

Tyrone shook his head with an ironic chuckle. "Ellis was never short on words. Nor is Titus."

"I meant when it came to expressing inner personal thoughts and feelings. Sometimes he had to be provoked."

"Like Nigel."

Avatar tilted his head to the contrary. "Not as severely. Nigel's shielding of thoughts and feelings is defensive due to his past crippling while Ellis' nature was more private."

The discussion stopped when Titus returned carrying a bowl and flask. Sticks poked into the bowl. Unaware of the conversation, he spoke immediately upon entrance.

"Actually, you're in luck. Tonight they have noodles and not rice. It's mixed with a bit of dried fish, vegetables and sauce. I tasted it and it's not bad."

Allard struggled to sit up, so Ridge helped him. He frowned at seeing the sticks. "I can't eat with those infernal things."

"That's all right. I can feed you," said Titus.

"Be fed like a child? I don't think so."

Titus held the bowl and sticks out for Allard, who took it and began to eat. He tried to catch the noodles in his mouth before they slide off the sticks but missed.

Tyrone chuckled and rose. "Maybe you'll do better with less of an audience." He, Avatar and Ridge left.

"Here, let me." Titus took the bowl from Allard.

"I feel like an inept old man."

"That's the pain talking." Titus deftly twirled the noodles on the sticks and held it for Allard to eat.

"Now you take some," said Allard. "I've not seen you eat much."

"I'm not hungry." Titus prepared another helping for Allard, who shook his head.

"I won't take another bite until you do. We'll share it," he added at Titus's reluctance.

Titus ate. They continued sharing alternate bites until finished. Allard drank some of the rice wine from the flask then Titus helped him to lie down on the cot. Soon, Allard fell asleep.

Egan entered. "You sleep also."

Titus shook his head. "I'll watch him."

"No, you need sleep. I know you haven't slept well and if you don't rest, you won't be any good to him." Egan took Titus by the arm and guided him to a mat across from Allard. "Sleep in peace. I won't let anything disturb either of you."

Titus smiled and closed his eyes.

Chapter 13

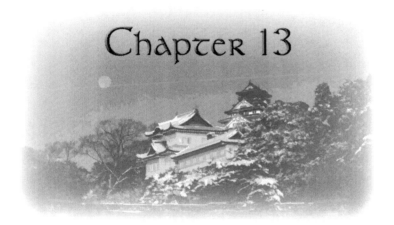

THE FOLLOWING MORNING, THE CARAVAN BEGAN A MORE gentle descent into the valley. Akido circled overheard. Ridge sat on the tailgate of the wagon carrying Allard, observing the dragon. Allard sat with his back against the front seat of the wagon, which made room for Ridge. Titus and Chad rode ahead of the wagon, leaving the ranger to tend Allard. A grunt drew Ridge's attention from watching Akido to Allard.

"Problem, my lord?"

"No, just moving to get some circulation to my rear quarters. It gets numb sitting in one position for too long," he sarcastically groused.

Ridge chuckled.

"I get the impression they don't like us," said Allard. He made discreet motion to the platoon of soldiers walking a short distance behind the wagon.

Ridge noticed Makito and Jiru among the group. They spoke in hushed tones so as not to be overheard. Makito appeared most animated in his disapproving expression. Granted, the caravan being attacked twice since leaving Kaori gave ample reason for displeasure.

"Or the strategy of shifting blame is working," muttered the ranger.

"What?"

Ridge didn't immediately answer Allard as he tried to be casual in his observance while considering the situation. Many unanswered questions remained. Thus far all the information came from Hodi and Kentashi, and based upon suspicion, no real intelligence.

Captain Hodi rode from the front of the formation to the following platoon. Ridge heard Hodi inquire of the commander of his troop's status. The man reported all was well. Hodi told the commander to have Makito and Jiru report to him when they stopped at the river. After the exchange, Hodi rode further back to another platoon of soldiers.

Allard beckoned Ridge to move closer. "Did you hear what they said before Hodi arrived?"

"No. They spoke so not to be overhead and I didn't want to give them more reason to dislike us by using my power to eavesdrop."

"I thought Guardians could do so without detection."

"We can, but it requires focus on those speaking. And they are watching us. Too obvious if I suddenly become interested in them."

Conversation ceased when Hodi passed on his way back to the front of the caravan at a gallop. He slowed his horse and assumed his position beside Kentashi.

"Hodi did request Makito and Jiru report to him when we stop," said Ridge.

Allard looked askew. "I thought you didn't eavesdrop?"

Ridge grinned. "He spoke loud enough to be heard, even by you."

"Ay." Allard grew curious in asking, "Makito and Jiru, are those the two who gave you and Virgil trouble?"

"Let's just say they aren't pleased by our presence. We're a bad omen in their minds."

Allard smiled "Well, you *spirits* do tend to cause a stir whereever you go."

Ridge chuckled. "Don't let Avatar hear you."

"Don't let me hear what?"

Ridge flinched, his head snapping around.

Avatar walked beside the wagon. He wore a satisfied smile at the ranger's surprised reaction. "Losing your hearing?"

Ridge tried to act nonchalant and asked, "Is there a problem, Lieutenant?"

Avatar's smile didn't waiver. "No, I just came to see how Lord Allard is doing."

"Better. The pain is minimal and I can move without too much discomfort."

"Good. I'll still have a look when we stop."

"No, tonight will be soon enough. I've already been the cause of too much delay."

"It's a serious wound, and of unknown powers."

Allard remained stubborn in his defiance. "I said tonight! The more we keep moving the less likelihood of trouble for the *captain*." He moved to glance over his shoulder toward Tyrone, only grimaced when he turned too far.

"He will not sacrifice your well-being," Avatar continued his argument.

"No! My duty has already been compromised. I won't risk further embarrassment." He curtly waved Avatar off and turned aside in a huff.

Ridge shook his head in warning to Avatar. Without another word, Avatar left.

<hr />

By mid-day the caravan reached the base of the mountain where a river flowed and continued on toward Yuki and beyond. Kentashi called for a halt to rest and water the horses. They would reach Yuki by nightfall.

For half a mile along the gentle riverbank, riders, drivers, soldiers and horses refreshed themselves. Allard sat on the tailgate of the wagon. Ridge stood beside him holding the mortal's arm as if helping him to stand. The others arrived.

"Do you think it wise for you to get up?" asked Nigel.

"I can't sit for hours without moving. Beside, Ridge said standing and walking is good for my circulation."

"*He* said moving was good for his numb rear," said Ridge.

Allard held the ranger's arm and carefully got down from the wagon. He gingerly put weight on his leg and smiled when standing on his own. "Not so bad."

"You look better. The color has returned to your face," said Mirit.

"I feel better. Whatever Raiden's paste contained is doing a wonderful job." He released Ridge to take a few steps away from the wagon but winced. Tyrone caught him to keep him from falling.

"You're not totally healed, so don't force it," said Tyrone.

Allard spoke in a firm yet measured voice. "I need to walk. I am no good as a diplomat if I cannot stand before the emperor when representing my king."

Tyrone kindly grinned. "Very well." He helped Allard to walk, but kept him close to the wagon if he needed to sit down.

Movement caught Ridge's attention. A hundred yards away at the tree line, Makito and Jiru approach Hodi. A conversation began, with Makito gesturing toward the Allonians.

"I'm going to find some more plants for Lord Allard's wound," said the ranger.

"We still have the paste the dragon gave us." Titus pulled the jar from his pouch.

Ridge cocked a smile before departing.

Virgil took the jar from Titus and bent to put it back in the boy's pouch. The gesture gave him the opportunity to speak privately in the boy's ear. "Ridge's way of telling us he is going to scout for trouble."

"Oh," murmured Titus. "I hope I said nothing wrong."

Virgil grinned, shook his head, closed the pouch and straightened to his full height. Egan glared after Ridge, then a moment later, followed the ranger. Virgil caught up to Egan after a short distance.

"Is something wrong?"

"Let's just say, I'm not enamored with his scouting skills."

Ridge disappeared into the trees and Virgil stopped Egan from further pursuit. "Why?"

"Personal history."

"Obviously. You two haven't exactly been on speaking terms since we left."

"Is there a problem?" asked Avatar.

"Egan thinks so."

Egan stared at the trees so Avatar followed the line of sight. "Evil?"

He still didn't speak, rather kept his intense focus on the trees.

"No, Ridge," said Virgil.

Avatar motioned for Virgil to leave. He waited a moment before confronting Egan. "Speak, what's the matter between you and Ridge?"

Egan's eyes never left the trees. "He cost me my first charge."

"Lord Willis? I thought he was kidnapped and assassinated by Farley's men."

"An assassination I could have stopped if Ridge found Willis in time."

"From what I recall hearing, it was a plot to rid the king of Willis."

Anger made Egan confront Avatar. "You weren't there! So don't lecture me on what you heard."

Avatar seized his fellow warrior's arm and switched to speaking in the Ancient. "Be mindful of your words and volume." He drew Egan's attention to the others, but the mortals paid more attention to Allard and refreshment. When he turned back to Egan, his voice grew low and husky. "I know well the pain of losing a charge to an assassin. Granted, I learned years later Nigel survived, but blaming Ridge isn't the way to deal with what happened."

Egan matched Avatar in volume, but harsh in tone. "You didn't see the ranger's confusion, his inept tracking, or find the mutilated body of the one you swore to protect. I won't let him endanger my present charge." He jerked from Avatar and marched to where Titus helped Chad aid Allard back onto the wagon.

Avatar grumbled a complaint, "Kell, why didn't warn me of this?"

"Did you say something?" asked Tyrone, also in the Ancient.

For a moment, Avatar regarded Tyrone, wondering how much to say in reply and opted for discretion. "Nothing that won't keep until we return home."

"You mean the tension between Ridge and Egan?"

"My attempt to be discreet didn't work, did it?"

"You should know better than to even try with me. I witnessed Egan's hostility toward Ridge in Straden, and heard his vehement denouncement of not needing his help. When Kell insisted, I knew there was a reason. I even confronted Egan, but he remained stubbornly silent, except to assure me he won't fail Titus. Did he tell you why?"

"It goes back to the loss of his first charge. He feels Ridge is responsible for not finding him soon enough for Egan to save him. But," he shook his head, a thoughtful gaze at the trees, then back to Tyrone, "I sense something more. Something beyond either of them."

"And you were grumbling because Kell didn't tell you beforehand. He seems to have a habit of not telling all his knows, which keeps most of us guessing."

Avatar laughed. "You don't know how true a statement that is. However," his humor faded as he continued, "I have to stem the bickering. Come, Ridge will alert us of danger. I'm concerned about Egan. Unbridled anger in a Guardian is not good." He escorted Tyrone back to the wagon.

In silent stealth, Ridge made his way through the trees to a vantage point nearest Hodi, Makito and Jiru. Taking a deep breath he concentrated his focus on Makito, stretching his senses to listen.

"We cannot speak freely. The spirits understand us," said Makito.

"In a few more hours will we reach Yuki and they will trouble us no more," said Hodi.

"Yes, our task will be complete," agreed Jiru, clapping Makito's shoulder. "They will become Lord Norkiru's trouble. Especially the two with hair like a concubine's robe." He laughed at his own joke.

Makito grew cautious. "It's not funny. They are a bad omen."

The conversation became interrupted at hearing Admiral Kentashi call the caravan back to formation.

"Remember," began Hodi in harsh warning, "keep your tongues for a few more hours and all will be well."

"Hoshiki willing," grumbled Jiru.

"I said keep your tongue, idiot!"

"Raiden has ears," Makito added his warning.

"Go!" Hodi shoved them on the shoulder to send them on their way.

Ridge shrunk back into the trees and returned to the others. The mortals were mounted and joining the formation. Egan sent him a glowering glare before following Titus. Avatar took up position behind Nigel and Tyrone while Virgil walked beside Mirit.

"Ridge!" Allard waved him to the wagon as it began moving.

The ranger jogged after and easily hopped onto the tailgate.

"Were you successful in gathering plants?" asked Allard.

"That has yet to be determined until I show them to the others."

Overhead came a familiar call. Akido headed back toward the mountain. Also, two birds appeared, and locked in a fight. A large red bird with a single long paddle-like fantail attacked a smaller white and yellow bird. The smaller bird tried to get away but the larger bird was persistent, until finally the smaller bird appeared injured and flew in an awkward pattern toward a patch of trees. The red bird continued in the direction of Yuki. The whole scene lasted only a few seconds.

Ridge noticed Jiru and Makito smiling, pointing at the birds and departing dragon. This conversation he could easily hear and both expressed pleasure at the defeat of the smaller bird. Ridge's consideration passed from the soldiers to the others up front. They also paid attention to the activity in the sky.

Melancholy filled Mirit's face and in her voice at Akido's departure. "I guess it's his way of saying good-bye and wishing us well."

"He said the valley is dangerous for him," said Nigel.

"Those birds could hardly hurt a dragon."

Tyrone went from watching the birds and dragon to surveying the valley. They headed southwest. Further to the south the valley went on for miles while to the west beyond Yuki, lay another mountain range. To the north were the foothills of the mountains they just crossed.

"The valley is very flat and open with only patches of trees. I reckon Yuki to be about five miles. We should be able to see trouble before it arrives from any direction," he said in observation.

Nigel also made survey of the valley. "Norkiru must be very powerful to build in the middle of open terrain."

"Waldron sits on top of a plain."

"Not this large. Nor surrounded by mountains capable of hiding a night approach.

"I saw an outpost on our descent. It could easily signal an alarm." Tyrone pointed over shoulder.

"Really, where?" Nigel looked back.

"On the small plateau about half mile up the slope. It is cleverly hidden from the untrained eye."

"I'm hardly untrained."

Tyrone chuckled. "Speaking of clever, I wonder if Ridge found any more plants."

"We won't know until we can confer about Lord Allard's wound," said Avatar. His eyes and head made a warning move toward Kentashi and Hodi, who rode ahead of them.

Kentashi turned in the saddle to speak. "I send man ahead to inform Lord Norkiru of our arrival."

"I thought his sentries at the mountain outpost would have already alerted him to our presence," said Nigel.

Kentashi laughed. "Very good, Highness. Ay, signal has been made."

With a sudden thought, Tyrone glanced back at the mountain before speaking to Kentashi. "That's why we stopped at river. Not to refresh the horses for a short journey across the valley, but to give the sentries time to send the signal."

"How?" asked Mirit.

"The bird."

Again Kentashi laughed with pleasure. "You as smart and observant as prince, Captain."

Mirit covered her mouth to stop a squeal of laughter but Kentashi turned to face forward and didn't hear. Nigel and Tyrone heard her.

Chapter 14

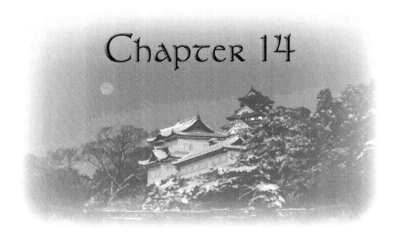

Yuki's massive size made it larger and more impressive than Kaori. The walls rose over fifty feet high and stretched for half a mile. The roofs and building were of similar architecture. Slate tiles turned up at the ends and apex, all displaying the splendid material and quality of workmanship. Unlike Kaori the statues weren't of dragons, rather fierce looking catbird creatures with long fantails and sharp claws but no wings.

The massive main gate of ornately carved wood and ironwork stood opened. Two rows of soldiers in formal dress uniforms and plate armor lined the way to the gate for about a hundred yards. In the enormous and beautiful courtyard, troops were mustered in tight formation.

"You receive royal welcome, prince," said Kentashi.

"Indeed," said Nigel. A private smile passed to Tyrone.

The main building was twice the size of Kentashi's home with five huge marble steps leading to a porch. In regal dress, Lord Norkiru stood on the porch. The colorful embroidered clothes made him appear younger than his sixty years. Three men flanked him with two similarly dressed to Norkiru while the third wore plate armor and ceremonial uniform.

Trumpeters stood on the wall and at farthest extent of the porch. They sounded a call when Kentashi, Hodi and the Allonians entered the courtyard and didn't stop until the group drew rein at the bottom of the steps.

The Allonians followed Kentashi and Hodi's example of dismounting. Servants dressed in uniforms of fine, unusual fabric hurried forth to take the reins of the horses, lowly bowing at the waist. Ridge helped Allard to join them. Once there, he shook off Ridge's hold to climb the steps on his own. Tyrone held back to help Allard. Hodi also stayed back, leaving Mirit and Nigel to take the lead with Kentashi. Titus, Chad and the Guardians followed Tyrone.

On the top step Kentashi stopped and bowed. He spoke in Allonian. "My gracious Lord Norkiru, I have honor to present Prince Nigel of Allon and his wife, Princess Mirit."

Norkiru nodded to Kentashi, his gaze brief on Nigel, but more intent upon Mirit. "Princess no woman dress."

"She is the Queen's Champion while I am the King's Champion. Surely Lord Allard's letter informed you of this fact, my lord," said Nigel.

Norkiru nodded in the customary short, stout manner they saw frequently from Kentashi. "Which is Lord Allard?"

"I am, my lord." In ginger, painful steps, he mounted the step to stand beside Nigel. He bowed to Norkiru.

Norkiru deeply frowned at seeing Allard's injury. "How?"

"Sheshian attack," said Kentashi. "Prince also slightly hurt."

This news disturbed Norkiru. He turned to the two similarly dressed men conversing in hushed tones. He waved them silent then motioned to the officer, who nodded and withdrew from the porch. Norkiru returned his attention to the Allonians.

"Sheshian not attack here. Please, come."

Before accompanying the others, Kentashi spoke to Hodi, the latter bowing before descending the stairs, calling orders to the caravan.

Inside the main house foyer, Norkiru bellowed Natanese commands that sent servants rushing to attend the guests. They did the customary surrendering of weapons, removing of boots and receiving house sandals.

"Princess, go with womans. Lord Allard to physician, heal wound," said Norkiru.

Before anyone could speak agreement or object, Mirit and Allard were whisked away.

"Prince, follow me." Norkiru led Nigel, Tyrone and the others further into the house. "Who these?"

"This is Captain Fraser of his majesty's army and his son, who is newly apprenticed to my squire, Chad," said Nigel.

Norkiru barked another order and two male servants appeared. He took hold of Titus and Chad and began to take them away. "They go to kitchen and—"

"No!" said Nigel then amended his tone to explain. "Chad is instructing the boy on how to serve a warrior. They will remain with the captain and myself."

Norkiru fought to hide his displeasure. He made curt snort, and dismissed the servants. "These?" he asked concerning the Guardians.

"They are good, powerful spirits. They save us from Hoshiki," said Kentashi.

Wary and uncertain, Norkiru eyed the Guardians.

"We mean no harm. We serve Jor'el and the mortals of Allon," said Avatar.

"They will also remain with us and not disturb you and your house," said Nigel.

Norkiru again nodded. "Admiral, see to care. We meet again at dinner." He made a slight bow to Nigel.

Kentashi escorted them toward the back of the large house and upstairs to an elaborately decorated and furnished chamber. The large bed appeared to be a cross between a normal mattress with pillows and the mats they slept on in Kaori. It sat upon a raised platform with elaborate decorations hanging around the head area.

"This one for prince, one across hall for captain."

"Do you know where Lord Allard and my wife are?"

Kentashi kindly smiled. "They brought back when well cared for. You see. Princess more better dressed." He bowed and departed.

They heard voices and the noise of water coming from behind a paneled door in the room and went to investigate. Four male servants worked to prepare a bath.

"It's been a few days, a bath is welcomed," said Nigel.

"I hope they have one ready and waiting for me. Only no *womans*."

Tyrone's humor was short-lived when Nigel stopped his departure.

"I don't like the idea of Allard and Mirit being separated."

"Neither do I, but I'm not sure what we can do."

"I can move unseen and learn of their whereabouts," said Ridge.

"We are guests. I don't think it would be wise for you to go snooping. It may be taken as a sign of hostile intentions. Spy, even," said Tyrone.

"The princess is nearby," said Virgil.

"Do you sense danger?" asked Nigel.

"No. Whereas Ridge might snoop, I can find her without appearing intrusive."

"Do so."

Virgil left.

"One problem down." Nigel stopped speaking when the Natanese fixing his bath emerged and spoke to him, all making bowing gestures.

"They say all is ready, Highness," said Avatar in translation.

"I'll summon them if needed."

Avatar relayed the instruction and the men left.

"You said one problem down, what did you mean?" asked Tyrone.

Nigel didn't answer Tyrone rather asked Avatar; "Why did the statue resembling a catbird look eerily familiar?"

"The beast that attacked Necie and Tristine. Only no wings, so they don't fly."

"What's this?" asked Tyrone in surprise at the answer.

"Mother?" asked Titus, also concerned.

"During the Morvenian visit when we were younger," said Nigel, his face growing steely in recollection. "I wasn't the only one they tried to kill. Necie and Tristine were the first attempt, fortunately no serious injury. Then father, but also saved from harm by the Guardians. They almost succeeded with me."

"The Morvenians?" asked Chad, a bit confused.

"No, Musetta."

"With the help of Morrell," said Avatar, his expression lethal.

At Tyrone, Titus and Chad's concern, Nigel explained, "We didn't know about Musetta and Morrell at the time. In fact, we suspected the Morvenians were behind the attempts since we discovered strange stones after the Guardians killed the creatures. We devised a clever ruse to confront the Morvenians using the stones. They called them *devil stones* claiming they contained an evil magic but denied bringing them to Allon. A few months later, Morrell sent me over the cliff, killing my horse and leaving me for dead. I can only guess he didn't fear discovery."

"Jor'el had other intentions," said Tyrone.

"Ay. Anyway, after Musetta's attempted coup, Father, Kell, Avatar and I discussed the possible connection and how she used the Morvenian visit to cover her earlier actions."

"You believe she meant to wipe out the royal family and blame the Morvenians."

"Ay. I didn't see the creatures, but based upon the description from Mahon and Armus the statues on Norkiru's roof seem too close for comfort."

"And confirm the presence of the Dark Way," said Avatar.

Titus' expression turned fearful so Egan placed a hand on his shoulder. Titus looked up at him. Egan smiled, but that did little to allay his disturbance.

"How long will we be here before we go home?" he asked his father.

"I don't know. It depends upon the rapport we establish with Lord Norkiru, and if he decides we can see the emperor."

Nigel turned scoffing eyes to Titus. "Wanting to return home so soon? I thought you wanted to see the emperor? Isn't that why you stowed away?"

Titus recoiled at the rebuff.

"I think your bath is getting cold," said Tyrone. He took Titus by the hand and left. Egan and Ridge accompanying them.

"I think Titus is getting a cold dose of reality," said Chad.

"Speaking of cold. The water has cooled down," said Avatar from behind the panel. He wiped off his wet hand on a towel. "I'll take your uniform to be mended and cleaned."

"There is another packed if it isn't ready in time." Chad indicated Nigel's personal chest.

Across the hall, Tyrone found a hot bath waiting.

"If you don't mind, sir, I'd like to take a bath first." Titus moved away from his father and started to undress.

"I don't mind, but we can always send for warm water if you want to talk about anything."

Titus shook his head, finished stripping and got into the tub.

"Forcing him to speak won't help," whispered Egan.

"And not speaking will?"

The Guardian didn't flinch at the rebuke and said, "He's stubborn, like his father and uncle."

"You can be as impertinent as Armus and Avatar."

Ridge snorted a sardonic laugh. He sat near the door, appearing to inspect his staff.

Egan drew Tyrone away from the tub and Ridge. "Take heart, he is coming around. At least, he has stopped physically and verbally rebuffing me. Although, he is more attentive to Lord Allard and Chad."

"I noticed, which is why I haven't interfered. Allard spoke to Ellis like few could, and was of great help to Tristine during the Tunlund crisis. Personally, I appreciate his friendship, intelligence and skill. Chad learned and experienced much since attaching himself to Nigel. Maybe they can succeed where the rest of us have failed."

"You have not failed with your son. His machinations are of his own design, and based on a false pride. He is being challenged by this journey, so let Jor'el have his way and take no blame."

A small, relieved smile appeared on Tyrone's face. "Thank you."

"Ahh!" said Titus. "I need a towel, I got soap in my eye!"

Egan flashed a rakish grin. He crossed to the tub and pushed Titus under water.

Titus fought to get up and when he did, a towel smacked him in the face. He took it and wiped his face while listening to laughter. His eyes clear of soap, he saw them beside the tub and asked Tyrone, "Why did you dunk me again?"

"I didn't. Egan did. I gave you a towel to dry off since it's my turn to bathe."

The women ushered Mirit through the main house, up some backstairs and finally into a large, beautifully decorated room with wonderfully crafted furniture. She tried several times to communicate, but none of them spoke Allonian and their endless, unknown chatter grew somewhat annoying. By the sight, sounds and smell, a scented bath was prepared. She flinched when the women began to undress her.

"No, wait. I can do that myself, thank you." She tried to be polite but grew firm when two of women persisted in their efforts. "No!"

The eldest woman spoke curt words to Mirit and waved for the others to continue.

"I said I can do undress myself!"

There came a knock at the door followed by "Princess?"

"Virgil!" she said in grateful relief.

"Is there some trouble?" he asked through the door.

"None of them speak Allonian and I can't get them to leave me alone."

He chuckled. "Are you decent?"

Mirit didn't immediately answer, busy slapping away hands still attempting to undress her. "Ay!"

The door opened and Virgil entered. The older woman confronted him with rapid-fire words and angry tone. He calmly replied in Natanese. She scowled but didn't dispute.

"Tell them I can take a bath by myself," said Mirit.

Virgil did so and the woman gave a lengthy reply. When she finished he translated for Mirit, though tried to keep a smile from his face. "It is customary for servants to undress, bathe and dress guests of their master. She doesn't understand your reluctance and wonders if there is a deformity you wish to hide."

Mirit flushed. "No!" She slapped another hand away. "Tell her it's not *our* custom, and modesty guides my actions, not any deformity."

At his translation, the woman sent a rude, scoffing sneer at Mirit. He promptly reprimanded her. The woman appeared surprised and repeated *donoshi?* He gave an affirming answer and she fell to her knees before Mirit. Her head touched the floor and barked orders for the others to do the same.

"Apparently, they were unaware of your royal status. They ask forgiveness for touching your exalted personage," he explained.

Mirit looked at the women gathered around her feet. "A simple *I'm sorry* would suffice."

The older woman rapidly spoke, her head still bowed to the floor.

Virgil said something to her before speaking to Mirit. "They worship their emperor and his family as gods. You are of foreign royalty thus you are a foreign goddess."

Mirit rolled her eyes. "Why can't anything be easy? Tell her, though I am of foreign royalty, we aren't worshipped."

He shook his head. "You won't convince them. Natan has been closed to the outside world for centuries. Their beliefs can't be undone by one conversation." Again the woman spoke and he translated. "She wants to know how angry you are and what is their punishment."

Mirit scowled with a futile sigh. "No punishment. It was merely a lack of communication. Also tell her I will undress and bathe myself. When I need help, I will summon them."

He did so and the woman tentatively looked. Mirit kindly grinned and motioned for her to rise. She did so. Virgil instructed the other women to stand and ushered them out of the room. After closing the door, he wryly smiled to Mirit.

"Anything else, princess?"

"You're enjoying this too much, you know that?"

He chuckled. "I'll be right outside the door." He left.

For the first time since leaving Kaori, Mirit enjoyed a relaxing bath. So much happened she didn't have a moment to reflect or even rest. She began to consider the events, but pushed the thoughts from her mind to allow herself a moment of blissful peace, breathing in the wonderful, soothing aroma of the scented water. She didn't know how long she remained in the bath until she woke from a light dozing at hearing some noise. The water grew cool so she got out.

She wrapped herself in a large luxurious towel before investigating the noise. Her clothes were not where she left them. Instead, eight garments of various shapes, sizes and cloth ranging from white, red to peacock blue were neatly laid out on a bed. She assumed some were undergarments. Picking them up for examination, she couldn't figure out how they were worn. A pair of wooden sandals rose rather higher than the house sandals they were given.

Virgil spoke through the door. ""Princess? Are you finished yet?"

"Ay, but my clothes are gone."

"They said they were taking them to be cleaned."

"And left some clothes in their place."

"Are the clothes acceptable?"

"I don't know. I can't tell what they are or how to wear them."

"Will they serve while yours are cleaned? Or do you want me to fetch your other garments?"

"I suppose they'll do, although I'd rather wear my uniform."

"Understandable, but perhaps this can be a step in diplomacy."

Mirit held up a garment next to her with a thoughtful frown. "Ay. Send them in." She moved behind a dressing screen when the door opened.

He complied and remained inside by the closed door.

The older woman in charge approached the bed, barking orders at the other women. She picked up two of the white garments and moved toward the screen, speaking in a contrite voice.

"She wants to know if she is now permitted to help you," said Virgil.

"Ay."

The woman joined Mirit behind the screen. Soon Virgil heard frustrated grunts from Mirit and the woman speaking, but wasn't asked to translate. When Mirit let out a yelp he asked, "Princess?"

"I'm all right," she grumbled.

The woman appeared and demanded the red and sliver garments and sandals before going back behind the screen. Shortly, Mirit stepped out. She stood noticeably taller by several inches, and walked in a manner suggesting she had difficulty keeping her balance. The woman steered Mirit to a full-length mirror.

The clothes hung on her in a most unflattering manner. The sleeves were huge and open while the dress flared from the high-waist out to a hoop like skirt ending at her ankles. She frowned in surprised concern. "Oh, this can't be it."

The woman spoke and Virgil translated. "That's just the under-layer. You still have the gown, waist band and headdress."

The woman ordered two of the younger women to place the peacock blue gown over the under layer. They wrestled with the sleeves, so the woman spoke to Mirit and tried to raise Mirit's arms. Understanding the request, Mirit lifted her arms straight out at shoulder height. This only made the garments look worse, like a deformed scarecrow with no hands.

From behind Mirit heard muffled laughter and caught Virgil's reflection in the mirror. At her scowl, he stifled his amusement by placing a discreet hand over his mouth.

183

Once the younger women finished placing the gown on Mirit, the older woman expertly buttoned the front of the dress from Mirit's throat to her waist. The rest of the gown remained open to reveal the red and silver under-layer. Mirit went to lower her arms, but the woman vigorously shook her head and said something a kin to "no" so she kept her arms up. The woman spoke and others brought over a slender folded garment of embroidered gold, silver and red. She took one end and the others stepped back, unfolding the garment until they were about ten feet from Mirit. She motioned and spoke for Mirit to grab the ends of the sleeves in her fists and raise her arms over her head. The woman wrapped the garment around Mirit's waist.

Again, by way of the mirror, Mirit saw Virgil fight to maintain his composure. He avoided looking at her during the time it took the woman to finish and neatly secure the waistband. With a grateful sigh of relief, Mirit lowered her arms.

The woman instructed several others to bring over a stool for Mirit to sit in front of the mirror. Once sitting, she frowned while examining Mirit's hair, then muttered under her breath.

"Is there a problem?" asked Mirit.

"She's never see such a style of knots," said Virgil.

"A braid, not a knot. Here." Mirit tried to reach up to undo the coiled braid but the sleeves prevented her from reaching the braid. She tried to push the sleeves down so she could move her arms freely, but the woman became frantic and seized her arms. "I guess that was the wrong thing to do."

"Apparently." Virgil spoke to the woman, who replied and he translated. "It's not proper for your exalted personage to touch your hair, which is considered unclean."

Mirit rolled her eyes and put her hands in her lap. "Very well. You undo my hair so she can see how it's done."

He balked with slight embarrassment.

"Oh, don't encourage them by refusing. You know my hair isn't unclean."

His hapless expression shone in the mirror. "I don't know how."

She laughed. "This should amuse the others. A warrior reluctant to deal with a female's hair."

That stung! He straightened his shoulders in a display of pride and moved to stand behind her.

She attempted to curb her amusement to instruct him. "Take out the pins and undo the braid."

The woman stopped him from proceeding. She spoke and he replied. "What?" asked Mirit.

"She says your hair style can accommodate the headdress." He stepped back.

Mirit smiled, but her humor was short-lived when the woman put on the headdress. It measured two feet tall and four feet wide with dangling beads all along the brim.

Virgil translated some more of the woman's speech, and tried not to show renewed amusement. "She wants to know if they can apply the cosmetics now. To veil your exalted goddess face from being seen by commoners."

"No! Tell her I've had enough."

The woman frowned in disapproval at Virgil's translation, but bowed to Mirit and ordered the others to leave. She then bowed twice to Mirit, backing away and speaking as she left.

After the door closed, Mirit stood to confront Virgil, but forced to brace her feet to maintain her balance. "I feel as ridiculous as I look!"

He could no longer containing his humor and heartily laughed. "It is Natanese royal attire."

"I'm an Allonian princess, not a Natanese royal mannequin!" she scolded and his smile vanished. She moved too fast and nearly tripped, which made the headdress slip. She stopped to keep it from falling off her head. "This is ludicrous! I can't even move."

He pursed his lips in chastised consideration before speaking. "At first I thought this might be a good exercise in diplomacy, but after watching you, and being amused, I was wrong. You *are* an Allonian princess and I won't see you publically humiliated by being forced to wear unfamiliar clothing. I'm apologize for laughing, Your Highness." He bowed in submission.

She kindly smiled. "I'm not angry with you. The question is what to do now? Risk insulting them by refusing to wear this ridiculous costume or stay as I am?"

"Let me take you to the prince and get his opinion before the others see you. If need be, I'll fetch your uniform, even if it isn't clean."

"I packed an extra uniform just in case." She only took two steps before wobbling on the sandals and the headdress slipped. She steadied the headdress with one hand while grabbing onto his arm with the other. "I'll need you to help me keep my balance."

Bathed, shaved and wearing a Natanese robe, Nigel inspected the clothes Chad placed on the bed. He picked up each of the three doublets only to toss it aside, frowning and dissatisfied.

"I did pack another uniform, remember?" said Chad.

"Ay, and it maybe best to maintain my Jor'ellian military status and leave the diplomatic façade to Allard."

"It's not the clothes irritating you, but Mirit's whereabouts."

"Ay. At least Allard is well. If only we'd hear from Virgil."

"The fact we haven't can be good. He's probably with her." At a knock, Chad paused in opening the trunk to fetch Nigel's other uniform.

"Come!" said Nigel.

Avatar returned carrying what appeared to be an overgrown sack. The Guardian wasn't alone; Mirit and Virgil accompanied him.

"Thank Jor'el—" began Nigel but stopped in mid-sentence, flabbergasted. She wore an exquisite Natanese dress of peacock blue with an intricate gold, red and silver pattern woven throughout and matching headdress. For a moment, he and Chad could only stare at her.

She made a teasing frown. "It's not like you've never seen me in a gown before."

"No. But it's so different—yet stunning." He noticed she looked him straight in the eye. "You're taller."

Holding onto Virgil's arm, she stepped off the sandals, which brought her down to her normal height, four inches shorter than Nigel. Only this made the dress drag on the floor. Holding her head erect and stiff, she crossed to the full-length mirror, mindful of the headdress.

"The fabric is gorgeous and no corset, but the layers are heavier. And these sleeves," she waved them while speaking, "are hard to move in much less do anything but flap, and look silly doing it. I can barely walk in those stilts or move without the headdress slipping."

Avatar chuckled. He removed Nigel's dress uniform from the sack and laid it out on the bed beside the other suit. "The Natanese are swift and superior tailors. You can't tell where your suit was ripped."

Nigel inspected the impressive workmanship. "Indeed." A knock came at the door. "Come."

Virgil opened to admit the others; all cleaned and highly polished for the evening.

"Allard. How are you feeling?" asked Mirit.

Allard didn't reply. He, Tyrone, and Titus stared at her. Even Ridge and Egan looked amazed.

"You don't have to gawk at me!" She tossed an annoyed glance to Virgil, the Guardian apologetic in expression.

"The clothes are so unusual yet ..." began Allard then balked.

"Stunning," said Nigel when Allard was at an unusual loss for words.

Titus took hold of a sleeve and it extended about three feet from Mirit's body. "Where are your arms?"

She snatched the sleeve from him.

"I suppose they could come in handy if she wants to learn how to fly," quipped Tyrone.

This time she turned to face Virgil. "We have our answer."

"I'll unpack your other uniform."

"No need." Avatar pulled out her cleaned, repaired and pressed uniform from the sack.

Mirit began to hurry to the bed, but the headdress fell off and she caught it. She continued to the bed. "Where did you get it?"

"With Nigel's uniform."

She tossed the headdress onto the bed and tried to pick up her uniform, but had difficult due to the sleeves. "This is ridiculous! If I'm to be on display, I'd rather do so in my uniform. Hand it over the screen to me," she said to Nigel.

"The Natanese may be insulted," said Allard.

His statement stopped her from going behind the dressing screen. She turn upon him with a decidedly determined expression. "Why should they be? We came here to as official representatives of Allon."

"But is it worth the risk?"

"I don't see any of you being made to alter your appearance."

"We weren't asked."

"So because I'm a woman I'm to be treated different than the men in the delegation?"

Allard tried to curb his impatience. "We're speaking of their culture, Highness."

"Exactly, *Highness,*" she repeated in rebuke. "I am an Allonian princess and the Queen's Champion. If anything I should be insulted at being forced to compromise my station for this costume. And disappointed by your lack of support, my lord."

First stunned then remorseful, Allard said, "Highness, I didn't mean that."

Tyrone intervened, his tone kind. "No, you spoke like a diplomat. However, Mirit has made her point very clear."

"You agree?"

"She is correct about her official status and royal rank."

"I truly didn't mean any disrespect, Si—Captain," Allard corrected himself.

"I know." Tyrone smiled and steered Allard toward the door. "We will all wait in the hall," he said to Nigel.

Fifteen minutes later, Nigel and Mirit joined them, and both dressed in their uniforms. Allard held onto Titus trying not to put too much weight on his left leg.

"Is your leg troubling you?" asked Nigel.

Allard shook his head with a forced toothy grin, but the feigned denial obvious.

"He's been standing too long while waiting," said Chad.

"We tried to get him to sit," added Titus.

"You may retire," said Nigel.

"I will not be further remiss in my duty." He made a submissive nod to Mirit.

"My lord," she began with a soft smile. "I apologize for my reprimand. I know your heart and dedication to duty."

He smiled. "Thank you, but I am in capable hands at the moment." His gaze went to Titus.

Tyrone regarded his son. "I hope so. If not, it'll be by my hand you retire."

Captain Hodi approached. The officer from the porch accompanied Hodi; a stout man with a sneering face, especially toward Mirit.

"This is General Ryo, Lord Norkiru's commander. He no speak Allon," said Hodi.

"He doesn't have to, his displeasure is plainly seen," said Nigel. "Avatar, tell the general to show respect for a royal princess."

Avatar complied and Hodi added a stern comment. Ryo immediately changed his expression to regret and bowed to Mirit.

"He offer apology. Not see woman so dressed," said Hodi.

Ryo spoke, making a gesture to follow him.

"He come to escort you to Lord Norkiru."

Titus and Chad aided Allard in descending the stairs, though by his taut jowls and level brow he endured tremendous pain with each step. His grip on Titus' arm tightened in an effort to keep his balance when they reached the bottom.

"Are you certain you want to do this, my lord?" asked Titus in a discreet voice.

"I have a duty. And until I'm either totally incapacitated or dead, I intend to do it. Do you understand?"

The meaning behind his statement and question were not lost upon Titus. "I'm beginning to understand, my lord."

Allard flashed a small, pleased smile.

Kentashi greeted them, but looked confused and concerned at Mirit. "Forgive, princess, but not dressed proper Natan."

"She is dressed properly for representing Allon, Admiral," said Nigel, yet continued at Kentashi disputing expression. "Would you have all of us change our attire and negate why we are here and whom we represent?"

"No, but woman—"

Tyrone intervened. "Would you, a warrior, tolerate being made to shed your uniform and feel dishonoring of the Emperor by doing so?"

Kentashi stared up to Tyrone, momentary disconcertion passing over his face. He shook his head. "No."

"The princess is no different. You have seen she is a warrior and is representing our queen."

Kentashi bowed to Mirit then did a brisk military turn on his heels to lead them to the dining hall. The room easily accommodated one hundred or more guests, but this night only Norkiru, Kentashi, Ryo, Hodi and the Allonians would be dining. Norkiru sat at the head of the low long table. He deeply scowled upon sight of Mirit.

Kentashi spoke a quick word to the Allonians. "Allow me." He didn't wait for a reply before approaching and addressing Norkiru in Natanese. By his expression, the explanation did completely satisfy Norkiru, but he nodded and Kentashi returned to the Allonians.

"Please, prince, sit on right hand of Lord Norkiru with wife beside yourself. Captain, sit on Lord Norkiru's left hand, Lord Allard beside yourself. I will sit next to Lord Allard, General Ryo next to princess with Captain Hodi. Guardians one either side with squires at end of table."

Once everyone was seated, Norkiru struck a small gold gong to signal the food to be brought. "Eat," he told them.

"With your permission, we shall bless our food first," said Nigel.

"How bless?"

"By thanking Jor'el."

Norkiru shrugged with indifference and reached for his food to eat.

Nigel took his cue, but instead of speaking in Allonian, he spoke a brief prayer in the Ancient.

"You believe Jor'el hear you in Natan?" asked Kentashi.

"I believe he can hear me anywhere."

Due to Norkiru's limited command of Allonian, the conversation consisted of simple questions and answers concerning the two countries. The Guardians translated when requested to do so, but the main discussion transpired between Nigel and Allard with Norkiru and Kentashi. On occasion, Tyrone added his thoughts, comments and observations. Mirit spoke a few times, while Titus and Chad kept quiet even though Norkiru commented several times about Chad and Ridge's red hair. Still, Titus paid close attention to what was said, who spoke and who didn't.

A few times he caught his father's eye. Sometimes Tyrone appeared pleased, other times thoughtful and concerned. Titus hoped those times were with what the Natanese said rather than his presence. They had little time to converse or even see each other. He avoided the earlier opportunity because he didn't know what to say. Still, the fact was not lost upon him that during the attacks on the journey and now in Yuki he witnessed a new side of his father's character, one of willing submission. Naturally, his father submitted to Jor'el. After all, he was the Almighty God of Allon, but to other mortals? His father did yield in private family disputes, but as king, he asserted himself.

Since arriving, each event forced Titus to reconsider his actions. The Natanese were so different he felt uncomfortable around them. At first he wondered if it the language barrier played a part in his discomfort, but after the dogmen, the firebird and the bugs, what Avatar said about the Dark Way made more sense. Despite his experience in Tunlund, his father, uncle and the Guardians were more adept in dealing with the Dark Way. Thus he listened and did not participate in the conversation. A change in attitude from what drove him to stowaway.

During the course of the evening's discussion the vast difference in customs, food, and clothing became evident. Where international trade and commerce were concerned, Allard showed his superior knowledge and skill. He held Norkiru's rapt attention when speaking of raw materials, especially those needed for war, as in forged metal capable of not melting under intense cannon fire. Indeed, he was a dedicated and loyal man, always speaking highly of his king. Titus noticed his father and Nigel well pleased by the Allard's efforts.

Two hours after dinner started, Norkiru called for entertainment. Titus had never seen such acrobatic ability and strength, and from such small and fragile looking people! The most awe-inspiring act where the men who juggled fiery swords. They watched a short play about the Zekar and Onedo, god of the underworld. The actors wore masks representing various gods and hideous creatures. Mirit grew uncomfortable during the performance. In fact, she became pale, shaded her eyes and held onto Nigel's arm. Titus couldn't tell if Norkiru noticed her uneasiness or he didn't care, and that annoyed Titus. No matter what role he assumed for the journey, she remained his aunt. Fortunately, the play lasted only a few minutes and its conclusion signaled the end of the evening.

Once safely upstairs, Allard navigated the hall by himself. Titus moved to take Mirit's hand. "I know the play upset you."

She squeezed his hand. "I'm well."

"Are you sure?"

She softly smiled. "Ay." She leaned over to say, "I'm proud of how you are behaving."

"It's not easy."

"I know." She paused at door to their chamber. "Good night," she said aloud to all before she and Nigel went inside.

Titus entered the chamber he shared with his father, Chad and Allard. The Guardians lingered in the hall.

Speaking in the Ancient, Avatar asked Ridge, "How was your scouting trip?"

"I'm not sure. They seemed happy about getting rid of us at Yuki, and Jiru mentioned the goddess who controls the night." Even speaking the Ancient, his discreet reference to Hoshiki rather than say the name since Norkiru's guards spaced along the hallway every twenty feet.

"How so?" asked Virgil.

"As we would say *Jor'el willing.*"

"Rather strange considering the way they reacted to us at Kaori, and the admiral claims to worship the one of the mountain."

"Ay, but a I heard nothing to raise alarm."

"That's not surprising," groused Egan.

The ranger stiffened and began to speak a rebuff.

"Peace!" said Avatar. His warning gaze shifted between Egan and Ridge, coming to rest on Egan. "Ridge says there is nothing to be concerned about, and I believe him. Despite the past we must trust each other to do our duty." He then instructed Ridge and Virgil, "Return to your charges and stay close. There is uneasiness in the air."

Egan also began to leave, but Avatar detained him.

"More tongue lashing, Lieutenant?"

Avatar drew Egan into a corner away from Norkiru's guards to speak privately. Still, he continued in the Ancient. "I know you are an Original and a former Trio Leader, and I'm only Kell's aide, but he placed me in charge of this mission. I won't allow personal issues to interfere with our task."

"I wouldn't do that. Ridge on the other hand—"

"Is good enough for Kell to trust. That should mean something."

Egan didn't reply since the statement had its intended effect of silencing his argument.

"What about Titus?"

The abrupt change in topic surprised Egan. "What about him?"

"His fooling you to stow-away and your tension with Ridge can't be helpful to your strained relationship."

"That's putting it mildly. Duped by a mortal boy. Did Nigel ever do that to you?"

Avatar fought back an impulsive smile to answer. "Nigel isn't the issue."

"He did. Well, at least you didn't have resentment clouding your relationship."

"I did with Ellan."

Egan stared at Avatar for a moment then nodded. "I remember. Thoughtless of me to say, I'm sorry."

"Accepted. Still, I didn't let it affect my duty to her."

Egan's earlier rigidity returned. "Nor have I concerning Titus!"

"*Shh!*" he warned, a glance to Norkiru's guards. They didn't seem to pay attention so he continued. "You are more concerned with Ridge's presence than Titus, as shown by leaving him to pursue the ranger when he did reconnaissance. Don't deny your preoccupation, I already endured your rebuke. So know this, just like I won't allow it to interfere with our mission, I will not let it jeopardize anyone's safety."

"I will not compromise his safety. In fact, that's what I'm trying to ensure."

"By focusing on Ridge and the past?" Avatar shook his head. "That is not the way to ensure his safety. I wallowed in self-pity after I believed Nigel killed. But you know that. You came to Melwynn to encouragement me. Knock some sense into me if you had to because of Willis. You expect me to do less in returning the favor?"

Egan's shoulders sagged, as all argument seemed to drain away. "I don't know what else to do to get Titus to accept me."

"Stop trying so hard."

"Is that how you handled Ellan?"

"Ay. Whether she accepted me or not had no bearing on my duty, a duty appointed by Jor'el, same as for you with Titus."

"I will protect Titus to the death."

"Only if Ridge isn't around."

Egan turned, intent on leaving when Avatar again detained him.

"Knowing Kell, there is another reason he sent Ridge. A reason I can guess deals with disharmony in our ranks, as told by certain behavior."

"Kell said as much during his rebuke before we left Straden."

Avatar scowled in annoyance. "And you scold me for unknowingly reinforcing Kell's admonishment to you?"

"I don't want to lose another charge! You should understand," he argued, but kept his voice from rising.

"I do. Yet in my spirit, I don't believe Ridge is a threat to Titus. However, your behavior is cause for concern." In urgency, Avatar gripped Egan by the shoulders so the warrior squarely faced him. "Don't let bitterness from the past consume you! It's too dangerous and the consequences unthinkable for you, for all of us. Please, Egan!"

For a long moment Egan stared at Avatar, his stiffness giving way to thoughtfulness. "I'll try," he said at length.

"Good enough."

"For you," began Egan with a small rueful smile. "Kell would have pinned me against the wall and held me there until I completely agreed."

"Because he can pull rank on all of us, I can't." Avatar grinned and released Egan. "Return to Titus." He watched Egan enter the chamber before making his way to Nigel and Mirit's room

"Well, did you find out the problem between Egan and Ridge?" asked Nigel.

"It goes back to Lord Willis' assassination."

"My ancestor?" asked Mirit.

Her question surprised Avatar. "Your ancestor?"

"Ay, though rarely mentioned because of his disgraceful life."

"Are you aware he was the illegitimate son of King Gowin, making him the half-brother of King Segar?"

"Ay," she admitted with some reticence.

"You are of royal blood? Why haven't you told me?" asked Nigel.

"As I said, Willis isn't well thought of by the family. His parentage couldn't make up for his treachery and debauched lifestyle." She grew stern with Nigel, waving a finger at him. "Say nothing to my father. He'd be ashamed and hurt if he discovers you know."

"I wouldn't think less of Mathias. Not all my ancestors are spotless." She frowned so he said, "Very well. Only it doesn't explain the tension between Ridge and Egan." Nigel looked to Avatar for further explanation.

"Egan was Willis' overseer. From what I remember being told, Grand Master Farley ordered Willis kidnapped to keep him from claiming the throne before Segar could be crowned. Kell sent Ridge to help Egan find Willis; only they were too late. Egan blames Ridge for not finding him in time to save him."

"You weren't there?" asked Mirit.

"No, I had duties elsewhere."

"Surely Kell knew about the tension between them when he sent Ridge and Egan with Tyrone," said Nigel.

"Naturally. Only he neglected to tell me, whereas *Captain Fraser* also had his suspicions."

"Have you two spoken about it?"

"Ay, when we paused on the plateau. I also told him Ridge is a skilled and dedicated ranger. Egan's attitude is of concern."

"As long as his attitude doesn't interfere with the mission."

"I told Egan so, and he assured me it will not."

"Perhaps I should speak to Egan. Willis' death proved beneficial for his wife and children when she married Baron Trevor. We consider him one of our most respected ancestors," she said.

"It might help. In the morning will be soon enough. Let him consider what has already been said."

Chapter 15

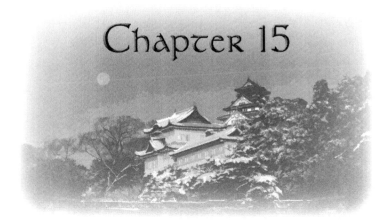

THE NEXT MORNING MIRIT DISCOVERED EGAN ACCOMPANIED the others to breakfast. Not a good time to discuss such matters so it would have to wait.

The meal was less formal than dinner and held in a smaller downstairs room. Allard appeared refreshed and said his leg felt much better. He sat between Tyrone and Titus, with the boy offering help when needed. Nigel and Mirit sat beside Chad, opposite Allard, Titus and Tyrone. Servants brought them plates of breakfast. Rice, along with some small pastries, figs and what appeared to be an egg pancake with a brownish-red sauce. Full teapots and cups sat in front of them.

"How do we eat this with sticks?" she asked watching Tyrone eat the pancake.

"Easy. Use the knife to cut the food into pieces and pick it up." He smiled and demonstrated.

"That I could have figured out by myself. I thought they showed you the *proper* way since they seem to have developed a manner of eating." She cut the pancake into six chunks. She began to eat, but just as it reached her mouth, it slipped from between the sticks. The others fought laughing.

"You put the chunks into the rice and hold the bowl up just like at dinner. The *captain* did fail to demonstrate the *proper* way," said Allard.

Tyrone simply smiled at her and continued eating.

Nigel curbed his humor for her sake and asked them, "Have you seen Norkiru or Kentashi this morning?"

"No, and strange our host is not joining us," replied Allard.

"Not really. On occasion, guests at Waldron must breakfast alone due to some urgent business," said Tyrone.

"Not normally, Captain," said Allard with a wry smile.

Tyrone chuckled. "No."

"Their customs are quiet different," began Mirit. "When attempting to communicate with the women I learned they worship the emperor and his family as gods and goddesses. In fact, upon learning I am a foreigner of royal status, they fell to their knees, faces to floor in fear I would punish them for touching me."

Tyrone almost choked on his food for amusement and took a drink to recover. Allard swallowed back a smile. Titus looked astonished and Chad smiled with curiosity. Nigel grinned at the reactions but Mirit wasn't accepting of their responses.

"It's not funny, *Captain*. They were seriously afraid."

"Sorry," he said in a strained voice of recovery. "How did you get them to understand you're not a goddess?"

"I wanted to try but Virgil didn't think it could be easily explained so we managed to work out an arrangement. Which is why I wore the gown—temporarily." She shot an arched glance to Allard, who flashed a grin of acknowledgment.

"Do they think all royalty are gods?" asked Titus.

"Ay."

"Can't that be good?" he asked, a bit confused.

"No," began Avatar. "According to some cultures similar in beliefs to Natan, the capture of another country's royalty, especially the *king*, would be robbing them of their god and make the country vulnerable to conquering." At his stress on the word *king*, he saw Titus understood.

The boy turned from Avatar to Tyrone when his father added, "Like they tried in Tunlund."

Allard leaned closer to Titus to speak in a private tone. "Remember, I said you placed us in a very awkward position."

Titus shied from everyone, uneasy and fearful. The conversation drove home the dangerous situation, especially for his father and what could happen if his identity was discovered.

Admiral Kentashi arrived. "Good morning. I hope everyone is well."

"Indeed, Admiral," replied Nigel with a smile to signal a change in tone. "I hope all is well with Lord Norkiru."

"All is well. Lord Norkiru arranged demonstrations of Natan strength and some goods for inspection of prince and Lord Allard."

"Oh, this should be interesting," said Allard.

Kentashi nodded, an agreeable smile appearing. "Please to go with me, if finished with fast breaking."

Nigel chuckled. "Ay, we're done eating breakfast."

"What I could manage," groused Mirit. She popped one of the pastries into the mouth and took a drink of tea to wash it down.

They follow Kentashi from the main house out a rear entrance. Nigel stopped and motioned to the statues of catbird creatures on the roof.

"What at those creatures, Admiral?"

"*Tigeti*, protectors of Norkiru and his ancestors."

"Are they companions of Raiden like Akido?"

"No," said Kentashi, his posture became notably rigid. "Norkiru's ancestors worship Kinkini, god of forest before defeated by Hoshiki two hundred years ago."

Nigel eyes narrowed in suspicious at Kentashi. "So Norkiru now worships Hoshiki? The one who sent those dogmen creatures after us?"

Kentashi shook his head. "Norkiru keep to ancestor tradition in honor of Kinkini, but tide is changing in Natan."

"How so?" asked Tyrone.

Kentashi moved closer to Nigel and Tyrone to speak in a low, confidential voice. "It complex. Like game played in Allon using pieces on board, knight, priest."

"You mean chess?"

"Ay. Some move one way, some another to hold in—how you say?"

"Checkmate?"

"Ay. Zekar make some men move in checkmate but Norkiru not listen to Hoshiki. Hope Kinkini will return."

"So the Zekar stirs up trouble between mortals?" asked Avatar.

"Ay, but new emperor wants to move forward. That why invite sent."

Tyrone glowered in displeasure. "You mean those invited are being used like pawns in a chess match to counter the Zekar?"

"Ay. Is that not how political game played in Allon?"

Tyrone attempted to stem his great agitation by averting his gaze from Kentashi but forced to admit, "Ay."

"That is hardly reassuring for us, Admiral," rebuffed Nigel.

"Indeed, more diplomacy would normally be employed," said Allard.

"I warrior, not diplomat. We deal arrow straight, not in pretty speech. Captain ask and I answer."

Before a piqued Allard responded, Nigel said, "We appreciate your candor, Admiral. Shall we continue with the day?"

Nigel and Allard proceeded with Kentashi, but Mirit hung back to walk with Tyrone.

"What have we gotten into?" she asked under her breath.

"More than we bargained for it seems," he replied.

"Indeed. And I'm becoming increasingly unsettled the more we learn."

He took hold of her arm as if escorting her. "Steady. As a goddess they won't harm you." He fought a smile of teasing.

A short laugh escaped despite her uneasiness. "It's not me I'm worried about." She glanced up at him.

They reached an open area near the western wall where various merchants set up booths or carts to display their goods and wares. Some booths were elaborately decorated with bright colored ribbons, flags or spiral paper columns twirling in the wind. The air came alive with various aromas and scents of food, spices and perfume. The noise and din of many voices bombarded the ears.

Hodi stood at the boundary of the open area. He shouted for a moment or two before getting the merchants' attention. He announced Kentashi and the Allonians. The merchants bowed low, some getting on their knees.

Kentashi spoke a few loud words in Natanese and waved both hands. Those kneeling stood when signaled. Great anticipation and curiosity shone on the faces of the merchants when he spoke of the Allonians. He addressed the guests.

"Goods of Natan: spices, cloth, rice, baskets and pottery. Please, inspect. Strength demonstration later."

The moment Kentashi finished speaking, the Allonians began to move among the booths. The merchants clamored for attention. One fragile older woman accosted Mirit with a bolt of cloth, insisting she feel it.

"The same cloth the robes are made from. Soft yet smooth and delicate. What is it called?"

Virgil translated the woman's answer. "She says it is the cloth of the gods. Spun on the looms of nature. They call it *silk*."

"Nigel, Captain Fraser." She beckoned them over. "The robe cloth."

Both felt the material. "Very nice," said Tyrone.

"Ay, we have nothing like it in Allon," agreed Nigel.

"Something your wife might fine interesting?" asked Mirit, making Tyrone smile.

"Actually, I think her younger sister would be more suited. Don't you agree, Highness?" he asked Nigel.

"Necie does tend toward the finer things." Nigel told Chad, "Make note of this material."

"Ay, Highness."

"There are some interesting spices and fine pottery over here," called Allard from across the area.

The others moved off to join him and Virgil spoke to the cloth woman. She widely smiled, bowing at the waist and saying what they believe to be thank you.

Titus wandered a few booths away from the others, Egan remaining with him. He stopped at a display of fruits, vegetables and bugs. "What are these for?"

The man spoke about his wares. He even took one of the bugs Titus pointed at and ate it, grinning the entire time. Titus screwed his face up in disgust.

"Crickets are a delicacy, like *squid*," said Egan, smiling.

The man shoved a cricket at Titus but the boy shook his head. He motioned to Egan. The Guardian took the cricket and ate.

"Not bad. A bit crunchy."

The man held another cricket out for Titus.

Chad arrived just as Titus accepted the cricket. "Are you going to eat it?"

"Egan said it's crunchy but not bad." Titus chickened out and shoved the cricket into Chad's hand. "You eat it."

Chad sent Egan a curious look, to which the Guardian smiled. Chad took a tentative bite of the cricket, his lips remaining in a sour frown. "Well, he's right, it's crunchy." He turned, cupping his hand over his mouth to keep from gagging as he swallowed. "I disagree with the not bad part."

The man laughed, indicating more crickets.

"No, thank you." Chad handed the half-eaten cricket back to him.

He shrugged and ate the half-cricket while Chad, Titus and Egan moved on.

Egan chuckled.

"Did you do that on purpose?" asked Chad.

"Guardians and mortals have different taste in food."

"You mean when you eat."

"*If* I eat."

"He did it on purpose," said Titus.

For two hours Kentashi accompanied the Allonians. They tasted and inspected various foods, spices and merchandise. By the time they were done they complied a list of goods for trade.

"You like?" asked Kentashi.

"There were some very unique and interesting possibilities, Admiral," said Allard. He grimaced in discomfort and held Titus's arm as they left the area.

"You've been on your feet too long, my lord," said Titus.

"Indeed."

Kentashi shouted to several nearby soldiers. They scrambled to carry out his orders. "You sit." He indicated a bench. "I send soldiers for chair to take you to demonstration."

Titus helped Allard to the bench.

"Are you able to continue, my lord?" asked Titus.

"I believe I can." He tried to rub away the pain.

Ridge knelt to discretely examine Allard's leg by feeling it and not raising the pant leg. He tried not to press too hard since Allard flinched at first touch. "Swollen from usage. Being off your feet is the only to reduce the swelling."

"He sit for demonstration. All sit," said Kentashi.

"That would help. Can he also have a stool to put his feet up?"

"Ay."

The two soldiers arrived carrying a portable chair in the middle of two supporting poles, each carrying one end. They stopped beside the bench, lowering the chair and kneeling, with heads bowed.

"Please." Kentashi motioned to the chair.

Ridge and Titus helped Allard onto the chair. Once Allard was seated, Kentashi barked an order and the soldiers lifted the chair and began carrying it toward the rear entrance of Yuki. Kentashi and the rest followed.

At the gate, servants waited, each holding a weapon belonging to the guests. Kentashi paused. "Outside Yuki you take weapons."

Once armed, Kentashi led them outside the gate for several hundred yards to a field marked off for various demonstrations. A lavish pavilion stood at the end of the field. Norkiru and Ryo already occupied the pavilion. A thousand troops consisting of archers, mounted soldiers and foot soldiers stood in front of the pavilion. The mounted soldiers and some infantry wore plate armor. Other soldiers were dressed in uniforms of cloth and well-crafted leather vests or breastplates. The archers carried extra large bows. Each group stood in precise formation with colorful banners displaying their unit's symbol. In front of the troops stood a line of drummers and trumpeters.

The Allonians and Kentashi walked the aisle created by the formation to the pavilion. Drummers and trumpeters played what sounded like a march or maybe a call to arms. They continued playing until Kentashi brought the Allonians to a halt at the pavilion steps. He bowed to Lord Norkiru.

"Prince and Lord Allard," began Norkiru. He indicated the empty seats. "No!" he snapped when Chad and Titus mounted the steps behind Tyrone and Mirit.

Chad bowed and backed down, drawing Titus with him.

Norkiru spoke in short sentences to Kentashi. The admiral translated for the Allonians. "Squires permitted for first night only as polite. Must now take place among servants."

"I understand." Nigel smiled and gave Norkiru an agreeing nod.

Once they sat, a footstool was placed so Allard could rest his foot.

Norkiru waved and trumpets sounded again. "Natan bow," he said.

The archers displayed their skill on foot.

"Very good," said Nigel.

"Not if Vidar were here," said Ridge to Avatar. They stood near Nigel's chair.

"Who Vidar?" asked Kentashi.

Nigel turned to Ridge. "You care to answer him?"

Ridge flashed a toothy embarrassed grin. "Vidar is the master archer of the Guardians."

Kentashi relayed the answer to Norkiru. The warlord loudly laughed and said something to the master of the games.

"Vidar do this?" asked Norkiru.

From one end of the field a mounted archer rode at full gallop firing and reloading with ease. He struck all five targets before reaching the end of the field. Two more mounted archers rode from opposite ends of the field and stuck the targets simultaneously without a single miss.

"Oh, my," said Allard in awe.

"Very impressive," said Tyrone.

Several more rounds of mounted archers showed various techniques of precision firing.

"Your archers are highly skilled," said Nigel.

"Allon archers same? Vidar maybe?" asked Norkiru with a proud satisfied smirk.

"We don't have mounted archers. After seeing this, it may be a future consideration."

Norkiru laughed. "We teach. Vidar learn."

Tyrone laughed and Nigel snickered to him, "That I'd like to see."

"Wouldn't we all," agreed Avatar, grinning.

"*Samaki* next. We eat, field cleared," said Norkiru.

"Samaki?" asked Allard.

"Natanese knights," said Avatar to which Norkiru nodded approval of the interpretation.

The refreshment consisted of finger food of fruit, vegetables, raw fish wrapped in rice, tea and rice wine.

The samaki took the field with great ceremony of colored banners and trumpets. Each wore plate armor, helmet, two swords, and elaborate decoration marking an individual or perhaps a regiment. Norkiru made a short speech and the rounds of mock combats began. Most took place simultaneously around the field. Some bouts were two combatants with various weapons, while others fought in teams. The bouts took an hour to complete.

"They coordinate well," said Tyrone.

"Ay, and they have stamina to compete for so long," said Nigel.

"Battle last time long. Must stay strong," said Norkiru.

"Ay," agreed Tyrone.

After the samaki cleared the field, two barefooted men dressed in the common shirt and pants appeared in front of the pavilion and bowed to Norkiru.

"Witness Natan real strength," said Norkiru. He waved to the men.

They bowed again and began slow deliberate arm movements and body gestures that seemed to be choreographed.

Mirit leaned toward Nigel and asked, "Are they dancing?"

He shrugged his ignorance. "There's no music."

Kentashi chuckled. "This is called *katani* our ancient form of martial arts. Hand-to-hand fight," he clarified when they didn't seem to understand.

"But they are not fighting each other. So what does this mean?" She mimicked the movement of the hands coming in toward the body from over the head.

"Bring in spirit of everything surround and give warrior strength from outside to inside."

"A form of meditation?" asked Nigel.

"Ay."

The men faced each other, bowed and assumed defensive stances.

Norkiru spoke Natanese to Kentashi, who replied before addressing the guests. "Lord Norkiru ask if Allon have like manner before battle."

"Jor'ellian do this, no?" asked Norkiru.

"Not calling upon the spirits, no. I pray to Jor'el and meditate before a battle," replied Nigel.

"Where get strength?" Norkiru motioned to the men, who fought in a unique style of punches, kicks and acrobatic moves.

"Well," began Nigel, mindful of how to answer as he watched the unusual fighting style. "Aside from years of hard training, a Jor'ellian is dedicated to Jor'el and his laws of morality and maintaining personal integrity before the Almighty and men."

"This give strength?" Norkiru flexed his arm muscles.

"Ay."

"Enough to face dogmen in battle and defeat them," said Kentashi to Norkiru.

"I suppose it could be seen that way," said Nigel.

"Don't be so modest, Highness" began Allard. He spoke to Norkiru. "The prince slew a spirit once."

This duly impressed Norkiru. "Ah! You show. Slay spirit." He motioned to the Guardians.

"No!" said Nigel; a quick rebuking glare at Allard. "These are servants of Jor'el, friends and allies. The one Lord Allard speaks of turned to evil."

"Then spirit slay spirit, see power."

Avatar drew to his full height, jowls flexed in anger. "For a Guardian to slay another Guardian in cold blood is forbidden and the consequences unthinkable. It will not be done for your amusement."

Norkiru bolted to his feet at the rebuke.

Egan and Virgil clasped the hilts of their swords and Ridge readied to grab his staff. Nigel and Tyrone placed themselves between Norkiru and Avatar. Mirit moved beside Allard to prevent him from rising.

"Lieutenant Avatar's tone may have been ill-advised, but he speaks the truth. Killing as you suggest goes against our law and conscience," said Nigel.

Kentashi spoke to Norkiru and they argued, but Norkiru made a stout nod from Kentashi to the Allonians.

"Lord Norkiru not understand reaction or reluctance to show strength. In Natan, strength is everything and no thought to slay to show it."

Nigel squared his shoulders, his face fixed and voice firm. "It is not the same in Allon."

"If not see Allon strength how Lord Norkiru convince Emperor you worthy allies?"

"Jor'ellian fight, kill samaki. Prove strength," declared Norkiru. The warlord's eyes were harsh and narrow upon Nigel.

"No," said Mirit. She moved to stand by Nigel.

Norkiru snarled at Mirit. "Prove Allon not weak or no Emperor!"

"My lord," began Allard in warning. "Remember he is a prince of royal blood. Would you have your divine Emperor or a member of his family prove their strength by fighting?"

Norkiru scowled but his expression softened at the argument. He spoke a few curt words to Kentashi, who translated for the Allonians.

"If not prince, then Captain Fraser." Kentashi surveyed Tyrone and ended with looking Tyrone squarely in the eyes. "He could slay many in battle."

Nigel clasped the hilt of his sword and said, "No—"

"I'll do it," said Tyrone, thought his eyes never left Kentashi.

"Captain!" said Nigel in stern objection.

A small confident smile appeared when Tyrone finally did turn to Nigel. "For the honor of Allon and Jor'el I will do what must be done for the sake of all."

Thought reluctant in feature, Nigel stepped back so Tyrone could pass him to descend the pavilion steps.

Norkiru smiled, smug and cocky. He whispered something to Ryo. The general bowed and left the pavilion. Norkiru resumed his seat.

"Did you hear what he said to the general?" Virgil whispered in the Ancient to Avatar. His question also captured the attention of Egan and Ridge. They flanked Avatar, all ready when Tyrone moved from the pavilion.

Avatar's silver eyes narrowed on Norkiru. He shook his head in response, still concentrating on their warlord host.

"Then how do we support *the captain*?" continued Virgil.

"I'll focus on him, you three remain alert. First sense of danger, we strike and dimension travel everyone back to the ship."

Titus and Chad stood close enough to the pavilion to witness everything. In anxious anticipation, Titus watched his father descend the steps. Their eyes met and he saw a complete look of confidence and reassurance on his father's face. That wasn't how he felt. His father must face a Natanese warrior, and this wouldn't be happening if he weren't here.

No, it would be Uncle. He looked back to the pavilion. Nigel caught his eye. Unlike his father's confidence, the scolding glare made him shy away.

"Jor'el, protect him," he weakly prayed.

Chad held clapped a hand on Titus' shoulder and whisper in the Ancient. "None of us will let any harm come to him."

A large Natanese warrior in full plate armor moved from Ryo to join Tyrone in front of the pavilion. The warrior bowed to Tyrone. He returned the greeting with the Allonian salute.

Tyrone heard Mirit's protest. "He has no armor!"

Norkiru replied, "If strong like Allon say, no need armor."

"I'll be fine, Princess." Tyrone flashed a smile of reassurance. She wasn't certain by her prodding look to Nigel. He appeared ready to spring into action at the slightest miscue. Tyrone's gaze passed to the Guardians. They would act the same as Nigel.

"Begin!" Norkiru barked the order.

The warrior turned to Norkiru, bowed, faced Tyrone and drew both swords.

Tyrone drew his sword and dagger then assumed the Jor'ellian first position. He prayed in the Ancient, "Jor'el, strengthen me for what must be done to honor you, to save Allon's reputation and protect my people."

A growling shout, alerted him to the warrior's attack. Tyrone parried, and in doing so, he and the warrior changed sides. The warrior again attacked using both weapons and Tyrone stood his ground. They exchanged a flurry of blows. The warrior went stumbling sideways when Tyrone caught him in the back of the left shoulder. The warrior immediately retaliated with a backward slash that clipped Tyrone's right arm, slicing his doublet, but not cutting him.

Tyrone heard Titus' gasp, but didn't dare look at his son since the warrior charged. He stepped aside and deflected the passing lunge. The warrior moved fast, and his shorter sword knocked away Tyrone's dagger. Tyrone didn't hesitate and gripped the hilt of his sword in both hands and used his added strength to shove the warrior's weapons down to the ground. He quickly stepped on the blades and clouted the warrior behind the neck, sending him sprawling to the ground when he lay stunned and groaning.

Norkiru shouted in Natanese. The warrior tried to rise but Tyrone's foot crashed down on his back and pinned him to the ground. He leveled the sword at warrior's face.

"I believe the show of strength is finished," said Tyrone.

Norkiru snarled and spoke in Allonian. "Slay him. Then done."

"Why? He is defeated."

"Slay him!" shouted Norkiru, slamming fists on the arms of his chair.

Instead of following the command, Tyrone removed his foot from the warrior, sheathed his sword and stepped back. The flush of insult rose in Norkiru's face.

The warrior stood. His fretful, uncertain glance passed from Tyrone to Norkiru. Suddenly, Ryo seized the warrior from behind and slit his throat. Tyrone reacted to the unexpected action by drawing the sword, deadly eyes on Ryo ready to engage.

"Father!" Titus raced to Tyrone.

"Titus, no!" shouted Nigel in warning the moment the boy moved.

Egan leapt off the platform. Titus reached Tyrone before Egan could get to him, so the Guardian stepped between Tyrone and Ryo. The general still held a bloody dagger, but made no threatening move, instead he stared up at Egan.

Tyrone lowered his sword and drew Titus back to the base of platform out of Ryo's reach. Only then, did Egan move, but still kept himself between Ryo, his charge and Tyrone.

"General Ryo only do what you do not, Captain," said Kentashi. "Strength and honor demand death in failure."

Tyrone's passion was slow to ebb. "There are different types of strength, including mercy and justice."

Norkiru bolted to his feet and spoke to Kentashi in angry loud words, gesturing between Tyrone and the others. Kentashi bowed. Norkiru left the pavilion, sneering at Tyrone and Titus in passing.

Kentashi's face betrayed his concern. "I fear too many different between Natan and Allon to agree."

"That is most unfortunate, Admiral. Because those differences can also provide instruction beneficial to both countries," said Allard.

Kentashi's thoughtful gaze passed from Allard to various members of the Allonian delegation, ending on Tyrone. "I will speak to Lord Norkiru. For now, return to rooms and await summons." He motioned for them on the pavilion to leave. The same two soldiers arrived carrying the chair for Allard.

Mirit held Nigel's arm as they walked with Avatar behind Kentashi.

Nigel leaned slightly toward Avatar and whispered in the Ancient. "I don't like the idea of surrendering our weapons."

"We won't." Avatar did a careful glance over his shoulder, his voice remaining in a private tone. "Egan, take the point." While Egan obeyed, Avatar continued, "Everyone, follow Egan. Don't pause, linger, or speak, just keep walking."

The tension of the situation was palpable and Titus clung to Tyrone's hand. He stared up at his father, unable to mask his fear. Tyrone moved his hand from holding Titus' hand to encircling the boy's shoulders. Titus drew closer to his father as they moved toward Yuki.

Egan walked ahead of the Allonians but behind Kentashi. Nearing Yuki, he began speaking in the Ancient under his breath. His focus shifted between Kentashi and those gathered at the gates. *"Bi Jor'el's ordugh, bi dall gu ruige claidheamh er stav."* He repeated the phrase, "By Jor'el's command, be blind to sword and staff." His fists clenched with the effort of concentration as he kept repeating the phrase.

At the gate, the servants bowed to Kentashi. The admiral continued moving without pausing, and so did the Allonians. No guard or servant even spoke. The servants remained in the bowed position and guards at attention as the group passed.

211

When they reached the house, Ridge carried Allard from the portable chair to his chamber and gently lowered him to sit in one of the wooden chairs. The others gathered in the room. Titus released his father's hand to help Chad fetch cushions to prop up Allard's leg.

"How did we get make it inside without surrendering our weapons?" asked Mirit.

"I used my special power of blindness. Or rather amended it to specifically suggest they didn't see our weapons," said Egan.

"At least something went right," groused Allard. He squirmed to get comfortable. "The demonstration certainly didn't."

"That's the pain talking. For I can't believe you would want any of us killed for political gain. Especially, *the captain,*" said Avatar.

"No, no, of course not," groaned Allard. He couldn't get comfortable so Chad adjusted the cushions under his leg.

"I don't know about anyone else, but I'm growing more uncomfortable with what we learn about them," said Mirit.

"Maybe staying in the gown would have helped," continued Allard in his sour mood.

"The gown wouldn't have stopped the fight nor Ryo from killing in cold blood!"

"Easy," said Nigel, in an attempt to calm Mirit.

"Difficult to do when I think what could have happened to—him!" She motioned to Tyrone, struggling to keep from saying his name.

"None of us would have allowed it."

Tyrone took her hand. "It had to be done."

"You should have let me. In fact, I was about to speak, since am the most expendable of the group," said Chad.

Tyrone shook his head. "No one is expendable. Besides, as well-trained as you are, he was much stronger than he appeared."

"This is supposed to be a diplomatic trip," chided Mirit. "We're attacked twice, Allard is wounded, I start feeling and seeing things, Avatar senses the Dark Way and *you* are forced to fight. When can we go home?"

"Hopefully when Kentashi convinces Norkiru we aren't totally hopeless." Allard cried out when he tried to adjust a cushion under his leg.

Ridge knelt to check the wound. This time he rolled up the pant leg to reveal the bandage. The leg swelled on either side of the bandage. Ridge unwrapped it to discover it once again angry red and inflamed.

"You must be great pain," she sympathetically said.

Allard didn't reply and screwed his face in an attempt to withstand Ridge's examination.

Tyrone spoke to the others. "Leave, so we can tend him. We'll let you know how he is when we're done."

<hr/>

An hour later, Tyrone, Titus and Avatar met with Nigel and Mirit in the couple's chamber.

"How is Allard?" asked Nigel.

"He must have endured terrible pain during the demonstration. I gave him a strong sedative and he's sleeping. Ridge and Chad are watching him," said Avatar.

"He never complained," said Mirit with distress.

"He wouldn't. He's too stubborn and determined to fulfill his duty," said Tyrone, his face and voice betraying uneasiness.

"How concerned should we be for his health?" asked Nigel.

In sobriety, Tyrone replied, "Very. All the remedies only have short-term effect."

"Then we should send him back to the ship and have Gulliver or Chase take him home," said Mirit.

"Can we, Father? I'll even go with him," said an anxious Titus.

Tyrone's smile at his son was plaintive. "I understand and appreciate your concern, but in his condition, the trip would not be a good idea."

"Ay, he must rest for a few days before being moved," said Avatar.

Titus grew troubled. "If his condition is that serious couldn't Eldric do better than the Natanese remedies? And what about dimension travel?"

Tyrone tried to be sympathetic. "Remember Avatar first used the medicine Eldric packed, and to no effect."

"Dimension travel is difficult on healthy mortals and only done when those injured or sick have no other alterative. Allard can rest here. He just needs to be more cooperative," said Avatar.

Nigel sat in the chair, a thoughtful sigh escaping. "Would be a shame to lose him like this. He is a dear friend to our family."

"No one said we are going to lose him," refuted Tyrone.

"Ay," began Mirit kindly for the boy's sake. "Ridge and Avatar know what they're doing."

"Indeed. I didn't mean to imply otherwise," said Nigel. "What I meant is we need to find a way to help him recover. I'll send word to Lord Norkiru for a stronger remedy."

Titus appeared only mildly satisfied. "I'll go sit with him." He left.

"I didn't mean to sound so morose, but you can't shield him from the possibility Allard may not recover," said Nigel to Tyrone.

"I know. Yet I don't want him discouraged either. He's taking responsibility of caring for Allard very seriously. More so than any task before."

"Which is surprising considering the tongue lashing Allard gave him after his discovery. At first I wasn't certain what to say, but Allard is never at a loss for words."

Tyrone shook his head, his expression heavy with regret. "During the trip we've barely had time to say much of anything to each other. Although sharing a tent or room, events prevent us from speaking. Chad mentioned talking to him."

"At this point, any understanding may come from Chad and Allard than from either of you," said Avatar to Tyrone and Nigel.

"Why?"

"Because you are both too close to the situation and it tends to cloud your judgment.

"And how you interact with each other concerning him," said Mirit.

With hopeful expectation, Tyrone spoke to Nigel. "I think that has changed, hasn't it?"

"Ay."

Tyrone smiled in relief.

Virgil answered a knock at the door. He exchanged a few words with the Natanese servants. "Lord Norkiru sends dinner to the chambers," he spoke, allowing the servants to bring in platters of food. "He says it is wise for all to take this evening and consider the future in the way best suited to each conscience."

"Wonderful," groused Nigel. "We may all be returning to the ships shortly."

"After what Kentashi said earlier about the Zekar it maybe for the best," said Tyrone.

One of the servants reacted to the word *Zekar* prompting Avatar to signal the mortals to remain quiet. They heeded the nonverbal warning and remained silent while the servants finished setting up the food. Virgil ushered the servants from the chamber.

"You think they understood us?" asked Nigel.

"Maybe not completely, but the Zekar provoked interest. At this point, it is best not to arouse any more suspicious."

"Us arouse suspicion?" she sarcastically said and went to inspect the food. Again, rice was the main stay with various cuts of meat, vegetables and sauce. She used her pinkie to dip into a dark, almost black sauce to taste it. She gagged, opening her mouth and hands waving in front of lips. Her reaction alarmed the others

Nigel moved to aid her. "Poisoned?" he asked with great concern.

She didn't answer, rather seized a pitcher of the local ale and drank in large gulps.

Virgil snatched up the offending bowl and sniffed the sauce. Avatar dipped his finger into the liquid and took a careful taste. His face screwed up in surprise and his voice strained.

"Not poison, but I don't think even Armus would eat it."

"Oh, too spicy!" She began to breath normally, swallowing and sniffling. "And it made my nose runny."

Tyrone and Nigel laughed.

"You think it's funny? Take a taste!" She snatched the bowl from Virgil and shoved it in Nigel's face.

Nigel pushed the bowl away. "We trust you and Avatar."

"My tongue still burns." She gave the bowl back to Virgil.

"What do you want me to do?" asked the Guardian.

"Get rid of it." She took another drink of ale.

He went to a nearby plant and poured the sauce into the pot.

Tyrone curbed his amusement to speak. "We should return to keep watch in case he develops a fever. We'll see you in the morning." He and Avatar left.

Curious, Mirit drew close to Nigel. Her eyes searched his face. "Has the situation changed between you two?"

He smiled. "After the clearing where Akido appeared and gave us the medicine, he surprised me by apologizing, saying jealousy prompted his actions. I told him I never meant to make him jealous or take his place in Titus' eyes. He looked relieved, like a burden was lifted. For first time in awhile, I felt at ease with him and not defensive."

"You are both honorable men with a long history of friendship no one wants to see strained."

"Ay. Now if only Titus would come around, all can be well again."

"Unfortunately, he shares his father and uncle's stubbornness. We can only hope, pray and wait."

Inside the other room, Chad stretched out on a small lounge, still awake. Egan stood beside the door and Ridge mixed some more salve in a small bowl to tend to Allard's wound. Titus sat in a chair beside the bed where Allard lay sleeping.

The day's activities deeply disturbed Titus. Each encounter showed the danger his actions caused his father. Although he accepted the necessity of their role-playing, the news of how Natanese viewed royalty as gods and prizes to capture or kill troubled him. But seeing his father fight the samaki unnerved him! His father's victory did little to allay his fear, while the situation grew threatening.

A simple diplomatic mission became a life and death display to win favor with the Natanese! And people who thought nothing of killing in a proud show of strength. That thought struck Titus hard, as it contrasted his father's choice of strength—strength enough to take on the mantle of a soldier to protect those in his charge. The voice he heard in his brain wasn't his father speaking, rather Egan declaring how he would protect Titus to the death just like Jedrek. The disturbing recollection made him look at Egan. When the Guardian caught his eye, Titus turned away.

"Something wrong?"

Titus jerked in fright at Egan's voice now closer. In fact, he moved beside the chair. Titus stared up at the Guardian, but couldn't answer.

The door opened and Tyrone entered. He approached the bed. Ridge tied off the new bandage and Allard remained sleeping.

"Any sign of fever?" Tyrone asked in a quiet voice.

Ridge rose to answer. "No, he is sleeping. The salve worked. The green scab is gone and the wound healing normally. He just needs rest."

"I'll make sure he does," said Titus, his voice a bit hollow.

Tyrone smiled and moved to kneel beside the chair. "Your diligence in caring for him is commendable."

The pleasure in his father's eyes muted Titus. How could he be pleased under such circumstances? Titus couldn't speak; he didn't have the words. Besides, what happened was his fault! He bit his lip and turned back to watching Allard.

"Very well. You watch him. I'll get some sleep then you can sleep and I'll watch him."

Titus nodded, chewing on his lower lip.

217

Chapter 16

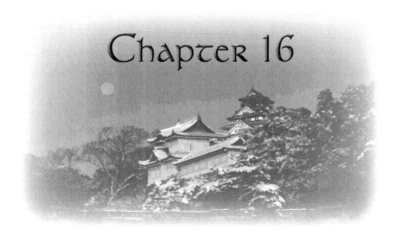

MOST OF THE NIGHT PASSED QUIETLY, BUT WITH THE APPROACH of dawn, Egan and Ridge grew uneasy. Tyrone dozed in the chair beside the bed where Allard rested peacefully. Titus slept in Tyrone's bed and Chad slept on the lounge. Nothing bothered the mortals, but the disturbing sense was palpable.

Ridge whispered, "Stay here, I'm going to find out if the others sense it." He didn't wait for a reply and left the room.

In the hall, Virgil and Avatar become alert and only slightly relaxed when Ridge arrived.

"No need to ask if you both feel it," said the ranger in the Ancient.

"Egan too?" asked Avatar.

"Ay. I think I'll take a walk."

"Be careful they don't see your staff."

Ridge flashed a cocky smile. "Obviously you don't know *who* showed Egan how to adapt his power of blindness to only shield certain objects." He left without waiting for a response.

"So the ranger's power is shielding," said Virgil with sarcasm, then added when Avatar scowled. "Another detail Kell left out?"

Ridge decided to try a back door and not go out the front entrance. The pale red light of dawn reached the compound. Four soldiers accosted him. All were armed with swords and carried spears, which they pointed at Ridge.

"Come no further, spirit," said one. "Go back inside with your kind."

Ridge put up his hands in a non-threatening gesture and spoke in Natanese. "I mean no harm."

"Then why carry a staff?"

Ridge concentrated on the lead soldier. "I'm not carrying a staff. You are the only ones armed." His gold eyes flared in brightness as he spoke.

The lead soldier frowned and momentarily hesitated. "Go back inside." He thrust his spear and Ridge stepped back to avoid being stuck.

Ridge shrugged and turned to leave. Jiru ran across his line of sight, crouched behind a pillar then darted in between two buildings. Jiru didn't see Ridge, nor did the soldiers notice what caught his interest. The lead soldier used his spear to poke Ridge in the side. This time the ranger snatched the spear behind the point.

"No need to get violent."

The soldier tried to pulled the spear free but wasn't successful until Ridge released his grip. "You go, now!"

Ridge moved only far enough from the soldiers to be concealed in the shadows. He stepped to one side to watch the soldiers return to their duty. Once they were out of sight, he spoke in the Ancient and dashed across the compound unseen by any mortal. He didn't stop until he reached the alleyway where Jiru disappeared. The disturbing sense grew stronger and he readied his staff, eyes shifting about and alert for danger.

He moved down the alley to the end. A distance of ten feet separated the rear of the building and the defensive wall. Jiru stood fifty yards away at a gate speaking to a cloaked man in hurried, hushed tones. Ridge couldn't hear the words clear enough to understand but when the cloaked man began to leave, Jiru seized him. The man pushed Jiru away but Jiru wouldn't leave and accosted him again. In a brief struggle the man's hood fell back. Hodi. Jiru gasped, not in surprise of recognition, but death. Hodi shoved Jiru away, jerking his short sword from Jiru's body.

Before Ridge could react to the slaying, an eerie screeching sound echoed. He heard the cry an instant before three smaller firebirds flew overhead. The soldiers on watch sounded the alarm. Hodi hastened to open the gate. Dogmen rushed inside, and for a brief moment Ridge wondered whether to engage the creatures or warn the others.

More cries of firebirds, and now the twang of bows and hiss of arrows. Ridge ran down the alley intent on reaching the others. From behind came the loud snarling of a dogman. Once out of the alley he turned, swinging his staff for added strength and force. The impact sent a dogman flying sideways into the building. Four others followed the first. Ridge assumed a defensive stance, staff in his right hand and poised along the back of his shoulder ready for action; the left hand free for balance or drawing his dagger. The dogmen circled him like wolves snarling and snapping. One made a feint attack but Ridge didn't flinch.

"You'll have to do better than that old trick."

Taking him at his word, they attacked in unison, but Ridge moved faster. His staff arched down and swatted two of them aside in a single blow. He whirled around and used the staff to take the legs out from under another one. The fourth one moved to attack Ridge from behind. Without looking, he pulled the staff backward, connecting in the creature's mid-section. He whipped about and cracked the creature's skull.

The first two recovered, only Ridge had momentum and smashed one in the face with the end of the staff. A third grabbed the other end of the staff, pulling Ridge off his feet. When the creature went to leap on him, he rolled to one side, sprung to his feet and threw his dagger. It struck the beast between the shoulder blades. Suddenly a blow from a claw slashed at him, ripping the back of his tunic and flesh. He went sprawling to the ground. He tried to get up, but it pounced on him and they rolled several times before he ended on top. The triumph proved brief when the beast threw him aside. He cried out when his injured back slammed into the wall, and he sunk to his knees in pain. The beast rushed Ridge, only Virgil intercepted it and cleaved it half.

"How badly are you hurt?" asked the warrior.

"I don't know." He reached up. Virgil helped him to stand and made quick examination of Ridge's back. "Well?"

"You'll live."

"What about the others?"

"With Egan and Avatar. I came to find you. Yuki is being overrun and we need to flee."

Ridge fetched his staff before he and Virgil began crossing the compound. The main gate became breeched, bringing them to a halt. Mortals in different armor and uniform swarmed inside. The new mortals and dogmen battled Norkiru's soldiers while overhead firebirds breathed down flames upon everyone.

"I hope they're not caught up in that," said Ridge in concern.

"No. They've taken shelter behind a stable along the east wall. But we have to get through this to reach them." Virgil went to draw his sword, but Ridge stopped him.

"We can move and go unseen."

"Unseen, but not unharmed if a weapon impacts us."

Ridge just smiled. "My power of shielding will protect us from both." He placed a hand on Virgil's shoulder to speak the Ancient. "By Jor'el's will, shield these frames from sight and harm till we reach our destination."

Together, they raced with incredible speed into the foray with Ridge repeating the phrase when he could. All around them the battle continued, mortal against mortal and dogmen against mortals. Almost appearing in slow motion compared to their speed. Neither Virgil nor Ridge slowed down, weaving through the chaos. They dodged mortal swords and swiping claws between combatants that took place without any hint or inclination of seeing the Guardians passing in their midst. When a dogman leapt at a group of Norkiru's soldiers, Ridge dove to avoid the beast, rolling and coming to his feet without missing a stride.

Virgil spun around to avoid a thrusting spear of one soldier into the belly of another then jumped over a wounded soldier. Finally, they reached the stables where the others remained hunkered down.

"Ridge? Are you alright?" asked Tyrone at seeing the torn tunic.

"A scratch."

"I have medicine." Chad indicated the medical pouch he now carried.

"Later."

From the corner of the stables, Titus watched in fear as the dogmen and invading soldiers cut down Norkiru's men. "Who are they? Why are they doing this?"

"That's not important. We need to leave," said Tyrone.

"The main gate is breeched," said Virgil. He turned to Avatar to ask, "Should we dimension travel everyone to the ships?"

Tyrone answered. "Once we're in a safer place."

"Ay," agreed Avatar. "An errant, sword, spear or flame could be fatal for all if interrupted before complete disappearance."

The sound of approaching battle placed them all on alert. Everyone was armed, but shrunk back into the shadows. Three dogmen mercilessly attacked two of Norkiru's men. Mirit closed her eyes at the savagery. Titus bit his lip to keep from making a sound. Tyrone shielded Titus from the brutal ending. Not until the dogmen left did Tyrone release Titus, the boy pale.

A wounded Kentashi stumbled and fell against the wall. Two enemy soldiers pursued him. Nigel scrambled from his concealment to grab Kentashi, intent on rescue. The soldiers shouted, angry at Nigel's intervention.

Egan placed himself at the edge of the wall and waved his hand in a circular motion while speaking in the Ancient, "You see nothing!"

The soldiers stopped and began muttering to each other, which allowed Nigel and Kentashi to reach safety. The soldiers ran back in the direction they came.

Astonished, Kentashi asked Egan, "How did you do that?"

"I told them they didn't see you."

"Thank you."

Nigel examined Kentashi's wounds, a long but shallow cut along the abdomen and a gash to the forehead. "Nothing appears too serious."

"I will live, but not know who of my men will survive."

"Is there a way out?" asked Tyrone.

"I can't leave Lord Norkiru."

"Yuki is about to fall!" Tyrone motioned to the battle and invaders making short work of Norkiu and Kentashi's men. Kentashi tried to stand when Tyrone grabbed him, which made the admiral fall to his knees, unsteady and weak. "Going to your death won't help. The only way is to flee and bring reinforcements to stop whoever is behind this."

"You would help me do this?"

Tyrone shook his head. "No. My responsibility is the safety of my people same as yours. You can't protect them or aid Norkiru if you die."

Kentashi returned Tyrone's stare before stoutly nodding. "There is a way out." He peeked around the corner. The sounds of battle drifted toward the main house. He motioned for Tyrone to follow and dashed into the shadow of the battlement.

Tyrone signaled Egan to follow Kentashi. Mirit, Titus and Virgil followed Egan. Chad and Ridge aided a severely limping Allard. Tyrone followed Allard with Nigel and Avatar keeping a rear guard.

They crept along the wall for several hundred yards, alert to any and all sounds or movement. Kentashi's abrupt raised arm stopped them at a corner. The sun had now completely risen, leaving no shadows in the compound to shield them.

"We must get inside that building." He pointed across the compound.

"We will," said Egan. Kentashi began to move, but the Guardian seized him. "Wait."

Overhead the firebirds screeched. Then they heard Akido's call and the dragon engaged the firebirds.

223

Egan bowed his head, closed his eyes and spoke in the Ancient. "By Jor'el's will, blind the enemy to our presence though we move in plain sight veil us in the black of night."

"Go!" urged Avatar to the others.

Everyone, but Egan and Avatar, dashed to the building. Egan used his power to blind the enemy by bowing his head, closing his eyes and whispering. Avatar waited beside Egan, sword drawn, watching both the progress of the others and shielding Egan.

Mirit pulled Titus out of the path of a falling soldier, which made him stumble, but she held unto him and continued moving. Soon he regained his footing and ran without her help.

Allard's leg gave way and he fell face first to the ground. Ridge deadlifted Allard and held him up to keep pace with the others. Kentashi reached the door first and practically fell on it to open it. He let the others inside, first Titus and Mirit then Chad, Ridge with Allard, followed by Nigel, Tyrone and Virgil.

Once the mortals were inside, Avatar slapped Egan's arm. "Done. Now, go!" He nudged Egan toward the building. He kept the rear guard, shutting and barring the door once inside.

"This way." Kentashi led them downstairs to a dark basement.

Titus ran into Mirit. "It's dark," he complained.

"*A'lasadh,*" said Avatar. He held up his sword to use like a lantern. The room appeared to be a shrine of some kind with various stone statues and altars. "Where to?" he asked Kentashi, the admiral wary in regard of him.

"There is secret way through statue."

"Which one?"

Kentashi moved toward a statue of a catbird like the one seen on top of Yuki's roofs. He pulled the tail and the statue slid to one side revealing a dark passageway. He went to take Avatar's glowing sword but the Guardian stopped him. "Everyone inside, then I close statue."

Avatar went first to light the way, followed by the others.

Tyrone laid hold of Kentashi's arm before entering the passageway. "You're coming with us."

Kentashi grinned. "Lever on this side close statue." He followed Tyrone and pulled the lever. The panel slid closed. He took the lead, Avatar behind him, his sword lighting the way.

Although narrow, the tunnel was tall enough for the Guardians to pass through without having to duck. Allard groaned, the urgency of flight hard on his wounded leg. Titus tried to aid him, but difficult in the constricted tunnel. "How much further? Lord Allard must rest."

"No," grunted Allard. "We have to hurry."

Kentashi paused at a sharp turn in the tunnel. "There are many steps to top."

"I'll carry him on my back," said Egan.

"I won't be a burden."

"Egan will carry you," insisted Tyrone.

Allard yielded, so Egan positioned himself on one knee for Allard to climb on his back.

"Follow Kentashi and Avatar, we'll be right behind you," Tyrone instructed Egan.

Many steps translated into about one hundred before Kentashi and Avatar reached the door at the top. Kentashi used his hands to search for and find the key to unlock the door. Even using the key, the door proved difficult to open for him to open.

"Let me." Avatar pushed with his shoulder. Sunlight came crashing through the opening, temporarily blinding the mortals. Avatar spoke the Ancient and his sword stopped glowing. Standing in the threshold, he guided the others out. Most blinked as their eyes adjusted to the light.

They emerged onto a small plateau about two miles north overlooking Yuki. Egan lowered Allard to sit on a nearby boulder. The others surveyed the carnage below. The worst appeared to be over with the invaders ransacking Yuki and the dogmen partaking of dead meat. Mirit guided Titus away from the brutal scene.

"Who would do such a thing?" the boy asked.

225

Kentashi's jowls tightened and he sneered. "That banner of Rukan." He pointed to the new banner over Yuki. "I did not think he so bold."

"He had help," chided Ridge.

"Ay. Hoshiki and Onedo."

"No, Captain Hodi."

"What?" exclaimed Kentashi with outrage.

"Just before the attack, I noticed Jiru acting strangely, so I followed him to a small gate on the west wall. He had an argument with a hooded man. When the argument turned deadly and the man killed Jiru, the hood fell off and I saw Captain Hodi. The firebirds appeared and Hodi opened the gate for the dogmen to enter."

Kentashi glared at Yuki. "He will pay for treachery!"

"In time perhaps, but we can't stay here in the open," said Avatar.

"Ay, if Rukan knows about our visit he may come looking for us," said Nigel.

"He already is." Virgil pointed to a troop of mounted mortals, dogmen and firebirds leaving Yuki and heading in their direction. "Now maybe a good time to leave for ships," he said to Avatar.

Akido's cry came for overhead. The dragon dove at the troop heading towards them, fire coming from his mouth. More startling was the deafening ear-piercing screech. Mirit fell to her knees and doubled over in pain. The others cringed at the noise. Tyrone knelt, holding Mirit in protective support. A large firebird swooped over the trees where they were heading. When it's shadow passed over them, she fainted.

"It's coming back!" shouted Titus.

The firebird made a large return arc to dive at them. Its deafening screech made the mortals immobile for the increase in pain.

"To the trees!" shouted Kentashi. He struggled to move.

Nigel started to make his way to Mirit, but Tyrone lifted her in his arms. Virgil and Avatar hurried to aid them to the trees. Chad and Titus helped Allard. Egan and Ridge remained with them for safety. Nigel staggered in step as he followed.

Akido intercepted the firebird at the tree line. The exchange of fire ignited the trees all around them. The intense heat and smoke obscured vision and made them choke. Soon everyone became separated.

Blinded by the stinging smoke, Tyrone took a wrong turn and he and Mirit tumbled helplessly down a slope. He didn't stop until his back smacked against a log. For a brief moment he lay winded and stunned, trying to catch his breath. Hearing a nearby groan, he pushed himself off the log. He grimaced in pain, as his whole body hurt. He noticed she lay on the ground about ten feet away.

"Mirit?"

She didn't answer so he made his way to her, anxious of her condition. Her eyes fluttered in an attempt to wake. "Mirit," he urged.

Her eyes opened to her name and his touch. "Tyrone?"

"Ay," he said with a smile of relief. "Are you hurt?"

"I don't know." She reached for him and he helped her sit up. Once sitting, she took several deep breaths and considered her condition. "I think I'm all right. What happened? How did we get down here?"

"You fainted when the firebird appeared and I carried you away from its attack. Unfortunately, I couldn't see due to flames and smoke and we ended down here."

"What flames?"

He indicated for her to look up the slope and the smoke overhead. "Akido arrived. He and the firebird ignited the forest."

"Where are the others?"

"I don't know. We became separated. Can you stand?"

"Give me a hand up and we'll find out." On her feet, she gingerly stretched. "Aside from being sore, I'm in one piece. What about you?"

He arched his back and winced. "I smacked my back on that log."

She stepped behind him and felt his spine and back ribcage. He flinched when she examined the right back ribs. "Does that hurt?"

"Ay!"

"Nothing feels broken. You must have hit pretty hard to cause deep bruising."

"I'll manage." He glanced up at hearing a distant call of a firebird. "This whole situation is out of control. Let's find the others and hurry back to the ships." Before he and Mirit moved two steps they heard Nigel shouting her name.

"Over here!" she called in response.

Nigel and Avatar rushed from the far side of the slope. "You two all right?"

"We're standing," said Tyrone in bravado.

"Don't let him fool you, he hit his back hard against the log, causing deep bruising," she said.

Kentashi and Virgil came from another direction. The admiral limped and Virgil sustained a cut on his right cheek and above his right eye.

"Prince. Captain. Any hurt?" asked Kentashi.

"Mirit and I fell down the slope and are sore, but no serious injury. You?"

"I fall and twist ankle."

"What happened to you?" asked Avatar of his fellow warrior.

Virgil acted sheepish in reply. "I couldn't see due to the smoke and ran into a tree. Don't tell Ridge," he added when Avatar chuckled.

"Have you seen the others?" asked Nigel.

"No, but Egan and Ridge were with them on the plateau."

"The question is, do we search for them or continue to Kaori?"

"Dangerous to make search with Rukan's forces after us," began Kentashi. "If those spirits as powerful as this one, they will reach Kaori safely." He indicated Avatar.

"Guardians! We are Guardians."

"Easy, Avatar," said Tyrone.

"We could focus on Egan and Ridge's spirit and track them," said Virgil, of himself and Avatar, but corrected his wording at Avatar's frown. "I mean essence, presence, not spirit exactly."

"See, I knew you spirits," said Kentahsi with satisfaction.

Virgil heaved a hapless shrug at Avatar. Both warriors stiffened in anticipation of danger and reached for their sword.

"Something comes. We must go, quickly. Which way?" Avatar asked Kentashi, but Mirit answered.

"This way." She pointed, and hastened in the direction she indicated.

Nigel hurried after her. "Wait! How do you know?"

"I just know. It's this way," she insisted and kept moving.

Allard stumbled again, this time falling onto all fours and taking Titus with him. He was exhausted, breathing heavy and coughing due to the smoke. "I'm sorry, I'm slowing you down," he gasped between breaths.

"It's not your fault." Titus also had difficulty breathing because of the smoke.

Allard looked around. "Where are the others?"

Titus tried to control his coughing to survey the area. They were in a small grove surrounded by thin trees, but smoke veiled any clear view beyond the trees. "I don't know, I can't see very far."

A branch snapped followed by a low snarl. Titus tried to peer through the smoke.

"Can you see what it is?"

Titus shook his head. He jerked around at hearing more sounds, only closer.

"Go! Find the others and get to safety," said Allard.

"No. I won't leave you!" Titus struggled to pull Allard to his feet.

From out of the smoke, two dogmen charged. Allard shoved Titus away and reached for his sword. He just finished drawing it when a dogman leapt at him.

Titus tripped and fell from Allard's shove and scrambled to his knees. He reached for his sword, but a dogman's paw struck his hand. The sword fell back into the sheath and he sat back on his rump to avoid the dogman's next swipe. The claws barely missed his face. He swiftly crawled backwards from the beast. It yowled in painful anger, arching its back as if struck by something. Momentum made it fall on top of Titus. The boy cried out in surprise and squirmed to get free when a foot kicked it off of him. Titus stared in befuddlement at the dagger logged in the dogman's back.

Chad pulled Titus to his feet. "You all right?"

"Ay." He swallowed back his initial surprise then cried out, "No!"

The other dogman's jaw clamped down on Allard's throat. Titus drew his sword and hacked at the dogman. The beast released Allard to deal with the boy. Chad aided Titus and landed a stunning blow to the beast's chest. It staggered back then arched forward with a yowl, struck from behind and nearly cleaved in two by Egan.

Egan knelt beside Allard and felt for a pulse.

"Is he—?" Titus couldn't finish, as fear choked his voice.

Egan nodded. He spoke a farewell prayer in the Ancient. He removed Allard's signet ring and stuffed it in his belt.

Titus moved toward Allard when a hand grabbed his shoulder.

"He's dead and we must flee," said Ridge

"We can't just leave him!" Titus tried to get free, but Ridge held fast.

Egan stood. "Let him go."

Ridge complied, stepped back and raised his hand in mock surrender.

Again Titus moved toward Allard, but Egan intercepted him. A gentle hand made Titus look at him. "Don't make his sacrifice be in vain. We must leave him." Titus fell against him, weeping.

Ridge became alert at more sounds. "We need to find the others."

Egan steered Titus in the direction Ridge indicated.

Mirit lead them in a northerly direction, and further into the foothills. Kentashi and Tyrone trailed behind.

"This not way to Kaori," said Kentashi. "She lead us into Hoshiki's domain."

"I thought Raiden ruled the mountains?"

"Raiden rule mountains east of river. Hoshiki rule west mountains and forest. Onedo's underworld beneath Hoshiki's mountain."

The news didn't set well with Tyrone. He hurried to catch up to her. "Mirit! Kentashi says this is Hoshiki's domain on the surface and Onedo's beneath. Are you sure of where you are going?"

"Something draws me this way and I sense it may hold the answer to what is happening and why."

Unconvinced, he inquired of Avatar and Virgil. "What do you two sense?" They appeared hesitant to answer. "Well?"

"Nothing," said Avatar with reluctance.

Mirit gripped his arm, urgency in her voice. "Please, Tyrone, you must believe me. The last thing I would do is lead you into danger."

"Tyrone? Is that not Allon king name?" asked Kentashi.

Mirit flushed at her passionate miscue.

Nigel stepped in front of Tyrone. Avatar and Virgil stood shoulder-to-shoulder beside Nigel to shield Tyrone. "Forget what you heard, Admiral," he warned.

"No, Nigel." Tyrone moved from behind them. "It's time he knows the truth."

"That you are no captain? I know. But not your true identity. Why keep it secret?"

Tyrone met Kentashi's glance and quoted, "Not know you well."

Kentashi smiled at hearing his words. "Still not explain why you in Natan in disguise."

"A series of unexpected circumstances, not intended, I assure you, Admiral."

"Remember, I tried to get him to leave when you arrived, but you said the emperor ordered all ships to port," said Nigel.

Kentashi nodded. "And boy? Is he your son?"

"Ay, and the reason I'm here."

"How?"

Tyrone briefly thought of how to reply then said, "At Kaori we spoke about our sons and how they learn by their mistakes. Mistakes that sometimes lead to unexpected circumstances. He wanted to come to

Natan, but I said no, so he snuck onboard. When I learned of it, I came to fetch him. That's when you arrived."

"Why lie?"

"Because the last time I set foot on foreign soil it was a plot to draw me from Allon to kill me, using my son as bait. I didn't want any misunderstanding about my presence to cause a repeat of past events. I do not have harmful intentions towards Natan. The only thing I want to do is get my people home safely."

Kentashi considered the answer.

"Lord Norkiru ordered me dressed as Natanese royalty to honor my *goddess* status. What would he have done if he discovered Tyrone's true identity?"

"He wanted us to kill each other to show strength," said Nigel. "Doubtful he would have accepted any harmless explanation."

Kentashi's gaze shifted between them, coming to rest on Tyrone. "As I say, you wise in words. This action shows same wisdom in deeds. For Norkiru would be much angry if he knew."

They heard the screeching of a firebird.

"We need to find this place quickly!" She grabbed Tyrone's arm.

"Ay. Lead on."

They hastened up the final ascent to a small plateau. In middle of the plateau, stood a round, pillared dome. At the apex of the dome was the figure of a catbird.

"There!" she declared.

"Are you sure? It doesn't look like much," said Tyrone.

The screech became louder and a large firebird, swooped down, shooting a stream of flame at them.

"Take cover!" shouted Nigel, and they ran to the dome.

<hr/>

Titus, Chad, Egan and Ridge heard the firebird and voices.

"Sounds like Mirit and Tyrone," said Ridge. He changed course.

They reached the edge of the tree line to the plateau just as Nigel shouted his warning. The others rushed to take shelter under the dome. The firebird attacked the dome with a stream of flame. A the fireball hit the top of the dome the same time white light sprung up from under the dome. The combined forced of both blew the top off the dome, shattering the pillars. Akido arrived and chased off the firebird.

"Father!" Titus ran to the dome, now reduced to rubble. "Where are they?"

Chad searched the ruins, a frantic Titus helping him. After a few moments, he stopped and shook his head in momentary disbelief. "We saw them go inside. They couldn't just vanish. Could they?" he asked the Guardians.

Ridge knelt to examine what appeared to be a broken and scarred tablet with writing. "Natanese, but some words appear to be Ancient." He handed a piece to Egan and pointed to a phrase. Egan's expression turned grim after reading.

"What is it?" asked Chad.

"This was a portal to another dimension," replied Egan.

"Does the table say where?"

"No, and I believe the firebird destroyed it so it couldn't be used again or the location revealed."

"What about another portal? Does it mention another location?" Chad tried to read over the Guardian's arm.

"No."

"Then what can we do?" asked Titus.

"Find them," said Ridge.

"You can do that?"

Ridge smiled at the boy. "I'm a ranger, and created to find things." He returned to the dome, knelt and placed his hands on the floor.

"Please, Jor'el, let him find them," prayed Titus.

For several moments Ridge didn't move. Finally, a satisfied smile appeared. He opened his eyes, stood and brushed off his hands. "That way."

Titus practically ran in the direction Ridge pointed, Chad at his heels

Egan grabbed Ridge to delay departure. With set features and low, threatening voice he spoke. "Be careful, ranger. If your tracking causes any harm to my charge, it will be your last act."

Ridge matched Egan in feature and response. "Mind your threats, warrior. I've bested more powerful ones than you, including Armus." He jerked away and hurried from the dome, Egan not far behind.

Chapter 17

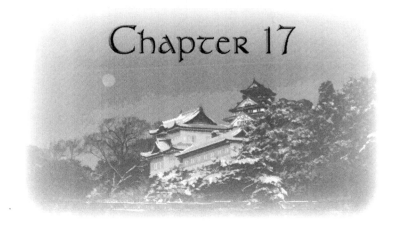

NIGEL'S EYES REMAINED CLOSED. HE HEARD VOICES, BUT real or imagined? One voice grew more distinct and very insistent in saying his name. Hands seized him and his eyes snapped open. Through a brief haze, he recognized Tyrone held him by the shoulders.

"Thank Jor'el," said Tyrone in relief. "I wanted to make sure you were alive."

Nigel sluggishly looked around to get his bearings. They appeared to be in a dim, cool, damp cavern. "Where are we?"

"Onedo's domain," said Kentashi. He stood near an opening with his sword drawn as if standing guard.

"The underworld? How did we get here?"

"The dome was a portal," said Virgil.

Nigel blinked his eyes, still a bit groggy. "Where's Mirit?"

Tyrone hesitated and pursed his lips. "We don't know."

"What?" Nigel got up too fast and clumsily fell to his knees. Tyrone helped him sit against the wall.

"Avatar and Virgil made a quick search but couldn't find her."

"She may not have been transported with us and is still at the dome. We were waiting for you to wake before making a concerted effort of focusing on her essence," said Avatar.

"You haven't been able to sense much of anything," groused Nigel. He rubbed his eyes in an effort to ward off the grogginess.

"Of Natan origin no, but we still can sense you and the others."

"Can we go back by way of portal?" asked Kentashi.

Avatar shook his head and pointed at the damage. "See the scorch marks? The firebird's attack rendered it useless. We'll have to locate another."

"Not before finding Mirit." Nigel pressed his hand against the wall for balance. He took a grateful breath when standing on his own.

Avatar and Virgil closed their eyes, and for a long moment, remained motionless. Virgil hissed in surprise and his eyes snapped open. "She's here! And in grave danger." He ran from the room.

"Go. I'll keep the rear," said Avatar to the mortals.

Mirit fought against grogginess to open her eyes. She stood between two pillars, held there by chains around her wrists and ankles. The pillars were located in the middle of an enormous cavernous room. Many torches illuminated the cavern, revealing various cages and instruments of capture or torture, but no one else.

"Nigel? Tyrone?" she called in a harsh uncertain whisper. She flinched when her voice echoed in the chamber then followed by a mocking laugh that seemed to come for all around her. "Who's there?"

No immediate answer came, but the laughter grew louder until she determined the direction it came. She cranked her head to see. A very tall, large being enter the room, definitely the height of a Guardian warrior, and massive in bulk, even more so than Armus. He had long black hair, fiery orange eyes, and wore the same plated armor of the Natanese warriors only black and trimmed with red-orange material. A sword hung at each hip.

Fear gripped her when he stopped in front of her, but she managed to ask, "Who are you?"

"I am Onedo, god of the underworld, Mirit, daughter of Willis."

"You know who I am?"

Again he laughed with mockery. "Why do you think I drew you here?"

She shook her head, fearful and wary. "I don't know."

He took her face in one large hand and tilted her head to look directly in her eyes. "You truly have no idea why you are here."

"No."

He released her. A wicked smile grew on his lips. "To help send my enemy into oblivion and prevent a blood debt from being repaid."

"I don't understand."

"I speak of Raiden. But you wouldn't know him by that name."

"I don't know him at all, except from what the Natanese have said."

"Your ancestor, Lord Willis, knew him well. In fact, he was Willis' Guardian Overseer until he betrayed him to Grand Master Farley by killing another Guardian in cold blood so they could assassinate Willis. Now he faces eternal oblivion for his crime. I intend to see he gets his final punishment and take total control of the region."

The explanation proved confusing, but she couldn't think past the obvious question. "Where does the blood debt come in?"

"Through the sacrifice, of Lord Willis' descendent—you."

Sacrifice! Frantically, she attempted to jerk free of the chain, and kept tugging until he physically stopped her. His face taut and fiery-orange eyes intensified, making her cry out in terror and turn away.

"By using you as bait I draw him out. He wouldn't miss his only opportunity to repay the debt, and when I have him, you'll both be destroyed."

A dragon's roar echoed in the chamber. Evidence of flames came from the adjacent corridor. Akido flew into the cavern, breathing fire. Onedo drew both swords and crossed them in front of his face to intercept the flames. He spoke in a mix of Natanese and the Ancient, and flung the flames back at Akido. The dragon dodged the attack and made a sweeping return arc to dive at Onedo, who ducked to avoid the dragon. Akido's back claws broke the chains holding Mirit's wrists. Onedo moved to seize her but a blast sent him flying across the cavern.

A very tall, slender and hooded figure arrived, a large sheathed sword strapped to his back. He knelt to deal with the ankle fetters. "*Sgaoil!*" he said and they opened. He stood, snatched her arm and began to hurry away

"Raiden!" Onedo leapt in the air, did a somersault and landed in front of them, both swords ready. "I waited too long for this to be over so quickly."

Raiden shoved Mirit aside and he drew his sword in time to block Onedo's attack. His hood fell back, revealing thick white hair, making him appear older than Onedo. But he proved fast and agile during the exchange of blows. When Raiden moved too far to one side, Onedo sent him tumbling from a strike by the pommel of his sword. Raiden barely got to his knees when Onedo leapt at him, both swords ready to strike. Akido's rear claws clipped Onedo, sending him crashing into a far wall.

Not waiting for Onedo to recover, Raiden scrambled to his feet. "Quickly!" He and Mirit raced down a smaller corridor. Akido's cry echoed behind them.

"What about Akido?" she asked.

"He'll be fine. I must get you out of here."

She stopped. "I can't leave the others."

"I've not seen any others." He pulled on her arm but she resisted, so he forced her to move.

"No! My husband and Tyrone."

"Tyrone?" Disconcertion reflected his bright violet eyes.

"Ay, King of Allon. The Great King of Guardians and mortals. Your king."

He searched her face and eyes. "Onedo told you, didn't he?"

"Ay."

An angry shout came from the cavern.

He snatched her hand. "I'll see if I can find them, but after I get you to safety."

Virgil led the group down a corridor when they heard a dragon's cry and stopped. "Sounds like Akido."

"How did it get in here?" asked Tyrone.

"Raiden and Akido are one," said Kentashi.

"However it did, the roar is coming from the direction we're heading." Virgil drew his sword. The others also armed themselves and ran toward the dragon's roar.

Virgil came to a sharp halt upon reaching the main cavern. Akido battled half a dozen smaller firebirds, flames crisscrossing through the air. From an adjacent room ten catbird creatures rushed towards them. They were the size of small mountain lions with the head and beak of a bird, sharp talons on their paws and a tail with fan feathers.

Avatar joined Virgil in front of the mortals to meet the first wave of attacking creatures. Two leapt at Avatar, and one was decapitated but the second took the Guardian down. His sword fell away on impact, but he managed to hold the creature's head at bay, the razor point of the beak inching toward his face. He managed to get his feet under the beast and kick it off. He rolled toward his sword, grabbed it and held it point up just as the beast leapt at him, impaling itself on the blade. He had to release the sword when the creature fell. Rising, he placed a foot on the carcass to jerk the sword free.

Tyrone fell backwards at Avatar's feet. The Guardian immediately placed himself at the ready to protect, but saw the dead body of another beast.

"Sire?" He gave Tyrone a hand up.

"I'm all right. I tripped withdrawing my sword."

A short distance from the beast Tyrone killed, Kentashi lay not moving. Avatar went to the admiral and felt for a pulse.

"He's alive." He glanced around to assess the situation.

Virgil dealt with two more beasts. One firebird remained but Akido was nowhere in sight. A roar alerted him and Tyrone to two more beasts charging them. One reared back on its hind legs and Avatar swung his sword cutting off the beast's front legs. It fell aside yowling in pain. Tyrone sidestepped to avoid the other beast. A back swing of his sword sliced its hindquarters. When it turned to attack him, he thrust his sword in its chest.

"Nigel!" shouted Virgil.

An attacking firebird drove Nigel back to the platform. A catbird raced toward him. He jumped onto the platform and turned, sword first to make a stand against the firebird and charging beast. When the beast leapt at him, he stepped back and a flash of light sprung up from the platform. He and the beast disappeared the moment the firebird sent a ball of fire at the platform igniting it.

Avatar raced toward the platform but forced to stop and shield his face from the intense heat of the flames.

"Do you see him?" asked Tyrone.

"I can't see anything! Nigel?"

"It's a portal. A flash of white light came from the floor before the firebird attacked," said Virgil.

They were surprised by water thrown on the flames. Kentashi held a bucket. "Spring there." He moved toward the spring when Virgil stopped him.

"No need for water." Virgil held his sword in front of his body and spoke in the Ancient; "*Na teintean gu deigh!*" and struck the platform. Instantly the fire turned to ice.

Kentashi took an impulsive, astonished step back.

Avatar looked askew at Virgil. "You could have done that earlier."

"I did." Virgil motioned to where three catbirds stood frozen.

"And the attack on the plateau?" chided Tyrone.

Virgil heaved an apologetic shrug. "I missed."

"Where prince?" asked Kentashi.

Avatar closed his eyes and took a deep breath. The effort of concentration needed showed on his taut features and tightly pressed lips. After a loud exhalation of release, he opened his eyes. "Alive, but not nearby."

Akido roared. The dragon hovered over a connecting corridor too small for him.

"She went that way." Virgil raced toward the corridor with the others at his heels.

<hr />

On the surface, Ridge, Egan, Chad and Titus tried to keep to the shadow of the trees and mountain. Several times, the eerie screech of firebirds echoed overhead, but they managed to elude being spotted. Before a clearing, they took shelter in a cleft of the mountain wall, watching the firebirds circling above.

"If we keep hiding we could lose any chance of finding the others," chided Egan.

"I won't lose the trail," said Ridge.

"What will you find at the end, ranger? Death or success?"

"What do you mean, Egan?" asked Titus, very concerned. "You think they're dead? Like Allard?"

"He didn't mean that," Chad rebuked the Guardian warrior.

"He meant me." Ridge tossed an angry glare at Egan before leaving the cleft. "This way!" he called back.

Titus grabbed Egan's hand. "Egan?"

The warrior hesitated in replying.

"We better leave before Ridge gets too far ahead," said Chad.

Egan ushered Titus from the cleft to follow Chad, only the boy resisted, staring up at him.

"How could you mean something terrible about Ridge?"

Egan scowled in regret and frustration. "I spoke wrongly. We Guardians do grow edgy and ill-tempered at times."

"You're not like that even when I provoke you. But you act mean to Ridge, and why wish him dead? I didn't think Guardians wanted to harm each other."

The question stymied Egan, along with the befuddled, fearful gaze of his charge. Avatar's warning plea sprang to mind, and in that moment he realized he did allow bitterness to control him and affect Titus. A hard tug on the arm broke his stupor.

"Egan?"

He forced a reply. "It's a long and painful story. I'm sorry to upset you. It won't happen again, I promise."

"Ridge found something!" called Chad. He was about a hundred yards from them, pointing to where Ridge stood at the crest of a slope.

"Father!" said Titus hopeful and ran to join Chad and Ridge. "Do you see them?" he asked Ridge, expectant for any signs of the others.

"No. I sense another portal up ahead. We might find answers there."

A flash of light appeared through the trees. They picked up the pace to reach the tree line of a small clearing. Screeching and snarling brought Egan beside Ridge, both ready for danger. Someone appeared pinned beneath a beast rising on its hind legs to strike. Egan's dagger flew, hitting the beast at the base of the skull. Ridge's staff sent the dying beast off its victim.

"Uncle!" screamed Titus. He fell to his knees beside Nigel, who lay motionless. Claw marks cut his neck and tore through his uniform to his chest. "Please, wake up!" Nigel didn't respond or move to his prodding and Titus whimpered, "No, Uncle."

Egan knelt opposite Titus and felt for a pulse. "He's alive, just unconscious." He placed his hand on Nigel's forehead and said, "Wake, son of Ellis." To his voice, Nigel began to move, sluggish and painful.

"Uncle!" urged Titus, vigorously shaking Nigel by the shoulders.

Nigel groaned and opened his eyes. "Titus?" He grunted in painful surprise when Titus fell on him to hug him. "I'm all right. Let me sit up." Titus and Egan helped him. After a moment of recovery, Nigel noticed the trees. "This isn't the cave. Where are we?"

"In a clearing further up the mountain," replied Ridge.

Again, Nigel glanced around. "Where are the others?"

"You were the only one who came through the portal."

"Is Mirit with you?"

"No, we saw her with you."

"What about Father?" asked Titus.

"He was right behind me. We've got to find them." Nigel got to his feet and swayed. He gabbed onto Chad to keep from falling. He took a deep breath to clear his head. "I thought I hated dimension travel but portals are worse. And my chest hurts."

"Claw marks from the beast."

Nigel took note of his wounds, not realizing he had been injured.

"You mentioned a cave," said Egan.

"Onedo's underworld, or so Kentashi said. It was more a maze of tunnels and caverns. We were trying to find Mirit when those creatures and several firebirds attacked us. We must go back for them."

Ridge stopped Nigel's advance to the portal. "There are scorch marks on the bottom." He picked up several rocks and tossed them onto the portal. Nothing happened. "We won't go back that way. Something must have destroyed it on the other side."

"They were right behind me when I stepped onto the platform!"

"It doesn't mean harm has come to them," said Chad, trying to sound encouraging.

"We were under attack! Can you find another portal quickly?" he asked Ridge.

"I found this one."

"Egan, take Titus and get back to the ship."

"What? No, I'm not leaving," protested Titus.

"Take him!" Nigel commanded before turning to leave with Ridge and Chad.

Titus ran in front from of Nigel. "No! Uncle. I'm going with you to find Father and Aunt Mirit."

243

Nigel seized the boy by the shoulders. "The king is missing and in mortal danger. You are the prince royal. If I can't find him, you will be king!"

Titus paled at the implication. "I don't want to be king. Not like this."

"You should have thought of that before stowing away. It's because of you he's here!" He shoved Titus at Egan and again, started to leave.

"Uncle, please! I want to find him. I need to find him. To tell him I'm sorry and I love him," said Titus with tears of despair.

Nigel stopped, anger and regret on his face. For a long moment he regarded nephew to bring his temper under control. "Aside from the fact he has become my brother and I want to find him for the same reason as you, I have a sworn duty to protect the king." When the boy shook his head to the contrary, Nigel spoke with urgency. "Don't you understand? You must be kept safe so I can fulfill my duty!"

"You and Father told me it's wrong to let others suffer for my mistakes. I never understood why until Lord Allard died protecting me."

"Allard?" repeated Nigel in dreadful surprise.

Chad gave a grim nod of affirmation.

Titus continued unaware of the exchange. "I guess I knew it in Tunlund with Aunt Mirit, but I didn't fully understand because Jor'el restored her life. Not Allard. Now we could lose Father and Aunt Mirit because of my selfishness! I don't want that to happen. Please, Uncle, let me come with you."

Nigel took a deep contemplating breath at hearing the passionate speech. "What about your responsibility to Allon?"

Titus squared his shoulders, trying to put on a brave face. "If the worst occurs, I will step aside and you can be king since you were born heir before I."

Nigel stared at Titus, taken aback by the offer. His reply was interrupted by Ridge's hand on his shoulder and warning.

"Something stirs. We must move swiftly."

Nigel nodded, though his focus remained on Titus. "A bargain. If we have not found another portal by midnight, you will leave with Egan for the ship and have Gulliver take you home. I will remain to search for them. No questions, no argument. Allon must not be without a king."

Titus swallowed back his emotions to reply. "Ay."

They left the clearing to move further up the mountain.

Chapter 18

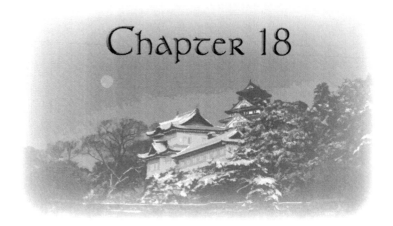

DURING THEIR ESCAPE, MIRIT CONSIDERED ALL ONEDO SAID about the past and Willis, then Raiden's appearance. Some things made sense while others didn't, like Onedo saying Raiden was Willis' Overseer when Egan claimed to be Willis' Overseer. How is that possible? Yet as much as she wanted to ask Raiden questions, the most important priority was finding the others. However, he moved in such haste she wondered how they would accomplish that.

"Do you know where they are that you're moving fast?" she asked.

"I told you, I'll find them once I get you to safety."

She stopped. "And I told you, I'm not leaving with out them!"

"If I take the time to locate them, Onedo will learn our location and come after us."

"I'll take the chance."

"I won't!" He seized her arm and pulled her to continue, but she resisted. "You don't understand what is at stake. You must trust me if you and your friends are to survive."

Being no match for a Guardian, she snapped in frustration. "All right! We'll do it your way. Now let me go, you're hurting my arm and shoulder."

He didn't immediately comply, looking squarely at her. "I hope you mean that, because the cost of failure is beyond anything you can imagine."

The truth in his violet eyes made her shiver and her voice barely above a whisper. "Ay."

He released her and they continued. His warning brought new questions to mind regarding the situation and fate of the others. Why did she feel so many disturbing sensations when the Guardians didn't? Oh, how she wished for the ability to concentrate and reach out her mind like Avatar and the others to know if they were safe or even alive. She shivered at the thought Raiden wasn't looking for them because he knew they were dead. No! Nigel would protect Tyrone while the Guardians would keep all of them alive. She had to concentrate on escaping the underworld and rejoining them. Any other thoughts were distracting and not helpful.

Rounding a corner, they came to a very narrow crossing over a chasm. The width was barely a foot wide and each side sloped down into the dark unknown with only a dim light far below. Raiden didn't pause in step when crossing the chasm, but Mirit did, wary and uncertain.

Nearly to the other side, he stopped. "Are you afraid of heights?"

"No. I climbed the main mast of my father's ship, but I'd like to see the bottom."

"Focus on me and pretend you're on the mast."

She fixed her eyes on him and began walking. Barely a half-dozen steps onto the crosswalk, it gave way and she slid down into the chasm, screaming. At the bottom of the chasm, she tumbled across the floor and into the opposite wall. Dazed, she lay not wanting to move until her heart stopped racing and she could breathe normally. First she heard then saw small rocks falling down the slope. Raiden slid down on his heels toward her. He just reached her, when someone slammed him face first against the wall and held him there.

"What were you doing to her? Answer truthfully or you'll feel my sword!"

"Virgil, no!" Mirit struggled to her knees and continued her hurried explanation. "He is Raiden and helped me escaped from Onedo."

Tyrone pulled Mirit to her feet and away from Raiden. "Are you hurt?" he asked, anxious of her condition.

"Only if you consider tumbling down another slope painful," she said and hugged him in relief.

Virgil grabbed Raiden's right arm and twisted it behind Raiden's back. "I asked a question. What were you doing to her?"

Raiden winced in pain and spoke through clenched teeth. "You will join me in oblivion if you kill me."

"Turn him around," commanded Avatar.

Virgil obliged, but held Raiden against the wall.

Avatar stepped up to study Raiden. When their eyes met, Avatar paled in surprised horror and uttered, "*Auch mallaich!*"

"Accursed?" echoed Virgil, at first stunned then angry. "I'll kill him." He reached for dagger but Avatar bodily prevented him.

When Virgil resisted, Avatar commanded in the Ancient. "*Seasamh sios!*" The order brought Virgil's attention to Avatar, the silver eyes narrow in warning. "Stand down!" he repeated.

"Ay, Lieutenant." Virgil stepped back.

Avatar regarded Raiden, cautious and not direct. "What is your real name?"

"My name no longer exists and even I told you, you would not remember me, Avatar of the Lightning Sword."

As if hit by a hard, stunning blow, Avatar's legs gave way, making him stumble and fall. Virgil took up a defensive position between Avatar and Raiden, sword drawn, but Raiden didn't move.

Tyrone aided Avatar to sit on a boulder. "What did you do to him?" he demanded.

"Nothing, my lord king. He nearly did something to himself."

"Don't listen to him, Sire, he's accursed!" Virgil raised his sword.

"I said stand down!" Even speaking a command, Avatar's voice was thick with emotion. "He is correct. Twice before I allowed passion to get the better of me, but thank Jor'el tragic consequences were avoided. The most recent happened in Tunlund." He spoke to Mirit. "On the battlefield, I met Hueil, who was going to let me kill him, unarmed and without a fight. If I had done so, you, Nigel and Titus would be dead and I cease to exist for I would have killed a fellow Guardian in cold blood. Just another way Hueil taunted me."

"But you didn't and we survived," she kindly insisted.

"Raiden still here, how not exist?" asked Kentashi.

Avatar's voice sounded stronger and some color returned to his face. "Physically he is alive, but in spirit he is nothingness. That's how I knew he is accursed. There is no life to his eyes, no trace of his Guardian essence. Anything he did in the past is forgotten, or worse, never happened."

"But Raiden help us, help my people."

Avatar shrugged, uncertain. "Here in Natan maybe different, I don't know, but in Allon, his existence and even the memory of him has been wiped out. Same as mine would have if I had succumbed. The punishment is remaining alive to watch, knowing your existence is meaningless."

Raiden shook his head, his expression doleful. "There is no difference here. When I physically cease, I will be forgotten."

"I'll not forget," declared Kentashi.

Raiden grin at the statement, but short-lived and poignant.

Avatar stood and squared his shoulder to assume a braced posture to look again at Raiden. "Why are you helping her?"

"To repay a blood debt to her ancestor."

Mirit became confused. "Onedo said you killed a Guardian, which allowed Lord Willis to be assassinated. Why help me but let my ancestor be killed?"

Raiden sighed with great regret. "The act has plagued me for centuries. I don't know if my explanation will suffice. I didn't mean for Willis to die. Everything happened because of unbridled passion." He sent a quick side-glance to Avatar and saw the warrior's narrow inquisitive regard, but returned his focus to Mirit as he continued.

"Perry and I never got along. Why, I don't know. I heard of his promotion to Trio Leader while I remained a mortal's overseer. At a chance meeting he made some snide comment and I struck, quick and deadly. When he vanished, I became horrified at what I'd done, but it was too late. I crossed the line and couldn't return to my charge. My absence left Willis vulnerable."

"Willis was Egan's charge," refuted Virgil.

"Kell gave Egan charge after I killed Perry in hopes of preventing the assassination. Although a half-brother, Willis was older than Segar, who wanted him dead to keep him from claiming the throne. My foolish pride cleared the way for Grand Master Farley to use the Dark Way to kill Willis."

Virgil's jowls tightened. "Egan believes the whole situation was his fault and has carried guilt for centuries."

Raiden heaved a hapless shrug. "In Egan's mind, he was Willis' Overseer. I can do little to change his belief since I no longer exist."

The explanation didn't satisfy Virgil but Kentashi spoke before the warrior further accosted Raiden. "I still not understand how he can exist but not exist. He does many wonders."

Avatar answered. "Because he no longer possesses his Guardian essence, his power has no lasting effect beyond the moment. It is better to be dead than never to have existed," he murmured the last sentence.

Mirit took hold of Avatar's arm, her face sympathetic. "You're neither."

He flashed a small smile at her encouraging effort. "It is also the reason we haven't been able to sense him and why you have."

"Ay. He is *nothing* in our ranks," added Virgil.

"But you sense evil," said Kentashi in confusion.

"Onedo," said Tyrone.

"No, Onedo is like me," began Raiden. "He is the one Farley employed to kill Willis and thwart Egan and Ridge from finding him and preventing Segar from becoming king. Before being forced by Jor'el to flee, I pointed Vidar after him. In the process of evading capture, he too killed a Guardian by the name of Corwin."

Pricked, Virgil stirred again in anger. "Corwin was created the same time as Jedrek and I!"

Tyrone stopped Virgil from advancing on Raiden with a hand on the Guardian's chest. He asked, "Does Onedo know you told Vidar?"

"Ay, and he followed me to Natan seeking revenge. We've battled for centuries under new identities. After learning about the invitation, he took advantage to start a civil war to gain complete control of Natan while killing any Allonians in the process. However, once your presence was discovered, it became more personal," he said to Mirit.

"Will repaying the debt help to redeem you?" she asked.

Raiden kindly grinned but shook his head. "No. Once a Guardian betrays Jor'el and his station, there is no redemption. However," he added at her distress, "it will help me face my destruction with some consolation. Now, we have talked too long. I sense Onedo is moving his forces toward this part of the cavern." He took the lead.

Virgil stayed close on Raiden's heel with Kentashi following. Avatar took Mirit's arm as escort. Tyrone remained with them.

"Where is Nigel?" she asked Avatar.

"We don't know. He disappeared through another portal when we battled some of Onedo's creatures. Virgil tracked you."

"Can't you sense where Nigel is?"

"I have tried but I don't think he's in this world any more."

She stopped, turning pale with fear. "He's dead?"

"No!" said Tyrone in a quick effort to calm her. "He means Onedo's underworld, this dimension."

"Ay," said Avatar, abashed by his miscue. "Nigel's probably back on the surface and the separation of the dimensions prevents me from sensing him." She struggled to get her emotions under control so he took her face in his hands to get her attention. "Mirit, I'm truly sorry. It was bad choice of words. I *know* Nigel is alive. I just don't know his exact location."

"I'll be all right. It was just a shock to hear on top of what Raiden said."

"Shock I understand," he said with normal dry wit. "When I saw nothingness in his eyes, it rocked me to the core. I never before came face-to-face with one who is accursed and devoid of all life." His voice fell to almost a whisper. "At that moment I realized, I was looking at myself and what I could have become."

"You didn't, and I can't tell you how grateful I am for that. I saw Nigel's grief in Misow when he believed you would die from your wounds. He bitterly wept and I couldn't comfort him. Not that he would accept comfort from me back then, but all the same, it broke my heart to see his grief."

Avatar wryly grinned. "I too am grateful everything worked out. He'd still be a handful for me if not for you taking some of the burden."

She laughed then turned serious again. "You can track him once we're on the surface, correct?"

He tossed a smiling glance to Tyrone then back to her. "Of course. All I have to do is follow the trail of destruction he leaves behind trying to find you and Tyrone."

Virgil kept Raiden within arms' reach. Avatar prevented him from doing the unthinkable, but he would not trust an accursed Guardian with the lives of the king and Mirit. After the tenth turn in an endless series of tunnels, he finally asked, "Do you know where you're going?"

"East. The closer I can get us to my domain, the less influence Onedo has."

"What about just finding another portal to the surface?" asked Tyrone. He and the others had closed the gap.

"Because he'll be expecting us and have them guarded. Remember he wants to kill us."

"No, he wants to kill *you*," corrected Virgil.

Raiden stopped and accosted Virgil. "By using Mirit!"

When Virgil gripped the hilt of his sword, Mirit stepped in between them. "He's right. Beside, he has proven he wants to help."

Virgil stared over her head at Raiden. "He's accursed. I don't trust him."

"But I do." She gripped his arm to get his attention. "Virgil. I appreciate your concern, but in this you are mistaken. Please, if you can't trust him, then trust me."

The conflict of complying with her request made Virgil's jowls flex.

"She's been right so far," said Tyrone.

"If you say so, Sire," his grumbled in reluctant agreement.

"Proceed," said Tyrone to Raiden. He held Virgil back, allowing the others to move ahead of them. "I approve of your diligence, and agree we must be on our guard. However, what many of us cannot sense on this venture, Mirit can. I suspect that is due to the blood debt, or more rightly, Jor'el granting justice and mercy."

"Not to an accursed Guardian!"

"To Mirit, her family, Egan and Ridge. For too long justice has languished and now the truth is finally revealed."

Virgil's posture went from defensive to considerate. "I hadn't thought of it as truth and justice."

"No," said Tyrone with a kind smile. "Your first thought is to protect *your* charge. After all, isn't what she's become since arriving in Natan?"

"Avatar told me to stay close to her."

Tyrone's smile grew. "He didn't tell you to start sharing her senses. I've seen it grow since we left Kaori, and you located her. Only Jor'el can grant such a connection."

Virgil grew thoughtful. "There is truth to what you say, Sire. But how can I be her Overseer when Avatar is already Overseer to the prince?"

"Avatar's status has changed over the years. Although he and Nigel became reunited after the coup, more commands have been given to him since then. Allard was the natural choice to lead the diplomatic core of this journey, but by Jor'el's instruction Avatar became commander and for you to accompany him in watching over Nigel and Mirit. With Avatar being of the elite Trio, there was no need for Kell or Armus to accompany me when I came to fetch Titus."

Virgil looked somewhat surprised. "Are you suggesting I replace him?"

Tyrone shrugged. "I don't know, but before Avatar can be given a new assignment, someone must be ready to take his place since no royal can be without a Guardian Overseer."

"What about the bond between he and Nigel?"

"Nothing will change the bond, only circumstances change."

Virgil turned his attention to the group ahead of them. Avatar listened to something Mirit said and chuckled in response. "Does he know or suspect?"

"Probably, but we haven't spoken. Until we return home safely, say nothing. Just remain true to your task and let the rest happen as Jor'el wills."

"Ay, Sire."

A low rumble started and grew louder, making them stop to listen. Only the rumbling wasn't from above, it came from below. The ground started moving beneath their feet and rocks fell off the wall and the noise grew thunderous.

"Earthquake!" Kentashi seized Mirit out of the way of a boulder falling off the wall.

She cried out in pain when a smaller rock clipped her shoulder. More rocks fell from the crumbling wall and some started falling from the ceiling. One knocked Kentashi off his feet and she jumped back to avoid more rocks. Tyrone had difficulty staying on his feet. Avatar and Virgil tried to help the mortals.

"Take shelter in the underpass!" Raiden indicated a rock walkway overhead from a higher corridor.

"It'll fall on top of us!" Avatar protested. He helped Tyrone to stand.

"No! I'll hold it up. Now move!" Raiden grabbed Kentashi and made for the shelter.

Mirit stumbled toward the underpass so Virgil aided her. Tyrone fell again and Avatar practically carried him. They dove under the crosswalk just before a large part of the ceiling came crashing down.

Raiden lifted his hands over his head and spoke; "Rock be still and remain steadfast, shield us from the falling blast!"

Mirit cried out in surprise when a small avalanche slid in front of one opening of the underpass. Virgil shielded her from the dust and debris.

Raiden's face shone with great strain, yet his arms remained overhead. More rocks and debris fell on the other side of the underpass, blocking both sides. Still, the crosswalk held. A moment later the shaking stopped, but some debris still fell before settling. When everything grew quiet and the dust settled, Raiden collapsed to his knees in exhaustion.

"Anyone hurt?" he asked.

"No," said Tyrone. He brushed off dust from his hair and face. "Mirit?"

"My shoulder's a bit sore, but I'm all right." She knelt beside Raiden. "What about you?"

He weakly smiled. "I'll be fine in a moment."

Avatar examined both blocked openings. "We'll have to dig our way out."

"Quickly and quietly. Onedo sent the quake to finish us. If we can make it look like we were buried alive, we may fool him," said Raiden.

"There appears to be more of an opening on this side." Avatar indicated the way their were originally heading. He climbed to the top and began testing the rocks. Finding a spot where the rocks easily moved, he took one at a time and handed them down to the others. It was a laborious task and he didn't stop to inspect the work until he created a three-foot opening.

"Can you fit through?" asked Tyrone.

Mirit sarcastically snorted. "Of course he can't, but I can. I am the smallest here." Tyrone didn't appear to agree with her assessment, so she continued. "This is taking too long. Perhaps on the other side I can see a better way out."

Tyrone waved Avatar down. "Let her try."

Once Avatar reached the bottom, Mirit began to climb up.

"I'll be right behind you in case the rocks become unstable," said Avatar.

She reached the opening. Avatar stopped far enough to give her clearance to fit through the hole, yet close enough to aid her if necessary.

"Here I go." She wiggled through the opening, trying not to displace any rocks. Unfortunately, her hand slipped and she went sliding down headfirst.

"Mirit!" Avatar hoisted himself up to the opening and looked down. She sat at the bottom of the rocks brushing off debris.

"I'm all right," she groused and stood. She scowled in observance of the landslide. "The rocks go above the crosswalk and I can't get around to the other side. The hole is the only way and the rest appears stable enough to make it larger."

"Any sign of activity?" she heard Raiden call.

She couldn't see past the pile of rocks, so she moved further back, away from the crosswalk. "No—Akido?" she said the dragon's name then cried in fear, staggering and falling to her knees. "Nigel."

"What's wrong?" Avatar tried to fit through the opening when she didn't immediately reply, but couldn't. "Mirit!"

"Through Akido's eyes I saw Nigel and the others are in danger! We must hurry."

"Move back!" Avatar waved at her before disappearing from the opening and shouting, "Virgil!"

She barely moved away in time before a crash and half the rocks were blown away. In the opening stood Avatar and Virgil with their swords swung to opposite sides, both breathing heavy.

"I said quietly and without power," chided Raiden. "Now Onedo will know where we are!"

Avatar slammed his sword back in his scabbard and moved to Mirit. "Can you tell where they are?"

She shook her head. "Somewhere above us, moving parallel, I think."

"She's right. Akido is flying northeast," said Raiden.

"How did he get out? For that matter, how did he get in?" asked Tyrone.

"Through a secret fissure I created during one of my many battles with Onedo."

"So we can get out that way?"

"If it's still undiscovered or the earthquake hasn't blocked it."

"Dimension travel would be fastest," said Virgil.

"The fissure is safer!" Raiden took Mirit's arm and hurried in the direction he indicated.

⁂

On the surface, Titus huffed and struggled to keep up when Ridge led them down the other side of the crest. He couldn't see the ranger, but Nigel and Chad were about twenty yards ahead. They must be able to see Ridge. Titus tried to catch up, but slipped and slid down the incline toward a large stream at the bottom. He screwed his eyes shut preparing to hit the water when hands grabbed him and lifted him off the ground. His eyes snapped open to see Ridge holding him.

"Wouldn't do for you to get wet." Ridge smiled and set Titus on his feet.

Egan arrived in a rush. "Are you injured?" he asked Titus.

"No. Thanks to Ridge."

"Rest." Ridge pointed to a log.

"We don't have time," refuted Nigel.

"There is time. None of you have eaten since last night and your wounds should be cleansed."

For a brief moment Nigel regarded Ridge, the ranger's light golden eyes soothing. "Very well, but not too long."

Ridge grinned. "I found some roots. Not a hardy meal, but will serve. I was cleaning them when the young prince began playing." He picked up three pale yellow roots laying at the water's edge.

257

"Playing?" echoed Titus, making Ridge laugh. He accepted the root, tentative in examining it. "What is it?"

"It's harmless, I took a taste. Similar to a carrot and turnip." He gave a root to Nigel and Chad.

"Hand me the pouch and I'll tend the prince's wounds," said Egan.

Chad yielded the medical bag.

Egan took out his dagger and cut off a portion of the hem of his uniform to use as cleansing rags. He moved to the stream to wet the cloth.

"It tastes a more like a turnip than a carrot," said Chad.

"I don't like turnips," groused Titus while chewing.

Chad shrugged. "It's a change from rice."

Nigel chuckled then stopped to let Egan clean the claw marks on his neck and chest. He hissed and flinched. "That's cold!"

"Think how cold I would have been, Uncle," said Titus. He took another unpleasant bite of the root.

Ten minutes passed for Nigel's wounds to be tended and for the mortals to eat. Ridge led them upstream. Cliffs rose in the near distance.

"Do we have to climb again?" asked Titus.

"No. We're actually on the northern lower plateau of the Kaori mountain range. I sense a portal through that passage between the cliffs."

Suddenly a rumbling noise began, followed by the ground shaking. Chad caught Titus to keep him from falling. Nigel stumbled into a tree. At the cliffs, rocks around the passage started to crumble.

"Quickly! Before the passage is blocked!" said Ridge.

They made their way as best they could due to violent shaking. From the plateau side, five dogmen leapt at them.

Egan pulled Nigel out of the way and drew his sword. "Keep going!"

Nigel joined Chad and Titus in defense of cutting down the dogmen impeding their attempt to reach the passage. Nigel landed a blow that severed the arm of one dogman, sending it yowling in retreat. Egan killed one and Ridge batted another aside.

Akido arrived, roaring and sending flames at the three remaining dogmen to halt the advance. This gave them time to enter the passage. Except for two clefts in the rocks, it turned into a dead end and the only entrance blocked by dogmen held back by Akido's flames.

Egan seized Ridge by the collar. "You led us into a trap!"

Ridge knocked Egan's grip away. "No, the portal is here, I tell you!"

At a low in the flames, the three dogmen rushed the mortals. In thwarted anger Akido circled above the fray.

"Why doesn't he send more fire?" asked Titus. He dodged a dogman.

"Because he may hit one of us," said Chad. He wounded one dogman, but the beast proved relentless and kept coming.

Nigel dodged the lethal claws of another beast, slipping and falling on the rocky ground. He rolled away to come up behind it. His sword slashed deeply into the creature's back, which made it fall forward and into the one attacking Chad. Immediately, Chad and Egan's swords finished both dogmen.

Another dogman lunged at Titus. They stumbled toward the cleft.

"Titus!" Nigel moved toward his nephew when Ridge's dagger flew past him and lodged in the back of the beast's skull. The momentum of the strike sent Titus and the dogman into the deep cleft.

Egan seized Ridge by the throat, his sword level at the ranger's face. "He dies, you die!"

"No!" called a voice from behind and Egan found himself in a bear hug, his sword knocked from his grasp. He struggled to get free but heard a calming voice in his ear say, "*Bi samhac, Egan!* Be still," and in stunned realization he recognized … "Avatar?"

"Ay, my friend." Avatar released his restraining hold, but maintained a hand on Egan's shoulder.

To Egan's further astonishment, Tyrone carried Titus, the boy clinging to his father's neck. Nigel held Mirit while Chad and Virgil helped Kentashi. A tall, hooded figure approached him.

"Passion for your charge nearly caused you to make the same mistake you did with Willis, and for the same erroneous reason."

"How would you know?" asked Egan, guarded and demanding.

"Because I was there." Raiden removed his hood, pale violet eyes staring at Egan.

Egan paled in fear. "You are accursed!"

The declaration brought Ridge to stand beside Egan, and also stare in apprehension at Raiden. "Who are you?"

"Here I am Raiden," he answered, looking directly at Ridge. "But in Allon, my cold blooded slaying of a fellow Guardian allowed Onedo and the Dark Way to kill Willis and prevent you and Egan from finding him." He turned his focus to Egan. "Ridge didn't fail then or now, and you, Egan of the Iron Blade, bear no reproach, guilt or shame."

Egan flinched at the pronouncement as if struck.

Avatar steadied him in such a way as to make Egan face him. "I had to stop you from committing the worst act possible for a Guardian."

Egan's face and body relaxed in a wave of calm. "Thank you."

Avatar just smiled.

A warning from Akido drew their attention skyward.

"We must leave before Onedo discovers the fissure," said Raiden to the group then, "*Akido, feuch!*" The dragon acknowledged and flew off. "Come. We must hurry to reach my domain. On foot to avoid *more* trouble," he emphasized to the Guardians, but none disputed him. Although Virgil made a hostile sneer and Avatar was not pleased.

"I have to put you down now," said Tyrone.

When Titus' feet touched the ground, he seized Mirit's hand. She responded with a quick embrace and ruffle of his hair. He smiled.

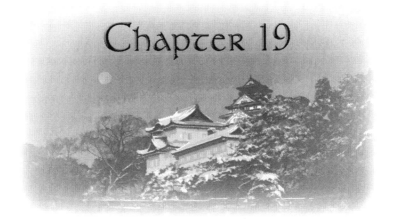

Chapter 19

RAIDEN LED THEM ALONG THE CLIFF WALL TO WHERE THE plateau began a gentle descent to an alcove off the main valley. On the other side of the valley rose a steep trail leading into the Kaori Mountains.

Titus' legs ached as he climbed the trail. He was tired and his stomach painful, more than likely from the horrible tasting root. Still, he couldn't lag behind, not after seeing how his uncle fought the dogmen even when wounded, or the prompting glances from his father, who followed him. True, he wanted to prove himself, but the situation had taken such a desperate, life-and-death turn that proof took on a different meaning.

Everything before became insignificant and petty, especially in light of Allard's death and fearing for the lives of Nigel, Mirit and his father. He thought he was mature and capable of handling any situation. This trip showed him the falsehood of his belief. Allard tried to tell him on the ship, but he wouldn't listen. Now he wanted to speak to Allard one more time and tell him he understood, to tell the old wise lord, how much he appreciated him. That being impossible, the only way to demonstrate his understanding and gratitude was by actions. Thus he determined not only to make it up the hill, but safely out of Natan and never to disappoint or disgrace his father again.

Titus slipped for the third time, but caught himself before completely falling. The gap widened between he and the lead group of Nigel, Mirit, Chad, Kentashi and Virgil. Ridge was out of sight in his shadowing of Raiden. His father and Egan came right behind him, with Avatar guarding the rear. Titus tried to pick up the pace to lessen the gap. After another hundred yards, stumbled again, this time falling to all fours. He felt hands helping his to stand.

Egan tried to be encouraging. "Not too much further. There's a cave halfway up. We'll probably stop there to eat and rest."

Titus followed Egan's indication. He sighed at seeing the steep distance of several hundred yards.

"Do you think you can make it?"

"I don't have a choice." Titus kept climbing with Egan close behind.

At a break in the slope, near the cave, Titus tripped and went sprawling to the ground. Egan reached to help him up, but he shook off the Guardian to stand. However, his legs would no longer support him. Egan caught him under the arms to keep him from falling.

"You're tired. There's no shame in saying so."

"Ay," agreed Tyrone. He took several deep breaths and arched his back. "We all could use a rest."

"You're tired, sir?" asked Titus in surprise.

Tyrone grinned. "I do get tired. Especially after battling firebirds, dogmen, catbird creatures, slamming my back against a log and surviving a earthquake-created cave-in." He held Titus' arm to guide him inside the cave. "I am half-mortal, but in case you haven't considered it, you are part Guardian also."

"I don't feel it," the boy groused.

"Maybe not, but considering the circumstances and age, your heritage is helping you to hold up very well." Tyrone sat on the ground and gingerly leaned back against the wall until he could completely relax. Titus sat beside him.

Raiden made a small fire.

"Do you think it wise?" asked Nigel.

"I can shield you. Besides, Ridge went to find game." He picked up a flask and handed it to Nigel. "Drink. Ridge said he refilled it when you paused at a stream."

Titus made a sour frown. "He gave us terrible roots to eat."

"I thought it tasted better than the rice," snickered Chad.

Nigel took a drink and handed the flask to Mirit. She took a sip and passed it to Chad, who passed it along to Tyrone when he finished. Tyrone held it out to Titus.

"You drink first, sir."

Tyrone grinned and took a swig. Titus accepted the flask and held it up to Egan, who shook his head in refusal and spoke.

"Rest. We'll stand guard."

After he drank, Titus corked the flask and set it down. He leaned his head back against the cave wall and closed his eyes. He wasn't sure how long he slept when his father woke him to eat. He hadn't even smelled the cooking game.

He yawned and asked, "What is it?"

"Venison," said Ridge. He sliced off a piece of meat to hand to Titus.

The boy glanced from the meat to the animal on the spit. "So small. Must be a fawn."

"No, it was an adult, only the size of large dog back home."

"Actually, it called, *morioshi,* forest dog," said Kentashi.

"Good and tender," said Tyrone.

Titus took a tentative bite then grinned. "Ay. Better than the root."

Ridge chuckled. "You must learn to survive on whatever edible food you find, no matter the taste."

"I'm learning a lot more than that," mumbled Titus.

Tyrone tossed an optimistic look to Nigel, who tried not to smile.

Titus noticed and grew somber. "I'm only sorry what it cost."

"Lord Allard's death is not your fault," said Egan.

"He was protecting me!" Titus sniffled and wiped his face.

"We fled an attack."

Tyrone placed a comforting arm about Titus' shoulders. "I understand your feelings, yet Egan is correct. You are not responsible for the attack."

"No, that is Rukan's treachery," said Kentashi with a sneer. "I can take all to emperor for safety until Rukan is defeated."

"No," said Tyrone. "Your offer is generous and appreciated, but we came here in hopes of establishing a friendly alliance, and will not be drawn into a civil war."

Kentashi gave his customary stout nod. "I take you safe to ships."

At the cave opening, Avatar observed the sky. "The day grows late. Is it safe to travel at night?"

"Risky since Hoshiki joined forces with Onedo, but I believe we can manage," replied Raiden.

"Who is Hoshiki? Another accursed Guardian?" chided Virgil.

Raiden shook his head with a sarcastic grunt. "She's not like any Guardian I've seen, normal or accursed. Her original name was River and she claims to have been an Enforcer. Never heard the term."

"River?" repeated Avatar.

"You said she perished in the Great Battle," said Egan.

"I believed I saw her disappear. But it must have been a ruse."

"You know her?" Raiden asked Avatar.

"Unfortunately. She was a fine warrior—before following Dagar. An Enforcer is a Shadow Warrior he infused with special strength by using the Dark Way. We've encountered them many times over the centuries."

"Often with limited success," groused Egan.

"Explains her disdain for Onedo and me since we are of the old way," said Raiden.

"Why would she join forces with him?" asked Tyrone.

Raiden shrugged. "I don't know. We're hardly on speaking terms."

"Rukan," said Kentashi. "He is devout of Hoshiki."

"You mean devoted," said Nigel.

"Ay. Make her supreme goddess of Natan if he wins."

264

Raiden smirked at the explanation. "She must have promised Onedo the power he wants if he helps Rukan succeed. Only I'm sure it's a hollow promise while Onedo has his own agenda. That is why we must proceed on foot and not dimension travel, as any use of power will draw her attention."

"You said this is your domain and you can shelter us," chided Virgil.

"I can, but as you saw on the way to Yuki, she has grown powerful enough to occasionally invade. Akido will keep watch and alert us."

"That's another question, how can the beast speak?" asked Avatar. "I've never experienced that before."

"Not to mention it looks like an overgrown kelpie," said Egan.

"It doesn't. I speak through it. A trick I learned centuries ago."

"I told you, Raiden and Akido are one," said Kentashi.

"So you manipulated a kelpie to create a dragon?" asked Avatar.

"No, the creature is native to Natan, but rare. The first *Akido, I* found as an abandoned hatchling shortly after I arrived. If not killed by natural enemies or hunters, one can live about a hundred years. I raise a new one to keep the appearance of oneness. Sorry for the deception," he said to Kentashi.

"No deception, since there is oneness if creature follow you and let you speak through it."

Raiden smiled. "It does, and it is a good companion. Now, we better get moving if we hope to make it to safety before she find us."

Mirit wiped off her hands after finishing her portion of meat. "We'll make it," she spoke with certainty. "If everyone is done eating."

Tyrone shoved the last of his portion into his mouth. Nigel tossed the bone into the fire just before Ridge extinguished the flames. Chad aided Kentashi to stand while Titus stumbled in getting to his feet.

By nightfall they reached the meadow where the caravan stopped on the way to Yuki to inspect the wagons before beginning the descent.

Raiden ran across the open meadow, urging the others to pick up the pace to reach the safety of the trees.

A shadow passed through the moonlight, making Mirit look up. Akido kept watch from above. Not paying attention to her footing, she tripped and fell into a ditch. She cried out when two very large insects, the size of mice, jumped on her.

Nigel knocked them off her using the flat of his sword. Tyrone pulled her out of the ditch. More insects materialized from the ground. The mortals used swords and daggers to kill the bugs or swat them aside.

Avatar raised his sword in front of his face and began to speak in the Ancient. Raiden seized him. "No! These are different. Light will bring more of her creatures to us. They are slow, run for the trees! *Eoin dion etroic!*" He snatched Mirit and began running.

The sound of crows filled the air, and a large flock flew over the treetops. Some birds dove and snatched up the insects. Others landed to devour the insects on the ground.

The group reached the safety of the trees, with no sign of the insects. After another quarter mile, Raiden paused to allow the mortals to catch their breath.

"Enough of this! We dimension travel them—" began Avatar, but gasped in painful surprise. He dropped to his knees then collapsed to the ground unconscious.

"Avatar?" said Nigel.

Egan moved to help Avatar, but also went down and followed in quick succession by Virgil and Ridge. All four Guardians lay unconscious.

"Egan!" Titus cried out in alarm.

Mirit watched in horror "What's happened to them?"

"Hoshiki!" sneered Raiden in anger.

Nigel knelt to examine Avatar. A small crossbow dart lodged in the back of the Guardian's left shoulder. "He's been shot!"

Frightened, Titus fell to his knees next to Egan. "No, not like Jedrek!" he whimpered and touched Egan's face. "Please, don't die, Egan. Please, don't die."

Tyrone knelt opposite Titus to examine Egan. Chad went to Ridge and Mirit examined Virgil. Each Guardian had a small dart lodge in the back of the left shoulder.

"They all have—" Tyrone gasped in distress and fell onto all fours.

"Father!"

Nigel rushed to Tyrone, who gestured to his back. A small dart lodged in back of his left shoulder. "He's been shot too."

Titus fought tears when he heard Tyrone say, "Pull them out."

"No!" argued Titus.

Tyrone fought to stay conscious and seized Nigel. "Stygian. Do it!"

"Brace yourself." Nigel waited for Tyrone to nod, grabbed the dart and yanked it out. Tyrone cried out and fainted.

Titus paled in fear. "Father? Is he dead?"

Nigel felt for a pulse and opened Tyrone's eyes to see pupil activity. "No, unconscious. Do the same to the others then we'll treat and bandage the wound," he told Chad, Mirit and Kentashi.

Being unconscious, the Guardians didn't move when the darts were withdrawn.

"Why do this, if not to kill?" asked Kentashi.

Nigel paused in treating Tyrone to hold up the dart. "These are made of stygian metal. One of the two elements capable of rendering a Guardian helpless and reduce their strength and power."

"Avatar mentioned dimension travel. She wanted to prevent that," said Raiden.

"What dimension travel?" asked Kentashi.

"How spirits travel from one place to another by disappearing."

"Ah, as you do," said admiral with understanding. "Why king? To do what you fear like in Tunlund and capture him?" he asked Nigel.

"Perhaps, but Tyrone is half-Guardian."

"She might be aware of that and sought to reduce his strength also," said Raiden.

"He can't dimension travel," refuted Nigel.

Raiden shrugged. "Just trying a give a reason to her action. But he will feel the affects of the arrow."

"How long will it take for them to wake?" asked Kentashi.

Nigel shook his head, more focused on tending Tyrone's wound. "A few moments, an hour, I don't know."

"I'll form a protective barrier until they recover." Raiden closed his eyes, bowed his head and gripped his hands together. Shortly, the night breeze ceased and the sound of nocturnal animals grew silent. Nothing stirred. It was total stillness and quiet.

Mirit stared up, but saw only blackness. "I can't even see the stars."

"That means we can't be seen," said Nigel.

"Feels eerie," said Titus, uneasy.

"Still, they can recover in safety, which is what matters."

Titus tenderly brushed the hair from Tyrone's forehead.

Nigel, Mirit, Chad and Kentashi tended the wounds using salve and bandages from the medical pouch. Each requested items from Titus, who complied without hesitation or comment.

Sheepish, Titus watched Nigel bandage Tyrone's wound. "I'm sorry," he murmured.

Nigel barely glanced from his work to answer. "I know."

"I can't wait to get home." Titus suddenly grew fretful. "I wonder what happened to Barrett. I hope Father didn't punish him severely. He helped me, though he didn't want to and kept telling me not to do it. I forced him with threats."

Nigel tied off the bandage. "You'll have to ask him when he wakes."

Titus glanced down at Tyrone. "So many things happened I didn't expect or intend."

"Unfortunately, that is common when one acts on selfish impulse." Nigel sighed with melancholy. "When I did so, my family suffered, especially Tristine and my father."

"Mother and Grandfather? How?"

"Long story." When Titus regarded him, confused and hurt, Nigel continued. "At first I wrestled with the sense I would not be king. It led to a series of events ending in the accident that crippled me. For five years I let my family believe I died."

"I've heard Mother and Father speak of it on occasion, but I don't fully understand. Why did you let them believe it when it wasn't true?"

Nigel frowned, deep and annoyed. "My struggle with pride and shame kept me from telling them. During my absence, resentment and jealousy took root in Ellan after she became heir. She found ways to abuse Tristine and beguile Father. Until she betrayed them and almost destroyed everything." His expression grew firm. "If I told them the truth, the situation may have been avoided and my mother and Darius would not have died during the coup attempt!"

Titus recoiled at Nigel's forcefulness.

Mirit moved to comfort the boy. "Nigel, is this necessary?"

"Ay!" he insisted, passion making his temper short. "I'm not the perfect hero he makes me into and it's about time he knows it. The hero lies here," he pointed to Tyrone. "He stood to up to evil and stopped the coup to save my family when I failed!"

Titus lowered his head, biting his lip with discomposure.

"That's enough," she told Nigel.

"He needed to hear the truth!" He moved a short distance away.

Titus sniffled and she stroked his hair. "You must understand, your uncle is very tenderhearted about those he loves, and sometimes it makes him sensitive and defensive or," she turned his face towards her, "indulgent. You know he loves you. Do you think it was right to take advantage of his love with lies and deception?"

"No," he whimpered. Tears swelled as watched his father, still unconscious.

"Nigel loves Tyrone and would die to protect him. To protect us."

Titus nodded and wiped his eyes. "He tried to tell me the same when he ordered Egan to take me back to the ship saying he would remain to search for you and Father. He said Allon could not be without a king if something happened." He turned moist eyes to Mirit. "I told him I would step aside for him if it did."

A small smile appeared. "You have learned something."

He sniffled and again wiped his eyes.

"Go tell him." She nudged him toward Nigel.

Titus took a deep breath. He crossed to where Nigel stood, facing away from them, arms folded and head bent, appearing more thoughtful than prayerful. "Uncle. Sir."

"Ay." Nigel's voice was short and features guarded.

Titus swallowed back the lump of anxiety in his throat to continue. "I was wrong in what I did. I took advantage of you and I should not have. I'm sorry."

Nigel's postured relaxed. "Well, realizing and apologizing is a start. Still, I see my fault in allowing your behavior to go unchecked."

"No, sir! I planned this! I guess I didn't fully understand what I was doing or how it would affect others." He glanced back to Tyrone. A sob escaping his compresses lips.

Nigel's hand on Titus' shoulder turned the boy's attention back to him. "I learned that lesson also. Love is a powerful emotion and can easily be abused or neglected if not anchored by duty. And duty is not based upon emotion rather what is right. Everyone needs a moral compass to determine right from wrong. Jor'el's Book of Verse should guide our actions, not how we feel or think about a situation or a person."

"I understand that now, sir."

Nigel smiled and clapped the back of Titus's neck. "I'm glad. Now let's sit with him and hope he and the others wake soon."

"They will wake, won't they?"

"Ay. The wounds aren't fatal." He guided Titus back to Tyrone.

For an hour they waited, checking each for signs of distress or waking. Kentashi first noticed a stirring.

"This one wakes," he said of Avatar.

Nigel knelt beside the Guardian and touched his face. "*Avatar, duisg.*"

Avatar's eyes opened at the command. "Nigel. What happened?"

"You, the other Guardians and Tyrone were shot by stygian darts."

Avatar pushed himself to sit up. "Tyrone? Is he all right?"

"Ay, but still unconscious. You're the first to wake."

Avatar held his head, blinking his eyes and taking a few deep breaths. "Must be more than a simple dart. How long was I unconscious?"

"An hour or so."

"Ooh, the back of the shoulder hurts." He touched his left shoulder.

"That's where the darts struck. We removed them and medicined the wounds."

"The ranger wakes," said Kentashi. He urged Ridge by nudging him.

Ridge bolted into a sitting position, seized Kentashi, surprising the mortal. It took a moment for Ridge to recognize Kentashi and release him. "Sorry, Admiral."

Kentashi rubbed his arm where Ridge gripped him.

Chad encouraged a groaning Egan while Mirit urged Virgil to wake. Both warriors were groggy but responded to their names.

"Father!" cheered Titus when Tyrone woke.

He grinned at the boy. "I'm not sure whether that was a good sleep or not."

"Unnatural." Nigel helped Tyrone sit up.

He groaned, flinched in pain and gingerly rotated his left shoulder.

"I can give you something for the pain, Sire," said Avatar.

"No. I need to keep a clear head. Give me a hand up." He held onto Nigel for aid.

Once everyone stood, Mirit approached Raiden. She touched his shoulder and spoke. "Raiden? The others are recovered."

At her touch and words, he collapsed to his knees, exhausted and breathing heavy. She knelt beside him.

"Are you all right?"

"In a few moments. That took longer than I expected."

"What did?" asked Avatar.

"He shielded us until all of you recovered. We couldn't even see the stars," she replied.

"What? You created a protective dome? I thought we forest Guardians were the only caste capable of that," said Ridge.

"As I said, I learned a few tricks over the centuries." He took a deep breath and got to his feet. "If completely successful, Hoshiki will have lost our trail and we should be safe for a few hours. Can you travel?"

"On foot. Dimension travel is out of the question until our wounds are healed," groused Egan. He felt his left shoulder and frowned in pain.

"She did it so you couldn't escape so easily. Once we reached the Kaori trailhead you will safe from pursuit."

"How so?" asked Tyrone.

"As part of our judgment, Onedo and I are not permitted to go beyond the boundaries of Natan. The distance between the trailhead and Kaori serves as a reminder by diminishing our strength. To go further we would immediately cease to exist and be forgotten forever."

"I won't forget," said Mirit.

"You will. Once you leave Natan, memory of me will fade."

"No," she insisted.

Avatar's hand on her shoulder made her turn to him. "It will."

The truth in his eyes was unmistakable and she bit her lip in discomposure.

"Do not be troubled for me, it is the justice I deserve and accept."

"River isn't accursed, so how can we be safe?" asked Egan.

"She willingly placed herself under the restriction for her own purposes. Once Onedo and I are gone, she can rule alone."

"That's why Natan has been isolated for so long, and why they picked this time to join forces and start a civil war to keep other countries from bringing in their influences," said Tyrone.

"Especially Allon. We should get moving before she rediscovers our heading." Raiden led them from the cave, again heading east.

<hr />

By dawn they reached the other side of the mountain and the large valley where the caravan spent the first night of the journey.

At the edge of the trees, Raiden brought them to a halt to survey the mile wide valley.

"Do you sense something?" asked Mirit.

"Just precaution. It would have been better to cross under the cover darkness."

"The longer we delay the more light." Avatar boldly stepped into the valley to begin a quick crossing.

Raiden began to object when Nigel said, "No use arguing when he's made up his mind." He followed Avatar.

"Look who's talking!" Mirit moved to catch up with Nigel.

Halfway across the valley everyone stopped at seeing two flashes of light appeared several hundred yards in front them, near the far tree line. All but Raiden readied their weapons.

From the fading light, Onedo and Hoshiki arrived together. Hoshiki stood Onedo's height with long black hair worn loose and vivid light green eyes. She also wore the Natanese amour only with purple cloth accents and the sword strapped to her back. Two large daggers were attached to her belt.

"Did you really think you could help them escape, Raiden?" she said.

Avatar stepped forward to confront her. "We will pass, River."

She bared her teeth in a sardonic smile. "You have no authority here, *Lieutenant*. Here I am Hoshiki, supreme goddess of Natan."

Tyrone joined Avatar. "You're wrong, River."

"No! This is between us, *Captain*." Raiden purposely used the title as a warning to Tyrone. He didn't wait for an answer before addressing his adversaries. "What do you want to let them pass?"

Hoshiki cast a conferring glance to Onedo, who nodded. She replied, "You and the female."

"*She* is out of the question. But," he said, spreading his arms wide. "If you want me, they pass."

Onedo smiled with satisfaction so Hoshiki said, "Done." She waved him forward.

"Make for the trailhead," Raiden told Avatar before heading for Hoshiki and Onedo.

Mirit didn't want to leave, her focus on Raiden. Titus seized her hand. "Please, Aunt Mirit."

She went with him, but her eyes slow to leave Raiden.

Akido appeared from over the southern ring of trees roaring a warning. From the same trees, dogmen and catbirds rushed the group.

"Treacherous wench!" shouted Raiden. He went to help the Allonians when a female war cry halted him. He drew his sword and moved in time to parry Hoshiki's attack. Onedo joined Hoshiki in attacking Raiden.

Hoshiki's thrust her hand out. Raiden ducked under a blast that struck and killed a dogman about to jump him from behind. Although he managed to avoid her, Onedo had a clear shot and his blast sent Raiden flying twenty feet and landing hard on his back.

Tyrone avoided one of the two catbirds leaping at him. He swung his sword and sliced off the front leg of the second creature. Something hit the back of his left leg yet he managed to keep from falling. Titus. A dogman charged them. Tyrone stepped over Titus and slashed at the dogman catching the beast in the chest as it passed. He lost his footing and stumbled. He used his sword to catch his balance and stand upright.

"Father?"

"I'm all right. You?"

"Ay." He pushed himself to his feet. "Chad!" he shouted in distress.

The squire lay on the ground unconscious with two catbirds fast approaching.

"Use your dagger!" Tyrone took the dagger from his belt. "Take the one on right, I got the left." He threw his dagger, striking the beast between the eyes, killing it.

Titus' dagger struck the beast in the neck. Not a lethal blow, but the creature backed away. Nigel arrived and killed the wounded beast.

Titus rushed to Chad and fell to his knees beside the squire. "Chad?" He prodded his shoulder, but Chad didn't move. He tried shaking Chad when Nigel, Mirit and Tyrone joined him. "He won't wake up."

Nigel felt for a pulse on Chad's neck and smiled with relief. "He's alive."

Mirit examined Chad for injury. The gash on the back of his head reopened. "Struck from behind again."

"We have to get out of here." Tyrone's attention shifted from Chad to the Guardians, who had difficult dealing with the creatures. "Our wounds are hampering our ability to fight."

Nigel sheathed his sword and lifted Chad to his feet then placed one of Chad's arm over his shoulder and his own arm encircled Chad's waist.

"Titus, help Nigel with Chad and make for the trailhead. Mirit and I will watch for more creatures," said Tyrone.

Kentashi came limping over. "Too many."

"Make for the trailhead with Nigel and Titus." Tyrone nudged Kentashi on his way. Again he saw the Guardians not fairing well against the creatures.

"We can't just leave them!" she said in distress.

"I don't like it either," his voice hoarse. "They have their duty and we have ours. Don't let their sacrifice be in vain." He turned her with a hand on her shoulder toward the trailhead.

A catbird knocked Egan hard to the ground. He landed on his back and aggravated his wound. The creature leapt on top of him and he struggled to keep its beak from gouging his face. His hand holding the creature's face slipped and the beak ripped into his right shoulder. He loudly snarled in pain. A blow sent the creature flying off him. Ridge. The ranger labored for breath and his face pale. He offered his hand to help Egan to his feet.

"We have to end this quick or we won't survive," said Ridge.

A few yards away, Avatar fell to one knee in his effort to swat aside three dogmen.

Egan snatched up his fallen sword when Avatar was forced down to both knees. "*Jor'el's neart!*" he shouted, and ran at incredible speed. He swung his sword at a dogman, cleaving it in half.

Ridge repeated Egan's cry, "Jor'el's strength!" In running stride, he planted the end of his staff in the ground to use like a pole vault and launched himself feet first at two of the dogmen. The beasts were knocked off their feet. Ridge landed in a crouched position, immediately straightened and swung at the dogmen trying to rise. He sent one flying but the other avoided his staff and sent Ridge staggering to his knees with a blow to his back. The intervention allowed Avatar to get to his feet and kill the dogman that downed Ridge.

The burst of energy weakened Egan. "We have to unite," he said between breaths of recovery.

"Ay." Avatar aided Ridge to his feet and shouted, "Virgil!"

In awkward and hurried steps, Virgil joined his fellow Guardians.

From various directions, the ten remaining dogmen and six catbirds joined in an attack formation, heading for the Guardians.

"We protect the mortals at all cost." Avatar placed the pommel of his sword in front of his face. Virgil and Egan did likewise, awaiting command. Ridge held his staff in front of him.

"Jor'el, hear us. Renew our strength even if this is our last stand—" began Avatar.

A loud roar interrupted him. Akido breathed a continuous stream of fire and ignited the valley between the Guardians and the creature. The charge halted.

Avatar watched to see if the fire barrier would hold. When Akido began the aerial assault of the creatures, he heard Raiden call to them, "Retreat to the trailhead!"

Mirit pulled up short of the trees upon hearing Raiden. Akido attacked the creatures and the Guardians retreated. Raiden was viciously knocked aside by a blow from Onedo. He landed about fifty feet away and when he tried to get to his feet, a dogman jumped him from behind.

It bit him on the base of the neck bringing him to the ground. She raced to intervene.

"Mirit! No!" shouted Nigel. "Stay here," he told Tyrone and the others.

Mirit's momentum added power to her swinging sword and sent a deep savage slash to the creature's back. It rolled away from Raiden, yowling in agony. Nigel arrived and helped her get Raiden on his feet.

He was in obvious pain from the serious bite. "I said get to the trailhead!"

"Not without you." She and Nigel held Raiden between them and hurried to the trailhead.

The Guardians arrived. Chad woke, but groggy, and remained on his feet with Titus supporting him.

Raiden shook loose of Mirit and Nigel. "Keep going and don't stop until you reach the Kaori overlook."

"You're coming," she insisted.

He swallowed back the pain to nod.

For the next hour they stumbled and weaved their way through the forest. Avatar kept the rear guard. He looked over his shoulder for pursuit, but no signs of Onedo, Hoshiki or the creatures.

Finally they reached the clearing overlooking Kaori. The Allonian ships remained moored with Kentashi's men standing watch on the dock.

"Your soldiers are diligent in their duty," said Tyrone.

"They obey until death."

Raiden stumbled and caught a tree to keep from falling. His face was now ashen. "This is where we part company. You're safe now." He swayed as if he would faint and Mirit caught his arm in support.

"You're wound needs to be tended."

He shook his head, swallowing back his increasing weakness to speak. "It's not the wound. I've come too far. The barrier began at the trailhead and ends here. I dare not go further. You must go and I return before my life force is completely drained."

"But they wait back at the trailhead for you!"

A wry smile appeared. "Either way, I thank you, daughter of Willis. You have made my eventual passing more tolerable."

"I won't forget what you have done."

"Alas, it has been ordained. There will be memories of mortal events and maybe vague impressions and feelings you won't fully understand, but Raiden will disappear from your memory." He staggered back into the forest.

"No, Mirit," said Nigel.

She stared after Raiden until he disappeared into the shadows of the forest. Feeling Nigel's gentle prodding, she accompanied him from the overlook.

"Consider what grace has been granted," said Tyrone.

"Grace? But he—" she began to protest.

"Grace to you, to Willis, to Egan and Ridge. Jor'el allowed Raiden one last act of compassion to those he wronged so long ago. The whole situation speaks to Jor'el's mercy and sovereignty."

"Ay," she said with relief. "Thank you."

Tyrone grinned. "What are brothers for if not imparting wisdom?"

"Making fools of each other," she quipped.

He laughed and gave her a fond embrace about the shoulders. "Leave it to our women to keep us humble and on the right path."

She gave him a toothy, teasing smile. "Remember that when I tell Tristine about your communal bath."

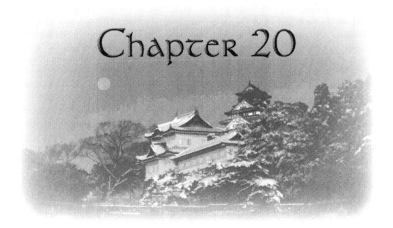

Chapter 20

THE SOLDIERS ON THE DOCK BECAME ALERT AT SEEING THE limping and weary group approach. Kentashi shouted a hailing call and two soldiers ran to greet the admiral. After a short conversation between Kentashi and the soldiers, the admiral translated.

"They say all is well with your ships."

"Excellent." Tyrone led the way to the *Protectorate*.

Gulliver and Chase ran to join them on the dock. "Highness. Captain," said Gulliver in relief. "We became concerned when word reached us of Rukan's attack."

Tyrone grinned. "No need to play coy any longer. The admiral knows who I am. Difficult to keep a secret during our escape."

Kentashi wasn't paying attention, as a soldier gave him a hurried report. "Soldier say Rukan's forces near Kaori. Best you—" Cannon fire interrupted him.

The soldier pointed to the fortress, chatting excitedly in Natanese. The cannons from the fortress returned firing. Kentashi barked orders to his soldiers, who ran from the dock, heading toward the fortress.

"We hold while you leave," he said.

"If you can, send me word of the outcome. I shall pray for your safety and for Natan."

Kentashi appeared visibly touched. "Thank you, Sire."

The cannon fire at the fortress became more intense. Kentashi nodded the stiff Natanese acknowledgment of a salute to Tyrone and ran off, shouting to his men.

"Prepare to sail. Have gunners stand by," ordered Tyrone.

The Sea Guardians raced back to their ships, issuing orders. The group boarded the *Protectorate*. Avatar and Virgil helped stow the gangplank and both flinched in pain after doing so. Still, they continued the preparations for departure. Tyrone, Nigel and Mirit made their way to the helm.

"Cast off all lines!" shouted Gulliver. "Deck gunners, stand by, eyes on the dock! Bow, aim on the fortress, stern, on the streets. Mister Kasey, have below gunners prepare to open doors once we're away from the dock."

"Ay-ay, Captain." Kasey ran down to the hold and repeated the order. After receiving an affirmative from the master gunner he called back. "All guns ready, Captain!"

Chad manned a deck-gun on the quarterdeck near the helm.

Titus hurried to join him. "Can you fight?"

"Ay. Now, get below, Highness, this could get nasty." He moved Titus out of the way of the gunner's mate.

"But I've been helping you, fighting with you."

"No," said Tyrone. "Ridge. Egan. Take Mirit and Titus to the cabins and stay there until we're out to sea."

"Chad is injured. Please, sir, I want to stay and help him."

Tyrone tempered his response to the concern. "Chad is trained, you are not."

Mirit intervened by taking Titus' arm. "Your time will come."

"Ay, one day I will be trained," he declared, and left with her, Egan and Ridge.

Inside the cabin, Titus jumped at hearing a ship's cannon fire and movement. "We're under attack!"

"No, we're casting off and that was a deck gun. Gulliver usually gives a warning shot when the enemy gets too close for comfort," said Egan.

At Titus' apprehension, Mirit added, "Gulliver and Chase will get us out of the harbor."

Titus crossed to the porthole and looked out. When he couldn't see well, he opened it. Egan shut the porthole.

"Leave it closed."

"I want to see what is happening!"

"Listen to your aunt and place your trust in Gulliver and Chase. And have faith in Jor'el."

Titus sat on a bench under the porthole, his expression worried. "This wouldn't be happening if I weren't here. It's all my fault."

Mirit sat beside him. "No. You are only responsible for your actions, not the actions of others."

"Father came to fetch me and Lord Allard died protecting me. Now they're coming after us!" He spoke in agitated words and gestures.

"They are coming to attack Kentashi," she insisted and snatched his hands to make him face her. "This is a civil war and we are caught in the crossfire. And would still be happening regardless of your presence—or your father."

"Indeed," said Egan. "Remember, Lord Allard was already wounded, which hampered his ability to escape. That is why he told you to leave him rather than endanger your life, not your presence endangering him. He died protecting his prince."

Titus shook his head and sniffled back his emotions. "I was supposed to look after him and I failed."

"No, the circumstances went beyond your control. Just like it did for others." She turned to Ridge and Egan, her expression prompting and pointed.

"What do you mean?" asked Ridge.

She stood to explain. "Grand Master Farley employed Onedo and the Dark Way to kill Lord Willis and thwart you and Egan from finding him."

"How do you know this?"

"Raiden. He informed Vidar of Onedo killing Willis. Onedo became accursed when he slew a Guardian named Corwin to escape Vidar. He followed Raiden to Natan to enact revenge and prevent him from repaying his blood debt to Lord Willis by saving me, Willis' descendant." She took hold of each Guardian's arm. "Don't you see? Neither of you failed, so there is no need to feel guilty, nor to be angry and bitter toward each other."

"I never bore bitterness toward Egan. I acted in defense of his aggression."

Egan sighed with regret and admitted, "I did concerning you, which is why I acted mean." He spoke the last part of the sentence to Titus then returned to Ridge. "I wanted to keep my present charge alive and would have taken action against you if anything happened to Titus. I'm sorry."

Ridge nodded. "Understood and accepted."

"Yet," began Egan, somewhat befuddled. "What connection did Raiden have to Willis? And why betray Onedo to Vidar?"

Compassion filled her face and voice in reply. "He was Willis' Guardian Overseer. You replaced him after he became accursed. Your first task to find Willis."

"No. I was always his Overseer."

Her expression changed to befuddled and she forced herself to continue. "All memory of Raiden was wiped away replaced by what you believe you remember." She flinched as if struck by a headache.

Ridge caught her elbow. "Princess? Are you hurt?"

She shook her head in confusion. "No. I suddenly feel I am forgetting something. What was I saying?"

"You told the young prince how Lord Allard's death wasn't his fault," said Egan.

"Are you sure?"

"Ay," groused Titus. "I still think he wouldn't have died if not for me."

She scowled. "You're as stubborn as your uncle and father!"

The ship lurched when struck. Egan caught Mirit to keep her from falling.

Titus threw open the porthole and looked out. "Now, they are firing on us!"

Two transportable cannons fired from the dock at the Allonian ships attempting to leave. One shot fell short of the *Sentinel* but the other blew off part of the *Protectorate's* bow railing, sending the anchor over the side.

"Secure the anchor! Don't let it hit bottom!" Gulliver ordered the warriors.

Avatar and Virgil raced to the bow. The anchor mechanism was broken by the blast and the chain spun free, the weight of the anchor dropping into the water.

"Grab the chain!" said Avatar. He and Virgil each seized the thick chain, but the anchor's weight pulled them toward the railing. Avatar stumbled and fell, smacking into the end of the broken rail. Virgil managed to catch his balance and braced himself in a wide stance, the strain evident on both their faces to hold the anchor.

"Can you get up?" asked Virgil through clenched teeth of effort.

"Only if I briefly let go."

"Do it!"

Avatar released the chain. The extra weight dragged Virgil toward the hole in the rail. He leaned back for added leverage then felt an easing when Avatar again held the chain, only this time behind him and near the mechanism.

Two sailors desperately tried to fix the mechanism.

Nigel rushed over. "Can it be repaired?"

"No, Highness, the latch has snapped off."

The ship lurched again. Nigel moved to the rail and gazed down to the water. "It's dragging and affecting the ship's movement—" A cannonball struck close to the ship and sent a powerful wave of water on deck, knocking him off his feet.

Avatar and Virgil slipped on the wet deck but managed to keep from losing hold of the anchor chain.

"They're getting our range!" shouted Tyrone.

Drenched, Nigel grabbed the rail to get to his feet. "You need to pull up the anchor!" he told the Guardians.

"Bho neart gu neart!" the warriors shouted in unison.

"Nigel!" called Tyrone.

He didn't answer, his gaze shifting between the Guardians and the water. The top of the anchor broke the surface. When the entire anchor appeared, he called to Tyrone, "It's free of the water!"

Tyrone issued orders for the deck guns to return fire.

With the anchor back on deck, "Secure it," Avatar told the sailors. Gritting his teeth in painful annoyance, he rotated his left shoulder. Fresh blood stained the back of his uniform.

"You're bleeding again," said Nigel. He examined Virgil. "You too."

"Fire!" ordered Tyrone.

The ship rocked when the deck gunners obeyed. For a moment, the smoke obscured any view of the dock.

"Go. We'll be all right," said Avatar.

Nigel reached the bottom of the steps to the quarterdeck and reported to Tyrone. "Anchor secure."

"Avatar and Virgil?"

"The effort reopened their wounds, but they insist they'll be fine."

"If we lost the anchor, I would have tried them to a rope and tossed them overboard," groused Gulliver.

Tyrone ignored Gulliver to ask, "What's the situation, Master Kasey?"

The first mate held the spyglass to his eye, watching the dock. The clearing smoke showed minor damage and some soldiers retreating. "The cannonade worked. No, wait." He removed the glass from his eye to report. "They are regrouping and preparing to fire again."

Two more shots from the Natanese cannons headed toward them. This time one struck the *Sentinel's* stern rail and the other landed in the water with a dull thud on the *Protectorate's* hull, but no damage.

Tyrone scowled in fierce anger. "Let's give them something to think about. Deck gunners, prepare to fire. Below gunners, fire after the deck guns!" He raised his arm and watched the deck gunners scramble to prepare, including Nigel, who made his way to the bow. After receiving signals of readiness, Tyrone lowered his arm. "Fire!"

All eight-deck guns simultaneously fired, followed by the fifteen starboard cannons. The ensuing multiple explosions on the docks and nearby buildings told of significant damage. When the smoke cleared, the docks where the ships moored were destroyed and buildings sustained heavy damage. Bodies of soldiers strewn across the debris and a few limped or crawled away.

Tyrone observed the grim aftermath with a fixed, unyielding expression. Nigel came alongside him, also taking note of the damage inflicted by their bombardment.

"Let's hope that's the end and they will let us leave in peace," said Nigel.

"If not, the next volley will use the firepower of both ships." Tyrone called, "Mister Kasey! Signal the *Sentinel*. She's to prepare her port cannons. If they so much as light a match, she's to come about and we'll give them everything!"

"Ay-aye, Sire." Kasey sent the signal.

"Hello, the watch!" shouted Nigel to the crow's nest. "Any signs of reinforcement coming from the fortress?"

Both men raised their spyglasses to survey Kaori. After conferring, one shouted. "No, Highness. The streets are clear."

"Gulliver. How long until we are out of the harbor?" asked Tyrone.

"A few more moments, Sire. The wind is with us. Thank, Jor'el."

"We'll wait until we are out of range before standing down." Tyrone heard Nigel's despondent sigh. "What troubles you? Kentashi?"

He shook his head. "Allard. It's bad enough he died, but it pains me deeply we are unable to bring him home for properly burial. Next to Darius, he, Erasmus and Mathias were my father's dearest friends."

"I know. I promise, his passing will be honored."

Nigel gripped the hilt of his sword and focused his attention on the dock. For several tense moments they watched for any aggressive activity. People on shore tended the wounded and dealt with debris.

"Captain!" shouted the watch from the crow's nest. "A ship moving from the east end of the harbor!"

"It looks like she's going to try block our escape, Sire," said Gulliver.

Tyrone took the spyglass from Kasey to view the maneuver. "Can we manage enough speed to outrun her?"

"I don't think so."

Tyrone shifted his view with spyglass between the *Protectorate, Sentinel* and the Natanese ship, judging the distance and timing. "Mister Kasey! Signal Chase to come about and a run parallel course between the dock and Natanese ship with all gun ports open. We'll run a similar cross from the opposite direction. When I give the order, I want that ship blown out of the water but be prepared to silence shore battery if necessary."

"Ay-ay, Sire."

"Risky to expose our broadside," said Nigel.

"If you have a better idea, I'm willing to listen. But we are leaving Natan!"

"I said *risky*, I wasn't disagreeing."

"Watch the starboard for any signs of land battery." Tyrone gave Nigel the spyglass. "Gulliver, once Chase has come about, we fire everything at that ship." He barely finished speaking when the Natanese ship fired several warning shots at the *Protectorate*. The cannon balls fell short and harmlessly landed in the water.

"They'll have our range once we turn into position," said Gulliver.

"We won't be still long enough to be hit. We'll signal the *Sentinel* she's to fire her deck guns while turning. We'll do the same. That should force them to keep their heads down. Mister Kasey!"

"I'm already sending the order," said the first mate.

"All cannons armed and ready!" shouted Tyrone, and his order relayed on deck and below by the gunmaster. "Deck gunners, prepare to fire in mid-turn. Doesn't matter if you hit the ship just keep them from firing until we are ready with our broadside."

"Ay-ay, Sire," said Chad.

The bow gunners echoed acknowledgement of the order.

"Gunmaster!" called Tyrone to the man at the hold ladder. "Fire all port cannons the instant we are at broadside."

"Ay-ay, Sire."

"*Sentinel* says she is preparing to come about, Sire," said Kasey.

Tyrone acknowledge the report with a nod. "Do the same, Gulliver."

Gulliver turned the helm hard to port and the ship began a sharp angled turn.

Tyrone grabbed onto the rigging to stand steady, yet continued to watch the Natanese ship. Two more shots fired, and came dangerously close to the *Protectorate,* causing large splashes of water to wash on deck.

"Deck gunners! Begin firing!" ordered Tyrone.

Chad and the seven other gunners sent a barrage at the Natanese ship then quickly reloaded for another volley.

"Land battery!" shouted Nigel, holding the spyglass to his eye.

Puffs of smoke came from an intact part of the dock. The cannon balls landed right in front of where the *Protectorate* was turning.

"Starboard deck gunners, fire on the dock. Port, continue on the ship!" Gunmaster! Have both sides fire when at broadside. Mister Kasey—"

"I'm signaling your orders to the *Sentinel,* Sire."

"Next shot from the dock will have our bow in range," warned Nigel, briefly turning his attention from the dock to Tyrone.

Two more puffs of smoke signaled fire from the dock and Nigel returned to watch through the spyglass. One cannon ball stuck and splintered part of the *Protectorate's* bowsprit.

"We must fire now! The next volley will hole us!" said Nigel.

"Steady!" Tyrone's eyes fixed on the turn of his ships in relation to the Natanese vessel. Both ships were nearly parallel.

"Tyrone!" called Nigel with urgency, looking from the spyglass to the helm.

At that instant, the ships drew parallel, "Now!" shouted Tyrone.

The thirty-eight guns and cannons of the *Protectorate* and twenty-five on the *Sentinel* opened fire. The roar of the guns was deafening and rocked the *Protectorate* on her keel. The impact proved devastating, shattering what little remained of the dock. The Natanese ship exploded when its magazine became struck.

"Quickly! Come about and head for sea at top speed," he told Gulliver and Kasey. He joined Nigel on the main deck, who again looked through the spyglass at the dock. "Any sign of regrouping?"

"No." Nigel lowered the glass and scowled. "Cut that a little close, didn't you?"

"We only had one shot. Remember, I asked if you had a better idea."

"For a moment I wished I had."

Kasey arrived. "Damage report from the *Sentinel*, Sire. She sustained a direct hit on the bow, but it's above the waterline and shouldn't slow her down. They'll make repairs on route. Unfortunately, two crew members are dead."

"Any casualties among our crew?"

"A few minor cuts but nothing serious or life threatening."

"Pray it stays that way." Tyrone returned to the quarterdeck, Nigel at his heels. They came upon the Natan ship. Debris littered the water along with dead bodies and badly injured crewmen fighting to stay above water.

"Total loss, Sire," said Gulliver.

Tyrone's face was set. "Keep going. They are close enough to shore to be rescued by their own."

"I wasn't suggesting otherwise."

Several tense moments passed as they waited to leave the harbor. No signs of more intercepting ships or cannon fire from shore.

"I believe we've made it," said Nigel.

"Ay. Come, we need to relieve some worry."

"Chad," called Nigel. They left the quarterdeck for the cabins.

Titus jumped off the bench when the door opened. He and Mirit sat at the porthole, watching and waiting. Tyrone and Nigel entered.

"Casualties?" asked Mirit.

"Where's Chad?" asked Titus with concerned.

"None on the *Protectorate*, thank Jor'el. Chad is having his earlier wound tended," replied Nigel.

"But we felt the ship struck."

"One hit the bow rail while another bounced off the hull. We're safely out of the harbor now."

"I told you Gulliver and Chase would succeed," said Mirit.

The boy nodded, his face worried. "So we're going home now?"

"Ay." Tyrone placed a guiding hand on Titus' shoulder. "Come. We all need to get some rest."

Chapter 21

REST WAS SOMETHING TITUS COULDN'T DO, THOUGH HE placated his father by allowing him to put him to bed and even place a blanket over him. From under the cover of pretended sleep, he watched his father move across the cabin to the other bed, carefully strip off his sword, belt and boots, get into bed and lay on his right side. When his father appeared to fall asleep, Titus lay on his back and stared at the ceiling.

Despite what Mirit, Egan and Ridge said about how the circumstances involving Allard were not his fault, his father would not have been wounded if not for him. He came to take him home and became caught up in a life and death situation.

The thoughts and gentle swaying of the ship gave way to fitful sleep. Images of events invaded his dreams, most notably of Allard's death. His eyes snapped open when someone touched him. In his dream, a dogman grabbed him, but in reality Egan held him by the shoulders.

"You were having a nightmare," said the Guardian in a soft reassuring voice.

Titus swallowed back his fright and sorrow. "Allard. I can't seem to stop seeing it again and again."

"Unfortunately, only time will help ease the pain and memory."

Titus sat up. His father still slept. He tossed aside the cover, placed a finger to his lips for quiet and motioned toward his father. He reached for his boots.

"What are you doing?" whispered Egan.

"On deck. I can't sleep any more and I don't want to disturb him." He tiptoed crossed to the door, carrying his boots. Egan followed, but Titus stopped him. "Stay with him. I'll be all right. Besides, I can't go anywhere else."

On deck, only the hands, Gulliver and Kasey were around. Titus assumed the others also slept, or the Guardians meditating to speed their recovery.

"Is there a problem, Highness?" asked Gulliver.

Titus sat on the bottom step of the stairs leading to the helm to put on his boots before replying. "No. I just needed some air."

He walked to the bow and stared out to sea. They were heading for home. The thought made him glad, sad and troubled at the same time. He was glad to be safely away from Natan and his father, uncle and aunt not seriously harmed, or worse. He experienced fear in Tunlund, and at Mirit's sacrifice, but he never experienced the depth of panic and horror he felt when Nigel lay unconscious and thought he was dead. What a relief when Nigel woke. But the thought made him realize how terrible it would be if his father died. He suddenly felt woefully unprepared for that possibility and the point driven home at seeing him shot. However, it wasn't just his father, Allard's death troubled him. Worst of all, they were forced to leave him behind, and he would never return home. The thought brought a new wave of sorrow and anxiety. What could he tell his mother? She would be angry and disappointed with him, but what about Allard's death? He was a dear friend of his grandfather and his mother very fond of him.

"Couldn't sleep either?" asked Chad.

"No," droned Titus. "How's your head?"

"I have a headache. The ship's surgeon gave me a remedy. I'm just waiting for it to take effect before I try to sleep again. What about you? Why can't you sleep?"

Titus shrugged, hesitant to reply.

"I can guess the reason. The same guilt and uncertainty I felt when returning from Soren."

"I really don't want to talk."

"I understand that too. But you're going to have face reality soon, and talking is the best solution for everyone involved."

Titus sat on the bulkhead and Chad withdrew.

***

Near dusk, Tyrone emerged on deck now clean, refreshed and wearing a new uniform. Titus sat on the bow bulkhead. Mirit and Nigel joined Tyrone on the main deck. They too appeared rested and wearing clean clothes.

"Has he said anything?" she asked.

Tyrone shook his head. "Nothing."

"That's surprising, he's usually very vocal," said Nigel.

Tyrone glanced along his shoulder at Nigel. "You weren't very vocal when you returned after so long. In fact, we had to provoke you into speaking."

"Sometimes we still have to," said Mirit.

"Point taken," agreed Nigel.

Tyrone patted Nigel's shoulder. "I think this situation taught him a deeper lesson than any of us could. I no longer see obstinacy or rebellion in his eyes. But I believe he needs time, like you did. Maybe that commonality will help when he finally does speak."

"I'll direct him to you. You've always been a better listener than me."

Tyrone laughed. His arm moved to encircle Nigel's shoulders. "I'm sorry this caused tension between us."

"You already apologized once, no need to do so again, brother."

Tyrone flashed a touched smile.

"The lesson came at a higher cost than any of us would have liked," said Mirit.

"Ay. Telling Tristine about Allard will be difficult," said Tyrone.

"I believe he thinks so too." She motioned to Titus.

"I don't know if continually telling him that he bears no fault will help."

"No, but I know something that will," said Nigel.

"I'll come with you, since I can guess what it is," she said.

Since Chad left, Titus became absorbed in thought and didn't hear anyone approach. He flinched in surprise when Mirit asked, "What are you looking at?" He shrugged, taking a moment to recover.

She sat beside him. With only room for one other person, Nigel stood by Titus.

"I'm looking forward to seeing home," she said.

Titus nodded.

"To seeing my father."

Again, he nodded.

"I'm looking forward to seeing my sisters, nieces and nephews," said Nigel.

Titus whimpered and bit his lip to keep from crying. Chad may be right but talking was too difficult and painful.

Nigel held the boy's shoulder. "You're thinking about your mother."

Overwhelmed, Titus bolted up and clung to Nigel, sobbing. His words broken and hard to say, "I'm scared. I don't know what to say to her."

"Fear kept me from my family." He tilted Titus' head up to look at him. "Don't make the same mistake I did and let fear stop you. You have an opportunity to do what I could not, to ask your mother's forgiveness."

Titus forced himself to ask, "Do you think she will forgive me?"

Nigel smiled, kind and certain. "She forgave me. In fact Tristine was so overjoyed she accepted me back without question or hesitation, deformed body and all. She'll do no less for her son."

He hugged Nigel again, his voice quaking. "Do you forgive me, Uncle?"

"Of course. I thought you understood that earlier."

Titus nodded, wiped his face and glanced to Mirit, shy yet expectant.

"I forgive you too. Have you apologized to your father?"

He shook his head. "I ... I can't find the words."

"You should, and soon."

"Chad said the sooner I talk about it the better. But it's so hard," he said and lowered his head to gather his emotions.

"Both Chad and Nigel know the difficulty, but you have started by talking sooner than either of them. The challenge is not to stop and continue the healing process. Especially the one you have wronged the most—your father."

"Will you help me, Uncle?"

Nigel hesitated, the conflict evident on his face, yet after a moment, he shook his head. "The best I can for you is to not help. I had to face my father alone and it was very hard, but afterward we became closer. Besides, he came all this way for you, he will listen."

Titus took a deep steadying breath. "Very well. I'll speak to him."

"What about Egan?"

The question briefly surprised Titus. "What about him?"

Nigel directed Titus' attention to where Egan sat on a nearby bulkhead, seeming to not paying attention. "Your plan included fooling him. How do you think he feels?"

Uncertain, Titus watched Egan for a moment. The Guardian kept his focus elsewhere only he sat in such a way that the bandage on his wound was visible. Titus bit his lower lip in distress. Despite his initial reluctance to accept Egan, seeing him shot like Jedrek frightened him. He admitted, "I have treated him badly since he took Jedrek's place."

"Ay. You made a mighty warrior of Jor'el look foolish and inept when all he is doing is trying to protect you and be your friend."

"I don't know what to say. Should I apologize to a Guardian?"

Nigel folded his arms in disapproval. "I take it by that last question you never have. Guardians are beings with feelings and Egan is diligent in his duty to you and Jor'el despite your admitted bad treatment of him."

Titus heaved an abashed shrug. "Things were different with Jedrek. Did you ever mistreat Avatar and apologize?"

Nigel guffawed, a little too loudly for Titus' liking, so he calmed his mirth. "Oh, ay. He put up with a lot of trouble from me, but because of him, I became healed."

"Really? I thought Jor'el healed you."

"He did. However, since the crippling came as a result of a Guardian's betrayal, Avatar broke all the rules in approaching Jor'el to petition for my healing." Nigel touched Titus' shoulder to add, "Avatar risked his very existence for me. The same as Jedrek and *Egan* have done for you. Such loyalty and devotion deserves respect and honor from those who are served."

Titus pursed his lips in consideration. He cast another glance to Egan, who still pretended not to be paying attention. "Seeing him shot did remind me of Jedrek," he began low and disturbed. "I'm glad he didn't die."

"Don't tell me, tell him."

Mirit added her encouragement. "Remember, the challenge is to continue and not stop the healing."

Titus swallowed back his emotions in an attempt to appear calm and collected upon approaching the Guardian. "Egan," he began, his voice betraying nervousness.

He faced Titus, his expression cordial as he asked, "Do you feel better?"

"I'm not sure."

"Gulliver says sea air helps to clear the mind."

"I've got a lot on my mind to clear," groused Titus.

"I suspect so."

Titus grew awkward. He sent a questioning glance to Nigel, who just nodded. He turned back to Egan and said, "How is your wound?"

"Not as sore. I'll be fine in a day or two. Guardians heal quickly."

"I'm glad. I mean, when you were shot, I thought about Jedrek."

To this Egan appeared a bit taken back and disappointed. "Oh, I see. You're upset at being reminded of Jedrek."

"No! I was upset at the thought of losing you too. I know I haven't been easy to deal with and I made you look foolish with the stupid tricks I'd play to get away. I even dragged poor Barrett into trouble." His words came quick, but with sincerity.

"He was punished for helping you."

Hearing it, made tears swell. " I'm sorry about that! And sorry for fooling you, for being so mean all these years! I promise, I'll try to behave better in the future and not put your life in danger again." His voice cracked in regret, looking down to wipe his face.

Egan lifted Titus's chin. "I forgive you. Despite your past behavior, I am fond of you. You have good qualities, a fine heritage and great potential. And if someday I do fall, know I do it willingly and without hesitation or regret."

Moved by gratitude and new appreciation, Titus embraced Egan. "I don't want that to ever happen. I don't want you to die!"

"Jor'el willing. But don't let fear guide your actions or responses. Let what you've learned make you stronger."

"I'll try."

Avatar stood on the quarterdeck observing all. Titus had been quiet and withdrawn since leaving Natan. Little wonder after everything. Some harsh lessons were learned, but good to see Titus accept Nigel's comfort and speak to Egan.

Tyrone joined him. "How's your wound?"

"Better. The salve and fresh bandage helped to stem the bleeding. You?"

"Sore." Tyrone noticed Titus with Egan. "I'm glad no harm is done to his relationship to Nigel and he has finally accepted Egan."

"Ay. However, other relationships have changed and will change."

As he spoke, Virgil took a seat on a chest near Nigel and Mirit.

"How long have you known?" asked Tyrone.

"For several months."

"Have you spoken to Nigel yet?"

Avatar shook his head. "Nothing is official. And I'd like to know what I'm doing before giving over my charge."

"Maybe that's why Kell sent Virgil?"

Avatar cocked a grin. "He wasn't Kell's choice, rather my choice."

The statement surprised Tyrone. "Really?"

"Kell wanted Gresham or Barnum for the journey, but neither felt right to me. When trouble started, I knew Virgil was meant to be here. My sense confirmed by the developing connection between he and Mirit."

Tyrone smiled. "It'll be a strange adjustment, but perhaps for the best. After all, you suffered with Nigel long enough."

Avatar laughed. He saw Titus return to Mirit and Nigel and Ridge approached Egan. They began conversing. More than that, they appeared jovial, which made Avatar curious. "Excuse me, Sire." He made his way from the quarterdeck to join them. "Well, this is a pleasant sight. You two on speaking terms."

Egan and Ridge regarded him with mild curiosity. "What are you talking about?" asked Egan.

"What do you mean, what am I talking about? You appear to be laughing like old friends."

Egan heaved a nonchalant shrug. "Why shouldn't we be? The prince and king are safe and we're heading home. In fact, Titus apologized to me and promised to behave better."

"I bet that surprised you," said Ridge with chuckle.

"Ay. Apparently seeing me shot changed his attitude."

"Jedrek," said Avatar.

Egan nodded, a new sobriety on his face. "He admitted to the memory and being scared of a repeat."

"Lord Allard's death also impacted him."

"Ay, but he made the same sacrifice Ridge or I would have done to save the prince, the mortals or each other."

Avatar grew skeptical. "What caused this sudden change? Stygian sickness?"

Egan and Ridge appeared befuddled and Egan said, "We still don't understand what you're talking about?"

Avatar made pointing gestures at each, speaking, first to Egan, than Ridge. "You've been angry at him since Lord Willis' death and you've been overly sensitive to criticism ever since. That's why Kell sent you, to rectify your relationship."

They stared at Avatar with guarded curiosity and concern. Ridge's focus remained on Avatar as he leaned close to Egan and said, "His senility is acting up again."

Avatar began to dispute when a hand clapped him on the shoulder.

"Are you scolding them and making something out of nothing like the elderly often do? They're finally at peace, why does it matter how it happened?" asked Virgil.

"Now what are you talking about?" asked Egan.

Avatar ignored Egan to asked Virgil, "Do you know the reason for their change?"

Virgil's brows grew level in consideration. "No, but something did and isn't that what's important?"

"Ay," said Avatar, his expression also changing to perplexed.

"You may be right about the senility," said Egan to Ridge.

"Only it's spreading." Ridge jerked his thumb at Virgil.

The watch called from the crow's nest. "Sire, Ships off the port bow!"

"Any flag or identification?"

"The *Tremain* and *Allon's Pride* and flying the royal standard!"

Tyrone smiled. "Tristine." He hurried to the port side. Nigel, Mirit, Chad, Titus and the Guardians already gathered. "She couldn't wait."

Nigel laughed. "You wouldn't have waited either."

A long boat launched from *Allon's Pride* heading for the *Protectorate*. On the long boat with the crew were Tristine, Kell and Armus.

Mister Kasey mustered marines for a royal arrival when the long boat pulled alongside. Kell boarded first. He wore his formal armor. Tristine came after him, followed by Armus. She wore the uniform of a royal officer.

Tyrone greeted his wife with a hug and kiss then wryly shook his head. "I'm very glad to see you only I wish you had waited."

"If the king can do this, why can't I? Beside, Kell assured me it was safe."

"Indeed, Sire. The success of the mission was never in doubt." Kell turned to Avatar and widely smiled.

Avatar made the Guardian salute, though his return smile held a hint of melancholy.

Titus stood next to Mirit and sheepishly regarded his mother.

"You appear unharmed. I hope this journey taught you something," said Tristine.

Titus began to cry and ran to embrace her.

"More than you realize," Tyrone spoke in voice sympathetic. "I'm afraid we are one less."

She heard Titus mumble, "I'm sorry." Her questioning gaze passed from Titus to Tyrone.

"Allard," he said in private whisper.

She winced in grief but tightened her embrace when Titus sobbed louder.

"My mission wasn't a complete success, Captain," said Avatar to Kell.

"It's my fault! He was protecting me. And he would be here if I had stayed home!" cried Titus.

"Let's retire to the wardroom," said Tyrone.

Titus clung to Tristine's hand in leaving the deck. Even when sitting in the wardroom, he wouldn't let go of her.

Tristine managed to find her voice to ask Titus, "How did Allard protect you?"

"We were fleeing the attack with dogmen pursuing us. I tried to fight, but I couldn't do much against them. That's when he told me to run and the beast killed him. Then father and the Guardians were shot by Hoshiki—"

"Shot?" she echoed in surprise to Tyrone.

"I think it we should start from the beginning," he said.

After several hours of explanation and supper, everyone retired to their various cabins. Tristine and Tyrone convinced an exhausted and remorseful Titus to go to sleep.

Titus seized Tristine's hand to prevent her from leaving the bed. "Do you forgive me?"

"Of course. I already told you, Allard's death was not your fault."

"No, I mean for what I did. For sneaking away, for putting Father's life in danger, for everything!"

"Ay." She smiled and stroked his head. "And I thank Jor'el he kept both of you safe."

"I thank him too. But how do you know when he's forgiven you?"

"Have you asked for forgiveness?"

"Ay, but I still feel bad." Titus sniffled, wiping his nose

"Feelings can often get in the way of reality. You asked my forgiveness and I granted it. How do you feel after that?"

"Better because you're not angry, but still sad about Lord Allard."

"That's grief. I too grieve for my friend, but it didn't stop me from forgiving you. Just like our feelings do not stop Jor'el from forgiving us when we truly repent."

"Maybe because he hasn't sought all forgiveness," said Tyrone in a pointed tone.

Tristine's gaze shifted between father and son, finally coming to rest on Titus. "Is there something left undone?"

Titus sat up. "Sir," he began, trying to be formal in voice and expression. "I'm sorry I acted in anger and disgraced you and placed your life in danger—" His voice cracked and he flung his arms around Tyrone. "I love you."

"I love you too." He took Titus' face in his hands, looking in the boy's eyes. "And I forgive you. My hope and prayer for you, is that nothing like this happens again."

"Ay, sir. Jor'el willing. And with Egan's help."

"Indeed, Jor'el willing. And I *know* Egan will help you." He smiled.

"Now how do you feel?" asked Tristine.

"Better, but very tired," said Titus with a weary, relieved smile.

Tyrone lowered Titus back onto the bed. "Be at peace and get some sleep."

He closed his eyes, and very soon, fell asleep.

Tyrone and Tristine sat at a table across from the bed to speak privately. He took her hand when she glanced back to the bed and visibly fought her emotions.

"Titus isn't the only one in need of forgiveness. I'm sorry for being pigheaded and ill tempered. Although no excuse, I had to deal with the situation personally."

She wore a plaintive smile. "I've thought a lot about the situation and accept the necessity for you and Titus."

"And for Nigel and I," he said then sighed in regret. "Until this trip, I didn't realize how jealous I became of him."

His statement surprised her. "Jealous? Why?"

"Manly pride. After Tunlund, Titus idolized him. Not that Nigel is unworthy of admiration, and Jor'el knows I love no man better. But I began to imagine things that weren't actually happening. When he spoke on Titus' behalf, I considered it interference. This adventure showed me otherwise." His tone changed to ironic. "Do you know what Nigel did when they discovered Titus onboard? He threw him in the brig with the intention of sending him back, only I arrived."

She cocked a confident grin. "I told you Nigel would keep him safe."

He chuckled. "In my heart I knew the same, only I allowed jealousy to blind me. My confession caught him off guard and he denied trying to usurp me in Titus' eyes."

"Of course he wouldn't. Jor'el knows, he loves man no better than you," she quoted.

He smiled and sat back to stretch his left shoulder.

"Take off your doublet and shirt so I can check your bandage."

He stood and did so, then sat so she could get to his back.

"A bit askew but not in need of changing. You are all fortunate the darts were small." She straightened the bandage and the wrapping around his torso.

"Avatar believes River used something on the tip to enhance the effects of the stygian metal, but I don't think so." He grunted when she pressed the bandage back in place.

"It's amazing she's been able to keep her identity a secret for so long. Better?"

He stood to dress. "Not hard considering how isolated and closed a society Natan is. She just used the culture to her advantage."

"What about our relationship to Natan?"

"There isn't any relationship. We never met the emperor nor established diplomatic ties or trade agreements. They are fighting a civil war. If I ever hear from Admiral Kentashi then I'll consider what to do. For now, they must decide their own fate." He again stretched his shoulder.

"You need to rest."

"After I speak to Nigel and Mirit and ease their minds about Titus. I won't be long." He kissed her cheek and left.

Avatar, Armus and Kell held a private discussion in another cabin.

"I'm glad to see Ridge and Egan are finally at peace with one another," said Kell.

"I wish I could tell you how, but all I can recall is our flight from Yuki and River's forces," said Avatar.

"That might have been enough. You were all fortunate to escape. She's grown powerful to solely command the Dark Way in such numbers."

"Ay," said Avatar thoughtful and a bit perplexed. "Still, I have a sense there is something more. That she had help."

"You said she was alone at the trailhead," said Armus. "Well, save for the creatures," he added to Avatar's chagrin.

"I'm still trying to account for Ridge and Egan reconciling along with Mirit's ability to sense the evil when we could not. Do you have any idea what it could have been?" he asked Kell.

The captain shrugged. "No. All I knew is that Ridge was to go so he and Egan could work out their differences." He laid a hand on Avatar's shoulder. "Do not fret about it or Natan's fate. You safely brought the king and prince home, and avoided embroiling us in another country's civil war."

"I feel responsible for losing Allard."

"Understandable, still, you are to be commended. Thus," continued Kell, a large smile appearing, "you are being promoted and given command of the Jor'ellian Guard."

Stunned, Avatar repeated, "The Jor'ellian Guard?"

"Ay. You've earned it," said Kell with great pleasure.

"Indeed. Congratulations, Commander," said Armus.

"Commander," repeated Avatar, still digesting the news. "I don't know what to say."

Kell laughed. "Well, you'll need to find the words to tell Nigel before we reach home. You're to report immediately to the Fortress and Temple."

They heard shuffling of feet outside in the hall. Armus opened the door and caught a glimpse of someone going on deck. "Nigel," he said to Avatar. "You can't wait. He might have overheard."

Avatar hurried on deck and spied Nigel at the starboard rail. "Nigel."

He nodded. "Commander."

"Ah, so you did hear."

Nigel shrugged. "I didn't mean to eavesdrop. I left my cabin to fetch a headache remedy and heard mention of the Jor'ellian Guard, which naturally piqued my interest." He tapped on his amulet. "You sounded surprised."

"I am, and deeply honored. Being among the High Trio was always good enough for me. Although, being assigned your Overseer was also an honor," he added and Nigel chuckled. "But the Jor'ellian Guard, is beyond anything I could have envisioned."

"Not beyond your abilities," said Nigel with a friendly smile. "You are a mighty warrior, intelligent, brave, loyal and a very dear friend. I am happy for you."

"And a bit sad?"

He nodded. "Ay, but that's being selfish."

"No, it's not selfish. I'm sad also." He leaned on the rail, as if assuming a casual posture. In reality, he brought his face level with Nigel, his voice private. "I never told you this, but you were my first and only charge. It has been more than an honor to be your Overseer, to watch you grow up, and consider you like my son in spirit."

Nigel's smile quivered with emotion at the confession.

At Mirit and Chad's approach, Avatar reverted to his usual wry humor. "Still, it's not like I'm leaving permanently and going to the heavenlies."

"Maybe we can install a portal between Waldron and the Fortress," teased Mirit.

Avatar laughed. Nigel smirked and asked her, "When did you know?"

"Tyrone told us when he came to say Titus is finally asleep."

"Only because you pressed him," said Chad.

She smiled. "I knew there was something he wasn't telling us."

Chad cocked a grin and shook his head at the Guardian. "Sad. We used to be on equal terms in our duty."

Avatar flashed a mischievous smile in reply. "Oh, it'll be worse once you get your knight's crest." He left laughing.

"My crest?"

Nigel widely smiled. "I was saving it as a surprise for our return. You'll be a full Jor'ellian. And I put in a word with the Vicar for your admittance to the Jor'ellian Guards."

Chad snatched a glance in the direction Avatar left then back to Nigel. "Did you know about him assuming command when you put in my name?"

"No," chuckled Nigel.

"I hope you're not too sad about Avatar and Chad leaving your service," she said.

"Somewhat, but it's also a new beginning. So come. A promotion and crest deserve celebration." He took Mirit's arm and reached to take Chad by the shoulder to steer them to the cabins. "But I wonder who will replace Avatar?" he teased when passing a crate upon Virgil sat. The Guardian appeared to be busy with a rope and not paying attention.

"Join us, Virgil. You may want to get some pointers on how to handle him from your predecessor," said Mirit lightly.

Virgil dropped the rope hopped off the crate. "What do you think we Guardians do when mortals are sleeping?"

Explore the Kingdom of Allon

www.allonbooks.com

Featuring:

- Read excerpts of Allon books
- Original Character Art
- Interactive Map of Allon
- News and Events
- Photo and Video Gallery
- Links to:
    - Facebook - The Kingdom of Allon Page
    - Shawn Lamb's All-On Writing blog
    - Contact Shawn Lamb

Made in the USA
Charleston, SC
16 May 2013